ONE PROMISE KEPT

Incidents in a Tragedy

Michael Round

Best wishes

Michael Round.

833/1000

RAINBOW VALLEY BOOKS

First Published in 1999 by Rainbow Valley Books
Rainbow Valley Ltd
Bula Matra House
205 Sanderstead Road
South Croydon
CR2 OPH

ISBN 0 9535891 0 2

Published by Rainbow Valley Books
A Department of Rainbow Valley Ltd.

Produced by
Axxent Ltd
St Stephen's House, Arthur Road
Windsor
Berkshire, SR4 1RU

ONE PROMISE KEPT

Incidents in a Tragedy

One Promise Kept is Michael Round's first novel. It was written over a period of three years after retirement from the teaching profession following a heart attack. It was inspired during a visit to Wichita State University when he attended a modern day pow-wow whilst leading a seminar on English education.

The author lives in Croydon with his wife and extended family and is working on the sequel to *One Promise Kept*.

The art work was prepared specially for this book by Graham Delaney, a retired soldier from the Royal Scots Dragoon Guards, currently a serving police officer with the Surrey Constabulary.

This book is dedicated to the memory of Michael Round's aunt, Ellen Hicks, who died in April '99 at the age of 92. She also saw into the future with her blind eyes; took her wisdom with her – but left enough behind to keep others going.

Author's Notes for Readers

The incidents in this account should not be taken as being the truth. Truth was lost in the earlier telling. Many of the characters are imaginary and not intended to represent anyone living or dead. However, in creating names for the Native Americans, and the soldiers, I may have taken the name of a genuine contemporary person. This was not intended. There are inevitable exceptions to this when writing historical 'faction':

George Custer lived, as did Sitting Bull and Crazy Horse, so too several of the colonels, generals, war chiefs and warriors mentioned and of course Lincoln and Grant and their generals, also Chivington, Evans and Stuart. Black Kettle lived and died close to the account which follows, but the descriptions of the attacks on his lodges, written here, have both accuracy and license. The detail of his death is not as I have written. Equally the activities of Captain Benteen are not correct, I have characterised him and others. Most of the dialogue with Captain Benteen is entirely imaginary, as are other conversations.

Whilst I have followed the run of history, I put into the mouths of some of the people who actually lived words which they did not say, as well as words attributed to them at other times. Those with knowledge will recognise them. The intention throughout is to be respectful, for those on both sides were greater persons than I shall ever be, either in evil or good, or in the taking and giving of lives. They made history; I am merely playing with it, altering its context, in an attempt, perhaps, to be there; to share some of the pain and in doing so take a little of it away from them.

There was indeed, for example, a real Yellow Hair who took up a handful of dust when a peace treaty and land deal was made and said that since the Wasichu had taken almost all the land they should take the remaining ball of dust. Though these words come from *my* Yellow Hair they were borrowed only because they need to be said again, and with them spoken I salute the real Yellow Hair who, I have no doubt, was not a winkte.

The purist will know that *winkte* is the Lakota people's word for a male homosexual. The Cheyennes called them *hee-man-eh*. To help the flow of the text I have used winkte (not in italics) throughout, for all the tribal people mentioned. I have also tended to use the word 'Sioux' to cover people who today might better be called Lakota.

I have also mixed up, but not carelessly, certain words, paint emblems and customs which may or may not be attributed to a given people, place or time. I have also been somewhat free with the timing that certain weapons touched the scene, but only the true expert will notice these 'errors'.

I have also taken incidents and moulded them anew into my description of events, an example being: the circumstances surrounding the quarrel between the wives of Sitting Bull, which are based on Stanley Vestal's account in *Sitting Bull, Champion of the Sioux* (UOP Reprint 1988). The later incidents concerning Snow-on– Her, one of the wives, are entirely imaginary and have nothing to do with the real Snow-on-Her.

Within the context of these pages the Crow Nation of the time, and others, are sometimes spoken of with haughty disdain. This is because those proud and beautiful people are being described as if by their enemies. No doubt they held similar views regarding their foes. No disrespect is meant by the author.

I have tried to recreate a time which is lost for ever, and may never have been anything like we all imagine it to have been – thus my account also becomes fantasy. However, in writing I have attempted a certain integrity in catching the way in which lives were led during those wild frontier days.

In following the guidance of history I make no endeavour at a plot. Life does not have a plot; like history itself, life is "one damned thing after another".

For the moment it is enough to let me apologise to another people's ancestors for what my ancestors did to them, for had I been there I would have been no less blameworthy than they. We all are caught in the cocoon of our times.

However there is one very beautiful notion which is in the essence of what I write. It is the Cheyenne idea that anything that ever happens in a place is always there. So perhaps we *can* go back and live it all again, as in the pages of a book, waiting to be turned.

Note on Brevet Ranks

A brevet rank was awarded to an officer for distinguished service in the field. They were honorary ranks but did carry some punch since an officer could be given a command at his brevet rank rather than his regular rank. They were more than 'acting' ranks since the officer remained in that rank. In the event of units being joined together in battle or campaign the senior rank prevailed whether regular or brevet. So a regular colonel could find himself under the command of a regular lieutenant who held the brevet rank of brigadier general. At the close of the American Civil War all officers returned to their substantive ranks. However they were often referred to by their brevet rank. Accordingly Lieutenant Colonel Custer would refer to his adjutant, Captain W.W.Cook, as 'Colonel', since he held that brevet rank from the Civil War. Custer, of course, held the brevet rank of major general and was called 'General' by officers senior and junior to him and in the press.

Within the text I switch ranks in an arbitrary way since calling a brevet rank might be a matter of respect or sarcasm. So Captain Benteen (brevet colonel) might well be somewhat spiteful in referring to his colonel commanding (Custer) as 'General'.

Until 1870 the officers actually wore their brevet rank. From that date administrative reforms no longer allowed the practice. Neither was the rule of brevet precedence continued with, though it was well known that brevet ranks were used socially.

It is interesting to note that Captain Benteen was granted the brevet rank of brigadier general in 1894. He catches the worth of a brevet by that time when he wrote to Colonel Goldin, with the rank underlined when he signed, at the close, *"I underscore to show you that after 19 years of waiting, the U.S. has showered upon me, drenched me with the Bvt of Brig Gen'l. for Little Big Horn and Canyon Creek."*

It was almost a posthumous award since he died the following year.

Acknowledgements

The author is indebted to Professor Tonya Huber of Wichita State University for the initial challenge to begin research for this book and constant encouragement to actually finish. Equally the book would not have been finished but for the praise and encouragement given, after a reading of some draft chapters, by Eve Fowler, sometime Mayoress of the London Borough of Croydon. The author is especially indebted to Clifford Eldred and Michael Harding, both retired teachers and soldiers, who gave unlimited time to the initial correcting of the manuscript, both scholars provided valuable criticism. Joel Dancingfire, of the Cherokee Nation, at present living and teaching in Connecticut was extremely supportive from the beginning of the project. His advice on the childhood of a Native American was inspirational. The author wishes also to thank Betsy Vieceli, of Carbondale, Illinois, presently a Psychology Instructor at Rend Lake College, for her encouragement. Thanks are extended to my wife and family for their toleration of mood swings directly related to the difficulties I had with some of the chapters. And finally thanks to the many internet friends who read, praised and advised in the early stages of the writing.

Spelling and Characters

On the whole the Anglo-English (rather than American-English) version has been used for spelling. On the advice of my preliminary helpers I have provided readers, at the end of the book, with a sketch of what happened after these events, and an indication of the fate of those main characters who were still alive at the end of this account.

*"The Wasichu made many promises and kept but one;
they promised to take our land, and they took it."*

War Chief Red Cloud of the Oglala Sioux

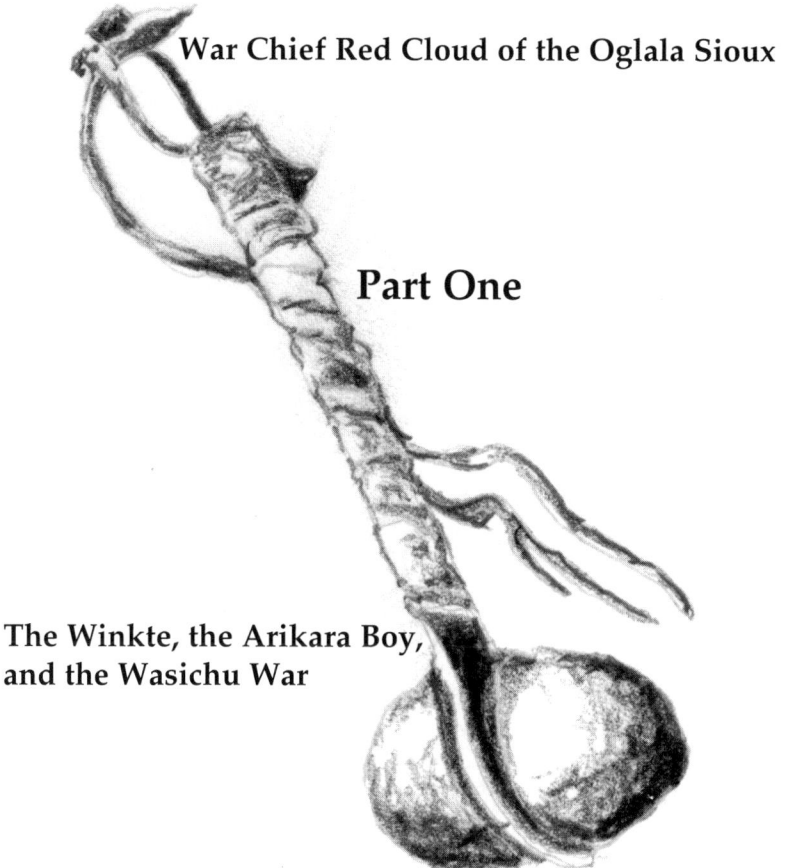

Part One

The Winkte, the Arikara Boy,
and the Wasichu War

Part One

1

First Coup

(10th Sun of the Sioux Moon When the Cherries Turn Black in the Wasichu Year of 1854)

"I am your winkte mother, your second mother, I am Yellow Hair the Warrior Winkte, much loved by your father, and I give you your secret Winkte Name." Yellow Hair's whispers were like insects at the ear of the child. The close lips tickled and the child chortled with the pleasure of the touch.

Smiling Mouth, infant of seven moons, looked on the face of his second mother and beamed. The words meant nothing but felt good. The face went to the ear again. The infant chortled with the expectation of it.

Yellow Hair, tall and handsome, was dressed in the lightest doe-skin robe of a favoured wife. Only at a distance did he resemble a woman. Closer, there was the chipped face of a warrior, and the experience of perhaps thirty winters. His male beauty, his female garb, were at once incongruous and complementary, eye-catching; and in the world of the Cheyenne there was a place for him, a two-spirit person.

"You have given the name?" White Hawk, older by three winters, stood in front of his man-woman. He was stocky; losing a young man's shape but taking on the power of maturity.

"I have given it."

"Is it a good name?"

"It is a happy name."

"Tell me!" There was a hint of pleading in the voice of White Hawk, Cheyenne war chief.

"A Winkte Name is secret!"

"You will not tell *me*!"

"You will die of pleasure at the hearing of it."

White Hawk looked at his friend and smiled, knowing that he would learn the name, perhaps also whispered in *his* ear, on a warm night when Yellow Hair was weak with affection. So White Hawk smiled and said, "Here – your reward."

White Hawk held the bridle ropes of three almost identical chestnut ponies, each a trained war pony, the best of mounts. The giving of a secret name by a winkte deserved a horse – but three! Two were mares, rare twins, and one a young breeding stallion – a gift almost unheard of in its generosity.

"Such a reward for me?"

"What is mine has always been yours."

"Liar!" the winkte laughed, for White Hawk was less than generous with his horses, was famous for it.

"Take them!"

"What is mine *remains* yours." The winkte knew at once that he had struck a target.

"Take them!" growled White Hawk.

Yellow Hair turned to Dances Quickly, first wife of White Hawk and mother of Smiling Mouth, and handed the infant to her. The winkte then took the horses' bridles. They were good ponies – good for war, good for carrying – a perfect gift for a man-woman. White Hawk had not lost his cunning.

"Go! Try them," said White Hawk.

Yellow Hair hitched up his robes with a feminine swish and deftly mounted the mare twin named Breeze. He had ridden her before, knowing most of his husband's animals by use and all of them by name, pattern and breed.

"Be careful, you can only ride one at a time!" called Dances Quickly. Her arms were folded in mock disapproval.

The man-woman turned his new pony away from the teepee of his man. The other two animals followed and were joined by a pack of four dogs. The dogs worshipped Yellow Hair and followed him everywhere. He walked them all out beyond the timber edging the shallow river, and onto the rolling grasslands, before heading towards the mountains, which were already etched against the sky by the lowering sun.

White Hawk watched briefly then laughed and turned away.

"Yellow Hair will not be back until the dawn," said Dances Quickly and moved closer to him.

White Hawk nodded, knowing that his good friend would go out into the night with the horses and the dogs, seeking the pleasure of the silence, the darkness, the possibility of dreams wrapped with visions. There was but a single moment of discomfort as he watched the dogs jumping round the horses then settling to pant ahead or alongside. There were no dogs left in the encampment... but no matter, Yellow Hair would return before the night was out.

Dances Quickly stepped closer still to her husband and touched his shoulder, "I hope he does not come back until dawn." She seemed to sense his unease, though making light of it. This was a safe camp, not far from the gathering of all the people of Chief Black Kettle. Many Cheyenne lodges, rich in warriors, were close by.

Smiling Mouth gurgled at the sound of words. He liked to hear words, liked the warmth of his mother as she held him loosely, safely. The infant lifted his hand to fondle his mother's ear – a sure sign that he was ready for a long sleep, but fighting it. Life was pleasure, sleep got in the way, but even sleep was beautiful.

)()()()(

Yellow Hair rode north. When clear of the small encampment he galloped Breeze. All three ponies moved together, heads forward sucking in the warm evening air in a wild charge. At first the dogs yapped at their hooves, but as the chase to nowhere gathered momentum the dogs concentrated only on the running. They quickly fell behind. They caught up, panting, when Yellow Hair dropped to a walk again and stopped to change ponies.

He mounted Winding Storm, the second mare, enjoying the sensation of the creature's breathing after the dash, feeling the ripple of her muscles between his thighs. Perhaps it was this sensuous contact which made him think of White Hawk and a flashing vision came to him as he remembered the killing of the fat Crow, and the moment which first sealed them. That was more than fifteen winters ago.

In his mind's eye he once more saw White Hawk about to die. Again he felt the surge of anger at the threat to the young warrior he had pleased the night before. He saw again the fat Crow brave kneeling on White Hawk, lifting up a hatchet to drive down into the youth's beautiful face. Yellow Hair was between them hurling himself from his speeding pony so that the axe chipped Yellow Hair's face in its downward strike.

Before a second swing had taken place, Yellow Hair's hunting knife had sunk into the startled Crow's fat gut. He fell across both youths, burying them with his weight, but was still at once, as if he had died of surprise rather than the long blade which had cut up into his heart. All the Crow had seen in the moment of violence was a young winkte's face and had felt embarrassment as the blackness came. *Wakantanka*, Great Spirit, the one god of the real people had been good to the young winkte that day.

Yellow Hair had been with the hunting party to entertain in the moonlight, to tend the wounds, to hold the horses. At fifteen winters he was slim and an unlikely warrior, but from then on, winkte or not, he carried a lance topped by a Crow scalp. Yellow Hair also owned the life of White Hawk from that moment. They were brothers and closer than the water is to itself as it makes the rivers flow.

Yellow Hair was greatly respected after that fight. As a winkte he was respected anyway, for the two spirit people had special powers and anyone who carried the burden of powers which were not asked for deserved respect. But Yellow Hair was also a counter of coups and took part in war parties beyond the level that was expected. He would sing and love under the stars, cook and tend wounds; but he would also join in the hunt and stand with the warriors in battle too. Always he rode on the left flank, no one understood why – it was a habit.

Yellow Hair smiled at the memories and rode on towards the failing sun. When darkness came he halted by a creek. The panting dogs lapped, the horses sucked at the water and then munched grass. As if needing his company, all of the animals rested by the single human, who lay in the soft grass, staring at the parade of stars. He was completely happy, completely tired and completely relaxed. Without meaning to he fell asleep, under that weight of darkness, until an hour before the first hint of dawn.

Waking, he sat up. Alarmed. He sensed from the air that the night was almost done. He studied the sky and found that the stars were gone behind a wide hide of cloud. He listened. Something had touched him, but there was nothing there except three ponies dozing on their feet and the dogs already beginning to wag their morning tails at the movement of the loved one. He had woken to the chill of the air and the dampness that had gathered on his robes. He shook himself, chose the stallion. He had been away from the encampment for too long, too long with the dogs. They were the night ears, the safety gatherers; they were in the wrong place.

"It is not right that we are here!" he half whispered to the dogs, who wagged their tails with joy at the sound of his voice.

They snuffled at each other, sharing the honour of his words, pleased.

"Fire Eye," they heard him say quietly and the stallion reacted, looked, snorted, and stepped towards him, head raising and lowering, now eager to be on the way. The mares moved in behind him.

Yellow Hair mounted, called unnecessarily to the dogs, and headed back to the teepees, knowing he would be there before the new sun came into sight. It would be alright, the camp was not so far away. He walked the horses in the darkness so that the dogs ran ahead.

They were almost half way back when the dogs suddenly stopped and sniffed at the breeze which was coming from the direction of the encampment. The pack leader barked and turned to look back at Yellow Hair. A borrowing of the light of the new dawn broadened Yellow Hair's horizon. An instinct took command, his legs tightened on the pony's flanks, which signalled a gentle gallop. Something had happened. Something called, silently in his head.

)( )( )( )( )(

He heard wailing first. As he rode in between the teepees the oldest of the old men, Fox Dog, called out, "They came in the night!"

Tear-faces gathered round the tall winkte and the oldest of the old men spoke again, waving a coup feather, "They came in the night."

Even the words of Fox Dog sounded bony. He stood to the front of the little crowd of mourners. He had said the words a dozen times. Yellow Hair nodded each time.

"We heard nothing."

Yellow Hair nodded.

"They were Crows!"

"Crows!" howled the old woman at Fox Dog's side.

The old man waved an eagle feather in his hand and Yellow Hair took it from him, glanced at it, and handed it back in disgust.

"It came from where the horses were, trampled by the horses."

15

"I found it!" announced the youngest of the old men with arms folded, shivering slightly with anger at his aching bones and wondering what might have happened were he to have been a lifetime younger and alert. They would have had a fight then, the filthy Crows, night killers. Now there was anger in him, and that was all.

"They left it where the horses were," said Fox Dog. "They took six horses!"

"Two they left," said the youngest, "they did not know what they were doing."

"Forget the horses!" came words from the old woman. Astonishing words, for horses cannot be forgotten.

But they nodded and then told Yellow Hair that White Hawk was dead.

They watched his face.

They saw nothing and this put fear in them for they did not understand this winkte.

Fox Dog waved the coup feather, "This is a Crow feather – see the cut!"

"Yes," said Yellow Hair. "I have seen the cut."

Later they all said the same thing – they felt fear as they watched the winkte stride to the teepee of blood. The fear grew as he turned into a warrior in front of their eyes, a fear which was threaded with admiration for what they saw emerge from within a woman's fine robe.

The people of White Hawk's campfire stood close by; the children and old women wept, howled, but watched as well. The old men stood grim faced. Through the openings to White Hawk's teepee they stared in awe as the winkte removed his woman's robes and stood naked. He did not glance at the dead; he did not howl or weep. This was very strange. It was not what was expected.

They watched as he selected a breechcloth, tied the thong, inserted the loincloth and tucked a hunting knife into the left-hand hip. Still he ignored the dead who lay round him within the teepee.

He found and mixed paint quite slowly in the gathering light of morning, and turned his golden face to black on part of the left-hand side and placed black handprints on his chest – the marks and colours of mourning. He wiped his hands clean and mixed the red tincture, hearing the sounds of approval from the others as he marked the greater part of his face with the blood colour of revenge. The old man with the feather watched the man-woman's broad back and narrow waist and had the uneasy thought that this man-woman was mostly man.

Yellow Hair took the powerful bow which was his own from the weapon place, and the war quiver with ten fine war arrows barbed with iron. Finally he picked up the war club of White Hawk. Only then did he turn to the body of his friend and with anger rising at the death face he knelt by his side and whispered in his ear, "I'll tell you his Winkte Name, it will please you."

And he did, but the ear that his lips caressed was very cold.

He rose and left the teepee without a glance at the others lying there and a silence came to the onlookers.

Yellow Hair had much fame with his people for his predictions of what was to come. He was respected for his courage and for his medicine. He was a winkte warrior and rare for that. But there was more. He was a *wicasa wakan* – a holy man.

He could heal snake wounds, stop a warrior bleeding to death, speak with spirits – it was known – but it was his visions that mattered most, blended with his battle courage. The contrary band wanted him to be with them, the Dog Soldiers wanted him to lead them, War Chief Sitting Bull of the Hunkpapa Sioux loved him as a son, despite his being a mere Cheyenne. But Yellow Hair was White Hawk's man, faithful (except sometimes), and they all loved him the more for it. Yellow Hair was thus many things.

He was taller than the real men, could outrun a *Ta-tan-ka*, bull-buffalo, they said; but this was not really true – but they said it. His own bow was heavy and his pull could put a war arrow through two men at twenty paces. That was true, it had been seen. They whispered that his love touches were breathtaking when he chose to drift away from White Hawk, and they looked over their shoulders when they said so in case their wives heard. He had a scar on his face, put there by a Crow when he was fifteen. The Crow warrior was dead; killed by this winkte when he was but a youth winkte. Yet, for all his powers, Yellow Hair had not foreseen this raid.

Yellow Hair had not foreseen his White Hawk lying in his own teepee with blood frothing around the greedy cut. So grievous was the slashing that the windpipe's interior was exposed. White Hawk's wife was at his side, dead. And White Hawk's mother too, with a wild look on her face, dead eyes open, mouth open, spirit gone. The anguish – she was Yellow Hair's own older sister, Sweet Water, mother of dead White Hawk, the most beautiful of men.

17

All lay there – blood-running scalped.

And the child was gone.

He who had dominated Yellow Hair's visions. The future warrior of warriors was gone, Smiling Mouth was gone. Gone! Yellow Hair's heart was in flames.

Yellow Hair formed a cold battle plan as he dressed. A message to Black Kettle, Great Chief, leader of their people, would bring a dozen warriors to follow his trail. He would leave good tracks, as he went ahead to scout for the killers. Another party must race ahead, angling to the north, to cut off the Crows. Meanwhile he could travel faster and more quietly alone, keeping contact with the killers. He would ride the gift ponies to exhaustion one after the other. He would fix where the killer Crows were, and then...

Yellow Hair told them what to do.

"Go!" said Yellow Hair.

The youngest of the old warriors snapped at the reins of his own best pony which burst away towards the north and the lodges of Black Kettle. He was a real warrior once more. There were braves enough there to feed on his message. Black Kettle would listen and follow the request at once. They could circle north and then towards the east and cut the raiders off. Yellow Hair would follow the killers and catch them first, but if they escaped him the men of Black Kettle would take them later – that was the request sent in the mouth of the young old man.

As the lone rider moved from sight the people looked at their winkte. He had stepped back into the teepee and was towering above the dead. It was as if he had forgotten something.

"I shall bring back their souls," hissed Yellow Hair at the still body of White Hawk. Then he glanced at his dead sister and the silent form of Dances Quickly, still, by her man's side. "I shall bring them for all of you."

Yellow Hair turned away and within a handful of paces was mounted on Breeze and whirling on the mourners, "We will have them all, except for one – he can go tell of our swift revenge. And the boy of White Hawk will live with us again, if they have not taken his life too..."

Breeze pranced eager to go. Yellow Hair steadied her and looked towards the sky. "*Wakantanka!* If I swear now to spare one of the murderers then perhaps you will deliver up to us the little one, if he

18

still lives! And if he does not – then they *all* shall die. *Wakantanka!* I promise it."

Yellow Hair called out to the sky, "I promise a life for a life – hear me!"

He kicked the flanks of Breeze.

All three ponies surged forward. The dogs yapped after him but, sensing that he was going far away and this was no game, their chase ranged only to the other side of the river, then they halted and threw back their half-wolf heads and howled to the morning sky.

)( )( )( )( )(

The young Crows had hit the little village at that silent point of the night when dogs sleep and night begins to die giving way to cool dawn. Death was not in their minds. They intended a coup-touch of the teepee, an entering in, silent as voles. They had arrows ready to place on the sleeping figures. They planned to place them and then slip away.

They spent the dark night crawling. They did this well; moving so slow, so quiet, with ingrained skill, deadly. Each moved with a play-killer's silence. Cleverly they sought out the Cheyenne horses as they moved in. To count a silent coup and take the horses as well would gain award markings to carry in the hunt and future battles – many honours.

They selected the teepee of the single warrior they had seen earlier, and became snakes as they squirmed towards the first of the poles which supported it out of the earth. They were lucky. Such had been the heat of the day, the teepee walls of buffalo hide had been curled up and secured high above the entire base to allow the free passage of air. Silently all five touched a pole. Coup! Their young hearts beat with the excitement of it all.

A signal from Runs Fast, and Red Horse wormed away towards a drop in the ground which led to the river and a water meadow where eight horses were tethered. At the first sound he was to move in quickly on the horses and take them. Otherwise he was to do it with gentle stealth, whispering in Cheyenne to keep the horses calm. He knew that the perfume of his body might also spook them so he approached from downwind.

Runs Fast, and the other three young Crows with him, slipped between the poles and were in the teepee. There were no dogs.

Three people were sleeping in the teepee. They saw in borrowed moonlight that an elderly woman lay to one side, snoring strongly. The man looked dangerously big in his nakedness, even in his sleep, with his back to his wife. They were not touching, escaping from one another's heat. It was Frog Boy who began the bungling as he stumbled – over an unseen sleeping infant, on a cradleboard set close by the old woman – just as he was about to place an arrow on the old woman's bed.

She did not wake but made a sudden movement in her sleep and Frog Boy in sudden panic drew his hunting knife and grabbed at her mouth thinking she had woken. She still made little noise, but it was enough to stir the man across the other side of the teepee.

The other three young Crows threw themselves onto the warrior and his woman at once.

Instinctively they took the man first. Big Elk and Runs Fast, the two of them, smothered him. Suddenly, with all of their strength, they had him in his breaking sleep. Eagle Claw took hold of the frantic waking woman, lying at the man's side, his whole body was on her, his hands silencing her.

All the power of the Cheyenne warrior's terror was not enough to counter the shock of four powerful hands invading his dreams. But with a vicious thrust he pushed his face against the hand holding it; his jaws clamped on an assassin's little finger. With a grunt he bit on bone and felt the finger drop free into the back of his mouth. He choked.

He heard the muffled agony, but the injured attacker did not scream. The struggling Cheyenne felt the knife as it went into his heart, carefully aimed, pushed in, life snatching. He felt the bleeding, rushing, but powerful hands on his mouth silenced his calls, almost crushing his jaw, as his throat was cut. His last feeling was that of the sawing cut and, as he passed through the screen to the world behind, he wondered if they were cutting off his head. Then oblivion.

Eagle Claw's knees, in the killing silence, were on the woman's face and neck, and three knives were working. These, and the quick blade of Frog Boy on the other side of the teepee, brought rushes and spurts of warm blood spattering faces and bodies throughout the teepee in the darkness.

"Scalps! Take scalps!" hissed Runs Fast.

They did. They took them warm and sucking.

The youths were frightened by the silence following the struggle noise. They paused. Listened. Then they began their flight as Frog Boy snatched up the infant on its cradleboard, holding its waking mouth with his free hand. He could feel it squirming, but it could make no sound.

They ran, bending low, towards the Cheyenne horses. Red Horse was waiting. The horses were jumpy but had accepted him when he crept amongst them – sensing him as a casual rider looking for a mount. Dawn was coming. It was the time for journeys.

They all hurriedly mounted. Unnoticed, Runs Fast's coup feather fell from his head. Two Cheyenne ponies pranced away in the confusion and were gone. They let them go. With the most subtle hint of light riding in from the east they were away, escaping with many trophies.

Moving ever more quickly they dropped out of sight of the camp, heading to where their own horses were waiting, held by the fool. They galloped past him, knowing he would follow. They rode hard, long enough almost to wind their horses. Then they walked, then cantered. They watered the horses when they could, and then cantered anew putting distance between the slaughter and themselves. By sun-up they were five hard gallops from their easy victory over the Cheyennes. They moved on twice that distance before they halted, tired, at a creek which had no name that they knew of.

They thought their tracks were covered, and were proud of their skills. They passed over rock formations when they were able; went through streams, entering and leaving on bedrock or through undergrowth, avoiding mud and small beaches; all the time trying to avoid making spoor.

They failed of course: horses left their droppings; grass was trodden; no man can move without leaving his mark, and nineteen horses leave a river of damage. But the signs they left were few. Only the best would be able to track them.

Yellow Hair, the winkte warrior was legendary amongst the Cheyenne as the finest tracker they had ever bred. The young raiders did not know it, but this was the beginning of a bad Crow day.

)( )( )( )( )(

Half a day after the killings, and the Crow raiding party needed to rest. They were in dangerous territory close by the river the Sioux called the Little Big Horn. Here lay good land often used by the Sioux and their allies; they called it the Greasy Grass. Once clear of the Big Horn Valley, another half a day north, they would be safe. But they needed to rest.

As they emerged from a dry coulee their horses sensed a first hint of water on the air; their coats began to shiver with expectation. Flecks of white sweat-foam were shaken off with the sudden movement. There were five riders, each with a spare horse trailing from a rope.

At first sight they all seemed stamped from an original pattern – dark tanned, slim, a shared age of about sixteen winters, a hint of perspiration covering each of them. They had the most traditional of Crow hairstyles, the sides plaited, the front crests swept back, though the crests were damaged by the hot breeze and sweaty ride. Each of them drooped forward as if weighed down by the sun. Each was handsome with the fine features of their Crow bloodline. The last in the line was Frog Boy. Strapped to his back was the cradleboard with the infant in it, silently sleeping.

As the tired group idled by there appeared from the coulee a sixth rider, smaller than the rest, even slimmer, but upright on the back of his horse. Ahead of him he drove six riderless horses. A seventh trailed from a fine buffalo mane rope he held loosely in his hand together with his own slack reins. In his holding of reins alone he was a copy of the others; for the rest it was as if he did not belong. His face was less defined, softer, almost stupid in appearance, except for his eyes, which shone with intelligence and alertness.

The heat was still overbearing. Even the riderless horses were sagging: heads dropped, stumbling too frequently, winded and thirsty. Mouth foam perfume and the sweet stink of tired horses welled round them, generated by the direct rays of the sun and spread by the constant hot breeze. The group involuntarily increased pace as the creek of fresh water came into view: cool, whispering, capturing the blue of the sky. The cloudy morning was completely burned away. A white hot sun ruled the plains and with it a flowing breeze burning to the skin.

For them, the creek had no name, it was merely a creek which they knew would shortly join the Little Big Horn. No people or tribe who passed by any place ever failed to give a name. Naming a place created maps in the mind. But these boys were fresh to the detail of this territory; they were still nervous, and not thinking of names, so they did not bother to give it a name. Nothing had happened for them at this place, but it was a good place to rest. Before they departed a name might emerge to remind them of the moment – Swimmers' Creek, Cool Place Creek – something would give rise to a naming, just as there had been something about each of the youths to give them a name.

Runs Fast, young war chief, very proud, saw that this was a tranquil place with no danger. It was he who had the idea of leading the raid, his first leadership raid. He received his new name as a ten year old when he spooked a grizzly and fled like an arrow. He was also a lucky boy for the bear could have had him had it wished; instead the great animal had watched the foolish human cub run and returned to his nipping of berries from a wild rose bush for no other reason than that is what he did.

It was that lucky boy, now a leader of youths, who said: "We rest here!"

The others looked around. Unusually, there was no discussion. They simply agreed that it was a good place to rest. They nodded agreement. They were tired.

"Good place," grunted Big Elk, the next in the leadership line, who could have been leader except for the coup feather of Runs Fast.

The animals surged forward and were in the water, drinking, drinking. The young men's movements were sensuous in their exhaustion as they slipped from the nakedness of their horses; dropped their weapons on the bank of the creek and then threw themselves into the coolness, splashing and for a moment shouting. They quickly fell silent with the ingrained caution that dominated their lives. They worked themselves into the centre of the creek where the water was half a man's height and long weeds stroked their ankles at the deepest point. Then the boy fool they called Little Knife came up with the stolen horses, plunging them into the water amongst the swimmers.

"Fool!" shouted Big Elk, slightly larger than the rest, already a man's thickening about his shoulders, paddling languidly on his back away from the gulping animals.

"We should be quiet!" hissed the fool to the rest. He looked back over his narrow shoulders from where they had come. He seemed anxious.

"Fool!" laughed Big Elk.

"It's not safe here!" said the fool, slipping from his horse's back and easing himself into the water. Oh – the coolness striking at his loins. He gasped.

The others took no notice of him; he was Little Knife and knew nothing at all.

He surfaced and stood in the creek looking back from the approach line, wiping water from his eyes. A thousand droplets covered his skin, turning his tight flesh darker and his hair into fronds of damp blackness. "We must not stay here," he said.

He was ignored for he was very low, an Arikara, son of a captive, favourite of Old War Chief for no good reason – just because Old War Chief fell in love with the Arikara bitch who was this boy's mother. Their parents whispered about it, so the boys knew it all. He was not despised exactly – but he *was* an Arikara.

The Arikara boy pushed his long hair from his face. The strands hung loose. He had no plaits. He scowled at the others.

"We must keep moving," he said, and shook the water from his head like a dog.

Only Frog Boy spitting water from his mouth heard this and grinned, "Spoken like an Arikara!"

It had been like this from the start – the pecking out of the feathers of the Arikara's confidence. It passed the time, it kept him in his place. Runs Fast was with his best friends. The Arikara had been forced on them, only half belonging to the group. These youths had played together for their entire lives, as boys and as envious youngsters looking at warriors going off to war or the hunt. Now they had done it! They had counted coup. Even with the Arikara getting in the way.

Little Knife the Arikara was always on the outskirts of their games, slowly being accepted, always taunted for being half a Crow at best. They were inexperienced in war, but knew much of play. Only Runs Fast had made a coup before: a year earlier when, on the flank of a buffalo scouting party, he was caught in the open by three wandering Cheyennes. He had killed one, and the rest had fled at the first sight of the other Crow buffalo hunters whooping to Runs Fast's aid.

The Cheyennes were the finest of riders and it should not have happened that way. Maybe they were over confident when they saw

24

the slim youth separated from the rest of his group. As they suddenly appeared from a hidden section of a dry river bed Runs Fast had released his hastily strung arrow in panic and struck their leader in the eye. It was a lucky shot, but deadly for all that. With courage springing from fear and instinct Runs Fast had ridden straight at the reeling enemy and struck him with his bow to count coup. As the horses collided the Cheyenne's had reared, hitting his rider in the face with its head, smacking the shaft deeper in. Death was instant. Runs Fast was a hero – that is why his friends agreed to go with him and let him lead, even Big Elk.

Everything was done properly. There was much discussion, more than three days of discussion. Advice and permission was sought, also given. The older men thought the eager youths would meet little danger since there was no knowledge of any hostile lodges in the Cheyenne hunting lands they intended to enter. It was well known that the Cheyenne lodges had moved north-east with the buffalo. For this reason, unusually, no seasoned warrior went as leader. Secretly the older ones saw the journey as an extended game. Old War Chief called Runs Fast to him.

"You are going?"

"If the wise ones say we are going. Yes. We are going."

"The journey is dangerous," smiled Old War Chief

"We know."

The chief thought him an arrogant pup and was pleased with the knowledge that the journey was not so dangerous. There would be no real honour in it, just experience.

"There are many Cheyennes!" the chief lied playfully. It was not really a double tongue, for that was not allowed; rather it was a game with words.

"We know."

"Take Little Knife!"

Runs Fast hissed as might a snake, but caught his breath for if the wise one was saying that Little Knife was to ride, then permission was going to be given for them all to go. They would go anyway, but permission was better.

"Take Little Knife – he dreams of war and is old enough."

"But Little Knife..."

"I want you to take him, look after him," came a sigh from the chief which meant that further discussion was unwise.

"Then we may go?"

"You may go – taking Little Knife."

The whoop of triumph was a signal to his friends sitting two hundred paces away. They rose to their feet as one to greet Runs Fast as he scampered away from the war chief.

The chief fell to admiring the youth's movement as he left, as does an old man looking on a ghost of himself when young. Runs Fast would make a great warrior but he had no head; the boy thought with his bow rather than his inner eye. Little Knife, despite his few years, had something special. Maybe he would be a vision master in the future, a medicine man, a *wicasa wakan*. His eyes, that was it – always open, aware. Even when he slept the eyes were flicking beneath their lids. A strange boy – but he had eyes, inside and outside. The others loathed him; the war chief loved him, which was sufficient for him to join the raiding party even if it was heading for an empty space.

Grudging Little Knife for being imposed on them, they made him useful, like a dog. He was always made to trail behind, but was alert, looking to the left, to the right, to the horizon, listening, watching, and absorbing the perfumes and insect sounds. They all did this too, but lacked the younger boy's intensity. He was told to stay with the spare horses when they scouted ahead, fetch wood, fetch water, go get the horses if they began to drift away at a halt place, stay awake when the others slept. He despised the others for making him do these things.

But he was there, even if it was as carrying dog, to do as bid. He did not care that they thought he was of no account. He was a youth; thirteen winters, *and* short for his age. Runt. But useful. And this *was* a raiding party. It was Little Knife who discovered the Cheyenne camp.

On the preceding afternoon Little Knife had moved out on the right flank and heard a dog bark. The yap was far away, carried on the freshening breeze.

"Hey hey!" he called, softly, with the wind in his face so that his voice carried away from the camp and towards his downwind comrades.

They all looked his way as he bounded his pony towards them.

"I heard a dog!"

"Where?" snapped Runs Fast.

"Listen!" the fool said.

Despite doubts they halted.

Far away the faint call came.

"There!"

"I heard nothing," said Runs Fast.

"Shhh!" Big Elk raised his hand.

They heard it, a faint bark, and then again – so they changed direction but, moving with little caution, almost stumbled on a small encampment of Cheyenne. They dropped from their horses and watched – four lodges, widely dispersed because of the thickness of the timber, lay close by a stretch of water,

"Fishing!" whispered Big Elk.

"Must be Cheyenne," said Runs Fast.

"They are!" said Red Horse.

"Yes," said Big Elk, for he had seen the paint style of the Cheyennes before, when he had ridden with his uncle to trade with them.

"How many?" asked Runs Fast, himself already counting.

They were able to count twenty women with but a single warrior and two old men.

"Just a fishing party," said Runs Fast.

"Old men and women," Big Elk's tongue ran across his dry mouth.

"What's *she* doing?" asked Red Horse.

They watched as a tall woman rode out of the small encampment with three horses and some dogs bounding round their legs.

"She's big!" said Frog Boy.

"Eat us all alive," grunted Eagle Claw, getting hard at the possibilities.

"She's taking the horses," said Red Horse, disappointed.

"Not all!" said Big Elk and pointed to a small herd enclosed within a roughly laid brushwood corral near the river's edge. "Look! There are eight of them!"

"They are what we want!" hissed Runs Fast through his teeth.

The youths remounted and pulled back a mile.

"We shall attack them!" said Runs Fast.

The others thought about it.

"Yes," said Red Horse, slightly shorter than the rest, stockiest of the slim built youths, like his father, born to be a big belly in his later years.

"Now?" Frog Boy frowned, uneasy.

"When the sun goes down," said Runs Fast glancing at the blue sky, eyeing the gathering clouds to the west.

Big Elk folded his arms, thinking.

"In the morning, before the light," said Little Knife, nodding at the clouds. "It will be a cloudy night."

"Oh shut up!" snapped Frog Boy and Eagle Claw as one.

But Big Elk thought about it. "Let us talk," said Big Elk and slipped off his pony.

The rest followed, dropping to earth silently. The horses, sensing a lengthy halt, drifted away, halted by an occasional hiss or soft call from their masters. They remained in the close vicinity, occasionally rolling in the yellowing prairie grass between bouts of grazing.

The young men sat in a circle and began to argue. It was some time before a battle plan was agreed. They *would* attack in the morning before the light. They were to ride through the woods and count coup on each one of the teepees, enter the last one and touch the sleepers, and then a wild gallop away from the rising sun with the Cheyenne horses. Easy. The insult to the Cheyennes would be profound.

"We can leave an arrow on each Cheyenne!" said Red Horse.

"Take the horses!" said Runs Fast. "We must take horses or they won't believe us when we get back."

The rest nodded at this.

"We heard a dog," said Little Knife.

They all glared at him.

"If we wake the dogs!" he cautioned.

"Maybe there is only one," said Frog Boy.

He was glared at too.

"There were plenty dogs!" muttered Red Horse.

"Go in on foot," said Little Knife.

"Stupid," growled Runs Fast and poked at the runt with his bow.

"Foot *is* safer," said Big Elk.

"Go in the deep night, creep very close, coup one teepee, and all of the people in it. Safer!" said Little Knife.

28

"The Arikara way!" growled Frog Boy.

"Less danger," said Little Knife.

"Crows do not fear danger," snapped Eagle Claw, but felt comfortable with the idea.

Little Knife shrugged his narrow shoulders and felt, not for the first time, a hint of pride that he was Arikara and not Crow. Little Knife kept the smile from his face as they talked about his tactical variation as if he were not there, and agreed to it as if he had not suggested it.

"Who will stay with our horses?" asked Eagle Claw.

They all looked at Little Knife with soft grins on their faces but it was the words of Red Horse that fixed it. "*Our* dog," he said, "Little Knife." And he patted him on the head as one pats an obedient hound.

The following morning Little Knife was lying in the dew grass with a rope to each pony wrapped round his wrists, half asleep, enjoying the cool of the summer dawn. He heard them approaching, returning from the raid, out of the dawn light, back towards him.

All of them were mounted on Cheyenne horses. Big Elk held two more by ropes.

Little Knife jumped on his own horse and yelled at the other Crow mounts waiting with him. They looked at him for he had a way with them.

"We counted coup!" shouted Frog Boy, galloping on.

"All of us!" Big Elk swept by.

"Scalps!" yelled Runs Fast, waving three blood-spitting trophies.

The whole pack of them was gone. Little Knife kicked his pony into a gallop and the well trained Crow horses followed, eager to move with the morning.

Little Knife drove his horse hard. Each time he got close to the others he heard triumph shouts of coup and of three Cheyennes lying in their own blood, and he saw that Frog Boy had a Cheyenne infant strapped to his back and Little Knife counted for sure six good horses captured. They had killed enemy! This was no game.

All *he* had done was stay with their own ponies bent only on grazing dew grass. Tears welled in his eyes as he rode after them. He blinked to clear his eyes and halt his dangerous anger. He hated them, Runs Fast he hated most of all. Being left with the horses he had had no chance of a first blood coup.

Now, half a morning later, they were dismounting in this 'good' resting place. Little Knife grumbled beneath his breath, "This is too early! They will be following us. If we halt they might circle ahead of us."

"What?" snapped Runs Fast turning on the thin-limbed boy. The sudden turn hurt Runs Fast's right hand which had a stump where there had been a little finger that morning. He glanced at it and saw that the bleeding had begun again, slightly, the wound opened by the water. The crimson oozed as he watched it, then he carefully put the stump in his mouth and moistened it, tasting salt, wondering what he would do about the white exposed joint in the years to come. He looked again. The bleeding stopped. The wound throbbed. He was bad tempered with his wound, but proud of it. It made up for the loss of the coup feather. He blamed Little Knife. It was as if it were Little Knife's fault – coming up behind, noticing the loss of the feather, as the dawn grew stronger, half a day earlier.

"Where is your eagle feather?" the Arikara boy had gasped.

Runs Fast's right hand had shot to his head. It was gone. And there was a surge of pain as his damaged finger caught in the strands of his hair. They were too far out of the Cheyenne place to go back. Runs Fast had cursed, and kept riding. Why had Little Knife been the first to notice? His silly high pitched voice was there again!

"This is not safe," said Little Knife, caressing the face of his pony.

"*I* say if it is a safe place."

"They will come after us – fast."

"Listen to me, rattler's brain! I'll think – you hunt!"

Runs Fast began to lead his mount out of the water.

"Hunt?" Little Knife brightened.

"Yes – over there!"

Little Knife saw nothing but low scrub, the tops of wild turnips and dead grass.

"Turnips. Go hunt turnips – our bellies are empty."

Turnips! Even that was without honour. Little Knife hesitated. Runs Fast bent, lifted his bow and raised it.

"Dig!" commanded the young man, youth muscles rippling across his naked chest as every segment caught the sun. "Dig – or I'll lay my bow across your Arikara back!"

Little Knife, muttering to himself, sauntered off. He had no choice but to dig turnips in the heat, and be jeered at. Women dig turnips.

As he walked away Runs Fast's hand rose to the back of his head as if in hope that the coup feather was still there, but it was not.

A sudden shout from Frog Boy, "Ducks!"

A flight of ducks was coming in, circling, turning into the breeze, drifting down towards the blue of the summer shallow water. There was one thing that Frog Boy did well. Swim. They all looked at him.

Grinning, he slipped away downstream to where the ducks were landing. In the time it takes to straighten a handful of arrows through the eye socket of a buffalo skull he was back with a fat dead duck.

The birds had landed on a deep slow moving patch of water. In winter there was a whirlpool there, in summer the pool shrank to the depth of a grown man sitting on another's shoulder, with peaceful catfish in the depths. Frog Boy had slipped into the willows, noiselessly entered the water and taken the duck with his hand from beneath, like catching eagles from inside a pit trap.

"Get dry wood!" Eagle Claw snapped at Little Knife.

"No fire!" said Little Knife.

"What?" asked Runs Fast.

"You want a beating? You really do, don't you?" snapped Eagle Claw. He was already getting to his feet, reaching for his unstrung bow.

"They'll see the smoke."

"There'll be no smoke," said Eagle Claw, doubtfully, thinking that there might be.

"They'll smell it."

"Who?" asked Runs Fast, lips in a slight sneer.

"The Cheyenne!" replied Little Knife.

"We are too far ahead. We have their horses, except for two. There were no other warriors but that one we killed. Light the fire!"

Even so, they cooked the fat duck over a very small fire. The plume of smoke did not go high, would not be seen from more than a mile away. They lit the fire with the flint that Runs Fast carried.

"Get more wood – quickly," the leading youth snapped at Little Knife.

"Go – fetch!" the rest howled at him.

When he came back, Runs Fast flicked Little Knife behind the ear, for no reason other than his personal pleasure, and sent him gathering even more wood in the heat, smiling at the sweat on the boy's scrawny torso.

Little Knife, searching for timber, brooded, muttering dark things about his leader. As he returned with an armful of bone-dry aspen he heard a squeal from the infant as it suddenly woke to unfamiliar voices.

"Here," said Red Horse, thrusting the squealing infant into Little Knife's arms. "Shut the brat up! Take it with you – give it water."

"Give it milk!" shouted Big Elk. "Your tits are big enough!"

The adolescent's enlarged nipples were sore to the touch. The condition would pass, but at this time they were a target for pinching fingers and wasp words. Once, the day before, Big Elk had come from behind and grabbed him so hard the boy shrieked with the pain of it. Little Knife wished for Big Elk's early death. He wished it would come that very day.

"Winkte!" shouted Big Elk.

"Kiss me, kissi kiss!" laughed Eagle Claw.

And Big Elk pulled his breechcloth to one side, "Here!"

They all laughed at that idea.

Little Knife, though his soul was dead with these embarrassments, obediently took the infant to the edge of the creek and thought of drowning it. He sat on a minute beach of copper sand and propped the infant on his knees. They stared at each other.

The infant stopped whimpering and gave an open smile to his new friend, and reached to touch his face. Little Knife took a scrap of dried buffalo meat from the top of his breechcloth and put it in his own mouth, chewed until it was a juicy mush. Then he turned it into still smaller pieces with his tongue and slipped the first into the infant's gummy mouth from his own. The child took it, and made a sucking and chewing sound all mixed up in the gathering of experience, swallowed and lifted tiny hands towards the face that was feeding him. They both smiled. Little Knife fed and watered the infant until the little one ceased to ask for more with his eyes and lips and was thus content.

Little Knife crept back into the group of young braves. He was feeling less alone with the infant chortling, strapped on his back, and a fresh pile of wood in his arms. Perhaps this time they would be satisfied. Big Elk was still awake.

"The squaw returns," he said.

Frog Boy opened his eyes, "Want to lie on your back?"

"On his belly!" said Big Elk.

"Both!" giggled Frog Boy.

Then he, with the rest, closed his eyes and left the Arikara alone. Perhaps, thought Little Knife, he would kill them all himself.

He sat down with his back against a hot boulder. He looked at them, sleeping. The fat little new friend was also sleeping, eyes tight closed in a little satisfied face, resting on Little Knife's bare legs. He turned the infant and propped him in his arms, squaw arms. Little Knife's face screwed up at the thought.

He looked across to the leader, deep in sleep, snoring gently. The other five were scattered about in the long grass, languid, dozing, with the cool air of the willow and cottonwood shade stroking their young coppery skins. Little Knife felt curiously uneasy. He tried to reassure himself. Except for their treatment of him things were not that bad – after all, he was *part* of the raid and it had been successful. He lay back against the boulder, and gently put the infant upright on his upper legs so that its feet were in his lap, its body gently trapped between Little Knife's part-open legs, its head level with his knees. The infant woke, but did not cry out.

"You are a nuisance," he whispered to the small face.

The face smiled, and the little lips dribbled.

Little Knife picked at one of the scraps of duck bone which had a hint of meat on it. He had scraps of everything; even the child was a scrap from the raid. He pondered, with gathering bitterness, on what they had told him – of what *they* had done whilst he lay with horses. A fresh surge of restlessness ran through him. They should not be waiting here, dozing in the shade. He was correct. Little Knife was not the only one looking on them that bright afternoon.

Less than a mile away, standing on Fire Eye's back, to secure a view above the protecting scrub, was a lone Cheyenne warrior. His powerful face was painted half black, half red, with such haste that the strokes were blending into his sweat and running in streaks to his waist, and then on to the flanks of his pony. The warrior's face was tight with concentration, his nostrils seeking messages on the air, his ears piercing the sough of the prairie wind. His eyes squinted to confirm the hint of smoke he thought he had just seen.

He dropped down onto the hot back of his horse. The animal was proud, tired, but still had the power for another hard gallop. The twin mares were ambling along, out of sight, far behind, blown, recovering, instinctively following

The youths had no idea he was there, fatal for them unless friendly spirits spoke to them; but this was Cheyenne hunting land, shared with the Sioux – and they were Crows. Crow protective spirits were far, far away.

Never before had the boys been in so much need of a spirit intervention, for the menace was as bad as it could be. For the watching winkte warrior, at best, this day was a most perfect day to die, for in so doing he could rejoin his man on the other side of the screen; at worst he would live to dance the steps of revenge.

)(×)(×)(

It was instinct that took the first of Yellow Hair's arrows into the sleeping chest of Runs Fast. He woke to it. He felt he was screaming, but no sound came. The second arrow took out a slice of flesh from Big Elk's shoulder. His pain-grunt woke the rest. He was scrambling to his feet when a third arrow buried itself up to its feathers in his chest and protruded two hands depth from his back. It was then that the war call of Yellow Hair destroyed what was left of their courage as he swept amongst them.

He threw himself at Big Elk who was trying to rise to his feet again. Yellow Hair heard a 'crack' at he hit the Crow with his full weight. Red Horse and Frog Boy dived for a tired horse each, struggled with them, mounted, and without looking back, fled.

They galloped with the panic of youth to the north, horses quickly wheezing and slowing, and were destined to meet Black Kettle's twelve Cheyennes waiting on ponies ridden hard to cut off that route. They would meet them in the time it took for a man to skin and quarter a deer. They tried to run back when they saw the trap, but were cut down with good arrows, smashed with clubs and their scalps were cheered on lances within moments.

Only Eagle Claw was left on his feet, no weapon in his hands, frozen at the sight of the big Cheyenne rising to his feet. Big Elk lay with a broken neck, his eyes beginning to glaze over, still and staring. Eagle Claw watched as the Cheyenne altered the position of the club in his hand.

Eagle Claw's hand moved towards the knife on his hip as he tried to duck the blow, but only flashes of light came to him, pain, and

34

then nothing. Yellow Hair turned to his first target, who was still writhing with the pain of the arrow, holding it, somehow having struggled to a kneeling position. Yellow Hair went across to him.

"Why did you slaughter my people?" Yellow Hair asked Runs Fast in the tongue of the Crow.

For a moment the wounded youth looked up at the towering Cheyenne. Their eyes met.

Yellow Hair hesitated, saw the beginnings of a smile on the boy's face. It was a good face. The Crow were a handsome tribe. Yellow Hair saw the faint trickle from the fine lips. Then the winkte warrior looked beyond the youth's good features and saw White Hawk's throat.

Runs Fast watched the huge Cheyenne lift a war club, then saw nothing more.

Yellow Hair, breathless, allowed the club to fall to one side. He saw three fresh scalps on a lance lying by the side of the Crow youth, one scalp grey with wisdom. Forcing down the rise of vomit he picked up the pieces of those he loved and strung them on his hip. He added the scalps of the fallen youths and as he did so he heard the call of a child.

He spun round towards the sound. He saw a copper movement against the green of the trees. He began to sprint towards the sound and movement but stopped as he saw a thin youth holding an infant in his arms rise up out of the undergrowth.

The boy seemed to have no fear in his eyes. He was holding the infant as if it were a younger brother or sister. He did not run. His eyes were startling, hawk eyes.

As the boy took in the size and warrior grace of Yellow Hair he stepped back in a moment of anticipation, knowing that he was looking at death.

"I fed him," whispered the boy quickly, in Crow tongue and made a movement with his free hand towards his own mouth in the traditional way.

The infant had turned its head towards the boy as he spoke and reached up to his face, fingers straining for the boy's mouth and making the sweet sounds of an infant in pleasure.

Yellow Hair was standing close enough to the boy to strike him dead. The boy gulped as he saw the intention in the Cheyenne's eyes. Yellow Hair saw the swallow, the movement of the throat. The boy's

35

eyes never left Yellow Hair's. It was almost a threatening look, fear mingling with a call to Yellow Hair to do whatever he had to do. Yellow Hair considered grabbing his small throat. Smiling Mouth became aware of Yellow Hair – the perfume of him, perhaps – and his face became an open mouthed smile.

Yellow Hair reached out his hands.

Little Knife handed over the infant, quickly but gently. Smiling and dribbling with delight the infant reached towards Yellow Hair's familiar face.

"Go into the trees. Disappear. Live a little longer," Yellow Hair said to the youth in Crow tongue.

As the boy braced himself to run away words formed on Yellow Hair's lips which seemed to come from madness.

He said: "Boy!"

The youth stopped, froze rather.

"What is your name?"

"Little Knife."

"You almost lost it – with everything else – this day."

Little Knife swallowed.

The warrior nodded that he could go. Little Knife turned on his heels and ran away.

He expected an arrow in his back, but nothing came. He dared not look back and drove himself out of the Cheyenne's sight, deep into the timber where he had gathered wood. He hid.

Yellow Hair watched him go and thought that maybe he should have killed him too, but he had promised to spare one. Then he looked at the dead around him. He listened to the breeze licking his ears, and he saw the blue of the waters. He thought he must give this creek a name.

The infant made a noise.

"I have names to give," said Yellow Hair.

The infant seemed to listen.

"Do you remember your Winkte Name?"

The infant smiled.

"Only the dead and *Wakantanka* are here so I can call it out loud. Your name is..."

Yellow Hair swallowed. Fresh tears burned the black streaks of paint.

"I wanted to please *him* with the secret name."

Yellow Hair bit his lip and held the infant against the sky, "*Wakantanka* I tell You his Winkte Name, his secret name so that You can tell *him* on the other side."

He paused as if to listen for the voice of *Wakantanka* – but there was only the wind dropping down from the plains above the creek.

"Listen to me, *Wakantanka*, I was his second mother once, now I am his second father until I die. Help me protect him and teach him. Listen to his Winkte Name! It is his father's name." He looked upon the infant. "You are White Hawk, as he was." Yellow hair blinked. "So that he lives again."

Yellow Hair hugged the child, marking him with black and red with sweat and paint.

He turned to face the creek.

"White Hawk's Creek!"

He shook his head. It had to be what had happened at the creek. He thought for a moment.

"This place is Mercy to the Crow Creek."

The place exists to this very day but has lost its Cheyenne name on the Wasichu maps. It is a small creek that flows west into the Little Big Horn. People call it Reno Creek.

2

Painted Horses

(Some days before – and moments after – on that hot day,
during the 10th Sun of the Sioux Moon
When the Cherries Turn Black in the Wasichu Year of 1854)

Little Knife had asked, very quietly, whether there would be any chance of honour; a fight, a real fight.

"We cannot say what will happen," Old War Chief had said. Then he leaned forward and touched the shoulder of Little Knife, to reassure him. "Maybe you will return on a painted horse."

"He'll never amount to anything!" The cackle of Old War Chief's first wife came from the gloom of the teepee.

"Hold your tongue woman."

"He's just a lying Arikara boy."

"Be quiet!"

"He will not come back!"

Old War Chief turned to her in annoyance.

"He'll break your heart one day," she muttered, moving into a darker curve of the teepee, pretending to look for something.

"He shall have a painted horse – full marked with war honours!" growled the old man.

The old woman had gone silent, shuffling in the gloom, doing woman things, whilst Little Knife still felt the shock of her words. An Arikara did not lie. Only loafers around the Wasichu forts lied. He felt the foul taste of the suggestion that he had a double tongue; then pride in the old warrior's predictions and the man's trust. That was then, before the raiding party set out – now Little Knife did not even have a horse.

Little Knife coiled his dry tongue round his dryer mouth. He lay in the undergrowth beneath a knot of willows and aspen. The trees were askew with the pain of old winter winds and the passage of several forgotten ice storms. The criss-cross of damaged trunks and fallen boughs broke the pattern of standing timber and helped hide his human form. Perhaps he was the first human being ever to be in this place, but he doubted it.

Rotting branches and debris from the previous autumn, winter and spring floods formed an even thicker lower screen beneath the summer foliage. His face was resting on a rare patch of sand. He saw a pebble, half covered. Panting, he scratched the pebble out of the sand, instinctively cleaning it with his fingers. The pebble was cool in the deep shade. He slipped the pebble into his mouth. The pebble was also dry, but a miracle took place in his mouth as the trickster pebble brought his saliva glands into play and the dryness disappeared, and with it the fear.

"He is playing with me," Little Knife whispered, and dared to raise his face with the return of his courage.

He could see nothing except tangled vegetation peopled with insects. Further away a brace of red-winged blackbirds chattered at him as they strutted through the bare branches of a dead aspen. Little Knife raised himself a touch higher, his breathing under control. He realised that he was unarmed except for his hunting knife in the buffalo skin scabbard attached to the thong which held his breechcloth. This sparse garment, the knife, and a pair of moccasins, were his entire possessions.

He rose to one knee and looked back to where the Cheyenne had been. He saw nothing, but he heard the sound of horses. He did not move. He made no sudden change of position, he simply turned his head and through a small gap in the timber he saw the Cheyenne on a tall horse. The warrior held the infant in one arm. Little Knife could see the tiny hand gripping the nearest plait, its little face looking at the Cheyenne's. As he passed from sight Little Knife saw that the Cheyenne's mount was followed by four, no, five others.

"There are many horses still free," Little Knife said to himself.

Cautiously, though the Cheyenne was too far away to hear or see, Little Knife made his way down to the creek. He sniffed the air, sensed nothing unusual, and with a careful look up and down stream he entered the water. Half way across he had to swim three strokes until he found a new footing but soon was on the opposite bank. Keeping low he hurried through the vegetation until it thinned as the terrain rose steeply towards the plains. He caught a final glimpse of the Cheyenne and saw that he now had eight other horses with him. The distance was so great he could not tell if they were the captured horses or a combination of the captured ones and those of the fallen Crows. He felt a surge of foolishness rise in himself – he should have noticed which horses were which when they were closer to him.

"But there are *other* horses still about," he whispered to himself again.

He made calculations. When the Crow raiding party halted Little Knife had hobbled the captured horses. Maybe those were among the eight that the Cheyenne had with him. Altogether the youths had nineteen horses with them – two had been taken by Red Horse and Frog Boy when they fled – the Cheyenne had eight – somewhere there were nine horses – much wealth! The Cheyenne must have decided to leave the other horses. This was a strange thing for a warrior to do. Maybe it was the child he was interested in. Maybe he had enough horses. But no circle of lodges has enough horses. This Cheyenne was strange, that was certain. Perhaps it was some kind of trap. Little Knife ducked out of sight at the thought, then very slowly rose up again out of the undergrowth.

Even as he watched afresh, the Cheyenne disappeared from view. Little Knife looked back at the river. He felt the belting heat of the afternoon on his back. He coiled his tongue round the pebble in his mouth and made it click on his teeth. Little Knife did not know what to do.

"I cannot go back!" he said aloud, but quietly.

The Arikara youth flopped down onto his haunches and began to think hard.

"They will kill me."

He pictured himself stumbling back into the place of the lodges, naked, blackened by the sun, legs worn by a long march, nothing to show for the adventure. They would not be happy that the Arikara boy lived, and the others were dead; even Old War Chief would not smile. He always smiled at Little Knife. This time he would not smile. All of the others killed. Not all!

"Maybe Red Horse and Frog Boy will circle and come back." He brightened and smiled at his whispers, but then further doubt made him say, "Maybe they are dead too. Maybe the Cheyenne will come back. Maybe there are more Cheyenne. I am talking to myself!"

He still did it, muttering, but his voice fell to a deeper whisper and he looked round from left to right, stood up, went on tiptoe, then dropped to his haunches again. Nothing. He was uncertain whether to move or hide. He felt extremely naked.

He heard the call of a horse.

"Ah!"

Alert, he stood, listened, and sniffed at the air, opening his mouth slightly to gather in the sounds and perfumes of the afternoon.

Little Knife let out a high pitched yelp which was his call for Blackback, his own pony. At once he wished he had not done so – so much noise. Then he heard a horse call back and his senses caught the direction and he broke into a run, making his way back towards the creek. Even as he covered a hundred paces he saw his pony.

At that moment the deep trouble that the Arikara boy was in began to dim because he was no longer alone. Better still, behind Blackback were two other horses – the yellow which had belonged to Runs Fast and another black, Big Elk's. Suddenly Little Knife was wealthy. The horses were standing by the bodies. Little Knife stopped, found he was biting his lip and stood still, heart thumping.

)(	)(	)(	)(	)(

Runs Fast's yellow had a good saddle with pouches made of buffalo hide. It was the best of the ponies and stood quietly by her master, occasionally touching the body with her muzzle. She looked round at the approach of Little Knife and snorted welcome, even stepping towards him.

"He is in another place, Morning Moon," said the boy quietly.

Her head rose and fell.

Blackback came trotting over as soon as she saw Little Knife and touched him from behind as he knelt by Runs Fast. There were flies where his scalp had been, and they hissed away in a panic crowd as Little Knife knelt, but only briefly – quickly returning one by one. A softly intoned call began to emit from Little Knife's mouth as he sang a prayer-song with an unexpected enthusiasm.

Carefully, as if he might wake his leader, Little Knife put his arms beneath the armpits of Runs Fast. The flies burst into panic. He lifted. Almost nothing happened. He gave a tug and slipped, and fell backwards with his own weight, full length, supporting himself on his elbows. It was no good, so he thought hard for another way.

41

He could lift the dead youth onto his horse, maybe, and take him back into the village, with Morning Moon painted for death. No. The weight was impossible to lift. He thought to make travois for them both. He glanced at Big Elk, strangely handsome, as if he were sleeping, the fly-scalp out of sight as he lay there. He pictured himself riding for several days in the heat with the dead youths bumping behind their horses on travois poles. He shook his head. He thought of being surprised by more Cheyennes, riding him down in triumph, strapping him to his dead comrades, tied to a tree or burning with them. He shuddered.

"What if the big Cheyenne returns here?" Little Knife spoke aloud again, and quickly got to his feet.

He decided to leave the bodies under boulders and then he could return with others to collect the bones for mourning. Glancing round, there were no boulders. The bodies were also too heavy to lift into the branches of the trees. He did the only thing that was possible. He dragged his old taunters, still warm to the touch from lying in the sun, into the shade of a large aspen tree. He eased them so that they were sitting with their backs to it. He placed their bows and weapons close at hand. He stood in front of them.

"I wish I could make you live again," he muttered, and in saying it he bit his lip once more, finding he meant what he said. He returned to the horses.

He found nothing in the saddle on Morning Moon except some white clay for making paint. Though the yellow was the best of the mounts Little Knife skipped onto Blackback. He linked all three horses with lengths of buffalo hair rope and struck north for the Crow people.

The sun had not moved far in Little Knife's journey when he sensed Blackback shudder with expectation and at the same moment he heard the whinny of a horse. He saw ahead two more horses, one moving lame. It was Old She Dog, his own second mount; the other was Big Elk's second mount. This was good. The other horse, Big Elk's second mount, stood with drooping head. As he got closer he saw that it was badly wounded. Three arrows were deep in its belly; there was a cut at its neck as if an attempt at slaughter had been made. There had been an ambush and both horses, one lame, the other injured, had been left to die. This was a bad thing, to leave the horses so. Little Knife did not know the mount of Big Elk, but Old She Dog was a friend. Old She Dog was a lead mare of great wisdom and had been given to him by the Old War Chief three winters earlier.

"Here!" the warrior had said, "take this wise old horse and she will teach you many things."

At that time Little Knife had seen only ten winters and even then Old She Dog was a scrawny one. The memories of it came back as soon as he saw her. The other boys had been laughing and pointing and jeering. But this was the Arikara's first important possession and very memorable for that. The horse, as with all things, belonged to everyone, in the culture of the Plains People, but bonding with a bow or a lance or a personal horse amounted to personal possession.

Little Knife had learned to ride with the rest when he was little more than a scurrying infant, hardly aware of his own capture, everything a blessed blur of innocence. Old War Chief had led the raid on Little Knife's village and raped his mother and taken her to his lodge together with the squealing Little Knife and made her a junior wife. Their child would have been Little Knife's brother had he not died and killed his mother at birth. Little Knife had no-one except Old War Chief, and the old Crow warrior had no-one but Little Knife, other than his grumbling first wife. The boy was to have been a slave, but became a son.

The old man was middle ranking amongst the leaders of the Crow people, ageing. As the years hurried by he smiled at Little Knife, and saw that the boy took on the spirit of a son. But the old man did not spoil the boy. True, he occasionally put a halt to the taunts of the other children, for the boy was always an Arikara in their eyes, but mostly he left Little Knife to develop his own strategies for survival.

"Let's hunt Little Knife!" would come the call from someone, without warning.

Little Knife was then gone, disappeared into timber, vanished beneath the water, dropping from sight in the prairie grass or a snow-drift. But they found him, sooner or later. It was not easy for the Arikara boy. So Little Knife developed the cunning of a vulture mated with a wolf. Old She Dog brought it all back the moment she came in sight.

Little Knife slipped from Blackback and walked across to his old friend.

"What is wrong, Mother?" he asked.

She dropped her head, her dark eyes flicking white, as she looked at him.

He knelt by her and lifted her front left and found a shard of rock caught in the whorl of the hoof. He pulled at it with his young fingers and it did not move. She did not jerk at the touch and he was relieved that she was not in pain; it was a matter of discomfort as she placed her hoof. He took out his hunting knife and drove it with care into the dead tissue, eased the point to the edge of the shard and twisted it out. She did not move. There was no blood.

"It is done."

Little Knife was about to turn to Big Elk's mount, to see what he could do, when he heard it gasp. Over his shoulder he saw it fall to its haunches and then, slowly, its neck relaxed, its head came down to the earth and it was still.

"Farewell," said Little Knife, quietly.

He returned to Blackback and was on her with an easy leap. He let go the ropes to the other horses for he knew that Old She Dog would follow him and that they would follow her. It was then that he saw the black vultures.

There were a dozen of them. More were coming in from the east, their quick laboured flapping followed by a short glide. At a distance, appearing to be a horizontal scratch against the azure sky, they banked and descended, their short square tails snapping at the air. They were dropping onto something not too far ahead but off Little Knife's line of advance. He shifted on Blackback's spine and the pony altered its direction to head for the bottom of the descending funnel of birds.

The two corpses were ripped and strewn amongst the talons and beaks of a mob of birds. Little Knife knew who they were. He walked the horses towards the arguing feeders and they reluctantly gave way only when he shouted at them. There was enough left of the naked youths for Little Knife to be certain. From the remains of Frog Boy he saw that his scalp was gone.

Little Knife spoke and it was a prayer: "When I see the black carrion eaters high in the sky I shall know that my brothers are watching me. Enjoy the wind and the freedom of the heavens."

He turned away and headed north again, believing in the chant he hummed as he rode.

〉〈〉〈〉〈〉〈〉〈

Runs Fast woke to the pain of a thumping head not knowing that Little Knife had saved his life by dragging him into the shade. His eyes first latched onto the flight end of an arrow sticking absurdly out of his chest, half a hand above his right nipple. Runs Fast touched it and the touch drove a rush of pain into him.

The arrow had missed his lung. All bones were untouched and only minor veins had been cleanly severed. He eased his hand to his back and found the other end of the arrow protruding from above his shoulder blade.

In dragging him Little Knife had snapped the arrow. The barb was gone. This was good because the binding that secured the arrowhead was lethal. Made of buffalo sinew the arrowhead was packed with deadly bacteria which, once inside a fresh host, would multiply and spread within an hour of entry if not removed.

Runs Fast, like all of his people, had phenomenal tolerance to wounds and infections. But he knew that the missile, left in place, meant death. Almost with instinct he took the flight end with both ends and with a wrench whipped the shaft out. He had to do it, and he did at once and returned to blackness.

He emerged from the new unconsciousness some moments later. The arrow was still clasped in his hands. A trickle of blood ran down his chest. He grunted with satisfaction knowing that the lack of pumping red meant that he had a chance.

Overriding his thought was the pain in his head. He dropped the shaft and lifted both hands to his forehead. The pain was intense, beyond bearing, and inside his skull, beyond his brow. To ease it he slid his hands higher.

He felt the wound and knew at once, and fainted.

}{ }{ }{ }{

Little Knife did not eat that day, or that night. He camped close to a dying stream that gave him and the horses water. He envied the animals as they contentedly rolled in the still green grass which bordered the stream and then ate for an hour before flopping down or remaining standing, to sleep. They gathered near Old She Dog.

Little Knife slept near her too, and wrapped her long bridle rope round his wrist. Twice she woke him as she ambled about in a half sleep, but each time she felt the pull of the rope as it went taut and moved a few paces closer to her master, easing the tension, regaining a kind of freedom. The hint of dawn woke him, carrying the call of a small flock of geese, passing overhead, flying north, very late in the year. Little Knife felt hungry. He must hunt.

But first he stood, then crouched and relieved himself there and then in the grass, unthinking, part of the universe. He stood, adjusted his breechcloth, stretched, sighed, looked east at the gathering light and counted the horses. All four were there. He went down to the stream and drank, filling his belly with *something*.

There was a sound, a sound that did not belong in this place.

He stood, listened. He glanced at the horses. They were looking east, towards the sunlight, ears forward. He listened intently, his jaw dropping as he gathered in the slightest vibration, filtering the morning calls of birds, testing the breeze passing his ears. He heard snoring. Snoring?

The wind was coming in from the east too, not strong, not enough to play with horses' manes, but enough to be felt on naked skin, cool with the threat of dew, a dawn breeze strong enough to carry sounds.

Little Knife took a hobble rope from the low saddle which had been on Old She Dog and put it round her front legs. She protested, more out of surprise than outrage, for it was morning and time to travel. Little Knife knew that if he moved off on foot she would tend to amble after him and the rest would follow and call to each other. Dawn was the time for journeys to begin. With Old She Dog hobbled they would stay with her.

Little Knife moved up a rise in the prairie floor towards the rising sun. He went two hundred paces and to his surprise the terrain suddenly changed into a dip-slope at the bottom of which was a curious widening of the stream to make a pond, now summer burned and half dried out. On the far side of the pond were four horses and three strange animals that Little Knife had not seen before. He had heard tell of a half horse that the Wasichu used. They were like horses, but shorter in the body, bony of leg, different heads. Very ugly.

Wasichu – the white men, the white-eyes – they were there too.

Little Knife had seen only one white man before and knew that they were strange and very dangerous, and extremely stupid. Now he was looking on three of them, sleeping, with no lookouts. Fools. He had heard that they were fools, and stupid. The noise of snoring now filled the air. Wasichu snore! No-one had told him that. They were like real people, like the old big bellies whose snores could be heard two lodges away.

Little Knife moved a little closer and stopped as he saw one of their horses lift its head. Little Knife kept snake-still, just looking. The horse was definitely alerted, but not to the point of calling out. Gradually the animal's head fell again as if the surrounding snoring brought security.

Little Knife decided to withdraw, but stared a little longer astonished at the scalp that the snoring man appeared to have growing all over his face. The Wasichu were very strange. He crawled back to the reverse slope, and then stood and began to trot back to his horses. His heart was beating fast. Little Knife was scared and hated the sudden thought that he wished that Runs Fast and the rest were there with the horses. He sensed them, on the air, laughing at his fears. At least he had his horses! Then real fear came, solid and threatening...

He saw a man sitting there amongst his horses; his treasure. His heart leapt into his mouth and he stopped dead. It was worse. The man was a Wasichu.

He was just sitting there, close by Old She Dog, just sitting, cross legged like a High Chief with a pipe across his knees. But it was no peace pipe across his knees; a long barrelled gun lay across them instead. Little Knife's mouth was bone dry. His hand slipped to the hunting knife at his side. The man made no movement. He just sat there. Grinning! It was the same smile as Old War Chief's, but this was a Wasichu. So, Wasichu smile too; they snore and smile and can creep behind your back! Little Knife now knew that Wasichu were truly dangerous.

Little Knife felt like a hunter crawling through the undergrowth, approaching buffalo on his belly, and coming face to face with a basking rattler. Keeping still was the only option. The man raised his hand from the trigger guard and beckoned the youth. Mesmerised, Little Knife stepped towards him, stopped, and the man's hand became agitated with another call. Little Knife moved closer.

The man said something. Wasichu also speak.

That was to be expected. But to hear them *was* a surprise; expected, yet a surprise. The words came from beneath a bush of hair, a kind of scalp beneath the nose. He had heard that a Wasichu might have more than one scalp but had not believed it. It was a little scalp that obscured his upper lip. It was frightening and a little disgusting.

Little Knife stopped. The words meant nothing. Then the man looked the naked boy up and down and said in Crow tongue, "You are a careless boy."

Little Knife was struck dumb.

"No tongue?"

Little Knife's jaw dropped.

"You alone?"

Little Knife nodded and felt completely stupid in doing so. Now the man knew he was alone and would kill him.

"You have a heap of horses for a boy."

Little Knife nodded.

"What's your name?"

Little Knife was silent.

"I am Grey Eagle," said the Wasichu and Little Knife could see teeth behind his lips, just like real people.

Then Little Knife's face registered doubt for this was a Wasichu and the Wasichu had strange names which meant nothing at all – the Old War Chief had told him so. But this Wasichu had a real name.

"What's your name, young warrior?"

There were no markings on the boy. He was just a kid with narrow shoulders and hips a mite too wide and tits, for Lord's sake, but good legs and a bright eye. He did not seem too scared. He had a knife. He was no threat, *if* he was alone. Frank Partridge had not even half-cocked the old Baker rifle. There had been no signs of there being more than one Redskin.

"What's your name?" he asked patiently, again calling the youth towards him with his trigger hand. The boy came closer and dropped to his haunches three paces short, and then sat, cheekily crossed his legs, and stared at the balding mountain man cum army scout.

"I am Little Knife."

"You a Crow?" The Wasichu smiled to encourage a reply this time.

"Yes." Little Knife sniffed at the air.

"You telling me the truth?"

Little Knife could smell this Wasichu. It was the smell of horses and doe-skin, a curious smell, acrid and sweet at the same time. He did not smell like a real person.

Frank Partridge had expected a look of outrage at the suggestion that he was a two tongued varmint, but the boy's face was without expression. His nostrils moved. The little devil was smelling him. He somehow did not look like a Crow. He had his hair in the high tuft of a Crow, but he had a softer face.

"You sure you Crow?"

"I was Arikara."

"Was?"

"Am!"

"Ah!"

They stared at each other. Frank was chewing a piece of dried buffalo meat. He was aware that the boy was watching his mouth.

"Hungry?"

The boy's eyes opened wide and gave away his thoughts, Frank reached into his pouch and threw him a piece, and it was gone from sight in a moment, being chewed, fast.

The boy now had a smile on his face and Frank gently placed his Baker by his side. The boy took his knife from his hip and placed it, mimicking, by his side. Then the boy eased himself forward and very gently he raised his hand and touched Frank's drooping moustache and quickly withdrew with a faint giggle of surprise and distaste.

Frank Partridge smiled and as he did so the orb of the morning sun came up from behind the slope and appeared to sit briefly on the boy's scalp. Frank pulled his hat a little lower to shield his eyes and began to question the Arikara-Crow boy on how it was that he was a boy with so many horses.

)( )( )( )( )(

"I cannot go back, with my friends all dead and nothing to show for the raid!"

Frank nodded.

"It is worse, for I am the Arikara boy. I lived, and the Crow boys died. I shall be blamed even though it was I who warned them, many times. Old War Chief will believe me, but the rest will not."

"Where will you go?"

"I do not know!" The boy's head dropped.

"I know."

The boy remained silent.

"Come with me."

Little Knife looked up into the eyes of the Wasichu and saw they were blue like the sky on water, which was strange, and very Wasichu for certain, and possibly magical.

"To the Wasichu Lodges?"

"No."

"Where?"

"To the Crow Lodges."

"But!"

"I know the Crow people." Frank waved his hand, "And you are rich in horses."

Little Knife frowned. This Wasichu knew the Crow people. He, Little Knife, had never seen this Wasichu and he was of the Crow. No Wasichu had visited *his* Crow people, except the strange one who sang songs and dressed in black and had a *bawk*. The *bawk* was also black with a cross on it picked out in gold. Little Knife had seen him only from a distance. Old War Chief did not like the Wasichu man who waved the *bawk* and sang strange songs and spoke of being saved. Old War chief said that Little Knife should not go too close for he was not in danger and did not need to be saved. So he watched from afar, did not get close enough to touch, and learned little of that Wasichu who seemed to have nothing to offer anyway. This Wasichu was very close and he had touched him already. Little Knife shuddered slightly.

"The morning is cold," said the Wasichu.

Little Knife nodded and said, "I do not know you, Wasichu. You have not been to my people." Little Knife dropped his head as if in shame that he did not know this man.

"But you are of the Elk Hunters."

Little Knife nodded. How did this Wasichu know these things?

"My clan are the Wolf Callers."

"Ah! I *have* heard of them." Suddenly he was eager. "I have heard they hunt with the Wasichu."

"It is true. There are few of them, far to the north."

"How is it that you are of that clan, for you are Wasichu, not Crow?"

Frank nodded, "They take me as their brother."

"Why?"

"Because I trade with them."

"What do you trade?"

"Good guns for good pelts, for the hides of buffalo too."

"My people do not know you."

"You can take me to them."

"They do not know you and will still hate me. Maybe even more if I bring a Wasichu with me."

"I have gifts."

"Gifts? To trade?"

"No – gifts."

"What gifts?"

"Beautiful things."

"The burning water?"

Little Knife had heard of a Wasichu water which was said to burn the mouth and the throat but gave visions and a sense of wonder. He had heard of this but never seen it, still less tasted it, but he had heard that it was a beautiful thing, better than a dream. There was a bad look on the face of the Wasichu. Had he said something wrong?

"I bring gifts not poison."

What was this strange Wasichu talking about? "Poison?"

"The burning water takes away the thoughts of a man and makes him foolish. It makes a man half dead, but gives him the feeling that he can fly. But no man can fly."

Little Knife shook his head at these ideas which meant nothing.

"I bring gifts – good hunting rifles and words from my Chief of Chiefs. I must talk with the Crow and learn from them, taking word back to my Chief of Chiefs, also bringing to your people secret things. Come with me. Help me."

Little Knife heard the words with amazement. He, the Arikara boy, *helping* a Wasichu. He felt the sun on the back of his head and wondered if he was being made sick by its burning. But this could not be, for the morning was young.

"But I bring nothing but death back to my people – my friends are gone."

"Do your people know of this?"

"No."

"Only you know?"

"Yes – I am the bringer of the news in my mouth." He paused for a moment, then said, "The mouths of my friends are silent for ever."

"I can help you," said the Wasichu. His blue eyes were burning into Little knife.

"How?"

"There is a way."

They were cut short by the call of a man's voice behind him. Little Knife turned his head and saw three men on the top of the slope and he became alarmed.

"They are my friends, have no fear, Arikara warrior."

Little Knife turned back to the Wasichu who said he was named Grey Eagle. The words that he had just heard from him had never come his way before and he liked them.

)( )( )( )( )(

The bad news of the death of young men came from a scouting party returning home from the east and crossing the path of the approaching band. They saw the small group of Wasichu with their curious half horses, heavy with Wasichu things. They saw in the lead a youth with his hair in the style of an Arikara warrior. He sat on an old mare and in her wake came three horses. The mare was painted for war.

Above her shanks were four mourning emblems and the sign of two coups alongside them; also a mark to show a captive, crossed out to show an escape. As the scouts trotted closer they saw the pony of Runs Fast with two coup marks and that of Big Elk showing one. The other horses also carried similar stripes to show that they had been ridden in the killing of enemy. It was the Arikara who was unusual.

The young Arikara was painted entirely white except for his face which was blackened with the mark of death. He sat upright on his old black mare looking like a spirit in his whiteness. He stared ahead, thin and proud. Only when they came very close did they realise that it was Little Knife and they took the news ahead so that five lodges began to howl with the anguish for those who could not be replaced.

The rest mourned too but the edge was taken from their sorrow for behind the Arikara boy came rare Wasichu and behind them came the half horses, and soon it was revealed that they had brought gifts and wished to trade for many other things.

The Arikara boy would not speak at first. His bright eyes seemed full of sorrow. He sat in the teepee of Old War Chief and let the Wasichu first hand over gifts – twenty rifles called Baker were given.

Food was shared, and with the falling of the sun, with the fire burning in the evening, and the sound of mourning close by, the story of the raid was told. The listeners heard how bad luck came with the losing of Runs Fast's coup feather. Then they were told of the fight for their lives by the Wasichu leader, Grey Eagle.

"We bring these things to a people who gave the world the warrior you call Little Knife the Arikara. We saw his courage. We saw him fight a great Cheyenne war party who killed his friends. We saw these things. Only our long rifles held them off, but we saw him strike down two! And then he galloped free, bringing horses with him."

Grunts of admiration greeted the words, and Old War Chief was beaming.

"You saw these things?" he asked again.

"We did, father," smiled the Wasichu who had no scalp to take and long whiskers from beneath his nose.

Perhaps his scalp had slipped under his nose, was the thought of Old War Chief, and he smiled at that. But he had heard of such things before, for the Wasichu were plenty strange. Old War Chief looked with care into the blue eyes of the Wasichu and saw that what he told was no lie and that his boy spoke true as well. But he did not trust this stranger. He was too rare, too far from a real person. Perhaps he had the two-tongue mind of a bad snake. But the old man let the evil thought wriggle away, as might the flickerer of tongues disappear amongst rocks.

"I see your pleasure in having a son so brave!" smiled the Wasichu.

Old War Chief nodded, smiled once more, and sucked at the pipe to avoid laughing out loud, tasting the smoke and finding it good. Old War Chief looked at the Arikara youth with pleasure and blew out the grey-blue smoke.

"How many did you strike down?"

"Two!"

The old man's eyes narrowed and he said, "Look at me!"

Little Knife's eyes stared from behind the soot black mourning face, startling in their brightness and truth.

"How many did you strike down?"

"Two!" The eyes neither narrowed, nor grew, they sparkled.

"You shall have two coup feathers to wear in your hair."

Little Knife shook his head.

"You can not have more."

He shook his head.

Old War Chief blinked. No youth would refuse coup feathers. A sudden doubt filled the heart of the old man. The boy might lie, but he dare not invoke the loathing of all who had counted coup and now were ghosts by taking a coup decoration without reason.

"You refuse coup feathers?"

"Let me ride with the Wasichu instead."

The old man looked very carefully at the black face with the hair now in the style of the Arikara, not quite right, but it would do. The boy was clever to refuse the eagle feathers.

"You took two Cheyenne, and escaped their revenge. You refuse your honours! You dare return dressed for your own blood after all these years, and now you would ride with the Wasichu? You would leave us?"

Little Knife nodded, his eyes never shifting from the old man's.

"Why?"

"I need a scouting boy to train," said the Wasichu, softly, easing into the discussion.

Old War Chief held up his hand, "Let the boy speak."

Little Knife's head dropped for a moment, then he looked up, taking in the old man's eyes, "I am always the Arikara boy. I do not belong. Let me go and I shall return with many good things."

"Why return, if you do not belong?"

"For you."

The old man looked at the boy and said, "You killed two Cheyennes?"

"Yes."

"And lived."

"The Wasichu saved me."

"Two?"

"Yes."

"Then take the coup feathers!"

The boy's jaw hardened, and he shook his head.

"Then ride."

Little Knife gave a whoop which drew the attention of a hundred ears.

Later, in the winter, the wife of Old War Chief, turned to her man in the warmth of the buffalo hides and said, "Why did you let the Arikara brat go?"

Since he had gone her man had been silent and morose. She pressed her knuckles into his ribs, "Why?"

"Because he lied to me."

"Lied!"

"Yes!"

"Ah! Maybe the Wasichu taught him how to lie."

"Maybe. Now sleep woman. I do not want to talk about that boy."

"He broke your heart?"

"Yes!"

"You are sad?"

"Yes."

"I thought so."

"Sleep woman!"

"I said he would."

"Sleep!"

With a sigh she snuggled closer to him. Her small triumph was lost for now she too was sad, sad that the old man was sad.

3

Next Dream

(Starlight, just before the end of the 10th Sun of the Sioux Moon When the Cherries Turn Black in the Wasichu Year of 1855)

Starlight. But he could not see it. Then the cool air, which came as a blanket with the starlight, formed the sensation which caused him to open his eyes. A party of wolves was close by, howling. They were moving in. He understood that. Wolves were howling. He could hear them. They called that they could smell dead men but were wary. He knew from their call that they had the future taste of meat in their heads. His brothers were the wolves. He knew that as well. He also knew that it was night.

He lay there, and felt his head to be a thumping thing, as if it were going to swell and then burst. He felt a wave of nausea pass over him, and his mouth was very dry. He knew that his mouth was full of swollen tongue. He also heard the wolves again and knew they were closer. As he lay there, engulfed in pain, he heard them come near but each time padding away, or jumping away at an imagined movement of the human who lay there. He saw through his pain that there were warriors, dead in the moonlight. Then he smelt the water and heard the noise of its movement. Thirst. He began to struggle to his feet.

His movements were a weight, spawning a supreme tiredness. As he stretched to his feet he felt giddy and retched, but nothing came from his dry throat. He stumbled the short way to the creek, and felt a powerful joy as his feet, clothed in moccasins, entered the water.

He staggered at the chill, and bent to scoop water as he advanced into the midstream. When his seed pouches announced that they were submerged, and for no reason, other than the potential pleasure of it, he plunged forward into the water.

He screamed beneath the surface and shot to his feet. His hands lifted to the scattering pain lizards in his skull and he put his fingers to the wound and bayed at the moon. He knew he was a walking dead man; he was a warrior without a shred of honour. The pain.

"Fathers!" he howled to his ancestors. "Oh my *Wakantanka* save me!"

They listened with grim faces, *Wakantanka* too, but said nothing in the moonlight, except one, from long ago, who slipped through the night sky from where he had been dancing with the stars and whispered into the youth's head, "But, my young blood, you are alive!"

"I am a dead man living," gasped the youth and fell forward into the water.

Again the terrible pain came with the chill of the water, and then, curiously, the burn, the rush, the vomit sensation of brains being spilled into a fire – subdued. He emerged, stood, steadied himself and with a deep breath slipped beneath the surface once more and swam with gentleness for as long as his breath could be held. The pain was not so great and began to ease further. The flow of cleanliness, the coolness, the wetness, all combined to soothe and quieten him. He trod water and reached down to find the riverbed. It was not as deep as he thought, so he thrust himself upwards once more.

With great care he stood in the silver light and touched his skull. He felt the broad patch of bone where his scalp should be. It seemed a vast expanse, but in fact Yellow Hair had been savage and quick and only a piece of scalp the size of a small man's palm had been wrenched away. The touch of his fingers did not hurt so much; the nerve endings were all gone.

He made his way back to the bank and walked a little way sniffing at the air. He caught the foetid smell of bulrushes and their sucking roots. He knelt and felt with his fingers and lifted out some mud. He put it to his nostrils. It was the right perfume. He looked hard at his hands, and found he could see well in the light of the full moon. He saw part of a finger missing and wondered why.

He made a paste in his palms, his injured finger poking out of the way, and then, biting his teeth together he compressed the mud onto his skull. He was surprised at the stinging sensation, surprised that there was not a huge bout of pain. Then he went back into the flow of the water, washed his hands, and drank from them. Finally he found his way back to the bank. He searched out a patch of cool grass and gently lay down.

He stared at the stars, deciding to wait for the dawn. Directly above was a blue star, distinct and separate. He did not know its name. He had a problem, which was increasingly terrifying. He did not know who he was, did not know his name, or why he was there beneath the stars.

)(<)(<)(<)(<

Happiness was in the spirit of Sitting Bull as he lay on his back looking at the same blanket of stars. He had his hands beneath his head. He had thrown his blanket over himself, for the air had begun to chill as it magically formed dew across the prairie.

Slowly Sitting Bull lifted his left hand and made as if to pluck a star, a large one, twinkling blue, from out of the heavens. He failed and smiled at his failure and then wished that he could fall asleep.

Far away a pack of wolves was howling a meat-call. Perhaps they were boasting to the moon, for the moon was full. It was the time when wolves and the moon could discuss things. This was what Sitting Bull was thinking. Then the call came again and it was definitely the meat-call. There was a carcass out there. It was not the majestic moon that held their attention. Wolves had little respect for anything when meat lay red and warm, or even cold.

Perhaps the pack had brought down a stray buffalo or quartered one from out of a passing herd. Perhaps it was from the large herd that Sitting Bull's hunting party was following. Something was happening, a fast ride away, but in the direction they were heading. They would find out when dawn came.

He lay with a slight smile on his handsome face. It was a broad face, the face that women loved and men found strong. He was in his prime, for twenty-four summers had come his way and there were many to come. His perfect body was svelte with power, a wound here and there, long healed; and the marks of the Sun Dance were old scars on his chest and back for Sitting Bull had passed through the ritual and heard the voice of *Wakantanka* and seen a Thunderbird. He was already followed, not just as a good war chief but as a good *wicasa wakan* who not only had visions but could interpret them and dreams too. Only the old gunshot wound in his leg was whispering misfortune as he lay there. But he lived with the wound, and the limp it gave and thought nothing of it. He was wrapped in a traded blanket of wool and felt warm and peaceful.

Sitting Bull listened to his good friends as they slept, listened to their breathing, distinguished the breathing from the night calls of the brothers and sisters who hunted each other in the surrounding prairie grass, tall in the summer. The wolves stopped. Sitting Bull listened. Then they began once more, and it was this distant chorus which opened the screen which led him to the edge of the other side, the place of mysteries where all the real people found sleep and one day the freedom which comes with death. His breathing deepened, almost to a snore.

The rush of urine from Low Bear woke him. Other comrades coughed and stirred. All of them had shifted in their sleep towards consciousness echoing the hint of light in the east. Soon the light of the quick rising sun would noose the high bluffs. The good day had begun.

One by one they glanced at Sitting Bull. Each was surprised that he still lay there, for it was his custom to stir first and go striding out barefoot in the morning dew, dancing on Mother-the-Earth. Instead, this morning, he watched them, a smile on his face, peering out of his blanket; a smile, so that they smiled too. Sitting Bull slowly gathered himself together to join his people and with a sigh got to his feet.

The youngest of the hunters stumbled away towards the horses to bring them closer to the small stream whose water fed the creek that the Crow youth, Runs Fast, unaware, slept by. The young men, for all of them were around the age of twenty winters, prime warriors, were now on the move, without orders, scarcely speaking. All but two of them were members of the Strong Hearts band. Sitting Bull it was who carried the Dog Soldier sash and was their leader because of it. He had been chosen for he was the best of them in war, and they knew it. But this was not a raiding party. Serious hunting was on their minds.

Each of the young warriors led two extra horses. Each horse had travois poles strapped to its flanks, to be used later to carry meat. Had they been closer to their lodges women would have been with them, but the herd of buffalo had been moving fast and drawn the hunting group away from the encampment. And now, though it was scarcely dawn, they were eager to make ground, for they were certain that a hard ride would take them into contact with the herd before the sun was high.

The herd was in the east, and a good breeze was coming from that quarter. There was the faintest scent of buffalo on the air. They were closer than they first thought; the herd had inexplicably changed its direction and was coming back towards them.

Little was said as the young men mounted. Some chewed a shred of dried meat, swallowed with mouthfuls of water scooped by hand as they crossed the stream. The horses also sipped a little water as they crossed. Mostly the hunters' eyes were on the horizon, sharpening with the growing light.

The smell of the herd was increasing. The horses had caught the scent too and were double-frisky with the dawn and the knowledge that they would soon be in action. All of the main mounts were buffalo horses. They could be used in battle. They could be used for travois travel. Their speciality was to run without fear alongside thundering buffalo. They would show no sign of panic at the threat of the huge beasts. The buffalo ponies were skilled in dodging the sideways slash of the monster horns, taking their riders close enough for the barbed arrows to whack into the muscle and sinew, cut through ribs and destroy great hearts.

"Soon we eat warm liver and proud hearts!" grunted Low Bear, his belly empty and his plump face aglow with expectation.

Sitting Bull turned to smile at Low Bear and nod.

"I think I have had a vision," said Low Bear and his horse stumbled, regained its composure and walked on.

"Steady!" he hissed to his horse.

"When?"

Sitting Bull was puzzled for no preparation had been made, he knew nothing of Low Bear having a vision. If the vision had come with no preparation then it would be special, even powerful.

"When I slept."

"Ah – was it not a good dream, just a dream?"

"It was real."

"Ah!"

They were silent for a moment as they rode towards the growing light.

"It was very clear."

"Ah!"

Sitting Bull knew that the story would unfold. Low Bear was a slow one when it came to the telling of an adventure; his weaving of the tale took time.

"I fought against the dead."

Sitting Bull looked across at his good friend and smiled at the expression on the other young man's face.

"Did you win?"

"No."

"Ah!"

"He came at me without a head. I shot my arrow at nothing and he came on towards me on a big horse."

"Nothing? What do you mean, you shot at nothing?"

"It was as if we were skirmishing with the Crow, yet it was not the Crow. I knew it was the Crow and it was not the Crow. One came at me and where his head was to be was just a fountain of blood."

"That was a bad dream."

"I think it was a vision."

"How real was it?"

"It was real."

"Could you smell the blood?"

"No."

"It was a dream."

"It was not a vision?" Low Bear's voice was disappointed.

"It was a bad dream. In a vision you would smell the blood."

"Does it mean anything?"

"Yes. All dreams come from somewhere and all dreams mean something. But when we search for visions then what we see is more important than a dream."

"But this felt important."

"Have you had this dream before?"

"No."

"Then you must wait for the next dream. The next dream will be important."

Sitting Bull saw that his friend had a look of doubt on his face, "If you have the same dream again we must talk about it."

"He came at me and was screaming at me, like the death owl in the night."

"You said he had no head."

"Yes. But he was screaming."

"How could he scream without a head?"

Low Bear thought hard about that.

"How did he see to guide his horse?"

"He was on foot."

"You said he was on a horse."

"I did. He was on a horse. But he was on foot. He just kept walking towards me. He had a knife, I remember that."

"This is a contrary dream," smiled Sitting Bull.

"At the end he was on foot."

"And you killed him."

"I shot at him – but it was as if I shot at nothing. It seemed that I should not have shot. But I did. And the Great Spirit intervened and took away my arrow to nowhere. What should I do?"

"You must wait," said Sitting Bull, conscious that the perfume of buffalo was getting greater.

"For what?"

"You must wait for the next dream. If you have another dream you will know what to do."

"How?"

"You will know – but if I am there I will tell you what to do anyway."

"How can you be in my dream?"

"By a miracle!" laughed Sitting Bull and with a tightening of his thighs he caused his pony to speed him to the front of his people, followed by Low Bear who had more questions to ask.

)()()()(

The hunt was a good one. The herd was not as big as they expected. They were able to ambush it. They scattered into the herd, working in pairs or as single hunters and took out thirty head. Sitting Bull worked with Low Bear and they did well; they shot down four: an old cow, a young bull, and two older bulls. The last two were crazy, for in the middle of the hunt the two animals suddenly rammed into each other. It was most unexpected. They seemed to expect to die. Later, Sitting Bull and Low Bear would tell the tale many times, but even the story of these stupid ones was nothing to compare with what they told about the boy warrior they took on the same day.

)()()()(

Not far away Runs Fast woke to the sound of flies and beating hooves. He sat up with a start and the whole of his sight line was a sea of brown as a mass of buffalo was spread before him.

The great beasts were scattering their way through the creek sending a vapour cloud of water into the air. They passed, two good arrow flights to his left, so he was in no danger.

He cursed himself for sleeping, and at once was aware of thumping in his head, which had more sound to it than the passing herd which itself made the earth tremble. In the midst of it he caught sight of a hunter on horseback and immediately dropped to his knees in caution.

"He is Sioux!" came the thought. He did not know why this thought meant danger.

Then he saw more of them and could be certain they were Sioux when he heard their excited whoops as they wove in and out of the streaming mass of animals. In swift succession they were drawing bows to maximum and leaning forward to let go into the chest and gut of their prey, all at a wild gallop.

In his mind he knew they were Sioux, and this was bad, bad. Why bad? Then he thought to himself that he was not Sioux, he was Crow, and he said the word.

At least he *tried* to say the word.

The word formed in his mouth but no word came out, merely a grunt.

"I cannot speak," he said inside himself.

He felt to have said it out loud, but no words came.

Then he concentrated his mind and said it again, and painful sounds came from his throat, but no words.

The youth dropped to sit, collapsed more like. He breathed deeply and his chest hurt. His head ached. His scalp was all but gone and he noticed once more that a finger was missing. And he was a Crow. They were Sioux. The buffalo were his brothers. He fought with his mind's eye to make sense of it and two men on horseback were in front of him. He stared at them.

Both were big men, young men but big. Both were painted for a successful hunt and had bows. Both carried shields on the sides of their horses, good round shields, which would deflect a lance and catch an arrow not fired too close. They had charged bows and were walking their horses round him. They were going to kill him.

"I'll shoot first," said Low Bear.

"Through his chest!" said Sitting Bull, thinking that it would be good to kill him quick.

"Look – somebody has taken his scalp!" said Low Bear, his voice touched with disappointment, also humour.

Sitting Bull saw that it was a boy; a youth more like, perhaps sixteen winters, maybe seventeen. His eyes were bright but where the white should be white they were very red veined. The youth was unsteady as he struggled to get to his feet. He had mud, cracked and breaking, on his skull. There was a wound to the top left of his chest. Sitting Bull saw that he had blood on his right hand. A finger was gone from there. This boy should be dead. He noticed the other bodies. He should be dead like them.

Low Bear had drawn his bow.

The boy felt to his side and found his hunting knife and drew it. He then began to walk towards Low Bear. He made a sign on the air to show that it was a good day to die. Sitting Bull kicked at his horse and moved between them.

"Wait!"

The boy stopped and looked at Sitting Bull. He began to crouch as if to strike at the new threat.

"Out of the way," growled Low Bear.

"Wait!" snapped Sitting Bull again.

He unshafted his bow and slipped the arrow into his quiver and the bow into its pouch, never taking his eyes off the youth. Then, with a sinuous twist, Sitting Bull threw his leg over his horse's neck and was on the earth. He limped two steps toward the boy and stopped. The boy faced him and pointed the blade towards him.

"You are hurt too much," said Sitting Bull in the dialect of the Crow. This boy was clearly a Crow. Sitting Bull's face was in an open smile. He had no weapon in his hands. He offered the palms of his hands towards the boy. The boy made an awkward slash towards Sitting Bull, but fell instead to his knees.

"Let me!" said Low Bear, coming behind Sitting Bull, stretching his bow to full pull again. Released, the arrow would have gone clean through the boy wherever it hit. Low Bear had a famous bow.

"Look," said Sitting Bull. "Look at him – he should be dead – yet he threatens us with a knife. I think this is your next dream."

Low Bear lowered his bow.

"But he's alive."

"Just, only just – so he is almost dead," said Sitting Bull and put his hand close enough to the boy to have it hacked off. The boy did nothing, as if he were already destroyed.

)( )( )( )( )(

Light Hair, First Wife of Sitting Bull, very pretty, plump and sweet, was not happy about the Crow.

"He will be my brother," said Sitting Bull. "He is named Next Dream and is the life son of Low Bear."

"He is a filthy Crow."

"He is ours now. Low Bear gave him his life, as does a father, *and* he dreamed about this same Crow before he met him. This Crow has a burden to carry with his wounds and that makes him magical by the carrying of it. He carries the mark of another's triumph."

"Burden – he's just lucky he did not bleed to death."

"But he lived – he is meant for something."

"He does not speak, he just sits. He sits and stares into the dark corners of the teepee and says nothing. He eats and he sleeps. He goes to the river when we are by a river and *lives* in the water. He..."

"He is ours."

"So be it!" she said, but she was no happier about the Crow than about the Second Wife, Snow-on-Her, that Sitting Bull had brought into her teepee earlier that summer. This was not a good year at all.

Next Dream gathered strength. He had many dreams of his own. They were bad dreams. He dreamt of cutting throats and a tall Cheyenne, of a crying child and a thin boy who was stupid. It was winter before he remembered who he was. And a moon after that, before he had found his tongue. Everything came back like a flood then, as if the making of the words gave birth to fresh dreams, which were tricked into frightening truth.

By this time he had gathered sufficient of the language variations of the Sioux to understand where he was and whom he was with. Even when he had not spoken he had listened with care and used the universal hand signs of the plains to make himself understood. Now he was able to tell them clearly the things that he had to tell. Sitting Bull had listened with great patience, reassuring his Crow that he

65

was safe in the teepee of Sitting Bull. Then winter came and with it a great deal of time to tell of many things.

Outside a blizzard was blowing and Sitting Bull was singing his latest song:

"In the snow the earth is dead
"When it melts the earth is fed."

There was a soft drumming to accompany the song as the young warrior tapped the back of his knuckles with the palm of his hand to hold the beat.

"I am Runs F… F… Fast of the Crow," said Next Dream.

"Of eighteen winters," smiled Sitting Bull.

Next Dream nodded.

"And I have twenty four."

"Which makes you w… wise."

Sitting Bull stopped tapping his hand.

"Not so wise, Crow youth, not yet."

The young Crow did not speak well and there was a slur to his words. Sometimes he stuttered as he searched for a word. When he stuttered Sitting Bull felt a combination of awe and compassion for this strange person to whom he had given life, given it together with his good friend Low Bear. Low Bear was also in the lodge of Sitting Bull that day. Sitting Bull had asked him to stay, for his wives were quarrelling again and they were better behaved when friends were present.

"Come to my lodge and we shall talk and smoke and silence the women," said Sitting Bull. Now everyone was silent as they looked at the young Crow.

"I remember," said Next Dream.

"Ah!" Sitting Bull smiled. "Then say your name again."

"I am Runs Fast of the Crow."

"Who gave you this name?" asked Low Bear.

"I… I… I… rem… remember it was a bear. I ran from a bear. I am Runs F… F…Fast."

"Here, with us, you are Next Dream."

"I am Next Dream Who Runs Fast."

"That is a powerful name," said Sitting Bull and pulled strong on the pipe, handing it to Next Dream. "But it takes the emptying of lungs to say it. *Next Dream* is better. It is your Sioux name and good for you."

Next Dream gave a smile which looked stupid. Sitting Bull studied him.

Next Dream was not stupid, but he sounded stupid at times. He had fine dark eyes and the muscles of his shoulders were developing well. He would make a good Sioux. Pity he was a Crow, born to die too young. But he survived. There was magic in that. His time had not come – so what was he being saved for? He watched the young man put the long straight pipe to his lips and Sitting Bull felt pleasure that two enemies could be at peace in this way. Not that this one amounted to much of an enemy.

Next Dream dragged heavily on the pipe and said, "We counted coup on the Cheyennes and one came after us."

"One?" asked Low Bear. He knew very well that it was one; he had heard the story six times at least. Sometimes Next Dream forgot that he had told the story many times, but it was a good story.

"A big Cheyenne who took the child."

"I have heard of this," said Sitting Bull. "I have a friend in the Cheyenne, he is famous as a healer and a winkte."

"This was no winkte," said Next Dream.

Sitting Bull was always amused by Next Dream's disquiet in this matter. "This winkte of the Cheyenne – the one I know, is also big," smiled Sitting Bull.

"This was no winkte." Next Dream was adamant; a faint rush of embarrassment thrust at the impossibility that a lone Cheyenne winkte could be so devastating.

Even though his memory had returned, the attack remained as a confusion in his mind. At such thoughts his head hurt, but it was an inside pain, not the pain which hurt his skull with a change of temperature.

As he sat in the sweet warmth of the teepee his skull did not pain him. He knew that if he went into the open there would be pain. It was his thoughts that were hurting and even Light Hair could not change them. The other pains she had eased with the fashioning of a beaver cap for him, which he wore, no matter what the weather, over the yellowing section of his scalp where scar tissue had formed to give a faint covering to the exposed bone. But the temperature still broke through. The only time he felt peace from the aching was when swimming in the warm months, soothed by the water.

"But what of this remembering?" began Low Bear.

Next Dream shrugged.

"You want to go back to your people?" Low Bear asked.

"Like this?" He pointed his injured finger at his own head.

"You are with us, quartered safely," soothed Low Bear.

Next Dream shrugged again and fell to wondering at the welcome that he would have.

"You are Sioux now," smiled Sitting Bull, receiving back the pipe from Low Bear, after it being taken from Next Dream.

"I ride with the Sioux," he said, but shook his head as if to disperse insects gathered there.

"What you need is a woman," came the voice of Sitting Bull's Second Wife, Snow-on-Her.

"It is none of your business," growled Light Hair.

"Be quiet, women," said Sitting Bull.

But they were not quiet.

"There are no Crow women here!" Snow-on-Her hissed.

"When I was a youth there was a Crow woman here." Sitting Bull was smiling at the memory already and blew out a great cloud of blue and grey smoke to help clarify the pictures in his mind.

"I remember it very well," said Snow-on-Her.

"It was a bad day," cut in Light Hair.

Seeing the look of interest on the Crow youth's face Low Bear said, "I will tell you, Next Dream, how it came about."

"He should not have interfered," snapped Snow-on-Her, nodding towards Sitting Bull, who continued to smile.

"You were but a child," said Light Hair. "You remember nothing."

"I was there!"

"So was I, but you were a child."

"I was there! I helped gather wood for the fire."

"Tell," said Next Dream.

"It is a good story," began Low Bear. "There had been a raid, a serious raid with some of our best people dying sweet deaths. We took many trophies from the Crows. There was a hand, I remember that..."

Light Hair interrupted with a laugh, "There was the ball-sack of a Crow – and his dangling weapon – all three parts were still held together by their rotting skin. He had been a very big Crow – I remember that!"

"You would!" Snow-on-Her sneered.

"Be quiet – I am telling of this thing," Low Bear pulled again on the pipe, deeply. He passed it to Next Dream to help remove the frown from his brow. "We had good trophies, it is true – there were some ears too – but above all there was a beautiful Crow lady. We danced round them and the women touched the trophies with sticks. Some saying…"

Snow-on-Her cut in, "I know what they said: 'No woman will play with you again.' That's what they were singing. They sang that to the ball-sack. I hit the big thing with my stick. I hit it so hard it nearly broke away from the forked stick they hung from."

"You were a little girl, you had no stick to use," Light Hair threw back her head with contempt.

"I can see them now, dangling there, useless, hanging on a forked stick."

Next Dream moved uneasily, aware of the laughing eyes of Snow-on-Her. She was looking at him, throwing her memories at him like stones. And she glanced at his thighs as she spoke. She glanced high.

"They dangled useless – like all Crows," she laughed.

"This is bad talk," said Sitting Bull. "Be silent." He had seen the disquiet on the youth's face.

"I touched the ears as well, and a woman did it with me and said, 'If *you* had been listening you would not have been killed.'"

"She did not say that," growled Light Hair.

"I heard her – and she said, 'If *you* had been listening you still would have your scalp.'"

The pipe, now in the hands of Sitting Bull, was suddenly pointed at his Second Wife and she fell silent, grinning, trying to catch the eyes of Next Dream. But his eyes were fixed on the fire in the centre of the teepee, and his mind awaited the words of Low Bear.

"We danced round the trophies and the women were sad. Some had lost good men in the fight. So they turned on the Crow woman. The men wanted her. The women knew it. *She* was going to have men, thought the Sioux widows, but *their* men were gone, dead, killed by *her* men. There was much hate in our women that day. Who was it that wanted to marry her into our people?"

"Grey Elk," said Sitting Bull. "I remember that afterwards he was angry with the women and pleased with me. The Wasichu killed him in the end, remember."

"We know that," said Low Bear. "The women who had lost their men wanted to give the Crow woman pain. First they ripped off her clothes. Maybe that was all they were going to do. Then some of the children said to burn her."

"It was me," said Snow-on-Her.

"It is your nature," smiled Light Hair. "You do not change."

"Listen!" Low Bear held up his hands for peace. "They took her to a tree. The men just looked. They tied her there. It was a pine tree, very tall. Then they collected brushwood. They piled it round her, the women taunting, the children rushing for more wood, and the men watching. They were smiling."

"You were there?" said Light Hair.

"I was there. So was Sitting Bull."

Sitting Bull nodded, "I had seventeen winters and they would not listen to me. I should have shouted and done something, but I knew they would not listen. There was madness in the women."

"She was a crazy woman, that Crow, a woman who had many men. You could see it in her face. We did not want her with us, the real people," said Snow-on-Her. "What was a woman doing on a raiding party? She was like a winkte – there for all the men. She was a many-men woman!"

"You say so," said Light Hair. "But you do not know."

"I know."

Low Bear sighed and waited for a new silence; then said: "They went for fire, they went back to the lodges to the fires inside to get a brand to burn her good, tied against the tall pine tree. Sitting Bull was not far away, and was full of sorrow for the woman."

"She was beautiful," said Sitting Bull.

Low Bear went on, "He watched them bring the fire and then they lit the brushwood. Sitting Bull had his bow, with a good arrow, and he was watching everything."

"It was a buffalo arrow, broad headed, flint, I remember it."

"He pulled and put the arrow right through her heart. The flames had begun to lick. He was in time to stop her screams. Her head dropped like this." Low Bear's head fell forward as he felt the force of the arrowhead going into his own chest.

"It was a very beautiful shot," said Sitting Bull.

"We were angry," said Snow-on-Her.

"The Crow woman was not angry," smiled Light Hair. "She died easy."

"The heart of Sitting Bull is very big," said Low Bear. And he looked round all of them in the teepee, with the blizzard on the outside. "All of you know that he has a big heart."

Thinking on this Next Dream raised his eyes towards Snow-on-Her and saw that she still seemed to have anger. Their eyes met and he sensed a form of triumph in her face.

He did not know that she was thinking that the Crow boy had eyes quite as beautiful as the woman they burned, even though she was dead, the arrow clean through her. She remembered how it suddenly caught fire and fell from her. And she remembered the smell and with a glance at all in the teepee she hoped they did not see her shudder.

){){){){){

That winter Sitting Bull had a very difficult time. The women fought continuously. He made the mistake of permitting them both to share his buffalo robes at night. Light Hair was his First Wife and he loved her. Snow-on-Her was his Second Wife, and he loved her too. She was so young and smooth. Beautiful. But it was her place to be the Second Wife. But she could not be satisfied with that. Much trouble was caused, especially at night.

The women wanted him to themselves. He could only take one at a time, and this also was not enough. So the women took to each one of them holding onto a leg and an arm of their husband, one on either side. Their hands fought each other on his belly, and he was not left alone at night. He sometimes went to see a good friend so that he could sleep.

And whilst this was going on, the Crow boy was also there, listening in the night. He sometimes caught the eyes of Snow-on-Her as she looked across at him in the flickering of the fire. Even as she took the thrust of Sitting Bull she looked his way. Mesmerised he lay, always, watching and waiting for the eyes.

One late spring morning, the snow gone, the air chill, the very first of the new grass easing into sight he was entering the teepee as she was coming out. They collided and their heads met. The pain, which burst around the skull of Next Dream, was immense and he called out.

"You are like a child!" she snapped at him.

He pulled her to him and she was silent. She could feel the immediate reaction of his man's weapon and her hand, drawn almost by instinct, ran to his groin and felt, and explored, easing into the thong which held his breechcloth. She found the thing pounding and squirming. He gasped and she looked into his face.

"*This* Crow still lives," she smiled.

As it grew Next Dream suddenly took her hand and snatched it away. There was a sudden fury in the eyes of the woman. Without warning, and with the hiss of a snake, she pushed his chest away and was gone outside in a moment.

He fell backwards onto the buffalo hides of Sitting Bull's teepee and thought crazy thoughts as his eyes grew accustomed to the lack of light in the lodge. Then the pain began to return to his head, only to be vanquished by the thought of the touch of a woman, in his secret place. It was what he wanted, and that was frightening.

It was at this time that the whispering began.

The quarrelling between the women never stopped. Sitting Bull, to escape it, took a raiding party out towards the Crow. The whispering began to root, and in rooting came back to where it began: Sitting Bull's teepee. The word was out that sweet Light Hair was not so sweet but that she was going with other men. The poison words, when they came back to the teepee, were put into the ears of Light Hair and she did not know what to do. She did not know where the words came from. The Crow shared their teepee – perhaps it was he – boasting of something that had not happened. She had seen Snow-on Hair look at the boy in a special way and she had even said the Crow had beautiful eyes, for a Crow. But she, the First Wife of Sitting Bull had eyes for no-one – so where did the poison words come from?

Next Dream also heard the words, but could not understand why the First Wife was being blamed. He saw her every day and knew that she was good. He felt fear that he also would be suspected. But he had only heard the words, he had not spoken them, he did not pass them on. What would happen to him when Sitting Bull who had given him back his life, returned to find the poison words going about that he was touching his First Wife.

Cold sweat broke on his forehead. Accused of something that he had not done, and worried about something that he might have done, for those fondling fingers haunted him. Scalping was preferred to this worry. Then one evening, when the sun was tired, he was alone in the teepee and Light Hair entered and said, very quietly, "I have something to ask you."

Next Dream tried to make his mouth go moist, for suddenly it was dry with fear.

"We have grown to like you," she began.

"I know this."

"There are words amongst the lodges which harm me, also you."

He gulped and said, "I hear them."

"They are not true."

"I *know* it."

"What do I do?"

The winter that had passed was the nineteenth year of Next Dream's life this side of the screen. He began to feel that he might not live to see another.

"There are bad words about you, First Wife of my Sioux father, and I do not believe them. They come from the tongue of she who shares this teepee. She wants you gone."

Next Dream felt he was listening to his own words rather than saying them. They were remote and dangerous words, true as well, but spiked with blood.

"What do I do?" she asked him, even though he was only a Crow youth.

"Only the women can work this out," he said with certainty.

"If the women really think I am not a one-man woman then..."

"Then go to them."

This was a clever Crow. She thought about what he said and suddenly the face of Moon-on-the-Water came into her mind. She was the old Cheyenne woman come to visit her half-sister. She was

73

not concerned with Sioux quarrels, she was wise, though her eyes were growing dim with her many years. *She* would know what to do.

"Tell no-one," Light Hair said to Next Dream as she went to stoop her way out of the teepee.

He shook his head, "I am silent already."

She turned back and bent to kiss him on his forehead, and he felt that maybe things could get worse, for his groin stirred at once. He was relieved when she turned away and hands did not drift to his thighs this time, and at once felt disappointment too. He was a hungry little Crow.

)(·)(·)(·)(

Moon-on-the-Water knew exactly what to do. She had a special blanket where she kept treasures to remind her of her husband, killed by the Wasichu, hated white-eyes. She took her husband's old musket, she selected an arrow from his best quiver, and took a hunting knife that she herself used on fallen buffalo and she placed them all in the centre of the circle of lodges. She stood there with Light Hair and began to chant in Siouan with a heavy Cheyenne accent.

"Light Hair is a one-man woman,

"One-man woman, one-man woman,

"Light Hair is a one-man woman, one-man woman,

"One!"

A crowd began to gather, all the one-man women were invited to stand with them. And they did, for they also had heard the poison words and felt for Light Hair. They had heard the words and did not believe them, so they stood with her.

When Snow-on-Her heard the call she went to look and listen and felt alarm. She too joined the others, for she also was a one-man woman, even though the eyes of the Crow youth were in her mind. The beating thing was in her mind. But no-one knew except the Crow. Nothing had happened. She had wanted things to happen, but nothing had happened. But this thing she had started was now dangerous. She saw that the men were gathering and she saw too that the Crow boy was there, and those eyes were looking towards her, triumph in them now.

The old Cheyenne witch began to call out again and the men were all around, smiling at this strange thing that the women were doing, a new dance, a new curiosity. It was very interesting. Then they heard that it was the one-man women who had gathered together. It was very very interesting, something that could be talked about later.

Then came the challenge. The old Cheyenne woman turned on the men. "These are the one-man women. You know them all. You are their one-man women men! If you warriors, you men, our men, if you have had another of these women come point her out. Take up the gun or the knife or the arrow as you do so – and if you lie, for no Sioux can lie and live – then let him die by that which he has in his hand. And if you tell the truth then the woman dies the same way."

And not one man stepped forward for the one-man women were all true.

Next Dream seemed about to step forward. The eyes of the Crow boy met Snow-on-Her and her heart pounded in fear, but he did not move again. He pretended that he had shifted the weight on his legs, nothing more. She sweated. He could have taken the arrow and pointed to her with it, but he did not. Now he was really favoured in her eyes. But no-one knew. She looked at him without a smile and she knew from his eyes that she had won a great battle before it was fought, that he was her slave. And she was at his mercy. The old woman was calling again:

"Bad words have gone through the lodges that Light Hair is of many men. But no man steps forward. And the Sioux do not lie. Let the poison words die instead."

There was a sough of agreement from the gathering. The old rumours were replaced by new ones – that it was Snow-on Her who had first put about the stories. Who else could it be?

The anger of Sitting Bull was severe, severe in its being unusual, when he returned from the Crow fight to a silent teepee. Clearly a great argument had taken place and they were recovering from it. But when he found out what had taken place he called Snow-on-Her to him and he walked with her to her father's lodge and he gave her back to him with three horses saying that that was all that she was worth. After that no man who wanted a one-man woman wanted her, for fear of other poisons being bred on the air around the lodges, even when they went to a new encampment. When away from her the people also commented that Snow-on-Her spoke fewer words than ever before. The women did not look her way if they could help it, for she was a creator of difficulties, a spinner of bad dreams.

Some old men, being fools, did look her way. She saw it in their eyes; a different kind of hunger.

Even though her tongue took care, the way in which she walked made up for it. Despite the dangers, several thought of taking her as a *Second* Wife. It had to be a Second Wife, for she had been elsewhere. Others thought different thoughts and hoped that their friends could not read their minds.

But Next Dream decided to take her, not as any wife, but as his first woman.

4

Snow-on-Her

(At the time of the dying of the Sioux Moon
When the Cherries Turn Black in the Wasichu Year of 1861)

Years later, when few of those young Sioux were still alive, and were old men, they talked about it still, but in whispers. They were united in their view that it was Next Dream who first had the idea, told them about it, and started it.

"Anyone can take her!" he boasted. "Look a... at her!" he said to others, before it happened.

Of course they had all been looking, ever since the time the women made the dance that was not a dance, when they all collected to show they were one-man women. The men in the lodges of Sitting Bull warmed to Next Dream after that. They felt sorry that he had to share the teepee which had so many squabbles. Then his urging that they look at the blameworthy one in a new light both excused them for what happened and wound him closer to them.

Next Dream had many friends amongst the youths too, though they still saw him as the Crow who came with a missing voice, finger and scalp. But when he rode with the Sioux he was one of them, and seemed to be without care. He was welcomed into the Brave Heart band, the elite four hundred led by Sitting Bull. He was fearless in battle and began to reap a fine crop of coups.

"We are Sitting Bull's boys!" they would scream as they whooped into the enemy from the north. And that was sometimes enough to turn them away without a fight. They said that Next Dream wanted to die anyway to get his honour back. But he did not get a scratch as he rode by the side of Sitting Bull. It was also whispered that he stayed out of shame, for the Crow would not accept him back even if he returned. Others said that it was good for the lodges that Sitting Bull brought in a man with such a burden. All of that bad luck which was with him was magical; a lot of misfortune had been used up. And it was proved in battle because now he had good luck. He carried enough bad luck for the rest to be free of fear. That is what they all said.

He had counted first-coup five times and killed a Wasichu walking soldier. He was big and handsome too. He had some good friends amongst the Sioux.

"Look at your Crow," Low Bear said to Sitting Bull after they brought back the Wasichu scalp.

"He is your Crow too. You had the dream."

"See how he struts!"

Sitting Bull nodded, but did not smile.

"I should give him a new name," said Low Bear

"Yes – you can do that, for you gave him his first Sioux name. You can take it back, or replace it. My father did it." Sitting Bull paused, a gentle pride came into his voice. "My name was Slow and my father's was Sitting Bull. He gave me his own name..."

Low Bear had heard this many times and quickly interrupted, "Shall we name him Strutter?"

"His name will be what he is known by – but remember his first Sioux name came from a dream."

"A vision, I think it was a vision."

"There was magic in it, anyway."

"Perhaps we should leave his name as it is."

"That would be good," said Sitting Bull.

"But he is a strutter amongst men."

Sitting Bull smiled, "It is his way – remember he is only a Crow."

Low Bear nodded gravely and did not mention the subject again.

Low Bear was proud of his Crow even if he spent so much time in the teepee of Sitting Bull. He liked the way he threw up his head, the special beaver cap heavy with eagle coup feathers. He could strut, just sitting on a horse. He strutted, even as he stood still; arrogant and sure of himself; with his height and his shoulders, the five coup feathers quivering in the stiff breeze. Several of the girls had giggled in his blanket as they stood in his embrace before the matchmakers. But he had few horses and had not taken a Sioux woman yet. Besides he was haunted by the eyes of Snow-on-Her, though only he knew that. He was haunted by the sight of her from far away. He laughed with the other maidens and they liked what they touched, but they were not for him. He searched for another fire.

It was the way she walked. Even when she was young she walked like that. It was what attracted Sitting Bull in the first place. It was what annoyed Light Hair, First Wife to Sitting Bull. There was a sultry movement to her hips. She thought herself beautiful. She *was* beautiful. She was slim, but had flowing hips, exaggerated in the loose dress she always wore. As she walked the dress remained poised, but the movement inside it could be seen as she generated an awesome sensuality, accentuated by the swollen beauty of her chest, also moving as she walked by. She would flash a smile.

Then her tongue would snake out, quick; come and gone; pink and moist. Older women saw it and sometimes snapped at her and took the smile from her face. They saw the danger, told her, warned her, threatened her; once they beat her. They thought it would pass, soon a young warrior would bring many horses and the dishonour would be over.

She would be finished with the shame of being sent home by Sitting Bull with three horses, because that was all she was worth. Some silly boy would find *four* horses for her, the women laughed, and she would have what she wanted every night – they laughed at that too.

Next Dream used to think about her as he lay in the teepee with the family of Sitting Bull or Low Bear, in the cloak of darkness and was very quiet with what he did. But the rest knew about it because of the perfume of his secrecy. His fathers would smile in the night gloom as the waft of it drifted on the air. Next Dream ached for her, very badly, dreamed about her, but he had too few horses. When it finally happened he had no need of horses. He was the first to have her after she had been thrown out by Sitting Bull.

Next Dream had been swimming. It was in the year of the bad fever, and Next Dream had been very sick. Many people had been forced to lie in their teepees for painful days, and ten had died, but the dancing of the *wicasa wakans* had driven off the illness. Next Dream had been one of the last to be touched by it, and the last to recover. They were camped then in the land of the Greasy Grass, further north than where the great fight with the Wasichu would later take place.

There was a pool there, now dried up with the changes to the meander of the Little Big Horn, but then it was much favoured by catfish, and summer Sioux youths. But on that day Next Dream was alone in the pool. He had been toying with the idea of catching fish, but had slipped into the water to swim instead, not bothering to remove his breechcloth, leaving his cap on his head after taking out the coup feathers. When the cap was wet it was soothing on a hot day.

The afternoon was sultry and the whole of the sky to the west was purple with a gathering summer storm. The air did not move but a small twisting wind had suddenly rushed by making the sound of a distant herd of buffalo, running for no reason. The cone of wind whirled towards the teepees, then changed course and in a frenzy dissipated itself and was gone. He stopped swimming and looked at it in awe. With its disappearance he began to swim again, almost lethargic, but thoughtful, pleased to have briefly seen one of the fingers of the Great Spirit. A film of dead grass and leaves fell onto the pool, and then the air was still once more.

Next Dream had seen twenty-two winters at that time, heavy set but with a keen Crow face which the Sioux maidens found so alluring. He was feeling a wonderful pleasure in being with himself, weaving down into the water and swimming beneath the surface, then breaking it and flashing the remains of his long black hair clear and then going through the movements again. He felt completely happy. The fever had gone. He felt no pain in his now crusty scalp in this warm weather. The protruding section of bone on his injured finger had long been pulled away from the knuckle by Sitting Bull, with a hissing shock of pain, then the flesh had closed over the knuckle and it had completely healed.

He was recovered, powerful, and sensual. The only pity of it all was that he was still with the lodges whilst his age band were at that very moment somewhere to the north where many buffalo had been sighted. Sitting Bull himself had taken out a large hunting party and this was certain to secure a good score.

Next Dream paddled on his back and looked towards the huge blackening cloud. A sudden fork of lightning zigzagged across its purple edges. Far away they struck, so there was a long pause before the sound of the Thunderbirds' wings arrived. He moved towards the edge of the pool, touched the slime of the bed and stood, his waist just clear of the water. The shock of seeing Snow-on-Her standing there, smiling, was such that he called out, "Huh!"

The dangerous thing happened quite quickly. She was smiling at him as he slowly moved out of the pool. The water turned his coppery skin almost to deep amber, and although there was no sun, the rivulets flashed like insect eyes in the night. He looked at her and thought at once of the way she moved. But she stood quite still, looking at him.

He was in front of her and could feel the blood flow at once. She looked down at him and saw it filling beneath the clinging of his breechcloth as it hung low with the weight of the water. He stepped closer and she was in his arms. Instinctively and wickedly his hands pulled up her lose robe. And he took her. It was the heat, her willingness, the moment. She was completely ready like a buffalo cow, just taking it, fast, jerking. The excitement was such that with a gasp his milk flowed quickly and he felt her nails pull at the skin on his back. The Thunderbirds called closer and the first of huge spots of rain slapped down on his naked skin. The storm broke.

In the coming weeks, as the year grew older, they did it several times, usually close to the pool. He told his good friends. He took Low Bear to her. She said she would not do it with him. But Next Dream had promised him. For a moment she looked angry that he should dare to give such a promise. Then Next Dream, as if to touch her hair, got close to her, and suddenly held her. She was thrown to the ground. His good father-friend took a long time and quite soon in his strokes her struggles eased and she was holding him tight and moaning, until he finished. When he got to his feet, still oozing, she looked at him and smiled, turned her face to Next Dream she said, "Now you!"

It was a brief time before the word jumped, like a spark from smouldering embers setting fire to the prairie. Next Dream's friends did it, secret arrangements were made, but secrets are not possible where the teepees stand close to each other; it is as if the buffalo walls themselves fall to gossiping. The young men had been playing this thing and the old men did not approve.

There were twenty-five of them – older men. They decided that she must go. She was a bad person. Sitting Bull heard of it and said that she was to be called Milk-on-Her, and they all laughed at her new name. Sitting Bull hoped that a new name would be enough. He was pleased when Next Dream said that he would get horses and that she would become his woman and it would be over then, and her name could be Snow-on-Her once more.

Light Hair heard of this and asked Sitting Bull if it were true, asked between the buffalo hides when he was finished and content.

"Yes, she will be the woman of Next Dream," he said.

"A one-man woman?" she asked.

Sitting Bull was silent.

"Can this be?" she asked

"She will be the woman of Next Dream."

"As well as everyone else's," growled the wife of Sitting Bull. "It is against the best way. It will make the lodges unquiet."

"I think it will work out in a good way," he said, almost asleep.

She shook her head in the darkness and knew that it could not be.

When news came that some Wasichu with many horses had shot at some of the young boys out hunting it was Next Dream who led a raiding party to punish them and capture horses. He wanted horses for a bride gift. But the horses were Wasichu half-horses and not right for a bride. Also he brought back a Wasichu girl, very white and pretty who screamed a lot – which Next Dream liked. Snow-on-Her burst into the teepee in the middle of it and beat Next Dream and the Wasichu girl, so Next Dream threw her out into the autumn air. She ran back to her father who did not want her either, but let her in out of the cold, and for no other reason.

The older men then had a clever idea and talked about it in old men groups. Sitting Bull saw the intention in the older men's eyes. He could have said something, but did not. Afterwards he was angry with them, but remained silent. If the older men had done nothing then the older women would have done something, and that would have been worse – that was the thought of Sitting Bull. Sitting Bull was very wise.

One afternoon the older men lay in wait for her by the river and took her away from that place, calling her "Milk-on-Her" all the time. She did not struggle. She thought they were going to kill her. She saw strange looks in their eyes. They put her on a horse, trembling, and rode with her until the sun was red enough to look at, then they did it.

Some did it twice. Some tried to but could not do it any more. This made them angry, so they blamed her for that as well. Afterwards, some said they did it more than twice, but this was not true – they were not young men. But it was true that they rode off laughing, leaving her there, telling her she was banished from the lodges of the Sioux, for ever. As the sun died she stumbled away until she came to woodland which led down to a different river and in the darkness she asked the river to clean her and take her to another place beyond the screen. She began to let all the breath out of her body and started to sink.

As her lungs were taking in water and she saw the edge of the screen which led to the green valleys she felt something animal take her in the water. She remembered very little after that, until she felt fingers touching her breasts, gently, and thought they were her own, until she saw a young Arikara standing over her. So she lay with her eyes fresh closed expecting it to start again, and not caring, because she thought that she was really dead and that the passing to the other side of the screen was no better, after all.

)( )( )( )( )(

When the problems of the Sioux were little more than seeds Frank Partridge said to Little Knife, "Meet me here at the close of the Moon When the Cherries Turn Black in *this* place, after one winter." This was on the very edge of the traditional hunting grounds of the Sioux not far from the camping place of the Hunkpapa Sioux, the people of Sitting Bull.

He was surprised at the tears forming in the young Arikara's eyes. He felt a curious pleasure as their sparkle was increased, their stare was more vivid. The scout felt a choke in his own throat.

"Listen, Indian, I will return. I am not going from your life for ever," the scout said quietly in the lilting tongue of the Crow that he spoke so well.

"Can I not come with you, Grey Eagle?"

"Not this time. I keep telling you this. I want you to stay here and be like the air. Be my eyes and my ears. I trust you. You have eighteen winters behind you. You are my man. Look for all that there is to see. Then, when I return, tell me of these things so that I can see."

So Little Knife remained as long as it took to watch Grey Eagle and his three white-eye companions on their tall horses drift away up the pass. Occasionally he heard them shouting encouragement mixed with curses at the grumbling mules, heavy with traded pelts, trailing behind the horses. He saw them halt at the top, far away, and he saw Frank Partridge look back and wave. He half smiled as he realised that he had thought of the Wasichu as Frank Partridge rather than Grey Eagle at that moment. It was because he was going

83

back to his own people. Little Knife waved in turn, throwing his blanket from side to side, like a war chief signalling a charge.

Now the winter was gone, the spring was gone, summer was resting, awaiting the first approaches of the fall. Little Knife was wrapped in his blanket, in the timber, out of sight, away from the river but close to the place where they must meet.

The night was warm and he was almost uncomfortable in the blanket. He lay awake, but with his eyes closed in the darkness. The moon was up but had vanished behind one of many huge clouds that paraded across the sky that night. The lack of light could almost be felt. Within it, night insects called with scratching legs; and an owl, resting close by, signalled with a chilling hoot that he was only *resting* whilst searching for souls. Little Knife shuddered and felt within the shroud of his blanket for the hilt of his knife. Then he felt foolish for if the night owl wished to come then the night owl would come and there was nothing that he could do about it. In a moment of courage he eased his blanket open, not only exposing his naked chest to danger but enjoying the sudden invasion of the cooler air from outside the blanket.

He opened his eyes and looked towards the dark sky and the lesser darkness of the clouds. He saw gaps in the canopy, occupied by stars, and concentrated his mind on his good friend the Wasichu who had taught him the Wasichu way. He had learned the shooting of the rifle, the words of the Wasichu, how to talk to the half-horses and how to drink the burning water so that it did not take away his mind.

Frank Partridge had been angry when he first found Little Knife drunk. He had taken the white-eye companion responsible and grabbed him by his throat. Then over the months he showed Little Knife how to drink enough for pleasure and when to stop. He was not totally successful. Little Knife smiled at that.

Little Knife felt an excitement within his chest that his Wasichu might be very close, maybe a day's march away. Perhaps he would come that very day with the falling of the sun. Then bad thoughts formed.

"He's dead," he mouthed the words. He thought about that and did not like it.

"Maybe he is delayed – there are many dangers. Perhaps he is lost!" He shook his head in the darkness and whispered aloud, "Impossible!"

The youth moved restlessly within the blanket, "Perhaps he is sick with a Wasichu sickness. The Wasichu are rich in sickness."

An unexpected whimper invaded his thinking.

His eyes opened wide but he remained very still. He did not even whisper inside his own head.

For a moment he thought it was a stolen soul being shredded by the owl, then he thought he had merely slipped in and out of sleep and had dreamed it. He eased himself onto his elbows and listened, to be sure. There was nothing. He dropped his jaw slightly to gather in the slightest hint of sound and heard it at once.

The sound was like a child waking and being surprised by the waking, but it was not a single sad sigh; there was a rhythm to it like weeping, but it was less than that. There was an anguish in it. Little Knife heard that it was human, a wounded human trying to ease the pain by emitting sound, but at the same time trying to stifle the call in case something evil overheard.

Little Knife eased himself out of the blanket and drew his knife. He crouched so that the sinuous power of his nineteen years was concentrated in his thighs and back. He could leap and run, or throw himself into defence or attack. He was ready for anything. But nothing advanced on him; just the sad and distant call. He rose to his feet and stepped through the undergrowth in the darkness, becoming completely animal, sensing his way rather than seeing it, testing the woodland floor with his naked feet, leading with his toes, so as not to make a sound. The moon, shrunk and orange, broke from the clouds and cast cold light. The warrior's night eyes, black with widening iris, gathered in the shapes of trees and as he distinctly heard the moaning of a woman he saw an advancing shape.

He stood as still as an old aspen trunk when no winds blew as she passed within three paces of him, not seeing him, and he could tell that she was sobbing. She was past him and moving towards the spot where the timber gave way to the river called Little Osage. He did not immediately follow her. He watched, letting her get twenty paces ahead. On the point of her vanishing, he moved after her. By this time she was clear of the timber. He followed but stopped where the trees stopped and watched her in the moonlight. He saw her snatch her clothes from her body, as if they were some kind of filth, and move into the water.

She did not throw herself in. She moved into the depths slowly. Soon she was up to her breasts, slow walking with an underwater pace by pace, determined, without a stumble. She was up to her neck. Her buoyancy lifted her and she floundered for a moment, and then seemed to swim as she was taken by the flow of water. Little Knife cleared away from the timber and crouched on the edge of the river. The moon came free of clouds, so he could see her clearly in the moonlight. She was struggling and not struggling. She pushed her face into the water and burst out of it gasping and then she did it again. She was trying to drown herself. Little Knife dropped his weapon and ran into the water.

She did not scream. But she fought him. He yelped as her fingernails scored his shoulder and his face. They both went under the surface and struggled in the flowing depths. His chest was bursting when she suddenly stopped fighting. He broke the surface and she bobbed alongside him, face down. He turned her onto her back and slid under her, awed by her nakedness, half-excited by it as he felt it, and he struck for the shore.

The river was flowing slowly with the lateness of the season. He found a foothold sooner than he expected. He stood in the water and took her by the hair and towed her ashore. Once he had dragged her clear of the water he knelt by her side.

She was breathing, deep like a sleeper without dreams. He growled softly as he looked at her unspeakable beauty, the flowing shapes, and the nakedness in the moonlight with water rolling from her. With the tips of his fingers he caressed her breasts, cool and yet warm, very firm almost like muscles, nipples huge and standing, very hard. The youth emitted another soft growl as he fingered them. He was himself impossibly aroused and hard. It jerked out of his breechcloth. Instinctively he touched himself and gasped as the violent shoot of milk spattered on the sand; an uncontrolled youthful explosion. For a moment he stood gasping and then, thankfully softening, he turned away and left her on the edge of the water.

He strode back upstream, until he saw the glint of moonlight on the blade of his hunting knife. He picked it up on the run, turned, and headed on for his blanket. Finding it at once he hurried to the woman, who was already beginning to move. He was on her in a moment and before she could begin to struggle again he had thrown his blanket over her, rolled her into it and pulled her to him as he knelt, entrapping her. He looked into her face and saw that she was astonishingly beautiful, despite her look of stark terror. He said to her in Crow tongue: "I will not harm you."

She said, "Dog!" in the language of the Sioux.

"I not harm you," he said softly in the Lakota dialect, for he had learned much from Frank Partridge and spent time with many of the peoples, visiting in peace, sometimes dressed as Arikara, sometimes Crow.

"Dog! Dog!" she snarled and then she began to sob and sob and sob so that her whole frame vibrated.

Little Knife had no idea what to do.

He tried to talk with her, but she would not speak. When he stood and indicated that she should follow him she did not move. She was not large. She was delicate. She was not like a man. He thought to pick her up. He knelt by her side and tried to lift her and found it was easy, for Little Knife had powerful shoulders, was certain in his strength.

She seemed unable or unwilling to struggle. With an instinctive move he lifted her completely in the blanket and then found she was heavy. He hissed air into his lungs and went the hundred or so paces back to the secret place where Blackback's Daughter was sleeping on her feet. When he put the woman down he almost fell on her. He found it strange that, as he was carrying her, she was shivering violently. Yet the night was warm, even the water had been only cool.

She lay there wrapped in the blanket. Little Knife had a fire prepared. Frank Partridge loved to eat food roasted on a fire. The fire was waiting to be lit for Frank Partridge. To light it meant to send the scent of it through the forest, to show light in the darkness and smoke in the dawn. The fire was a signal to anyone that someone was there, not animal, but human. It was not safe.

"Are you alone?" he suddenly asked. It was a stupid question, especially as she did not answer.

She was still shuddering. Then he sensed that she was falling asleep. The shuddering stopped. He moved back to where she had entered the water and found her clothes. He picked them up. There was a faint odour to them, the fragrance of female. Little Knife was again half excited, beginning to pulse, and lifted the garments to his face for the pleasure of it. At once he smelt blood, and there was something else. In the moonlight he stood and pressed the deerskins into his face. He snatched them away with sudden disgust. The pungency of much male seed had invaded his nostrils.

)( )( )( )( )(

"Well, God damn my eyes!"

Frank Partridge was grinning broadly as he carefully focused the telescopic sight, set on the new Whitworth .45 rifle. He looked away, rubbed his eye, and put it back to the sight. "Damn me!"

He breasted the slope of the pass just before noon. As he approached he had dropped from his horse, taken out the long Whitworth and lain down with his elbow supported on a bolder, for all the world as if he were deer stalking. He had viewed the run of the Little Osage at the point he hoped to meet Little Knife. A couple of minutes went by before he captured the thin blue thread of smoke that marked a small fire. He then saw the pony. A movement behind the pony caught his eye. The pony moved a little and exposed Little Knife sitting cross-legged in front of a squaw who was wrapped in a blanket. Hanging from a tree were items of clothing. Difficult to tell, but they looked like a woman's robes.

"Well God damn me, he's got hi'self a squaw!"

Frank shifted away from the boulder, flicked the protective brass shields across the lenses and slid the rifle into the left hand pouch running from his horse's neck. He slipped his toes into the stirrup and was up and turning the animal in a single graceful movement as the two of them became a single being. He eased her up the last vestige of the approach slope and began the fall down towards the river, marvelling afresh at its blueness in the brilliant late summer's morning.

)( )( )( )( )(

Snow-on-Her looked at the young Arikara. He was not handsome like the Sioux; his face was too sharp with its high cheek-bones. He was no fine-featured Crow either. His eyes were intense, powerful eyes; she was struck by his eyes. She felt a rush of annoyance at herself. After all those pains from men like him she was thinking whether this youth looked handsome or not. Such thoughts had already brought her much trouble. The soreness was there, enveloping her, making her aware of herself, of being a woman, and she thought she could still smell them on her flesh. At the thought she hugged herself a little tighter, still watching him.

He was slim in body but broad at the shoulders. He sat cross-legged in front of her. She had glanced at his thighs and seen the tightness of his belly. She took in the back-sweep of his jet black hair and the faint smile on his face. He was unsure of himself, inexperienced, a youth. She felt curiously safe.

"You warm?" he asked in halting Lakota.

She nodded.

"You food?"

He had placed the flesh of a catfish on the fire, and the odour was invading the air. She bit her lip. The nausea had gone. She felt hungry.

"You food?" a little eagerness was in his voice.

She nodded.

As he was passing a strand of fish, steaming and oozing smoke, he stopped. She had reached out a hand from the blanket, but the fish was drawn away. The Arikara had frozen. Then she heard it too. The sound of a horse calling.

When the youth's pony whinnied a reply the Arikara snapped his head round to look at her and hissed for silence. The mare shook her head and her mane flew into the air. She dared call again. The boy was on his feet. He had picked up a long barrelled rifle as he moved. She saw it was one that the Wasichu called a Baker and she heard the click as he pulled back the hammer and then noiselessly he slipped to the place where the timber kissed the summer-widened beach. Suddenly he stood up and waved.

"There are more of them," she whispered to herself. She shuddered.

)()()()()(

There was only one: a very strange one with no hair and a huge scalp beneath his nose. He was a Wasichu and had a Wasichu hat hanging on his back instead of sitting on his head. His eyes were blue and penetrating so that she could not look into them. He smiled at her, and nodded as if he knew all that there was to know. She looked away.

The young Arikara had food cooking for the Wasichu in less time than it took to gather a basket of wild turnips. The three of them sat before the fire when it was ready. She felt safe and Little Knife felt pleased, for she had helped with the cooking, saying nothing, just helping. Frank Partridge had lain against his saddle on the earth, watching, seemingly at peace. Even the horses, who knew each other, seemed pleased, snorting into each other's muzzles, nudging, running a little, then stopping to chomp the dried grass, close to each other, herding.

"Well," said Frank, "what have my eyes and ears got to tell me?"

Little Knife told of many things. He had been on a buffalo hunt with the Crows. They had clashed briefly with a large band of Hunkpapa and some Oglala. He had seen their leader who was a famous man, known for his wisdom, Sitting Bull. No losses had taken place, but one of the Oglala Sioux had called coup on a Crow who had been lucky to escape with his life. The Sioux was a youth of perhaps fifteen winters, a strange youth with loose hair wildly flowing in the wind and without plaits. The hair was curious, very light, perhaps he was half Wasichu. He wore a red hawk attached to his head, and his horsemanship was remarkable. He had white zigzags on his face, lightning perhaps. None of the Crows knew his name, but they called him Long Hair. They remained wary of him. The Sioux were bad people, they said, and this one was a very bad Sioux – perhaps he would die a youth, for if he becomes a man he will be a mighty one. Little Knife told the story of the Wasichu buffalo to prove the point. It was gossip that he heard from the Crow, but it would be accurate enough to tell his Wasichu.

"Ah, my Frank Partridge, it was a funny thing. Many Wasichu came in teepees on wheels which squealed like a dying animal as they turned round and round and round."

"How many?"

"There were five teepees on wheels."

"How many Wasichu?"

Little Knife held up his hands twice.

"They went away?"

"Most of them went away." The boy smiled, a winsome smile. "One girl stayed."

Frank looked irritated, "Were they killed?"

"The Sioux killed them all. It was because of the white buffalo of the Wasichu. Each of the teepees on wheels had Wasichu buffalo with them. They were miserable creatures, which could not run like the real buffalo. So two Sioux boys took one in the night. The

90

Wasichu chased after them. The Wasichu buffalo was useless and could not run fast, so the boys killed it with arrows and this made the Wasichu very mad. They shot at the boys with their long rifles but they were as useless as their beasts and they missed. The boys went back to the village of the Hunkpapa when most of the warriors were gone on hunts – but a raiding party of youths was formed, led by a few old warriors..."

"Next Dream," said the girl.

"What?" Little Knife smiled at her, puzzled, but pleased that she had spoken for the first time.

"Next Dream did it. They were my people. I was there. I heard everything."

"Who in tarnation is Next Dream?" asked Frank in English.

The girl looked blank.

Then he repeated, in Lakota, the same question. "What did he do?"

"Killed the Wasichu."

"All of them?"

"One girl was taken back as the pleasure thing of Next Dream," Snow-on-Her was frowning as she spoke.

"I have never heard of him," said Little Knife. "But I heard a large war party set out and caught up with the Wasichu. It was easy. They were slow, the Wasichu. The same youths who killed the white buffalo ran down on the Wasichu and shot arrows at them and made them mad again. The Wasichu came out on horses – four or five of them – foolish people. They chased the two youths, but their flight was a trap and the Wasichu were all killed. No Sioux was hurt, not a wound. Then they went back and did things to the woman and children."

"One Sioux was almost killed," she interrupted. "That was after, after they attacked the rest – the women and children. They all fought back, but they were women and children and the Sioux were strong youths and big men. Next Dream is big. One Sioux was almost killed – he went for a woman. She shot at him, but missed, then she shot herself." Snow-on-Her thought hard about that and then shook her head as if to rid it of attacking wasps.

"You are angry Frank Partridge?" asked Little Knife

"My Chief of Chiefs will be angry. Soldiers will come." There was a curious doubt in Frank's voice and Little Knife caught it.

91

"But many soldiers have gone away from the forts. There are no soldiers!"

"There is a war," sighed Frank Partridge.

"A war? With what nation?"

"It is a war of the Wasichu."

"The Wasichu fight each other?" smiled Little Knife. "I thought they were one tribe."

Frank Partridge shook his head wearily, "No – the Wasichu are many tribes, and tribes within tribes. Sometimes they make themselves tribes inside their heads."

Frank saw that Little Knife would not understand that – the nature of politics.

"But this war will end in a few months – and then the soldiers will come and make war on the Sioux."

"That is good," said Little Knife. "The Sioux think too much of themselves."

5

The Wasichu Warrior's Tales

(Late summer in the Wasichu year of 1863)

There were two of them. A man, a big man; and a boy. Little Knife was thrilled with the magic eyes that he had in his hands which captured the figures he was watching and brought them close. Little Knife lowered the field glasses and blinked. Now the pair were smaller than ants at his feet. He looked into the glasses again and the two seemed to be within easy rifle shot.

He began to pan away to the right where the river ran yellow with the sudden rains of the week before. It was less yellow than yesterday and in patches almost caught the blue of the sky, brilliant overhead, with a skirt of white cloud on the horizon. Little Knife caught the silhouette of an eagle against the clouds and was surprised, for this was not the place of eagles. Then he saw Frank Partridge.

"Let me look!" Snow-on-Her poked at Little Knife's bare arm.

"See – Frank Partridge is there. We have not lost his trail" he handed her the glasses. "Look where the sun is laughing on the water by the big trees."

"I cannot see."

He took the glasses from her and turned them so that the eyepiece was to her eyes.

"I cannot see," she grumbled again.

"You look in the wrong place. Look!"

She lowered the glasses and glanced at his hand to see the pointed way and then brought the glasses up again. The magic happened.

"Ah!" she whispered.

"Look beneath the sun and you will see Cheyennes!"

Without a word she eased the glasses to her left, "Oh – they are so close!"

"They will find Frank Partridge."

"We must go to him?" she asked.

"Yes. There is no danger I think. But yes – we will go to him. There are only two Cheyennes and one is a child."

Quietly, even though the distance was great and no sound could carry that far and the wind was playing on their faces holding back both sound and scent, they edged back down the low bluff and joined their horses.

)( )( )( )( )(

There was only one man there, by the running water in the late warmth of spring. He was a Wasichu. He was naked. His facial hair was blond with heavy streaks of grey; the colours emphasised by the bronze of his face.

His body was also tanned, unusually so. Yellow Hair had seen Wasichu naked before, but always dead on the sacred earth, freshly killed. Their necks, faces and hands were always grotesquely red-bronzed by the sun, as if painted. Sometimes their forearms wore the same sun paint, but mostly the Wasichu were white as death, even as they lived. A thought that worried Yellow Hair was that living Wasichu were like ghosts. This one was unusual for he was touched by the sun from head to foot. Yellow Hair was also startled to see he had no scalp. But he did have much hair beneath his nose. Yellow Hair had noticed that the Wasichu favoured this growing of hair which made them even more strange in the eyes of a near hairless real person.

Yellow Hair watched as the man, sitting on a rock by the side of the creek, cut at his beard with two knives stuck together and held in fingers. He had watched him cutting at the remnants of hair round the side of his head. Yellow Hair squinted, and saw that the man did have a scalp but had no hair.

"Hmm. This one is a bald eagle this grey one, a bald grey eagle."

He could see that the man was mature, maybe more than thirty winters, but was slim, with a youth's shape. Yellow Hair had seen few old Wasichu but those he had seen had been fat and soft. This one was well-shaped, hard. Dangerous to be so old and so well shaped, alone and still alive. He must have outlived many enemies. Care must be taken.

Yellow Hair watched with increasing interest as the man stood up and walked across to some clothing. He put on a waist belt to which

94

he attached a Crow breechcloth. He picked up a bow and a quiver and walked back to his horse, which was quietly grazing some lush meadow grass, untethered, obediently not drifting far away. The animal was a fine pony, Indian, the colour of dirty snow, unmarked except that round the right eye was painted a red circle.

Yellow Hair signalled to his war party it should surround the Wasichu warrior, but not kill him. The war party was eager.

)()()()()(

The three buffalo hunters had two wagons, and a single horse tethered to the lead wagon. Each wagon was half-filled with hides. A million flies rose and fell back, in clouds, as the wagon lurched from side to side. The hunters saw the two Cheyennes as they neared the crest of a steep undulation and knew that they must kill them. They could be scouts for an Indian war party. These two varmints could move quickly to it and bring it back for their scalps. They had thought themselves clear of Indians; the presence of these two was a dangerous setback.

They were experienced hunters and with the wind stiff in their faces they were certain that the Indians had not heard them. Surely they had not seen them either. The hunters began to feel lucky. They were perched high on their wagons and saw over the crest of the hill before the wagons were exposed. They stopped their mules, dropped as one from the wagons, so disappearing from the Cheyennes' sight even if they looked over their shoulders.

The three felt a sense of relief that the breeze was so strong in their faces; even the stench would not drift down to the Cheyennes. But they knew the Cheyennes would smell the hides at some point, or find their track, or see the corpses. They might come across the tracks of the wagons further down the trail, and cut back to follow them, to find the killers of their beloved buffalo. The hunters decided to pick off the Cheyennes before that could happen. This would be easy work.

Lying there, staring through the lengthening grass, they did not find it unusual that the two Cheyennes should suddenly split from each other and head for the river. There were five fresh kills down there. The Indians must have seen the corpses already. They would find wagon markings too and begin tracking. The hunters eased themselves forward bending low in the tall grass, almost invisible as they too headed towards the river.

)()()()()(

Frank Partridge sat and unstrung the Crow bow to ease the tension and was gently nudged by his horse, hungry to move from this place, aware that his master was readying himself. Frank Partridge stood looking at his possessions laid out in the sun after the cleaning and the oiling. He felt very satisfied. They were laid out for inspection as he might have done in the Crimea, a decade ago. Frank Partridge suddenly pulled himself to attention, his back to his equipment.

"Corporal Partridge, ready for inspection, Captain, sir!" he called out and saluted the wilderness. Then he spun round and faced the equipment, returning the salute to himself and said briskly, "At ease, Corporal."

He put his hands on his hips and stared at the equipment, "Most pleasing..."

Ben nudged him again, hard from behind.

"Can't you see I'm inspecting me!" he snapped at the horse.

Ben snorted and Frank Partridge caressed the handsome animal's muzzle. "Alright, Mister, we'll get going."

Frank Partridge bent and picked up the belt which held the heavy Navy Colt. He fastened it round his waist. When he bathed he always favoured the bow at his side. Neither Indian nor renegade would expect a white man to go for a bow. The tactic had twice saved his life. But once on foot his revolver belt was round his waist, the weapon hanging to his right, balanced on the left by a thick bladed knife some nine inches in length, wet sharpened to a razor-edge. On a blanket lay two rifles, one a Spencer, the other a powerful English Whitworth .45 target rifle.

If he were lucky enough to make a hit with the Whitworth, its bullet would knock a man off a horse almost a mile distant. He was deadly accurate with the rifle at 600 yards, a target rifle turned to use as a precision hunting rifle.

The long Whitworth was also popular with sharpshooters in the war raging in the East. The Rebels were killers with the Whitworths in their hands. Frank had had a Whitworth before and lost it fording a river. Frank Partridge had picked this one up on the field of the First Battle of Bull Run. A telescope, cased in brass, was attached to the blue steel barrel. At two hundred yards he considered he could give a walking man a choice of which eye he would knock out. He had seven of the special moulded bullets remaining to feed this killer of men and great beasts. He also carried thirty rounds for the Spencer.

The Spencer repeater had seven of the thirty rounds stored in the tube magazine; a second magazine, also charged, lay alongside it. He had purchased the gun from its disgruntled manufacturer back East in America. Spencer had been unable to persuade the Army to buy it in numbers.

"You goin' out West?" asked Spencer, the smoke and smell of the shooting range outside his workshop still on the air.

"That I am," grunted Partridge, looking down the sight, fancying the barrel to be too short.

"Take it!"

Partridge looked at Spencer and nodded. Partridge had the Army's ear and success in Partridge's hands would not go amiss. The Englishman had arrived in Washington at the outbreak of the war. When it was discovered he was an experienced cavalryman and a survivor of the infamous charge of the Light Brigade he was immediately put on the Commander in Chief's staff with the rank of captain of volunteers. Lincoln himself heard of him and called for him to visit.

"You are a rare man, Mr. Partridge, out of hell and into hell. Go tell my boys how to do it – but not that way!"

Training and weapon purchase was his main role, though many a passing general sat to listen to his account of the charge.

He later found himself attached to McClellan's staff in the field. With the Union cavalry alone grown to more troopers than Wellington commanded at Waterloo, Frank Partridge looked for another role and was asked to go out on the plains to watch for Confederate attempts to turn the strategic flank by raising trouble with the Redskins. What he needed was a gun to match the Whitworth so he went to see Spencer himself.

"Had we had a few of these to hand we might have driven the Ruskies back to Moscow," said Frank Partridge snapping yet another cartridge into the breech.

He fired half a dozen rounds in quick succession. That was useful, rapid fire, but when he targeted at a couple of hundred yards he had missed the target every other shot. But he missed nothing at a hundred yards, and it *was* fast.

"How much?"

"Take it! Army don't want it."

"I fancy some of the boys might buy it for themselves – that might be your way in."

Partridge pressed a couple of Dixies into Spencer's hand – ten-dollar bills from New Orleans – insisting he took them.

"Same as takin' nothin'," muttered Spencer, but he threw the two notes on the worktable, near his cash box.

As Partridge was leaving he turned and said, "Who you seen in the Army?"

"Why, some high faluting colonel, in charge of munitions and supplies," said Spencer

"I'll talk to the President. Write him a letter in a week. I reckon if you can get him to fire it, the Army will buy it."

As Partridge picked up his Indian saddle with two pouches for the rifles, the Spencer pouch on the right hand side, he recalled the conversation, like a phantom passing by. Right now he was Lincoln's honest eye on the frontier, wandering, watching, reporting from time to time. His journey line now was east, for he had things to tell his master.

He threw the saddle onto the first of his blankets, placed on the pony's back and slapped him hard snapping: "Ben!" as the animal impudently expanded its belly to make the fitting of the strapping awkward – eager to go, not eager for a saddle. A further slap and a sharp word made the animal blow out air, the belly sucked in, and the strapping was secure. He fixed his second blanket and two fat pouches behind the saddle, then he bent to pick up the unstrung bow and quiver. He halted in the movement, briefly, sensing something.

He continued the movement and picked the quiver up, flicked it over his shoulder as if the world was all at rights, but in picking up the unstrung bow he showed a studied slowness, as if there was a weakness in the implement. But he was not looking at it; his senses were alert to something else, feeling out in every direction.

He had heard movement, a soft movement – an antelope, a ground hog, armadillo, a man? He moistened his lips and stretched, as if without a care, but listened for and was rewarded by the subtle sound of a fresh movement to his left.

The breeze, a stiffening of the breeze, made the new grass bend and shape itself like a squall on smooth water, forming a pattern of changing light which filtered across the ocean of growth. No uneven movement could be seen. Except, there! A man. He sensed a man.

He turned his back on the spot, now knowing where the hidden man was. He listened for the pull of a bow, the click of a hammer. The danger was downwind. Frank turned into the breeze and sniffed deeply. He ignored the perfume of his horse. He ignored the hint of the rotting corpse of a rabbit, half eaten by a prairie fox, then left to decay. There was nothing: no smell of buffalo oils, no smell of warriors coming with the wind. Perhaps there was only one, downwind. He turned back to the danger.

"Greetings!" he called out in soft Crow tongue. To his ear the dialect was lovely, lilting, he enjoyed speaking it.

He half imagined that he could sense the form of a man, snaking in the grass, now stock still, the stillness almost showing. Frank had called out in Crow because of his strength in the language, but this was a Cheyenne traditional hunting ground. With less confidence he called out in that tongue: "Greetings!"

Nothing.

"I see you!" he called out also in Cheyenne, risking a half laugh, and pointing.

"The Wasichu is good," came back a deep Cheyenne voice.

A magnificent man rose to a knee and slowly stood up. Frank lowered his pointing hand, pleased that he had the spot exactly, though more by luck than judgement.

The Cheyenne was armed with a hunting bow, which was strung and arrow ready. A jerkin of doeskin accentuated broad shoulders; his legs, from a lifetime on horses, had a slight outwards bend to them. There was a scar on his face, a proud face with a well shaped nose. It was a nose which would, with age, become a hawk nose. On his jerkin were markings, on his face no paint. He was not at war this one, but deadly for all that. Frank noticed a score of coup marks and other drawings on the jerkin to show the number of warriors this man had killed. The jerkin was the man's biography, a garment of medals and honours. Frank had taken in the information only at a glance because he was concentrating on those eyes, dark as coal.

"It is a good day to greet a friend," said Frank Partridge, looking to the eyes for a show of threat.

"It is a good day to live," said the tall Cheyenne and began to walk towards him. The Cheyenne's eyes were cautious, crowfeet at their corners showed that they were not wide open; the man was very alert.

Frank took his own sinewy muscles into contraction, ready. He knew that this huge man, getting larger as he approached, could have taken him earlier, before Frank had been aware of the first betraying sound. He saw an inquisitive twinkle in the warrior's eyes. Frank was about to relax when he heard an almost insect noise of green grass being crushed. There *was* another. The Cheyenne laughed when he saw the awareness of the Wasichu. "Do not worry, Wasichu, it is my raiding party, you are trapped."

"Trapped – the bad spirits of buffalo dung to it!" This was a clumsy attempt at a Cheyenne curse, which brought a grin to the Cheyenne's broad face.

Even as the smile spread, Frank's hand shot to the butt of his revolver. He threw himself sideways to the green grass, rolled, drew, snatching the double action hammer back, and came face to face with grinning white teeth, eyes – amazing eyes – of a boy standing with his hands on his hips. Frank blinked at the boy who had the muscle tone of a youth but must have been ten or eleven years old. He had sturdy legs, shaped arms, and was naked but for a breechcloth of the finest doeskin. Here was as perfect a creature as any under the sun of God, was what Frank Partridge thought. And damned near to getting his heart blown out.

Frank eased the hammer of the Colt back to safety. The boy was lucky his few years had not ended at that moment – lucky it was Frank Partridge who held the Colt and not a fool. The boy's over-sized bow was arrow-armed but held down without threat. In that split second Frank had taken in the peaceful information and not killed him stone dead. Crazy boy.

"The war party?" asked Frank, sitting up, turning his head to the powerful warrior, who was grinning broadly.

"All of it!" laughed the big Cheyenne, hiding considerable relief – the Wasichu had moved like the strike of the snake whose tail rattles, but with the control of a true warrior. He was glad that he did not have to kill him.

⋇⋇⋇⋇⋇

Always with eyes meeting eyes they talked, standing close, but not too close.

"You head for the morning light?" asked Yellow Hair in Cheyenne.

"Until I reach the lake of lakes," answered the Wasichu.

His words were good, the tone made slightly filthy with the lilt of the hated accent of a Crow. This Wasichu had the breechcloth of a Crow and a Crow bow master had cut his bow; the feathering of his shafts was also Crow. This puzzled the big Cheyenne. The boy standing behind him had a blank look on his face too, as he overheard the words – 'lake of lakes'.

The child's bright eyes searched the Wasichu's eyes. He saw how they did not leave those of Yellow Hair – the source of danger. Suddenly Yellow Hair glanced over his shoulder, as if to see if the boy was still there. At once the Wasichu's eyes caught the boy's and the young one glanced away at Yellow Hair. The Colt was in Frank's hand.

"Bah! Bah!" Frank snapped and the gun pointed at one heart after another.

Their faces showed surprise.

"I had you both!" laughed the Wasichu. "Your eyes left mine!"

Both Indians were staring at his eyes at once – and Yellow Hair's heart raced. The six-shooter was lowered and slipped into the side holster. There was a greeting slap of leather. The Wasichu was smiling. Yellow Hair knew that this Wasichu was boasting. This dangerous Wasichu was also warning them not to be foolish.

"The Wasichu is fast with his hand, like the paw of a mountain lion."

"Faster!" laughed the Wasichu.

There was something in the movement of the big Cheyenne, a flow which was softer than might be expected from a warrior who had just been shown death. There was something very unusual about him, beyond his handsome features, the coup marks, the flexing of muscles which were at a man's peak. The boy stood alongside the warrior, very close to him and looked up at him.

"Why is the Wasichu in our place?" asked the boy.

"He travels towards the dawn," said Yellow Hair.

"Why?" asked the boy.

"I return to my people," said Frank.

"The Crow are to the north," said the boy and waved his arm towards their lands.

"My people are to the east. I only dress as Crow because they are my friends."

"We do not love the Crow," said the boy.

The big Indian was smiling and looking down on the boy.

"This Wasichu can speak our tongue well, take care," whispered Yellow Hair, wanting the boy to see his surprise at the Wasichu's command of the Cheyenne tongue. Most Wasichu found this a difficult task.

"I speak Crow better."

"And you have big ears," grinned Yellow Hair.

Frank smiled.

"Why do you ride so far?" asked Yellow Hair.

"There is a war that way. I have to return to my Great Warrior Chief."

"I have heard nothing of a war? Which clan fights? Which band? Which nation?"

"It is a war of the whites – a nation against itself."

"The Wasichu fight each other?"

"Greatly."

"This is a good thing. This is a bad thing." The big Cheyenne pursed his lips.

Yellow Hair looked at him, aware at the same moment of a gust of prairie wind shaking a nearby clump of cottonwoods, catching the Cheyenne's attention.

"It is good because the Wasichu are bad. It is bad because not all Wasichu are bad. Young men die in wars..."

"Do trees give birth to the wind?" came the bubbling voice of the child from behind them.

Yellow Hair noticed a look of surprise on the face of the Wasichu.

Then the Wasichu said, "Is it usual for a young warrior to speak without permission?" He added in Wasichu, "Ain't that damned rude?" He was smiling at the boy although his words had criticism.

"Ha!" laughed Yellow Hair. "This is a special boy. He invents custom. I think he will become a contrary warrior."

The boy blushed at the half honour, half insult – a contrary warrior did all things in an opposite way, everything, including having a total love of death. The movement of the cottonwoods had also distracted the boy and the question had sprung to his head. As the insult-honour passed him by he looked at the trees again and the question returned – the birth of wind.

"Have you ever seen the wind?" asked Yellow Hair.

"No father."

"Nor have I?"

The warrior caught the eye of the Wasichu.

"Nor have I," said Frank Partridge. He leaned forward to see the face of the boy. God – what fine features he had. "I have never seen the wind."

"Yet the trees bow and wave when the wind passes by," smiled Yellow Hair. "So the wind is a living thing, but without shape – it is there, but cannot be seen."

He looked back at the Wasichu's thoughtful face and said, "I am called Yellow Hair." He put out a gnarled hand. He had seen other Wasichu do this. It was taken.

"My Wasichu name turned into your tongue is 'Honest Bird'."

Yellow Hair seemed disappointed.

"What is wrong?"

"In my head your name was Grey Eagle when I saw you by the water."

"By thunder!" said Frank in English.

The warrior looked blank.

In Cheyenne: "That is the name the Crow offered me long ago."

"Grey Eagle, the Cheyenne do not *offer* names, they are *given*!" Yellow Hair looked at the boy as if in confirmation.

"Grey Eagle!" chirped the boy. "Thus it is given by the Cheyenne."

"Grey Eagle it is," said Frank Partridge and goose spots ran across his skin as he looked back at the trees and remembered that as a small boy he also had thought that the waving of branches gave birth to the wind. Perhaps he had been a special child too. He shrugged – childhood – that was long gone.

)( )( )( )( )(

103

Frank felt that he could trust the Cheyenne pair. They called their ponies. All three mounted and all turned their backs to the sun. They meant to stay with him. Perhaps he needed to impress them further. Frank's eyes searched ahead and as the three breasted a rise in the plains he saw a small herd of antelope feeding. They would do very well.

A mile away: they were shapes of gold against an amber background, green in full daylight but painted amber by the setting sun. Frank was aware of the boy suddenly bringing his feet up to his pony's back and climbing so that he stood with perfect poise on his pony as the three continued to walk their mounts forward. The boy turned to the warrior with a face alive with excitement, his arms hung out for balance. Then he flopped back astride his pony, looking into the warrior's face and nodded towards the antelopes.

"Yes, you may!" said the Cheyenne warrior.

The boy slid his bow out of its case by the front left shoulder of his pony and yanked the string into place. The three continued to advance, the breeze in their faces, their route taking them closer to the small herd.

At a range of half a mile Frank decided to show the Cheyennes something. He reined in, dismounted and took out the long Whitworth, almost 50 inches in length. It was at that moment that there was a triple *crack crack crack* of heavy bullets passing between them.

All three horses jumped and reared with shock.

Frank's horse fled, and the other two threatened to unseat the Indians.

From behind the scattering group of antelopes Frank saw the mingling of three puffs of smoke. He dropped to his knee and brought his rifle up. He squinted through the sight, adjusted the lens, so bringing his apparent firing position to within 150 yards of his target – he saw three men, reloading. They were in buckskins. They were white. They were reloading! Gawd damn!

Frank looked over his shoulder; "Skiddadle!" he yelled. "Go, ride!" in Cheyenne.

The boy was already gone.

The big warrior was a hundred yards to the rear, turning his still excited pony so as to come back. Gawd Damn!

"Go!" Frank screamed, then turned to face the threat.

He stayed kneeling on one leg and squinted into the sight again. His eye watered; he blinked and focused. He steadied on his target and squeezed his trigger.

Cramppff! He was almost thrown backwards by the mule kick of the Whitworth. There was a pause and he could hear the Cheyenne pony coming up behind. Frank did not look back but watched and saw the distant figure on the left of the three throw up arms and appear to leap in the air.

"I'll be damned!" said Frank, already whipping out the ramrod. He thrust it down the smoking barrel, feeling with it for any particle of the bullet left behind. He had found that the bore of the Whitworth could foul if the bullet had been badly rammed home. The bore was clear. The *whizz-crack* of a ball passing his shoulder startled him and he heard the Cheyenne horse behind him jumping again. A second ball *thwacked* into the earth a yard in front of him.

"They'll get me next time," he growled.

His powder was barrelled, tapped down; the carefully moulded bullet, five left, was in the barrel's mouth. With all his strength he rammed it home. If it went in easy, it would not foul. It went in easy. He pulled the hammer back, flicked the dead cap away with his thumbnail, and searched in the pouch of his belt for a fresh cap to put over the nipple. The reloading had already taken fifty seconds. *Whizz-crack-twack!* and a bullet kicked up soil between his legs.

"Jesus!" said Frank Partridge. "They're good!"

The cap was placed, the hammer cocked from safety; up came the Whitworth. Focus. One on the right – breath out – hold it – squeeze – holy shit – it's waving about.

He saw the puff of smoke suddenly appear around his target. "Shit!" he said and steadied himself in expectation.

Hizzzt! The bullet was way overhead.

"Not so good,!" muttered the Wasichu Warrior in English.

Cramppff! the Whitworth roared. Pause.

He saw the ground spray in front of the two, and they suddenly upped and started to run towards the crest of the hill. They had three hundred yards to run, uphill in knee-length grass. Time enough. Frank Partridge coolly reloaded. As they neared the crest he was ready. Suddenly the big Indian was in front of him.

"Out of the way!" Frank snapped.

Instead the Indian threw himself on the earth in front of him. As he curled into a ball Frank knew what the warrior wanted him to do. Frank dropped onto the cool grass, and, using the offered man as a log he steadied his elbows against him, aimed at the figure to the left, brought up the barrel just a touch, shifted a hint to his right, felt the breeze on his left cheek and squeeeeezed.

The Whitworth bucked hard against his shoulder. He heard the Indian shout something obscene in Cheyenne and put his hands to his ears. Frank watched. Again a figure threw up his arms and went to earth.

"Good," said the Cheyenne.

"Good, hell and be damned," said Frank, "I was aiming at the bastard on the left, and hit the one on the right."

"Good," said the Cheyenne.

"I want the other," said Frank, scrambling to his feet.

"Good," said the Cheyenne.

They were both on their feet and running towards the Cheyenne's horse.

"Ben! Ben! Ben!" bellowed Frank. His own horse was three or four hundred yards away, ambling back, stopping to munch on a desirable area of grass here and there. The animal's red-eyed head came up and it shook itself.

"Ben! Gawd damn it! Here! Here!"

The horse began to walk forward then broke into an idle canter. As soon as it came nervously close Frank leapfrogged onto its back. In a single movement the big gun was in its side holster. Before he had even taken up the reins he was turning the animal with his knees toward the crest of ground behind which the enemy had gone... gone! Suddenly a horse appeared.

"The bastard's coming back. Got spunk! Gawd Damn!"

Frank leaned forward and pulled out the Spencer as Ben broke into a gallop. The first round was already in the breach. He pulled back the hammer, and as he did so he was aware that the Cheyenne was already a hundred yards ahead of him heading for the approaching Wasichu. He had a war club in his right hand and was whooping out a battle call; the club trailed a tuft of human hair.

Galloping horses closing others over two hundred yards occupy moments. Within them the Indian snatched his pony across the path of the oncoming rider and was alongside him, the club held high. It weighed four pounds; a large stone set in fine wood, lashed with the gut of a buffalo – it could crush a man's skull with a single stroke.

The enemy Wasichu would blow the Indian off his horse long before that, for sure. Frank had already brought up his Spencer, but the warrior was across his line of fire. The two were passing him by, the white man upright in his saddle as if on parade. The Indian struck. But it was an infant of a blow, that would not swat a butterfly. He just touched the rider on his shoulder. He was counting coup, damn it.

"Coup don't count with the Wasichu!" screamed Frank. "*Kill* him!"

Next moment Frank had a clear shot. Up came the Spencer, but the man fell out of the saddle before he got to snap the trigger. Frank's jaw dropped.

The Indian was whooping, and riding round and round the figure on the ground. Frank eased his horse with a jerk on the reins and a soft word, for Ben was mad as hell and wanted to gallop into the night. The words, as he leaned forward, his mouth near his animal's right ear, were aimed to cool the bastard down, but he was still rearing and backing. Frank got smacked in the face by the back of his horse's head as he tried words again.

"Ben! You bastard! Damn and blast you!" bellowed the Wasichu named Grey Eagle. The horse, snorting, came to an excited rest, shaking its head, throwing froth to the air.

"First coup!" shouted the Indian, leaping from his own prancing pony.

"This still ain't the right time to count coup!" snapped Frank. "This is a killing day." It was then that he saw the feathers of a hunting arrow sticking out from the shoulder blades of the dead man. Frank sat on Ben and watched, without remorse, as the warrior deftly took the scalp.

"Second coup!" said the Indian holding up the dripping blond scalp. He turned and looked back up the hill, still waving the trophy.

Below the crest, where the antelope had been, now scattered to the winds, and where the assassins had waited, there sat a diminutive figure on a white horse. He held above his head a hunting bow.

"God damn me!" said Frank. "Just look'ee at that!"

107

Frank eased forward and took out the warm Whitworth, and glanced through the sight. He saw the boy on the horse alright. He also saw what might have been two dark handkerchiefs hanging from the bow. He knew they were something else. He lowered the rifle and replaced it in the long pouch.

"That there is one hell of a lad!" he declared. "But he ain't gonna live long running off like that!"

"Special boy!"

"That's for sure – one heap of a good boy!"

"Warrior boy."

"For sure!" said Frank in English. Then he thought hard, remembered something and switched back into Cheyenne.

"If he is a heap good warrior and he is a boy, he special... he contrary warrior, a warrior when he should be a boy," said Frank.

"Contrary!"

Frank nodded.

"You know about contraries?" asked Yellow Hair.

"I know. I have heard."

"It is special." Yellow Hair's face broke into a smile.

"I know."

"White Hawk is very special – special for me."

"Sure looks that way," said in English.

Yellow shook his head, not understanding, and said in Cheyenne, "I fear for him."

"Yellow Hair," Frank used the name for the first time. "It is not he you should fear for, but the enemy of that heap of boy."

"The Grey Eagle speaks true."

They waited as White Hawk, came trotting up. From his neat breastplate of quill feathers flowed a streak of running blood. It was as if he had been shot through the heart, but the blood belonged to others. The child was safe.

)( )( )( )( )(

Frank set to examining the bodies. The man shot by the Indian kid was around thirty years old. He had a sabre scare on his cheek, the stitch marks still livid, and perhaps six or nine months old. His breeches were Confederate grey. Deserter maybe. He was armed with a Colt and a Whitworth too. He was still clutching it. It was unloaded. The fall had broken the stock away from the action. The rifle had not been cleaned recently.

The other two had long range rifles too, Prussian, not as reliable as the Whitworth. Reb deserters turned buffalo hunters? Frank gave the rifles to the Indians. The Whitworth man had no prepared bullets; he must have been using balls rammed down – not so good beyond 400 yards and messing up the rifling as well.

A search of the clothing and bodies of the men revealed nothing other than they were in their thirties. One had a tattered jacket, which had a button belonging to the 1st Tennessee Sharpshooters. Renegades? Frank wondered why they had opened fire.

He speculated that they had seen him about to fire and thought he had taken a bead on them. Three to three – the odds were in their favour – all they saw were three Redskins. But they were using common balls rather than bullets. That gave Frank the advantage, but now just three bullets were left for the Whitworth and Frank could soon find himself in the same position – using balls instead of bullets. Gawd damn!

Hands on hips, Frank looked at them, shook his head, having an uneasy feeling about them run through his veins. He decided to leave them out there as carrion. After all he was a Wasichu Crow out with the Cheyenne and both nations would do the same.

One thing that Frank Partridge did not notice was that the man who had been his right hand score had a hole in his upper chest, which had passed right through severing the aorta. The hole was too small for a Whitworth. It had entered from the right

〉〈〉〈〉〈〉〈〉〈

It was the appearance of Little Knife on their right flank that caused the hunters to bolt up the hill. Little Knife fired at a little over 200 yards and took out the one running closest to him. His shot hit a split second before Frank's long range strike. Little Knife then dropped from sight.

"Shoot the other one!" hissed Snow-on-Her.

"No!"

"Why?"

"My Wasichu told us not to follow him. He will be angry."

"Stupid foolishness," she hissed.

"Be quiet!"

They watched the action, saw the Cheyenne warrior count coup, heard his call of triumph.

"What is wrong?" asked Snow-on-Her.

"Hush!"

"Tell me!"

Her man's face showed fear – not fear, awe.

"It is him!"

"Who?"

"The big Cheyenne."

"What big Cheyenne?"

"Him!" was all he said.

)()()()()(

Yellow Hair's ears, surrounded by the insects of the night, were also invaded by the distant, far distant, call of a lone white wolf. Yellow Hair's eyes stared at the upended bowl of night which hung thick with stars, the soul people of all time. Yellow Hair was thinking very hard about the child. There was a problem.

At so young an age he had counted coup! He had taken the life of a Wasichu. Only a Wasichu, it was true; but even Wasichu were men, despicable, but men. The question was the status of the boy. At present he could not make milk, he could not marry, yet he outranked a brave; he was a warrior.

A brave was one who went to war but had not killed or counted coup, actions which were the very measure of a warrior. He thought very hard about these things, all the time staring at the stars with a smile on his face at the pleasure of the problem. He fell asleep and at once was swimming a river, in warm sun; his dream was in colour. The trees were dripping with green, and the grass grew around the grey and brown trunks, fish swam against his nakedness and he felt the pleasure of it until gunfire threw up water round his head. He felt terror, so that he woke to the sound of insects and again the distant wolf, further away in the night and its secret loneliness.

For a brief time he listened to the deep breathing of the strange Wasichu who thought he was a Crow warrior, but was still a Wasichu; he was a man, but he was not a human being – only the Cheyennes were real people. Were this Wasichu a Cheyenne he

110

would be a warrior for sure, and a war leader. This man was cool and brave, and yet had no scars. Wounds were honourable, but he was a warrior without wounds – both lucky *and* skilled. This Wasichu was definitely a dangerous man. Yellow Hair wanted to know more about him.

Those thoughts gathered around him and took him back into the dream world, but this time there was no terror, just visions which were lost in sleep, forgotten on waking, phantoms of pleasure lost for ever.

)(
)(
)(
)(
)(

"Tell me again," said White Hawk, looking intently at Yellow Hair.

The Wasichu looked startled, still not used to the idea that the boy should speak without call. He was either a boy or he was not. The tall Indian looked ahead as the three rode towards the new sun and the distant rise of hills, dominated in turn by the rocky outcrop. His voice, when it came, was deep, almost in a rhythm, a song of words.

"We go to a sacred place, high above the world, where we can see the rising sun. We go to a place where no trees grow, a place too high for the wolf. In this place there are no mice in the low grass, for there is no grass. But the great eagle is there high above the hills, whose sacred task it is to greet the dawn. Once there we shall look into the brightness of the eye of nature and see the future. This is a sacred place that only eagles know. From there you can see across the world towards the great green of the forests and the river which cannot be crossed without a canoe. No human beings go there, nor Wasichu, nor Sioux and definitely not Crow."

He glanced at Frank Partridge with a winsome smile, which was returned.

"There is nothing but the rising of the sun and the sharp scent of eagles up there. That is how it is, this secret place, sacred to those who told those who told him, who told me."

"Who was that, father?" asked the boy, knowing perfectly well already.

"The first was an old old man who had seen the other side and returned many times. He told my grandfather's father, who lived in the great woods. It was a time before the Elk Dogs were given to us by the kindness of the Great Spirit."

"It was the Wasichu who first brought the Elk Dogs," said Frank Partridge, almost as an aside.

They rode in silence.

Yellow Hair had not appeared to be listening. He *was* listening, but was feeling an unusual irritation at the profanity which had just been uttered.

"I read of it," Frank insisted.

"Read?" Yellow Hair thought about this. The Wasichu had said a curious thing, for in the way he used the Cheyenne word he had said that he had studied the walls of a teepee, looked at the drawings on it, he had read what others had seen and recorded. So, the Wasichu Crow did not *know* – he had only read the skins of buffalo.

"We Wasichu have things we call 'books'." He described a book.

Yellow Hair nodded as if he understood exactly.

"Do you understand?"

"Yes – *Bibell*," he said, in English!

"Bible!" said Frank Partridge in Wasichu and slapped the warm shoulder of his horse in delight so that it danced a step wondering what was happening in the mind of its rider

"*Bibell*," nodded Yellow Hair and then returned to the safety of the Cheyenne tongue. "Once a Wasichu came to us dressed in black. He was a mad man. He rode away from us waving his *Bibell* We caught him. He knew some Cheyenne words. He told us the book was powerful magic and was called *Bibell*. He was a Wasichu medicine man, but knew nothing. All he had was *Bibell*. And that was nothing."

"Bible."

"Yes, *Bibell*."

"What happened? You kill him?"

"No – he was a mad man – like he was in a bad dream – and as you know it is dangerous to kill a mad man for you may also destroy a special spirit who has taken him over – even in a Wasichu. He shouted at us that the end of the world was coming – he was very funny. Our world will last for ever and cannot disappear. He went into some woods and a big cat killed him. That was curious because the big cats fear people. Maybe it was a bear – the bear fears no-one. But *Wasichu* bringing horses to us – that is *very* funny!"

Both Cheyennes laughed.

"I tell you that many many moons ago," Frank waved his arm in the signal of Plains sign language that it was a time far back. "It was even before the time of your grandfathers of grandfathers – white men came across the ocean sea and brought to this land the first horses. Those Wasichu were dressed in iron!"

Both Indians shook with mirth.

"I tell you true! These Wasichu frightened the warrior souls of those to the south."

"They are poor warriors," nodded Yellow Hair, indicating that he understood the ease with which such people could be put in fear.

"And then one day several of the horses decided that they would go away from all the murder that they were seeing. Horses do not like murder. They like a warrior to meet a warrior. They enjoy the hunt. But horses have bad dreams when they see murder. Bad dreams..."

Yellow Hair nodded, for he understood that horses dream. He had talked to them many times. When he was a boy he tended the herds, first of his family clan, then of the band led by his father. He had felt sleeping horses dreaming as he lay with them in the fresh grass on warm evenings. Once he had slept with his head on his favourite horse of that time, Tramping Deer.

His mind went back to that earlier, happy dusk, he had fallen asleep with his own head on the animal's neck, talking to it until the dream time. He had woken to feel the movement of the animal, a shuddering, and he knew that the creature was galloping in his sleep across perfect grass with a herd following him. Horses dream. The Wasichu was talking sensible talk. The Wasichu was still talking. He must listen to him.

"...bad dreams. So the horses walked away from the Wasichu. They planned it. There were five. Two warrior horses, and three maidens. Their leader was called Yellow Spot. He was a brave horse, and had patches of yellow on black from his nose to his long flowing tail."

Frank Partridge was describing exactly the pony of Yellow Hair and brought laughter into the eyes of both Indians.

"To get a safe distance from the Iron Wasichu they galloped until dark night came and they could not be seen. They rested by a stream, which had fine meadows; they went on with the dawn. They roamed away always from the high point of the sun, in its journey

113

across the sky, moving in the direction the Wasichu call the north. They knew that they were in a safe place when they came across a mighty herd of buffalo.

"The buffalo laughed at them because they had no horns. They did not laugh when they saw the speed with which the horse could move. Then the chief of the buffalo thought about this thing and he began to laugh even more and said their speed was necessary to escape from the buffalo. The horses were very sad at this and went away by themselves. Do you know what they did then?"

White Hawk shook his head.

Frank made a gesture with his arm!

The boy laughed, he also blushed.

"It is true – they made love! They were lonely! After the five horses had made love and had become twenty, so that they made a buffalo sound when they galloped together, they found a Kiowa warrior hiding in some bushes."

"Kiowa!" cut in White Hawk.

"Be quiet! I am speaking," said Frank Partridge.

"Yes, be quiet," said Yellow Hair, "Grey Eagle speaks things I have not heard before."

"The Kiowa was frightened at first!"

Yellow Hair nodded in agreement with that possibility.

"So he put an arrow in his bow. Then he saw that the horses had no horns and that their eyes were large and wise, also kind. Then he was very surprised because the leader of the horses had a special gift. He could speak Kiowa."

They all three laughed at that.

"It is true!" said Frank Partridge still laughing a little.

"It is surely true," said Yellow Hair.

"Father! How can...?"

"It is true. Be quiet and listen," grinned Yellow Hair.

"The leader of the horses said, 'Thank you for not shooting us.' to the Kiowa, who was very ugly, as they all are."

Yellow Hair nodded and smiled.

"The leader said, 'What are you doing here?'

"'Hunting the buffalo!' said the Kiowa. 'But it is not easy. Every time I get close they run away!'

"'If you will get on my back I will take you to them,' suggested the chief of the horses, who could speak the tongue of the Kiowa.

"Of course the Kiowa was very wary of this idea for he was not brave, being a Kiowa. But soon he mounted the horse. Five times he fell off. Gradually he got the idea and they set out after the buffalo. The clan of horses followed to see what would happen. The leader of the horses searched out the buffalo chief, who had led the laughter. As he raced alongside the mighty one, the buffalo began a sudden turn to rip and tear with his great horns, as brave buffalo often do. At that moment the Kiowa pulled back his bow. He was an ugly man, but very good with his bow. The arrow found the buffalo's heart. And that is how the horse came to the sacred warriors of the plains and put fear into the hearts of the buffalo."

"I have heard it other ways," said Yellow Hair.

"So have I," laughed Frank Partridge, and with his horse sending vibrations of excitement through his legs he tapped the flanks and broke into a canter. "But I tell you," he shouted back, "the horse was a gift from the Wasichu!"

The Cheyenne kicked their ponies to follow, laughing, and not believing a word of it.

)( )( )( )( )(

The following evening Frank Partridge became aware that Yellow Hair was looking at him carefully.

"What is it?" asked Frank.

"You do not belong here, but you are content."

Frank nodded.

"Why are you here?"

"You ask me a difficult thing because the place that I come from is across the big water."

"What is the big water?" asked White Hawk.

"Oh it is a place where the sun comes from, and beyond it is my own land."

"Does the sun come from your land."

"Yes," said Frank Partridge, thinking that it was the easy way out. "That is why the Wasichu are so powerful."

Yellow Hair looked doubtful, but said, "Yes – but you – what is your story?"

"Well, once I was a warrior for my Chief who was a woman."

"A woman!" said White Hawk.

"In my land, things are different. This woman is a big chief. She is the one the northern tribes call 'Grandmother', even on this side of the big sea. There was a big war between my tribe and another tribe called Russia. It is very complex, very difficult to tell you these things because you know nothing of my people and my land, as I know nothing of yours.

"Oh – I have travelled across your land and understand the land. I understand the buffalo and the bear and the birds in the high places, but I do not understand your people as much as I would like. I was a warrior, a little chief, a two stripe chief, very low. I was in a regiment, like you belong to a society or friendship band. But in my way of doing things we fight as one. There was a battle and our two star chief received an order from a three star chief who had received an order from a four star chief, and there was confusion."

"Did they not use blankets to signal?" asked Yellow Hair.

"No – maybe it would have been better had they done so. My band of friends with two other bands galloped towards wagon guns and for every six who rode three were hurt or killed."

"So many, so many squaws without their husbands," nodded Yellow Hair gravely.

"This made me sad. I hated our star chiefs and one day I spoke to the one star chief and said he was a fool."

"Ah!"

"For this they decided to beat me and take the flesh from off my back."

"Ah!"

"But before they could beat me I became very ill with a sickness which made all that was in me come out and I was about to die. They said I could be a warrior no more. They sent me across the sea to my own country and they never did beat me because they thought I would die."

"The Wasichu are very soft," said White Hawk.

"I returned to my father who was a man who lived amongst the great canoes which sailed across the big water. He was a good man but before I became a warrior my mother died. My father in two seasons took another woman as his wife. I could not stay to see another woman in my mother's bed so I became a warrior until I learned to hate the star chiefs."

"That is very sad," said Yellow Hair wondering why the Wasichu could not have a Second Wife at the same time as a First Wife, never mind after her death. He would ask about that later.

"Then when I returned to my country my father helped me take a great canoe with fire in its belly to make it run fast across the water and canvass wings on poles to make it fly with the wind. I came across the big water to this land of yours."

"Ah!"

"I then saw terrible things. I saw a place where men sold men. The men who were sold were black. I saw one of these black men..."

"I have seen a black Wasichu, with hair like the scalp of a buffalo," said Yellow Hair.

"When?" asked White Hawk sleepily.

"Long time ago – let the Wasichu speak."

"I saw one of these black men, who had run away, be beaten until he was dead. I went north to the Wasichu lands where a man could not own another man. It was then that a war came to be, a war over whether a man could own another man or not. When my Wasichu brothers learned that I had been a little chief with horse soldiers they asked me to be a chief in their Army and made me a two silver bar chief. I again saw terrible things done to men and asked that I should be released for I did not belong to their country. Then a famous warrior, a two star chief named Sheridan, said that I could come out to where the sun goes down and see that my brothers the Red Men do not join with the Wasichu who buy and sell men who were not white. I have come to watch and speak and save the Red Man from the fork tongues of the southern Wasichu. And here I am."

Yellow Hair and Frank Partridge smiled at each other for they had looked down on White Hawk and seen that he had fallen asleep.

6

Visions

(The next day, in the Sioux Moon When the Calves Grow Hair)

In a rain gulch leading towards a gap in the high hills slept an ancient coyote. The high heat had driven him into a careless sleep. His legs quivered in the shade of his favourite rock. In dreams he chased succulent rabbits through easy terrain, catching them with sharp-teeth jaws, dream jaws, flinging them up with such violence that they were broken-neck dead before they thumped to earth. He was oblivious to the real world in which three warriors passed him by; the first large, the second pale and slim, whilst the third might have passed for a midget.

Yellow Hair in the lead was exhausted, fighting half-dreams himself, struggling against closing eyes as he rode Kills-a-Snake his dappled pony in the heat of the day.

Slowly, cautiously, Kills-a-Snake, trod upwards. The man and the horse were a single soul, locked, each entwined into the other's movements, their hearts in rhythm. Those ponies behind stepped in the exact tracks explored by the lead animal for they were watching its movements instinctively – the ground was uneven and strewn with rocks which could snap a fetlock if leaned on awkwardly. High above a soaring eagle focused on them briefly, without fear, and then wove away to look for prey much smaller.

A grey squirrel also spied on them, from high in a solitary fir, the last of the tree line, flitting along a branch, stopping, sitting back on its tail, out of sight of the eagle, unseen by the riders, of no interest to the horses. Insects were heavy on the air. A blue sky formed a porcelain arch above this world.

Yellow Hair slipped in and out of the threatening veil of sleep. He was half-aware of a sudden thump and found himself looking up at the snuffling face of Kills-a-Snake.

"Hey, hey, hey!" he sang at the worried horse. "I have fallen."

Then he saw the grinning faces of his comrades. He said nothing but made growls at himself and wondered which one of them would be the first to say something to bite his heart.

Yellow Hair was not hurt. He had dropped out of his dreams. He lay back for a moment as if he intended to be on the earth. The nuzzling of his faithful pony disturbed him.

"So you let me fall, my friend," he said gently to the pony as he climbed onto its back.

The Cheyenne stretched his arms to show he was wide-awake and urged his pony onwards up the pass. He knew the trail would soon open up to the panorama of a vast expanse of prairie, far below. He also knew the others were following, knew they were still grinning, so he did not look back.

"I was dreaming," he called out, not even looking over his shoulder.

"Of what?" laughed the Wasichu and was pleased as the boy laughed in unison.

A fall in sleep had happened to Frank Partridge half a dozen times; it was the sun, the mountain air, or the eternal rolling grasslands of the plains; long times in the saddle. Now he was content to have that broad back in front of him once more, leading the way.

"He was dreaming a winkte dream," whispered the boy.

"Winkte?" queried Frank Partridge

"Yes – he is a winkte, and he is my father," said the boy sensing Frank's doubts.

"A winkte!" Frank was looking at the broad back in front of him in disbelief. "You sure?"

The boy laughed and nodded, he was sure.

"And he is your father?"

The boy grinned.

"Sure is a strange world," grunted Frank.

With the boy asleep, the Wasichu had asked Yellow Hair for his story, asking how he had been given his name.

When he was born, the Cheyenne had explained, his head had been covered by an amber-gold mass of hair, most unusual, for no Wasichu had touched his mother. It was thought then that he would develop special gifts. By the time he was three winters old the pigment had given way to hair the colour of a raven's back. But the name given to him, with slight embarrassment, by his father, within a week of his appearance in this world, had stuck.

"And I have something more to tell you," said Yellow Hair with a curious smile.

"What is that?"

"I am a two soul person."

"I don't…"

"I am a man and a woman."

"A damned hermaphrodite," the Wasichu had muttered in English beneath his breath in disbelief.

"I am a winkte."

For more than an hour the Indian had explained that even the Sioux, war tribe above all, had a place for the winktes, for winktes were special, with powers that were of men and women too. The winkte was no curiosity with the Sioux, or with the Cheyenne, where they could be the wives of brave warriors. They were special for they could hunt and fill the cooking pots, and cook as well. When the men were away the winktes were man enough to protect those left behind from the Pawnee or the bear. But when the decision to go on the war path was made the winkte could follow too, accepted into warrior sleeping robes of fur, when far from maidens. The winkte could tend wounds but when the fight got hot could strip to a warrior stance and find the moment as good a moment to die as any warrior.

Frank had listened with amazement but when the time came to sleep he made sure his blanket was tightly wrapped round himself. Yellow Hair had seen this and was amused for to touch the entrails of a wolf would be better that to entwine with a Wasichu. But he had to think hard about it to convince himself, for the night was cold.

Frank had been woken by the boy tickling him with a twig. Yellow Hair was already up and a rabbit was cooking on a tiny fire. He had looked at the big warrior again and decided that the story had been a jest. How could such a man be a…? It was all too much. As the Wasichu still followed the warrior through the boulders of the pass he remained unconvinced.

Meanwhile giving the matter no thought, for it was not important, Yellow Hair was anxious to reach the apex of the trail so that the awesome view could be presented to White Hawk for the first time.

It was a view across a land which looked as if it might last forever. Beyond the image were the mountains, unseen, but there; and beyond them lay the ocean sea, and what was beyond that was not important to a traveller who was nothing but a grain of sand at the feet of such vastness. Yellow Hair needed to sing about it.

"*I am nothing,*" chanted Yellow Hair. "*I am nothing! I am everything! I am everything!*"

Yellow Hair began to sing the chant of life – to stay awake. He did not rhyme words as the Wasichu might; he rhymed entire ideas – ideas which permeated all that the Plains People did, and gave them a special insight into truth itself.

Frank Partridge listened to the chant and knew that he too was trying to stay awake. Now he felt the heat of the day on his bronzed shoulders and fell to studying the warrior ahead of him, focusing on him, absorbing his shape and movements. His hair was jet, catching the sunlight with its natural oils as it was pulled across his scalp to form braids which dropped across his shoulders and hung out of sight down his chest. From the rear of his head, held by a thong of kidskin, were three carefully arranged wing feathers of the Great Eagle.

Overhead a similar hunter rode the thermals, swooping in front of them for a moment so that Frank looked towards it. The bird suddenly dropped down the hillside and then began to glide once more away from them – it had seen a movement in the solitary fir, and was no longer interested in the riders. Frank's eyes returned to the warrior. And with the boy's words in his ears, he again looked at the Cheyenne, as they rode up the pass and could not believe it.

The sun's light almost turning the black of his hair to a sheen of blue, Yellow Hair's thoughts were focused on the cave up there, now close; the secret place in which bears lived in the summer moons, but now, at the close of summer, it would be empty. But he would be careful; bears did strange things and thought like men.

Yellow Hair longed for the moment of arrival, for first sight of the cave as if it were a home lodge. He needed to think, without half his mind on the passing by of rocks and animals. He needed the subtle invasion of a vision – some guidance.

"Grey Eagle – tell me of your war!" he turned to the Wasichu.

"What can I tell – other than it is a bad thing."

"Tell!" said Yellow Hair.

"Yes!" piped up the young voice.

"I smell the breath of the green things and they keep my mind away from that which is a ghost inside my head," said Frank.

"Tell us," said the boy.

For a moment Frank was silent then he said, quietly, "Such blood have I seen. I have seen men turned inside out like the cur that we might sacrifice in the dance of the dog. I have seen warrior courage as white men raced towards white men and they killed each other, rivers of them, creating lakes of blood."

"This is a good thing," said Yellow Hair. "Soon maybe they will all be dead and all the white women will not know white men at all. Maybe they will come in search of the real people."

"Tell of the bands who charged the wagon guns," called White Hawk.

"No more."

"Just one small story."

"There was a three stripe chief," said Frank. "He rode by my side. He held a lance. My band carried lances, not longknives. We were riding towards the wagon guns – it was the big fight with the Russian tribe. Suddenly his head was gone and still he rode on with his lance at the ready. He rode a long way and then fell from his horse."

"A long way?" asked the boy.

"Yes."

"Without his head?"

"Yes."

"That was very good," smiled the boy.

Yellow Hair had been considering what the strange Wasichu had said, and then went on, "If all the Wasichu warriors kill each other, there still must be boys too young for war in the Wasichu teepees with their squaw mothers. Yet they will grow! Maybe they will rush to the real people also and ask that we be their fathers – and we will say 'NO!' to them, so that the pale race will go away for ever – breeding its wickedness no more."

"But there are Wasichu girls as well – we shall breed for ever," said Frank Partridge

"Sitting Bull took a Wasichu as a son," said the boy.

"Where did you hear that?" asked Yellow Hair.

"Old Chief White Antelope told me." said the boy proudly.

"Yes – Sitting Bull has strange ways – but he is Sioux," explained Yellow Hair.

"The Sioux and the Cheyenne are too often as one," remarked Frank.

"You speak like a Crow," said Yellow Hair. "You are envious of the combined nations which can destroy all who come."

The Wasichu shook his head, "Not so – I am still Wasichu and I tell you the Wasichu are like a sea; there are more than you can dream on – there are villages as large as the whole Cheyenne Nation. There are villages as many as there are Cheyenne Warriors. There are plenty Wasichu!" Frank Partridge sounded bitterly emphatic, and Yellow Hair was impressed.

"Let me think about these things," said the warrior.

Again the ears of Yellow Hair's horse flicked back to listen. This was the horse which, even as a foal, stamped a rattler to death and was famous for it.

"Wasichu have strange names," said the boy suddenly. "Fronk Partridge."

"Your memory is good!" said Frank.

"That is a strange name for a warrior, a name that means nothing and does not touch the spirit."

"What name?"

"Fronk."

"It is the Wasichu way of naming. We do not give names from the natural world – but it is my true name. Partridge is the name of my father. Frank is my name. The two are my name. Wasichu always have at least two names."

"That is no name," said the boy.

"We Wasichu name people after their families and..." Frank searched for a word to cover the idea of 'saints'. "...and warrior spirits."

"And what of the wagon guns?" asked Yellow Hair, "I have heard that you have guns so big their bullets are the size of a man's head."

"Bigger," said Frank.

"This is very bad medicine," said Yellow Hair thoughtfully.

"And there is another gun which shoots bullets as fast as a rapid drum beat," said Frank. "The chattering guns, the Killers of Many guns."

"Do the Wasichu have plenty such guns?" asked Yellow Hair.

"Aye, my friend – plenty guns and plenty bullets – they fire plenty bullets until they choke on themselves and can fire no more. Greedy guns. I have seen wondrous things – but I tell the real people something which is very true, and which you do not believe."

"What?" asked the boy as he urged a stumbling horse alongside the Wasichu warrior.

"We Wasichu are dangerous. When one dies another takes his place, and if you killed us all then more would rise from out of the waters. The Wasichu are a sea of people – I have told you that!"

"The real people are many"

"But not enough," grunted Frank wearily.

Yellow Hair shook his head.

Frank said, "Listen to me! You will not believe me even when they come out of America, out of the rising sun and march right across the land to the other side. And as they do this more Wasichu will come from where the sun sets, from the other side of the mountains. They will come on iron horses which run on wheels along an iron road. The Wasichu will meet where the buffalo run safe. This is what will happen. And they will take your lands."

Yellow Hair shook his head at such nonsense.

"Look!" Yellow Hair pointed, for he had caught sight of the cave and his mind moved from the war things of the Wasichu and their stupidities and now thought only of bears sleeping inside the cave which was much more important than the foolishness of Grey Eagle the Wasichu.

Careful. He reined in and all three stopped. The heads of all three horses shifted up and down as they adjusted the bit-less war bridles in their frothy mouths.

Yellow Hair sniffed the air and could smell the old scent of bears, not recent, not for two days, perhaps more. One had put down a sign at the entrance, a urine marker to show that he had passed this way and that the mountainside was his. Three days ago, Yellow Hair concluded. But who knows? Careful.

"Brothers!" he called.

Leaning forward on his horse to stare into the cave, ready to turn and run in a moment, he called again in a half-chant voice: "I am here and I am your friend."

He slipped an arrow into his bow, and deftly swung his leg across Kills-a-Snake and dropped lightly to the ground. He felt the heat of the earth strike through his moccasins. He crouched slightly and the fine buckskin of his coat was pulling at the arching of his powerful back. He was aware that the Wasichu had drawn his small rifle from its pouch and heard the quiet noise of metal as a round was slipped into the breach. This gave Yellow Hair a curious sense of safety.

Yellow Hair moved in silence towards the black mouth of the cave. His eyes cleared and he concentrated on the cave. Bending again he moved into the entrance. He could smell bear very strongly, also wolf, but the cave was empty. He stood upright and waved his hand to the others. Here they would make camp.

They prayed together that night, kneeling, looking out at the sunset, with bellies full of a fresh brace of rabbit killed lower down the mountain with arrows. They watched the orb of the sun with great intensity, hoping that the spirit of the dying day would assist them towards a great peace, and it did.

Yellow Hair's head dropped suddenly. He was tired and his thoughts meandered to his boyhood in and out of his half dreams and attempts at forcing visions . Without warning, for no reason at all, he saw the creek named after him: Yellow-Hair's-Crows-Creek. He glanced at Grey Eagle with slight embarrassment for clearly Grey Eagle thought himself a Crow and might sense the nature of the dream-thoughts. But the Wasichu was still facing the sun, his eyes closed as if in sleep. The boy also was looking intently at the sun, now sitting on the horizon.

Flights of water birds close by the mountainside were crossing the path of the sun's dying glow. Yellow Hair let the memories flood in from his time of seventeen winters. He had been inexperienced, with an easy gentleness in his manner, riding back to the lodges in the setting sun. Two idle Crows, part of a larger scouting party saw him coming and waited for him. They saw he was a youth, and alone. They then committed their greatest and last mistake. They sprang their trap.

Their first two arrows ripped clean into Yellow Hair's sweet mare and she was felled dead at once by their penetration and the shock. He jumped clear, only to find that his bow was broken, snapped in two. He looked around for his attackers.

They had come at him on their horses, missing him with second shafts. Though his bow was snapped he had a battle club with an iron blade cut into its outer edge. It hung from his hip. He broke the leg of the first horse as they came too close in their blood hunger. Its rider was spilled at his feet, in perfect range for his swinging club and was dead before he could even kneel. Yellow Hair saw the split head, suddenly recalled in his memory, saw it in the light of a similarly tired sun glistening on the exposed membrane. It had been this same time of the day, also in the Sioux Moon When The Calves Grow Hair. Perhaps memories have a time to reappear.

"Hey hey, hey!" said Yellow Hair aloud, startled at the clarity of his memory. The other two were staring at him, startled at his sudden words. He ignored them.

How clear it was in his mind's eye, as if yesterday, though from fifteen years before. The second rider had turned in a flurry of mud and creek water but, as he rode back with arrow aimed, Yellow Hair had thrown the club into the man's face so that he too fell. Later, he declared it was a club with much magic in it. He was also angry because the club had vanished into the creek water and he never recovered it.

Yellow Hair, unharmed and in a craziness that made him a killer, was on the Crow in a moment, his sheath knife out and buried with a thump into the Crow's heart. As he got to his feet the Crow was alive, surprise on his face. He was very handsome. Yellow Hair remembered that he was very handsome. He gave Yellow Hair a nod of admiration and was dead with the nod

Yellow Hair took both their scalps. They had much hair, beautiful braids, the Crow people loved their hair. The scalps were heavy and warm as he held them up to show the setting sun.

He felt the happiness again at the present time and howled again at the memory, startling his comrades afresh and waking the coyote far below. The coyote jumped to four trembling paws, not knowing why he had been woken. All it could hear were the gathering sounds of night. The coyote forgot the curious noise from the place of bears as he felt hungry and began to snuffle around for beetles, anything, even though the biting of them would nudge his old aching teeth into fresh sharp pain.

"He is seeing visions," whispered the boy to Frank Partridge.

It was no vision, Yellow Hair was simply recalling the slaughtering of the injured Crow horse, a deep deft cut and an apology. Then the careful pursuit on foot, and the sweet words on the air to gather in the other Crow horse. He caught it and mounted it and called it Two Scalps. It was three nights and days before the horse responded to that name and Yellow Hair had sometimes wished he knew its Crow name.

The pony served him well for three years before it broke a leg in a buffalo hunt. Yellow Hair had cradled its great head in his lap and whispered to it as he gently cut its throat. It kicked. Then it slowly relaxed, trusting its master since there was no more pain. Then a horse darkness came over its soul and it went to the land behind the real world, and ran free once more with good legs rippling with power, rushing to his waiting Crow master who called him by his real name once more and on into eternity.

All of those things were still happening, thought Yellow Hair, for everything that has ever been in a place, still is there, for ever. Even something, which has not yet happened, really has happened in the future, and is also taking place for ever. Yellow Hair shook his head at that thought. Perhaps every moment is immortal. Perhaps, thought Yellow Hair, I am already dead. He pinched himself and found he was alive.

"Hey, hey, hey!" he called, so that Kills-a-Snake and the other two ponies drew up their heads and looked towards the warrior.

They were hoping that soon they would go further on their journey, which was already a mystery to the four-legged ones, for the journey seemed never to come to an end.

Yellow Hair suddenly turned to his companions, smiled, and said, "It was nothing – just a memory."

)()()()()(

"Why are they going up there?" said Little Knife.

"For visions," replied Snow-on-Her.

They watched from the south wall of the gulch, lying flat, hidden by a patch of yellowed buffalo grass.

"I know this place," she added. "They must come down the same way they went – we do not have to follow them."

She lay slightly behind the young man and was looking at his spine, admiring it, studying the run of the depression down to the firm mounds hidden beneath his breechcloth. She eased up to him, suddenly feeling a need to touch him.

He looked at her, as she came alongside, and saw something in her face and frowned, puzzled. She touched his shoulder and pressed him gently away from her so that he moved for her and turned onto his back.

"What?" he asked.

She placed her index finger in his navel.

"What?" he asked.

Her fingers moved downwards and in a single movement had forced their way beneath the doeskin. He seemed frozen, imprisoned by her hand, now out of sight.

"I think this is necessary," she whispered.

"Yes," he growled.

"You are little only in name," she whispered.

"Yes," he growled.

Afterwards they lay entwined in each other, naked and slippery with sweat in the afternoon sun.

"You not a woman with snow in her hair, not cold," he said, his command of her language not perfect.

"That is my name."

"You are my woman."

"I would like that."

"I shall give you a new name."

"What is that?" She snuggled close to him, enjoying the firmness of his frame.

"Warm Sun."

"Mm – I like that. But it is not my name. Let me keep my name."

"Why?"

"Because I am me, and my name is me. To change my name makes it a bad name. They think me a bad woman for what they did to me. But it was what they did that was bad."

Little Knife laughed lightly, "Then keep your name, but you are not a bad woman any more."

"I never was," she lied.

That night they slept wrapped in the warmth of each other and decided to go up the mountain and join Frank and face his wrath. But instead he found them first.

)()()()()(

128

The following day Frank Partridge left the Cheyennes. It was just after dawn. They had secret things to do and he had to continue his journey. At the foot of the eastern slope he halted.

At first he thought it was the carcass of a stray buffalo then, as he approached he saw he was facing the barrel of a Spencer, pointing out of two blankets, all entangled.

"Well damn me," said Frank Partridge, "it's my favourite Arikara."

"Do not be angry," said the boy.

Frank looked at them half struggling to hide their nakedness, and laughed. "I guess I knew you'd be close."

"We are coming with you to see the Wasichu kill each other," said Little Knife. "Do not send us back."

Frank nodded and rode past them. He was out of sight when they were dressed and mounted. They had no difficulty in catching him up. Their journey then became a rhythm of nights and days as they progressed to where the sun rose.

A month later, in the middle of the day, Frank Partridge halted and did something the others thought to be strange. It was just after they heard a sound like distant thunder, despite the sky being cloudless.

Carefully he unpacked a rawhide suit, replacing his scanty Crow hunting outfit. Remounting he looked less Indian and more white man. On each shoulder there was the sign that he was a silver two bar chief. This was a surprise to Little Knife, but it pleased him. They then headed east once more. It was in the evening when they heard the rumble of thunder again, but it was not thunder. Aided by advice obtained from farmers and a wagon train headed south he learned the approximate position of Grant's army. It was Grant whom he had to see; maybe Sheridan would be there too.

7

The Wasichu War

(3rd day of the Moon of the Red Grass Appearing in the Wasichu year of 1864)

"What's the excitement?" asked Custer.

"Injuns!" The plump corporal, breathless from his gallop, flopped forward in his saddle, gathering breath as he spoke to his famous 'Boy General'.

George Armstrong Custer, brevet brigadier general of volunteers smiled. It was a smile that hid confusion in his mind. Behind him close on two thousand young men sat on horses waiting his command. The air stank of gunpowder – giving that foul aroma of rotten eggs as it mixed with the broken damp earth. The black smoke was slow to disperse and seemed to congeal with the mist moisture of the morning. The already hazy sun was almost entirely obscured by battle smoke and one mile to his front was half of Lee's Army, also obscured. What was the fat corporal talking about?

"What do you say, soldier?"

"Injun – we've caught Injuns – an Injun, one a squaw. There's a man with 'em, got a captain's bars but don't talk right. We fancy he's a spy from the South.'"

"Lord! Indians *and* a spy!" said Custer, and he watched a ripple of red and black to his front and left as the Rebel battery fired again. "Lord, Corporal – what is that to me?"

He thought for a moment that he saw the trajectory of a brace of shot as they curved towards the outlying infantry skirmishers of the 7th Pennsylvanians also to his left. *Duft! Duft!... Duft! Duft! Duft!*

Five balls landed short of the main line. None of the skirmishers appeared injured. He saw the sods of turf shoot into the air with the impact. The earth was wretched, drenched from the recent downpour. The shot glued into the soil and failed to bounce towards the main line.

"Try again lads!" bellowed Custer to the Rebel gunners who were far too far away to catch his words, but it brought a laugh from his own men to the rear. Then others, further down the line, shouted, "What did he say? What did he say?"

For a moment Custer recalled discussions, led by those grey West Point instructor captains, regarding the opening play at Waterloo. He had a sudden insight into the first moments of that battle, so far away in time and distance, gone for ever. The ground was sodden that morning. Then his thoughts ran across his last days at West Point. He smiled. The trouble. The waiting. The fear that he would not be commissioned. His inner certainty that nothing could stand in his way. Two years ago – it seemed at once a lifetime and yesterday. He smiled.

Now there was a star on each of his shoulders and all those boys at his back. The grey captains were still talking about Waterloo, they still captains, and he a general. What the hell was this man talking about? The ripple of light and dark again to his left.

The enemy battery was firing at extreme range, guns elevated to the full, helped by the rise in the terrain on which they stood, jumping back on their wheels as they fired, close to blowing over backwards. They were getting round shot off at around 40 seconds a time, good work. The present had come back to him.

The fat man seemed to want some sort of answer; he had coughed. And now he was staring at the general taking in the excess of gold braid and the flowing golden locks bursting from beneath his general's gold-edged cavalry hat. His more familiar straw hat had given in to the steady rain and fallen to pieces. Damned man was staring. Damned man, coughed!

"Well?" asked Custer looking his way, tearing his eyes from the flashing battery, excited by its threat, knowing that his front ranks had their eyes on him, waiting for a signal. The corporal also looked away towards the ripple of fire and knowing what was coming, held his breath. There was a continuous racket of horses prancing and eager behind them, the stench of them, and the noise of leather and gossiping in the ranks. Cavalry in the field.

"Let's go git 'em!" came a shout from behind.

Then the voice of the fat man interrupted. He spoke quickly, anxiously. The shot had not arrived.

"I thought the General should be told..." he began.

Duft!..... Duft!...... Crack-duft (a scream). *Duft! Duft!*

"After, afterwards!" Custer was already looking to his right, beyond the corporal, who was struggling to hold his horse steady as tufts of sod splattered around them.

A courier was approaching, fast, riding a big grey. The courier was a handsome youth with a shock of red hair and no hat. As he came to a halt alongside the brigadier general his mount went down on its back legs, slithering in the mud. The corporal's horse reared out of the way, startled.

"General Sheridan says you are to retire, sir, and move to the rear of the Pennsylvanians, and then strike across from the far left and turn their flank. The general thinks their line ends there." He pointed. "It's in the air, and the general's heard their cavalry is still ten miles to their rear, sir. Their flank is in the air, sir."

"Go *behind*, the Pennsylvanians?"

"Sir!"

"Flank in the air!"

"Sir!"

"Waste time in going in the opposite direction?"

"General Sheridan says....."

"Bugler!"

"Sir!"

Custer leaned forward, drew his sabre and waved to his colonels on left and right. They knew the signal and were calling to their own buglers.

"Sound the advance Bugler Sergeant Major!"

"Yes Sirree!" called back the Michigan blacksmith, now a warrior.

The courier gamely protested, but Custer's brisk tongue was directed elsewhere, and his ears were deaf to the young man. With a shrug of tired shoulders the courier backed his horse and awaited an order from the young general. None came for him.

He watched as Custer called in his aids with an airy wave of his gloved hand. The young courier's face was a picture of growing astonishment. He heard Custer order that the brigade advance at the trot, straight at the battery, columns of four, within each of three regiments. There was to be a hundred yard gap between each regiment. Then the brigade would wheel right in column, face front and on the bugle's command, at half a mile, canter up the hill and finally charge on the battle call – straight up the slope at the guns. They would be on them within five minutes. The gunners might get off a dozen firings if they were lucky. Custer could see no supporting Reb infantry up there. So there *was* no infantry. A young major asked how Custer knew. The general smiled and said, "Trust in Custer's luck."

The whole staff laughed at the certainty of it.

There was a pause. The horses sensed the promise of movement and heads shook, foam flew, horse kicks slapped back, troopers' voices cursed their mares and geldings and the larger stallions seemed to swear right back. Custer trotted to the front of the brigade.

There was a muttering of excitement from the regiments behind him. The young courier had followed Custer. The general noticed him.

"Well?"

"Sir, permission to join the charge."

"Whatever will Sheridan say about that?"

"I'll blame you, General."

"Everybody does! Stay close! What's your damned name?"

"Clinton sir!"

"Stay close young Clinton and you'll see some sport today."

Custer's spurs barely made contact; the charger began to move. A touch to the reins held in a single hand and Custer was cantering his horse in a circle, twice. The courier spurred behind holding close like a magnet. As the Boy General came out of the second turn, his sabre was above his head as he changed direction and trotted towards the rise. This was the signal.

Twenty bugles sounded the advance – and it was done.

The earth began to grumble with the weight and vibration as a full brigade of Union cavalry on good mounts advanced towards the moment for a charge.

The gunners saw them coming, took the opportunity; they managed to get off three salvoes but they fell either too far or too short or threw up mud in the gaps between the regiments. The brigade was gathering too much momentum, the gunners' nerve was going. They had heard that Custer himself was opposite them – worse, it was Sheridan's Corps holding the line.

The brigade began to execute the right wheel and at the miracle moment of alignment the bugles called. A grumbling canter began and then the gallop and on to a thundering charge.

The brigade lost a dozen horses as legs snapped in a mass of unseen gopher holes, but the guns were taken with ease. The ill-uniformed gunners had panicked, mounted, and ridden like madmen for the cover of some trees on the reverse slope leaving their smoking charges to the Union brigade. The limbers had been too far back and the riders with them had turned as soon as the heads of the brigade came into view.

The rest of the engagement was a messy affair, hampered by falling rain. The Confederates withdrew. Two companies of riflemen in the woods took out a dozen of Custer's men and the charge lost momentum. The Rebels skilfully slipped out of an attempted entrapment. Pursuit was not taken up; the regiments were wet, dispirited, and had not eaten for two days. Behind them the victual wagons arrived, and that was the end of it. The Cavalry Corps bivouacked. Sheridan sensed his command had lost its wind rather than its spirit. They needed to catch their breath.

'Little Phil' Sheridan, when he rode up with his staff, growled at Custer, but with a smile on his face – declaring Custer should be shot for disobeying orders. Custer smiled at him, looking at the round Irish face with its neat moustache and the parchment skin tight on the good bone structure. Sheridan nodded with the neck Lincoln had said was too short to be hung by.

"General," said Custer, "It was *his* fault!"

Custer pointed at the courier and to Sheridan's astonishment the general and the soldier burst into laughter.

"What's your name again?" asked Custer.

"It's my lad Clinton ain't it?" said Sheridan, "Been with me since more than a year? Will not take a commission damn and sod him."

"I have been with you *that* long, sir?" The young man had a clear Irish brogue.

"Can I have him?" asked Custer.

"Well, if he can cause the kind of trouble you say he caused today, you can keep him. He ain't worth a bucket of spit."

The young Irishman laughed at the general's compliment.

"Corporal go get some dinner!" said Custer.

Courier Clinton looked over his shoulder. There was no one there.

"It's you I'm talkin' to, you fool. You're promoted. You can turn down a commission but I'm damned if you'll turn down my stripes!"

"Thanks General, I'll find meself a tailor."

He saluted and turned to go, then stopped. "Er... General, I am right glad to take responsibility for your victory."

"Food!" growled Custer, "Go get some damned food!"

"That I will, sir, right away."

Sheridan beamed at the exchange. He liked his cheeky courier and wished he had bars on his shoulders, could not understand why he turned them down. Irish, that was it, like himself.

The corps commander was very pleased with the way the battle had gone. He had seen the chance too, even as Custer was advancing, seen the advantage that Custer had given him and he came up with the rest of the cavalry in support of Custer's charge. The mere sight of the mass of four thousand horse had caused the advancing Confederate cavalry to wheel away as soon as the Union horses came in view. Pressure was off the Union Army. If the rain stopped they would make a good advance come the dawn.

"Well, General?" said Sheridan as they turned from watching Clinton walk his horse away to a nearby cook section.

"Well, General?" said Custer.

Sheridan suddenly gave his handsome young brigadier a hug in place of bullets in the chest and invited him to a glass of port before the hour got too late.

"What you mean, sir, is do I have port in *my* quarters!" said Custer.

"Its an alternative, General," smiled Sheridan.

"General Sheridan, sir, I would be right pleased if you would grace my quarters for dinner this night."

As they spoke and sat on panting horses a shift of wind eased the gloom and they could see the remnant Confederates' skilful withdrawal.

"They slipped away! We'll rest the men awhile," said Sheridan to his staff, "and grip 'em tomorrow! General, where're your blasted quarters?"

ᚷᚷᚷᚷᚷ

Just after midnight, the fires were burning fitfully in the drizzle, and a mist mingled with the residual gun smoke so that the very trees smelt of war. In the far distance an occasional patter of gun-fire sounded where forward pickets touched an outlying enemy sentinel, but the main bulk of the armies were not in striking distance. The night was too grim for either side to carry out an attack, but both had alert outposts, just in case – after all Lee was in the field and so was Sheridan. Nothing was certain.

The light breeze veered carrying the distant sound of wounded crying out in the field hospital which was set deeper in the stand of timber, out of sight in the darkness. A heavy port wine in two glasses looked like liquid ruby in the light of the lamp which hung in the awning of Custer's tent. It was then that Custer remembered the fat corporal and his news.

)(()(()(()(

Frank Partridge sat beneath a wagon gun, enshrouded with a damp horse blanket. In front of him was a mound of blankets inside of which were entwined the silent bodies of Little Knife and his woman, fast asleep, damn them. It was strange that he was thinking that this foul night was a Wasichu night, that he was home. They seemed to be at home wherever they lay their young heads.

Five paces away two guards stood in the rain, their cavalry capes as wet as rain itself. They were leaning against their carbines. Frank swore they were asleep. He should never have approached the rear pickets of the army whilst it was fighting a battle. They had been arrested on sight and awaited an officer to clear them with a passport. Now they appeared to have been forgotten. Frank had pointed to his jerkin with the bars, but he had no documents on him. He did not even bother to explain himself. He was given two useless choices by the sergeant: "What are you, buffalo hunters or renegades?"

"Yes, hunters – coming back for supplies," Frank said.

"You'z a Reb, you zound like von of zem Rebs."

The young sergeant who had caught them had a strong German accent, had been on the continent for five years, Pennsylvanian German out of Brunswick. Frank Partridge's English accent seemed to him like the fancy Reb officers they had shot the day before.

But the Indians made the situation uncertain so they waited for an officer before they shot them, and sent a corporal on a borrowed horse to headquarters to tell them what they had found.

Frank was dressed in the winter clothing of a Crow warrior, except for his jerkin. He leaned his back against the wheel of the field gun, drenched to the skin, shivering. The field piece was smashed and lay awkwardly on its side in the position it had landed, after a direct strike from a 12 pounder Reb ball. The entire barrel had cracked from the impact. Frank's other horse blanket was draped over the ruins to provide cover, but was sodden from an earlier downpour and gave him no protection. The chill, working its way into his body, caused him to rock slightly and there came from his lips the hint of a chant, more like a whispered moan, repeated and repeated. Thus, with this prayer, he was oblivious to the cold.

Suddenly he became aware that there were men in front of him. He looked up and in the gloom of the light from the camp fires he saw a short man with a sword at his side, and a taller man. Both were young; the taller one resembled a very large boy and had hair as long as an Indian chief, but it was gold, where a chief's might be grey mingled with jet. He also had a cavalry sabre at this side. He recognised them at once.

"General will you talk some sense into the fools in your damned command!" Frank growled.

"Damn me black – Mister Frank Partridge!" Sheridan leaned forward to take a closer look.

Custer had his hands on his hips and a smile played on his face, but there was no humour in it.

Frank made as if to stand.

"Stay put, Chief!" snapped one of the guards.

"Soldier!" snapped Sheridan at the sergeant. "Release this man, he's a ... a Presidential staff-courier. Damn it this is Captain Frank Partridge." He had hesitated for a moment and almost said, "Damned Presidential spy."

The sergeant was slow in his movement even in obedience to a major general's command. "Thez here iz Indian's!" That was an end of it for him. "Shall I zoot them?"

"Damn it! No!" snapped Sheridan.

The sergeant reluctantly stood to one side. Frank was on his feet, dripping, rubbing his iced hands.

"How come you're here, you damned Englishman?" asked Sheridan.

"They would not believe I wasn't no Redskin or Rebel," said Frank.

"To be expected," said Sheridan, looking him up and down.

137

"Just passing through the rear lines, making for Washington, or Grant's headquarters. Heading for the rail road."

"You'd better get dried out," said Sheridan.

The blankets on the earth began to move.

"They come as well," Frank pointed at the blankets.

Custer raised his brow.

Sheridan looked carefully, aided by the light of a lamp held by an escorting corporal. Two Indian faces blinked from the blankets. "They're just kids," said Sheridan.

"Bit more than that, General," said Frank.

"Long time since I seen Indians," said Sheridan.

"They're with me."

"Bring them then," said General Sheridan.

)( )( )( )(

Dried, warmed, fed, freshly dressed in the uniform of a staff major, borrowed for the night, Frank Partridge sat with Sheridan and Custer by a fire in the front of the Corps Commander's tent. The young Indians sat in close to the same fire munching on turkey and bread, whispering to each other from time to time.

"See their little two star chief," whispered Snow-on-Her.

"Yes."

"He looks like a puppy dog."

"And the one with long hair, he looks like a fir tree with straw on top." Little Knife nodded at Custer.

They giggled to each other, the more so as Custer's eyes came their way.

"See," she whispered, "his eyes are very blue like the sky."

"I see, I like his face."

"Do you think that Wasichu have big things."

Little Knife pushed her shoulder for the rudeness.

"No, the Wasichu are a small people."

She looked round at the massive army within which they sat and knew that this was not true in every matter.

The rain was falling more in the form of a mist so the fire was able to hold its own, huge, fed with great chunks of fir recently blown away by ball and shell.

138

"So Captain, tell us about the West, the Redskins and all," began Custer.

"General you ask too much. There is too much. All I know is, as sure as hell is hot, I want to get back there out of all this!"

"So why are you back?" asked Sheridan.

"Well sir, it ain't no secret that the Rebs have stirred up the Indians and there just ain't enough soldiers out there. It is a question of where to place the new regiments. I'm headed to Washington to tell them where's the greatest need."

"New regiments going out West?" asked Custer.

Frank Partridge and Sheridan looked at each other.

"You not heard?" asked Sheridan.

"What?" said Custer.

"We're going to send some new regiments out West. Regiments that cannot fight the Rebs."

"What's the use of sending the halt and the lame?" asked Custer.

"They're good trained soldiers," said Partridge.

"Some of the best," said Sheridan. "What they call 'em?" asked Sheridan sucking on a cigar.

"Galvanized Yankees," said Frank Partridge.

Custer's jaw dropped.

"Yes – Reb prisoners – signed up with the Union for deployment against the Redskins," smiled General Sheridan.

"Better that than the prisons," said Frank.

Both generals nodded at that.

"And we need help out there!" Frank was emphatic.

"How so?" asked Custer.

"Well, general, like I said, I reported back to Grant some months back that there just ain't enough soldiers out there. I ain't come across no Confederates stirring trouble myself – but I know they have worked up some of the Sioux. The Indians – especially the Sioux – are mean as hell over their hunting grounds being passed over by wagons and all. Then there's the telegraph – soon as they lay the wires on the poles the Redskins come and cut 'em all down. I told the general we must have something like five or six thousand soldiers out there, in addition to what is there at the moment – that's just for protection. I lived with the Crows, I know what they are about. The Crows will run with us, but they are too few. We'll be up against the entire Sioux nation, and the Cheyenne and a lot of other lesser nations. They are going to go to war sometime soon – and that won't do our own strategic west flank much good."

"You speak like a staff officer," said Custer.

"He's read a lot," laughed Sheridan.

Frank smiled, "Just the Bible, General."

"Ah – the good book. I heard they have already started to recruit for the new regiments," said Sheridan.

"It's all agreed, General – seems Lincoln is for it – six regiments of volunteers are going to be raised and sent out West at once. I'll be headed out to do some scouting, raise some Crows for service, and the Arikara." Frank nodded towards the two by the fire.

Custer looked at them. They were smiling. The brave nodded to Custer, Custer nodded back. Handsome bastard, thought Custer. He looked back to Frank Partridge.

"The savages should not present six regiments any problem," said Custer. "Keep 'em quiet at least."

"Civilised war is one thing," Frank waved his hand into the darkness towards where Lee might be, "but war with the Indians is like having a fist fight with a thick mist."

Custer snorted.

"It ain't easy, General!"

"After the Rebs, the Reds!" laughed Custer.

"I sure hope not," grunted Frank.

"What do you mean?" asked Custer.

"Well, General, them Indians have been out there for centuries. We ought to be able to let them be and get a treaty to create trails through their land without war."

"When this war is over there's going to be a hunger for land. We can't let the primitives stand in the way of that need for land," said Sheridan.

"Indian land?" questioned Frank.

"For sure," said Sheridan.

"Then there'll be a war," said Frank.

"I read a piece in the Washington papers," began Custer, "quoted a Senator – can't remember which one... talked about the people going out to the West. He came up with an idea which sounds right for me – 'manifest destiny'. Ain't nothing can stop us going out there and taking all the land we need. Fortunes are to be made after the war."

"*After* the war," said Sheridan.

"After the war," smiled Custer. "Why, General – whatever *shall* we do after the war?"

"We cannot dwell side by side. Only seven years ago we made a treaty by which we were assured that the buffalo country should be left to us forever. Now they threaten to take that away from us. My brothers, shall we submit or shall we say to them: "First kill me..."

Chief Sitting Bull of the Hunkpapa Sioux

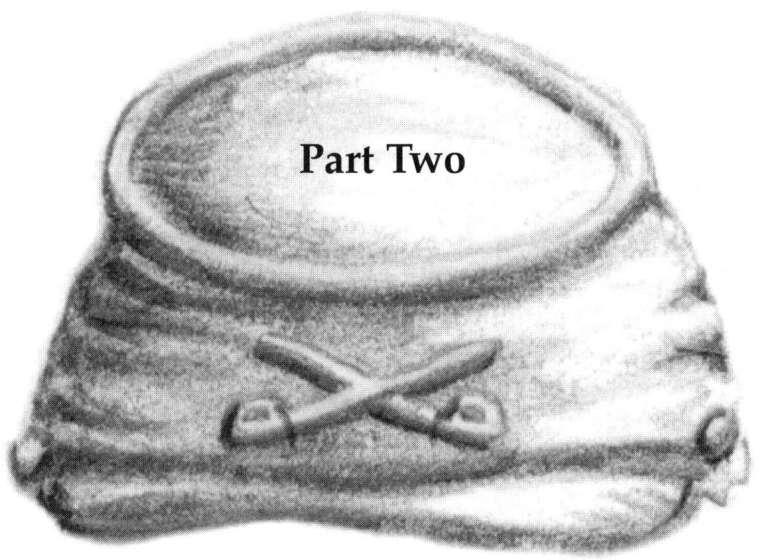

Part Two

**Warrior Priests,
Flags of War and Peace**

8

"All acquitted themselves well..."

(In the Cheyenne Year of the Long Sadness, which the Wasichu counted as, one thousand eight hundred and sixty four years after the birth of the Lord Jesus Christ)

Merle Clinton was already feeling a retching coming on when another of the bystanders said, "Them was the McKenzies." The bystanders' lack of emotion got into Merle Clinton, the acceptance of the horror of it all. As he rushed for the door of the saloon he was gasping for both fresh air and revenge. Folks looked at him in surprise. It was his uniform which startled them.

Clinton had ridden into town with twelve supply wagons. The heavy wagons protested every inch of the way, dragged by the teams of oxen, rather than pulled: oxen plodding, grumbling, stoic despite the hiss and crack of whips and the urging on of the humans around them. They jerked across the numerous ruts of the three hundred feet wide beaten roadway which was the Platte Valley Road, gradually passing through the Platte Valley over a period of seven days, suffering two minor attacks from hostiles.

The teamsters and escort put the whooping braves to flight with a final massive volley which missed them all except a horse which sprang into the air, fell, spilling his rider. At once two of the Indians wheeled back and rode either side the fallen rider. Leaning down they scooped him out of the buffalo grass and were gone, a final half dozen bullets cracking round their feathers.

The grizzled wagon-master watched. He put his hands on his hips, "Them was Cheyennies – worst of all of them red buggers – but we seed them off right enough!"

The sweating members of the column, mostly immigrants from the German states, no longer trembled as they had when they passed a dozen wrecked vehicles from earlier clashes and as many burned out homesteads. They felt lucky, confident, and increasingly superior. They were almost sorry to arrive at Denver without further incident.

Clinton, for his part, was relieved to arrive safely and immediately delivered the US Army dispatches to the Governor's Mansion. He was looking forward to a couple of days of ease, for he was his own man. Once rested he would have to plan his journey to Fort Rice.

Clinton was saddle sore from constant use of the two horses issued to make the journey to Denver but at least he had the thrill of riding alongside the sergeant in charge of the twenty man escort of 1st Colorado Volunteer Cavalry. He had 'felt' cavalry for the first time since leaving Custer. That was a good feeling. But it was the Sergeant's turn to be impressed when he heard Clinton's stories of the big war back East.

Clinton presented as a handsomely gaunt, rather than merely thin, young man: the sort of youth who has 'outgrown his strength', as his mother might have said before she fell victim to a cholera epidemic. The fever took old man Clinton, also Merle's brother and sister. The little sister went last of all, on Merle Clinton's sixteenth birthday. He kept a little bible in which their birthdays were recorded, neatly, in pencil. His eyes were to water on each of her birthdays, until he died.

All the dreams held by the little Irish family vanished in that New York hovel. So Clinton ran away, to war, as bugler boy, running from domestic death to face it square, with an expectant eye in a place it deserved to be. He also found a new dream – to ride with the cavalry.

Rostered into the 6th New York Volunteer Infantry, he was thrilled at the sight of horsemen riding by. Events moved quickly as Lee's Army drove north. There was no chance for a regimental transfer. The 6th was placed in reserve at Gettysburg when Meade's Army of the Potomac blundered into Lee. Merle Clinton only heard the rumble of the battle over the line of bloody hills, far away. The rumble was almost soothing for those not in action; in fact he saw nothing of the fight, but was thrilled when Custer's Michigan Brigade trotted by, withdrawing. Clinton thought he saw the 'Boy General' nod his way with a huge smile, as Clinton waved his hat at them. Clinton fell in love with those horse soldiers anew.

Ten minutes after Custer had gone by Clinton's colonel heard tell that it was Custer's brigade making dust down the valley, already out of sight.

"Can you ride?" snapped the colonel of the New Yorkers at the nearest soldier, the boy Clinton.

"Sir?"

"Can you ride, boy?"

"Yes sir!" came half a lie, for Clinton had ridden a mule, and as a scrawny boy had taken his father's mare to market when the old man took their two drays to sell, to raise the sea passage.

"Then take this to the general of cavalry who just passed this way."

"It was Custer, to be sure, it was!" said Clinton.

"Of course it was, soldier – my classmate at West Point. Take him this," snapped the young colonel, handing over a scrap of paper, folded, the combined corners turned and ripped to form a seal.

A small miracle and strong young legs heaved Clinton via the high stirrup into the saddle of the colonel's second mount. Clinton carried the scribbled pencil note in his pocket as he jerked the charger towards the distant dust. A combination of good luck, exhilaration, and tight gripping spindly legs kept him in the saddle. Somehow he managed to pull the horse up about a hundred yards beyond the head of the column. As he steadied the horse Custer cantered up. A brilliant horseman himself, Custer could see that the boy was having a hard time with the horse. He grinned as he took the note from the boy.

"Take it easy, lad," said the young general.

Clinton blushed with pleasure at the hero's words. He stared at the flamboyant uniform, the red necktie, the curling blond hair and the beautiful moustache of the young god.

Custer had laughed at the note, scribbled a reply on the back of the paper and Clinton was trotting and galloping back before a quarter hour was gone, taking a long route for the pleasure of it.

"You took a damn long time, soldier!" the colonel had snapped, an hour later.

"Yes sir!"

"Enjoying the ride?"

"Yes sir! Your hoss sure is a fine..."

147

The colonel waved away the words of gratitude and pleasure. The scribbled words brought a grin to the colonel's face.

"You did well lad!"

"Yes sir, to be sure!"

From that moment Clinton was the colonel's dispatch rider, then loaned as a brigade messenger. Finally Sheridan singled him out as one of his battle couriers. A year later, Custer stole him when Clinton had skidded in front of Custer's Wolverines at the clash with Lee's rear guard.

There was an innocence about Clinton. So, important men smiled at him, and girls looked his way, smiling too. His shock of wild red hair made him both attractive and memorable. He was earnest and brave and much respected by the troops who saw him galloping across a front of battle, countless times, with half the Confederate Army trying to blow him to the Promised Land.

"Go Red, go!" would come the yell from the Union infantry regiments. Then they would blast away at the opposite line, in echelon, as their red head boy passed them by.

He had a charmed life, and always got through. This continued until one day he was lying in a recently cropped wheat field near the headquarter tent of Custer's 3rd Cavalry Division. Out of the blue, he was appointed to help take to Washington the seventeen battle flags the division had captured. He also had letters for Mrs. Custer. Earlier letters to her had already got into Rebel hands – this time Custer wanted to be certain of delivery.

She had been very sweet and charming and Merle Clinton felt himself falling in love. But Washington was a busy place for an experienced courier. The moment it was known he knew the courier duties he was given dispatches to take from War Secretary Stanton to the commander of the District of Colorado – the other side of the world, to be sure. His dearest wish was to rejoin Custer – he told a journalist some forty years later – he was getting 'an iron arse' with all this courier carrying. He had the misfortune at the same time to meet with Major General Benjamin Butler, a meeting which made certain it would be years before he joined Custer again.

"Who are you?"

Clinton was sitting on a bench outside the staff offices of the War Secretary awaiting his leather pouch of dispatches. He looked up and saw a portly man in a smart uniform, a major general's.

Clinton got briskly to his feet.

"Not seen you before."

"No sir."

"I'm Butler."

Clinton looked blank.

"Major General Butler!"

"Ah – yes sir – I heard about you, sir," Clinton had heard tell that the man was an idiot, was a 'political' general, but a good organiser.

"Well?"

"Sir?"

"Well – what are you about, young Ginger-me-lad?"

"Dispatches for Colorado District, sir."

"You goin' to Denver, Ginger?"

"Sir."

"You wait here, m'lad."

It was half an hour before the major general came out, clutching the dispatch case.

"Got a job for you lad, come with me."

The major general walked a way down the corridor, then out onto the veranda which overlooked the stables at the rear of the offices.

"This here is your dispatches for Chivington, and there's some words for the Governor as well. All in here!" Butler tapped the rounded dispatch case. You're to take a couple of the best mounts from the stables here and make your way to Denver. Stay with the wagon trains and the escorts. There's a lot of hostiles out there."

He saw the furrow of bemusement.

"Indians, Ginger, lots of murderin' Indians, don't you know. Just keep that red hair on your head, lad. But after Denver I want you to go up to Fort Rice. There you'll find a regiment of Yankee Volunteers under Colonel Dimon. You're to take this letter to him, and he will then keep you with his regiment or send something back to me."

The major general tucked a buff envelope into the dispatch case. He looked at the young soldier and smiled, smiled from dark eyes divided by a long sharp nose, thin, like it needed breaking.

"But...."

"But you want to get back to Custer?"

149

"That I do, sir."

The major general seemed to wince, then smiled without humour, pleased to be taking something away from Custer. "Well, son, this war has not got a lot more to run. By the time you get back it might all be over and the whole Army broken up. I hear tell you want to stay in this Army – regular like."

"To be sure, General, I ain't got nowhere else to go."

"Then out West is the place to be, believe me," the major general smiled and put his arm round the young corporal. "And I'll tell you something else – when you get to Fort Rice there'll be an extra stripe for you anyway."

Clinton did not say he would prefer to ride back south to Custer; he kept the grudge to himself. Going out West would be different. Maybe there was something in what the smart general said. All that was a month ago. Now he was in Denver, looking at corpses and it was his eighteenth birthday.

Once he had delivered the dispatches he was free from any duties – he belonged to no-one for a change. The young soldier rode to Camp Weld, just outside town, begged a meal from the cookhouse and then sought and obtained permission from the orderly officer to ride into town.

What first caught his attention was a noisy gathering outside one of the brash new saloons. He eased his horse to one of the nearby rein-poles and from the excited comments learned of the homesteaders' laid-out corpses in the saloon. He went to go in.

"Twenty five cents son!"

He had not noticed the gnarled tanned face of a grey-beard skeletal man, sitting, bent forward, on a little bench at the entrance.

"Money for the rest of their family," smiled the skeleton, yellow teeth letting slip a coil of smoke from the yellowed pipe in the corner of his mouth. His face was parchment-tight with the last throes of consumption it seemed. He coughed from out of his soul and for a moment his face was crimson. He was a skeleton, just alive, just about. Only his eyes, steel-blue and watery, seemed to be certain to make it through the day.

"What's going on?" asked Merle.

"It's the McKenzies – what's left of 'em." This was followed with a violent fit of coughing.

"What?"

"Redskins cut 'em up – they'm on show – nasty like!"

Merle paid the twenty five cents, left the skeleton coughing in gratitude, and worked his way to the back of the saloon where the bodies were laid out. A white sheet marred with smudges of brown covered the bodies. Citizens lifted the coverings from time to time and universally gasped. Denver's town authorities had decided to exhibit the ruins of the McKenzies, the skeleton had explained, "So as the folks'll see f'sure what them dirty Injuns does!"

The Arapahos and the Cheyenne had been on the warpath for months. They were raiding the homesteaders, killing anyone they could whether travelling alone or in small bands. Denver's folk felt themselves nigh cut off. Even the escorted wagon trains were not always getting through, turning back before half-way points with heavy casualties or broken nerves, and the railroad was months away, maybe years, some said.

The Army proper was nowhere to be found, except for elements of the 1st Colorado Volunteers, thin on the ground. Further down the Platte the 7th Iowa was spread right back to Omaha. There were not enough guns to counter, let alone contain, the threat from hostile Indians. Something had to be done. But authority was needed, authorisation for the raising of another regiment. Clinton's dispatches brought that authority. Now it was a case of money and the raising of taxes.

A large party of buffalo hunters came in earlier in the day with a cart-load of hides, together with the corpses of Mr. and Mrs. McKenzie and the ripped up bodies of their two kids. All concern for avoiding the expense evaporated – though a regiment of cavalry in the field cost a million a year.

This was the second time corpses had been on display, the first had been the poor Hungates. The people had been mightily angered by that sight, the papers full of it, demands for action, revenge, annihilation.

"Here comes the preacher!" came a yell.

Clinton had recovered from the need to vomit, in the fresh evening air of July.

A strong breeze was falling from the backdrop of mountains which, behind the city of Denver, were still etched in ice against the gathering red dusk. There was a faint perfume of pine on the air, almost cool, as it ruffled hair and beards and sent eddies of dust to catch the last of the sun's rays as the orb dropped behind the snow-caps.

Clinton looked towards the yell and saw three men easing themselves off their horses. He recognised Governor Evans at once, sad-eyed and grey. Clinton had handed him the dispatches personally. He guessed that the tall dark-bearded man who led the way with a huge chest, which seemed to be trying to escape from his uniform tunic, was the famed preaching colonel, John M. Chivington, local District Commander. The third man was a major in the uniform of the 1st Colorado, a short man made all the shorter in the wake of the preacher. The major sported a blotched face with curiously red eyes which a medical man would see as a touch of scurvy. They walked by the young man, and swept into the saloon. A small group of chattering onlookers immediately hurried after them. Clinton gulped, swallowed and followed, immediate inquisitiveness overcoming potential nausea.

)( )( )( )( )(

A week before Clinton's train came into town, Brevet Colonel of Volunteers James M.Chivington had been stroking his beard facing a large mirror, the silver blown at the chipped edges.

"Conference, pow-wow be damned," he growled.

He picked up the nit comb and worked away, pausing from time to time to glance at the comb, studying the trapped flecks of scurf.

"They ain't getting no talkin'," he muttered, as he combed and searched.

Suddenly he recognised a single nit, about due to hatch. He eased it off the comb and with care placed it on the thumb nail of his left hand. With his right he squeezed and felt the 'pop' of a life ending.

"There you go!" he said. "There you go – no man's life blood for you, my sad little soul."

Chivington stopped as if struck by a bullet.

He looked at himself in the mirror. He caught his own eyes and felt a surge of inspiration run through his veins. He knew that God was speaking again.

That rush of blood was the word and the word was within him. The word was the flashing idea, the flow of logic – fleas drink the blood of men, nits become fleas – so simple. He had just destroyed a nit. The flea of its destiny would never be – the reverend colonel's own blood was safe – so simple.

"Blood," he whispered to himself, watching his own staring eyes. "Red blood!" He nodded at the confirming voice, "Redskins!"

The reverend colonel let the words and ideas weave and run on and said aloud, "Indians kill good whites. Dead Indians ain't going to kill nobody. It's a simple matter: kill all the Indians – no whites die no more. Simple. All of them! A journey of extermination – that's the way we have to go."

He looked into his own mind's eye and saw children. The Lord suffered all the children to go to him. Slowly he shook his head. The route was clear, there was no other way. So be it. He spoke the word clear and certain, "All!"

Chivington spent a lot of time with Governor Evans and Major Anthony working out the details. The Redskins had to be jerked right out of Colorado. The fiddle-fading had been going on too long. The consequences of the inspiration were nothing but good and could carry them both to Washington – the governor to the Senate and Chivington to the new House of Representatives. Anthony would get a silver eagle. They had promised a star – yes, yes – but the eagle would have to do.

In the almost refined parlour of the governor, with the scents and drapes imported from the East, they had the first taste of what the future could bring, a promise of luxury and power. But first they needed excuse, the following of the people, the raising of men to go on the white man's warpath.

The strategic view of the president and the general of the army was clear – do not stir up the Redskins until the main war was over. Containment! Talk! Pow-wows! Very well, talk to them, even talk of peace to them, and *then* rub them out. The savages would never keep their word anyway. What did they know of Christian decency? They were good for utterly nothing. They were in the way of progress.

For Chivington, the plan they had woven did not have containment in any line of it. The dream of that other plan was on his mind as he pushed his way through the saloon, past the smell of drink, cheap cigars and buffalo hunters' rancid clothes. Then something more wafted on the dirty air. The colonel could smell corpses.

As the onlookers parted to let the great men through Chivington was able to see the unfortunates laid out, four of them. "Bless their poor damned souls," he whispered aloud.

"There they be," said the major.

"Murdered!" growled Chivington.

"Right enough General," said a face close enough to have heard him.

"Just 'Colonel'," said Chivington without looking at him.

The major gingerly lifted the white sheet for the others to see. The body was at least a day old and the flesh had begun to swell so that the dead youth, maybe fifteen years old with a touch of hair above his cold lips, looked well fed, almost hearty, but white with death, blood full drained from the lips. Several of the watching people backed off as the sheet was drawn away from the nakedness. The body appeared untouched, except for burns on the abdomen, but the mouth was open as if emitting a hideous scream, locked open, dead eyes open too. Curiously his mass of red hair was intact. For some reason they had not taken his scalp.

"The fiends lit a fire on his belly," growled the major.

"Aye!" said Chivington.

The governor put out a hand to support himself against a wooden pillar.

There was just one other mark on the youth – a single arrow in his chest which had passed cleanly through his heart. The feathered end lay half snapped across the white chest. The other three bodies were less fortunate.

The major lifted the sheet away from the next in line and revealed a bearded man, into forty years or more, his shaggy beard, ginger, flecked with grey. They had cut open his chest and stomach, numerous arrows were in his body, mostly broken off with the moving of the corpse from place to place. The thighs were slashed open to display absurdly white bone, and that private place at his groin was gouged out flesh and nothing more, a ruddy hole.

This is perfect, thought Chivington and blinked back a smile.

The major went to lift the sheet from the woman who had been scalped.

"She is worse, sir," said the major.

"Enough!" said the governor, feeling his knees weaken. He fought to keep his voice steady.

"There's the little violated girl child as well," the major nodded towards a smaller shape alongside the mother.

"Do not insult the poor souls further with our eyes," said Chivington, half pleased that the governor could not take the horror so well as he. "Do we still talk to those savages?"

"It is arranged," grunted Governor Evans and turned away from the dead, struggling through the pack of people, gorge rising.

The silenced onlookers let them pass, easing out of the way but at the door the skeleton looked up and said, "Will you do nothing, sir?"

"Nothing?" the governor spun to face the grey beard.

"What will yea be doing then?"

"Not 'nothing', sir, not 'nothing'. We shall do much!"

Governor Evans took a step further – fresh air was needed. At last he was in the street, in the air. He breathed deep. Even the dust tasted good.

"Then what?" came a call from the entrance, and it was picked up by the rest now oozing out of the saloon.

"Y'all know I've made a proclamation calling the chiefs in for talks." He walked further from the porch.

"Then what?" asked the skeleton.

The governor stopped, turned and faced them.

"I'll tell you what! I'll have a punishing expedition raised!"

"Ain't no more men," smiled the skeleton.

"We have our Bloody 1st!" came a half shout from the shadows.

"Send the preaching-colonel!"

"Revenge!"

"Burn the bastard savages out!"

A surge of invective and hatred ripped into the air.

"Hear me!" shouted the governor.

The shouting and demands continued. The governor raised his hands again, and his voice.

"Silence!" bellowed the preacher from alongside the governor.

"Hear me out! Thank you, Colonel. Now y'all listen!" shouted the governor. The effort of throwing his voice brought some colour back to his face.

He was greeted with a partial silence which lay on a grumbling whisper, like in a Temperance gathering.

"We shall raise a new regiment of volunteer cavalry – I have the authority. Instead of your shouting – who'll be first to step forward?" called out the governor.

"Me!" Clinton heard himself shout.

"Well done Soldier!" shouted Colonel Chivington.

"There you go lads," called the governor. "A trained soldier steps forward with stripes on his arm. You'll have more of them for your daring lad!"

"Where's the rest?" butted in Chivington with a bellow and a waving of his hat.

A rush of voices buried Chivington's next words, ".... who'll ride to glory with me and the Lord? We'll wipe them out to the last heathen one of them."

Within three weeks the peace talk was called with the Cheyennes and their cousins, but even as they talked seven hundred Wasichu braves had signed their mark for a hundred days with the colours. Colonel the Reverend Chivington was in command and drilling them for war.

They called the new regiment the 3rd Colorado Volunteer Cavalry. It immediately picked up the nickname, 'The Unblooded'. They smarted under the twisted battle name, taken from the 'Bloody' 1st Colorado. It lost the name shortly after dawn on November 29th, 1864 at a place they called Sand Creek.

)K)K)K)K)K

The heart of Yellow Hair was heavy and lonely. The continuous prairie wind was pressing steadily at his back, thick with ghosts and so causing strange thoughts. His mind overflowed with memories of the boy. Sometimes he felt a phantom just to his right hand side, just behind in the wind, close enough for the muzzle of the boy's pony to occasionally touch his leg with affection. He even fancied he heard the trilling of the flute the boy played so well, but when he looked round there was nothing, just the rush of air at his turned face so that he had to squint as he faced into it. Yellow Hair contemplated what his feelings might be like if the boy were dead rather than in a safe place.

He thought hard about that, and then he smiled, for White Hawk was not only alive, he was truly safe. He was in the lodge of White Antelope, the old war leader, who was camped with the people of

Black Kettle under the protection of the good Wasichu in the fort they called Lyon. The boy was thus three times safe. He slept with famed chiefs who had been to see the Great Father of the Wasichu in Washington Far Place. They spoke of it often saying they liked the eyes of the Great Father and believed his words, which were slow words, but wise ones. A very special gift was given to them, a piece of Wasichu magic, their honour flag.

When the time came for a dance or when his camp was to stay in a good place for a moon or more, then above the teepee of Black Kettle there flew the honour flag of the Wasichu. The flag had beauty, with stars for heaven and bars of white for the Wasichu and red for the real people. When that flag was on high they were safe from all Wasichu attack. They had been told that this was so – this was the promise that came with the gift, a magic gift, an honour gift.

The peace gift had been given Chief Black Kettle by one of the Great Father of the Wasichu eagle chiefs. In addition both he and White Antelope had a beautiful round disc presented to them. They wore it on their chests many times; it had been taken from the hand of the Great-Father-Called-Lincoln himself. If this was the standing of Black Kettle, even in this bad time, then Yellow Hair was happy that the boy was under the protection of such leaders, chiefs who had the ears and trust of the Wasichu leaders.

He knew this was so for Black Kettle had told him, and White Antelope, very old, had sucked on the pipe and nodded that what Black Kettle said was the truth for he was also there. In this very year both were to meet with the Wasichu Chief of Colorado, in the place of their lodges the Wasichu now called Fort Weld, which the red men named Great Buffalo Crossing When the New Grass Grows. Yellow Hair remembered these things, and the talking about them.

Yellow Hair, with the wind coiling against his back as he rode, thought back to how the chiefs of the Arapaho and Southern Cheyenne sat in the teepee of Black Kettle, in the evening and into the night. They spoke of many important things.

He remembered because he had been there; with White Hawk in the gloom, behind the great men. He smiled at the memory of the boy's eyes twinkling in the light of the fire, listening, listening, watching. White Antelope had the wisdom pipe and sucked deep.

Black Kettle said carefully, "When we meet them I shall say to the silver leaf chief of warriors, and the eagle chiefs, and the man they

157

call Governor, who we might call Bear Coat Wearer, I shall say these words..."

Black Kettle's words were stopped as White Antelope's pipe was passed to his friend. White Antelope, once warrior now a famed peace chief, with the high cheek bones and wise eyes of age, he whose every utterance was one of truth had worry on his face. He said, "Your words with the Wasichu must be careful words."

Black Kettle sucked deep on the offered pipe. He slowly allowed the coiling grey-blue pleasure escape from his nostrils and from his mouth at the same time. White Hawk, half-hidden in the flaps of the teepee of the great one, looked with admiration at such skill.

The pipe lowered as Black Kettle said quietly, "I shall be very careful. I shall say, 'Wasichu chiefs – all we ask is that we may have peace with the whites.' When I say that I shall look into the eyes of those men to see that they are listening. I shall say to Bear Coat Governor, 'I want you to give all the chiefs of the soldiers here to understand that we are for peace!' I shall look into the eyes of their Silver Leaf Chief Chivington. I know that big Wasichu and do not like him. His eyes are small, and his heart is cold. He is a medicine man *and* a war chief, but he is not like the Great Sitting Bull who has similar honours. Sitting Bull's medicine is goodness, Chivington's is evil. Even when he listens he does not listen. He who has fleas jumping in his beard..."

Everyone in the teepee laughed.

"We are lucky to be free of beards," smiled Yellow Hair.

"We are human beings and they are Wasichu!" said Black Kettle with great firmness and a hint of sorrow for them because he tried hard to love the Wasichu; they needed to be loved.

White Antelope scratched his face where a scraggly thin hint of grey hairs grew.

Yellow Hair saw and smiled and said, "Your beard is as a desert compared with the Wasichu... which is good, for their fleas need forests. You chin is safe from their jumping legs."

"Hear me," interrupted Black Kettle. "I speak of important things!"

"Hear him!" begged White Antelope with a jesting look of hurt.

"I shall say to those Wasichu chiefs in their place they call Denver, I shall say, 'We have made peace so that we cannot be mistaken by you as your enemies – for ever.'"

Black Kettle paused, took a further deep pull on the pipe and passed it back to White Antelope. It was passed as if there was nothing more to say.

But White Antelope spoke again, "Maybe they will give us assurances and gifts and we shall give them treasure blankets to show our truth."

"Yes," said Black Kettle, "but my words have a weakness and the giving of blankets has a weakness. Our young men are not all for peace. They still look for the old way, counting coup on the enemy. But the Wasichu are a different enemy. They are dangerous in their difference. And our Dog Soldiers have not listened to me."

Grunts of agreement met the words.

"The Dog Soldiers are always for war – it is their nature," nodded Yellow Hair. "We were all Dog Soldiers once."

"Truth," said White Antelope.

"They must be brought in, stopped!" said Black Kettle.

Yellow Hair shook his head, "They care too much for the killing of the Wasichu. Remember they are young and hungry for glory."

In the gloom of the teepee White Hawk wanted to be a Dog Soldier, but did not dare speak.

"That, and the taking of women and pleasure," muttered White Antelope.

"Truth," said Yellow Hair.

"And you know about pleasure," the old war chief smiled.

Yellow Hair turned towards the old man, smiled, and said, "Ah – then White Antelope can still remember what his weapon is for?"

It was the passage of the time it takes to chew and swallow a piece of old-man-buffalo before the laughter ended.

Now, as Yellow Hair eased his pony through an edge to the timber, partly cleared by the Wasichu, all the cedar gone for ever, Yellow Hair smiled at the memory of the long talk. Around the memory also mingled his winkte time when he squirmed in the arms of the Dog Soldiers of the day, now wearers of Bear Coats, war chiefs, fathers, or dead. Briefly the face of White Hawk The Father passed before his mind's eyes and disappeared as his pony stumbled without a change of pace.

"Take care my friend, we have mountains to climb," he whispered, leaning forwards to the tall ears.

Yellow Hair had been asked by the peace chiefs to ride north and circle east towards the mountains and watch what passed, to talk with the Dog Soldiers. When he found them he was to plead the words of Black Kettle, telling the hot bloods that peace was fortune, further war was disaster.

Black Kettle was concerned that the Cheyenne people were split in this matter of the Wasichu. The split was as futile as the big war which could explode from it. Black Kettle had seen in Washington, lodges made of rock like the face of a cliff, not made by the Great Spirit but by Wasichu hands. The Wasichu might be nothing in the face of a herd of charging buffalo, and were known to flee from brother bear, but they could build things which put fear into the heart and soul of any man who followed only the pathway of the winds.

Yellow Hair almost imperceptibly touched the flanks of old Fire Eye and tightened his grip on the horse-hair rein. Fire Eye halted. Yellow Hair stopped and sat perfectly still to take in the vista of the Platte Valley as it fell away before him. Had anyone been watching they would have seen both rider and mount look to their left flank in a single movement, alerted by something.

Fire Eye's ears were raised and pointing towards the sound which had carried on the warm air. Fire Eye knew the touch would come, the releasing of the minute pressure on his soft mouth. He felt the thought of his master before the touch so that when it came both rider and horse moved as a single being. They had heard the sound of distant gunfire, and were moving cautiously towards it.

)()()()(

Running White Horse was frightened. He was told to catch the Wasichu horses as soon as the attack began. But there were no horses to be caught. They were still safe behind the box of tree branches that the Wasichu had made. The Wasichu were too slow to make it necessary to catch the horses.

As the braves came yelling in for the attack, the Wasichu family left their clumsy lodge of logs and made a run for their horses. Why they did this foolish thing was impossible to understand. They did not even get close to the horses before they were ridden down.

There were four of them: a Wasichu man, full warrior; his squaw; a young brave good for war; and a girl too young for pleasure. The war-party braves were glad that the Wasichu had not fought from

160

behind the walls of their lodge. Maybe they would have fought had they known there was a large party of white buffalo hunters not seven miles away, coming their way. Now it was too late. But the braves did not know of the hunters either.

The woman had been thrust at by brave after brave. Running White Horse was to be last, because he was the youngest; his turn was fast approaching. He stood in panic with no horses to watch out for, knowing his turn was coming and feeling that he could not do this thing. He fingered himself and knew that he could not do it. They would jeer at him for sure.

She was fighting back all the time and the old Wasichu with the scalp on his face was screaming under the blades.

Running White Horse dared not even glance at the young Wasichu brave as he was staked out, even though he was showing courage. He was struggling all the time but not a sound came from his mouth.

The little girl, lay like the skin of a butchered antelope on the ground. She was left alone. A chance shot had removed most of her head, even the scalp was gone. She was uselessly dead. Then Running White Horse sensed the band-leader, Next Dream, looking towards him and the youth swallowed hard.

Next Dream, leader of the Dog Soldiers, stood naked and idly slipped an arrow into his bow. He lifted, pulled, aimed and released. The barbed shaft thudded into the old Wasichu man's side, a wounding strike. The Wasichu screamed, as one of the braves holding him down yelled abuse at Next Dream. He had felt the wind of the shaft pass his arm. Next Dream grinned and sauntered back to the Wasichu woman. She was struggling less now, gasping. He glanced down with pride at his newly hardening manhood.

"You have to wait a little longer!" he growled at Running White Horse. "I'm going again."

The young warrior smiled lamely.

"Finish!" Next Dream snapped at the heaving back of the youth presently at work on the woman.

The young Dog Soldier looked over his shoulder, saw that it was Next Dream and that he was ready again. He began a frantic rhythm, gave a low grunt and was still. Next Dream kicked at the sweat-wet leg of the youth.

Slowly, the youth pulled away and Next Dream dropped to his knees, massaged himself briefly and fell on her. He was inside her easily. As he pressed hard she suddenly lifted her head to meet him and managed to bite his chin. His reaction was immediate. He took her head and smacked it against the earth, again and again, until her eyes lifted, rolling upwards, but did not close.

"You killed her," said the youth he had relieved.

"Give me a knife," snapped the naked Next Dream, still working with his hips.

Running White Horse drew his and gave it to the leader. He scalped her, deftly, even as he rode her. Then he threw the weight of scalp at Running White Horse. It struck his belly and fell to the ground. He felt her blood splash up to his chest-flesh and glancing down watched it for a moment, gathering at the thong, which supported his breechcloth.

"Now," said Next Dream, "cut the Wasichu bitch to bits!" He threw the knife into the dry grass in front of the young man. Only then did Next Dream pull out of her with a soft growl of pleasure.

Next Dream got to his feet and walked across to the still moaning old Wasichu man, nodded to those holding him down. One by one they began to cut him, carefully, so that he stayed alive for the longest time, his cries mingling with the brave curses of his son. The old Wasichu could not see the other braves placing dry wood and old buffalo grass on the white-white flesh of his boy's belly.

"Light it!" yelled Next Dream over his shoulder. It was begun with flint and iron, but was taking time.

"Light it!" he shouted again, surprised that half of the warriors were looking away from him. He turned himself in that direction and saw a senior warrior on a large stallion appear out of the trees from behind the burning sod-teepee of the Wasichu. He wore leggings, but no shirt. He wore the regalia and markings of a war chief. A bow was across his lap, armed. He was Cheyenne. There was no problem, except that he was a senior.

Eagle Flies, oldest of the Dog Soldiers but too stupid to be the leader said, "It is the Warrior Winkte."

"Winkte!"

"Yes."

"He is no winkte!" frowned Next Dream, curiously uneasy as if remembering a dream.

The warrior came closer. He had less body fat than might a man of his apparent age. He was sharp-edged like a bull buffalo at the end of a rutting season, hard eyed, dangerous, more like a Dog Soldier. This was not a winkte.

The Wasichu youth began to moan as the start of the burning killed his courage. The flames were slow to develop for the wood was not fully dry. This was good; it would be a slower way for the Wasichu to go. He was grinding his teeth and blood ran from his tongue as he tried to stifle his own screams, but failed.

His father's last words were to show no fear. He bit his lip through as the flames grew, but it was too much. His screams began to pierce the air continuously. He was ignored by everyone even as the burning began to eat him.

The strange warrior came deeper into the circle of braves as the screams grew. Then, in a single movement, without warning, his bow was up. The arrow hissed close to the ear of Next Dream so that he involuntarily threw himself to one side. Before Next Dream had steadied himself the shaft was buried to its feathers in the chest of the Wasichu boy who heaved but once and then was still.

Next Dream screamed, "Who are you that you *do* that?"

He scurried around looking for a weapon, suddenly aware that he was still stark naked and heavy hung, half hungry with lust.

The big man slipped from his horse. The animal very slowly followed his master though he was not held by a rope. The warrior walked towards Next Dream who stopped searching for a weapon as he saw how big the warrior was.

"Your name, brother?" smiled the man.

"I am Next Dream of the Hunkpapa Sioux of the clan of Chief Sitting Bull, war leader, a man of men." The words were gabbled, angry, lacking pride.

"Oh?"

"Why, 'Oh?'"

There was a smoothness in the gait of the big man, a something about his voice, a scar on his face, and twelve coup marks on his legs, repeated on his horse. The animal had come close behind him and touched his shoulder with its muzzle.

"Ah," said the big man to his horse, "you thought so too."

The warrior waved his arm across the scene, "My friend thought we had stumbled on Pawnee or maybe Crow, such a way as this is their way." Again he waved his arm across the scene.

163

Naked or not Next Dream tensed and took a step towards the warrior and took the chance of saying, "Are you not a winkte?"

The big one smiled, "Not for you."

"Oh?" Suddenly Next Dream thought that he had the upper hand over this man-woman. Eagle Flies had been right; he could see it now.

The winkte was looking him up and down, a smile on what was a very handsome face.

"No, definitely not for you," said the winkte.

"Why not?" snarled Next Dream, his lip curling with contempt.

"I prefer men."

"I..." Next Dream, leader of the Dog Soldiers, was contemplating flying at this thing but saw there was no fear in the eyes of the winkte.

The tip of the winkte warrior's bow touched the chin where the bite had struck, "I am sent by Black Kettle..."

"He loves the Wasichu!" snarled Next Dream. "We destroy them! He is peace-Cheyenne; we are war-Sioux riding with war-Cheyenne, as our good friends."

"I am sent by Black Kettle to bid *all* Dog Soldiers to return to your lodges..."

"He has no authority over the Sioux," called out Eagle Flies.

The winkte sighed and patiently said, "I am sent by Black Kettle to bid all Dog Soldiers to return to your lodges."

"Why?" several called out.

"For he negotiates with the Wasichu and this work..." he waved his armed at the carnage. "*This* work does not help his word with the Wasichu."

"The Wasichu do not belong here, they..."

"I know it, I know it all, but what you do is not the right way."

A sudden scuffle took place behind them as some of the braves were quarrelling over the scalps of the old Wasichu man and his squaw. One of the braves went toward the dead boy.

"He is mine!" said the winkte. "Put out the fire, leave him be."

The young men obeyed. This one *had* to be obeyed.

"Black Kettle says..." began Yellow Hair

"Who *are* you?" Next Dream dared to interrupt. Something had happened in the mind of Next Dream, something which made him begin to sweat.

As he spoke, so the winkte's horse suddenly grunted and turned away behind the winkte.

"What is it?" asked the winkte over his shoulder, ignoring Next Dream.

"What is *your* name?"

The Cheyenne turned his head back, slowly, saying, "I am Yellow Hair! I am *wicasa wakan*, warrior and winkte, war chief of the Black Kettle clan... What is it?"

Again the horse had spoken to him in the wind.

The winkte ignored the intakes of breath for he was known amongst all of the Southern Cheyenne, and many of the Sioux. Even the band of Sitting Bull had heard of him, and Sitting Bull knew him from many seasons ago. His ranking was almost as high as Sitting Bull himself. Stories were told about him in the winter nights. But the winkte was unconcerned by their awe; he was more interested in what his horse was saying to him.

Something on the air caused all heads to look towards the south to where Fire Eye's ears and eyes were pointing. From the direction of his look, a scout with the wolf head-dress came rushing in, his horse wheezing with the long dash up from the riverbed.

Next Dream, not a stupid leader, had scouts far out in four directions; the southern one had come in.

"Plenty Wasichu!" the wolf scout shouted.

"How many?"

"Twenty!"

"Soldiers?"

"Hunters!"

The braves had no need for orders. They were mounting. Twenty Wasichu hunters would be well armed and fine marksmen, and even at long range might kill. Best to move on.

"Tell Black Kettle that if he wants us then he must come himself and take us back himself. He is Cheyenne and does not lead us. He has too many years."

"You will continue to live *because* he has many years and does not hear your boy words," smiled the winkte coldly. He turned his back to the upstarts. He had seen their leader somewhere. The unusual cap he wore covered a wound. He had seen him before...maybe not.

Yellow Hair mounted and watched the young men ride off fast, away from the approaching threat. He saw Next Dream look back but once. Yellow Hair could not see the hatred, but knew it was there. He smiled inside himself.

Yellow Hair walked Fire Eye between the dead, pausing only at the young man, whom he saw to be beautiful, for a Wasichu. The fire of the handful of twigs and dry grass on his belly had gone out. Little damage was done, but Yellow Hair knew what would have come and was pleased that he had put a stop to it.

"Perhaps we shall all meet on the other side, my friend, where the hunting is good and we shall live in peace. You will not be lonely whilst you wait for me, but you will soon have many more young men to run with, for blood is going to flow. At least you keep your scalp on the other side. You may thank me for that, when the time comes. Farewell."

He turned Fire Eye away and withdrew into the woods to watch what the hunters would do when they found the destruction.

)()()()()(

Governor Evans looked out from his 'work place' – the name he gave his office. The new curtaining and drapes at the window still permeated the room with the smell of thick fresh linen backing, slightly yellowed already by facing out to counter the morning sun. The windows were closed; all the glass was turned opaque with grit pitting after the long dust storm of the previous week. The glass would have to be replaced. Expensive. Everything was expensive. Everything coming down the Platte Valley, everything delayed, attacked, having to be guarded, shipping costs rising by the day. He turned to face the tall figure of Colonel Chivington. The colonel was staring at him, the broad handsome face frowning slightly, waiting for the governor's reply.

"We *have* to talk to them," smiled the governor.

"Why? Why not just take the field and be done with it?"

The governor nodded towards the papers spread on his desk, one standing clear of the rest – a brief letter from Lincoln himself, quite explicit. They *had* to talk. Feeding the Indians was cheaper than fighting them. There was a great war being fought, the letter had explained, reminding the distant governor with a hint of sarcasm from the great man's pen – Lincoln had written it himself. An Indian war was not wanted at this present time.

"The view of government is that feeding is cheaper than fighting," the governor said, and raised his brow in expectation of the colonel's retort.

"I am not talking about fighting Governor, I am talking about killing. If you kill the useless fiends, you no longer have to keep feeding them 'til doomsday comes!" There was an impolite edge to the colonel's voice.

They were interrupted. A sudden sharp knocking on the great double doors which led into the room echoed everywhere.

"Only Major Anthony knocks like that, a man with a heavy hand," snapped the governor. "Enter!"

The doors, oiled that morning, swung open and hit a chair placed too close. The red-eyed major glanced round at the chair, ignored it.

"Good mornin' Governor!" The major saluted, turned to Chivington, saluted. "Mornin' Colonel."

"What have you got this morning?" asked the governor. There was a single piece of paper in the major's hand, a telegraph message.

"I have this for the colonel, sir. I've also got a good interpreter. Just rode in."

The colonel took the message and read it.

"Who is he, this interpreter?" asked the governor.

"Hunter and scout, name of Partridge, captain of volunteers as well."

"Jack–of-All-Trades is he? Speaks the Cheyenne babble does he?" muttered the governor.

"I don't think speaking will be necessary!" cut in the colonel. He handed the brief signal to the governor.

The governor said, "Who's this from?"

"Colorado Department – Fort Leavenworth – General Curtis," said Chivington.

Evans read carefully, then said, "Chivington, listen to this! *I want no peace till the Indians suffer more.* He can't say that – President Lincoln has specifically..."

"President Lincoln is a long way away!" smiled the colonel.

"James, listen to me. First we talk, maybe after we do it your way," the governor smiled hopefully.

"No 'maybe' about it, Governor..." began the colonel.

The governor raised his hands for silence.

167

"James – first, we talk; then you take the field and make it as bloody as you like. We have the 3rd Colorado. They were raised to kill Redskins. Men signed on to avoid the draft – I'm no fool. They'd rather kill Redskins than fight the Rebs. We can't de-muster the regiment without the loss of a thousand votes or more. We both know that. But first we have to talk. I don't want to talk. You don't want to talk. But we *will* talk. We'll talk, d'you hear?"

The colonel nodded without a smile.

The governor returned to the opaque windows, "Does he speak Cheyenne?"

Silence.

"Does he speak Cheyenne – the interpreter?"

"I..."

The governor scowled at the major, "Well?"

"He says he does," replied the major.

"Well – let's hope he does. If he does – then we shall have our talk!"

The governor struggled with the latch to the window, won, and stepped out onto the narrow balcony, into the fresh air, and looked out to the east where the savages were riding, somewhere out there. He smiled to himself, thinking that Chivington was right, of course, which made up for him being nothing else.

)()()()(

September 28th 1864 – City of Denver

The chiefs came to Denver in a wagon. As it trundled through the main street, none of the onlookers cheered. Instead there was silence, slightly broken by occasional mutterings; a kind of wonderment took over. The whole of Denver came to see the display. Seven chiefs out of the wilderness, riding on the board seats of the flatbed wagon, drawn by big mules; that was some sight. A large garrison flag of the Stars and Stripes fluttered on a teepee pole above the wagon. The little cavalcade escorted by a troop of 1st Colorado rode through to Camp Weld. It was a spectacle not dissimilar to a funeral or a crowd of prisoners off for a hanging.

Evans was already there beneath a specially erected quartermaster's tent with the flaps open; it was a warm day. He stood and waited for the chiefs to be fed, and was astonished to see them eat three times that of any man he ever met. Then they were all sat opposite each other in two parallel lines; on one side the chiefs, on the other the officers and the governor. Two things struck Evans about the Indians: their stench, and their dignity.

Evans sat down on a large chair carefully placed to keep him slightly above the Indians. He stared at them for a moment and then looked towards the interpreter.

He liked Partridge, bald and grizzled, bronzed by the sun with eyes made the bluer by his tan. He spoke Cheyenne sure enough – he had gone straight to the youngest of the chiefs and thrown his arms round him. Seemed to know him well. He sat with them to eat and talked ten to the dozen. He also had a young Indian with him, lighter built than the Cheyennes. Frank Partridge said he was an Arikara who was his own scout. Evans noticed a curious interaction between the young Arikara and the big Cheyenne. The boy appeared to be in a state of reverence towards him, especially when words passed between them and the big Cheyenne had laughed. Now Partridge stood on the right hand side of the governor, ready. The boy dropped to the floor at Partridge's feet, crossed his legs and stared at the chiefs.

"Ask them what they want," began the governor.

"Peace," said Black Kettle.

"Ask him this then," the governor leaned forward. "Why is it that he makes war on *children*?"

"We have come to talk about these things," said Black Kettle quietly, and Partridge translated perfectly.

"The Cheyenne are cowards. Only cowards kill women and children." There was almost a snarl in the governor's voice.

When the words were turned into those of the chiefs' the governor expected a reaction, but their leader, the one they called Black Kettle, was impassive. He even smiled and after a moment's thought said, "We cowards came in your wagon through all your tribe without arms, with trust. We left our young men far away. We came in trust. We came as if walking through fire. We took a risk with our trust. That is how we cowards came. We want peace with the Wasichu. We would hold your hands, we would have you as a father to the people. This war is a dark cloud which brings fear and sorrow. We would send this cloud away. These chiefs with me will do what I say. They will take good news to our people. We want to hear good news from you to take to our people."

"But still your braves ride with murder in their hearts," snapped the governor.

Black Kettle shook his head slowly. He wore a head-dress with four eagle feathers and as he shook his head one of the feathers shed a shard of down. The chief looked at the fleck of white as it landed on his knee. He leaned forward and blew it away and then he looked into the governor's eyes, hard, clear, "I want you to understand that we are here for peace. That is why we have come to this place that you have made your own. We do not want to be mistaken for enemies of the Wasichu. We have come to talk not to bark – hear me in these things."

Frank Partridge listened carefully and translated, and then he added, "He speaks true, Governor Evans."

"Translate Mister Partridge, do not opinion on the matter!" Chivington butted in.

Frank swallowed the obscenity which rushed to his tongue and forced a smile. "I know these people. He speaks true." Frank watched Chivington's face flare at his words.

The governor grunted and glanced toward Chivington who raised his eyes upwards in obvious contempt. Evans turned back to Frank Partridge. He nodded towards Black Kettle and said, "Ask him why it took so long for him to come to see me!"

"What does it matter?" said old White Antelope. "We have come." This was said direct to Frank Partridge in Cheyenne.

"I will tell him what he wants to hear, my old friend," said Black Kettle to White Antelope and then turned to Frank Partridge. "Yellow Hair has told me that he calls you Grey Eagle and that you are a good Wasichu – I do not think the Bear Coat Governor is a good Wasichu but we will tell him what we have to tell him. Say this in the Wasichu tongue: 'We came as soon as the season would let us come, we came as soon as we could speak with our people about our journey. We came as soon as we could make our young men quiet. We came free and without fear to see you. When we return I want to tell our people that we have held your hands, and the hands of the eagle chiefs of the Wasichu, and that you will let us live near the buffalo in peace – I tell you true that if we do not live near the buffalo we shall starve.' Tell him these words Grey Eagle."

170

Governor Evans heard and bit his lip and saw that the Indians were not shifting. The time had come to dig a trench. He brought a smile to his face but said, "Why is it that we still have war, if you have done these things? Still your young men ride and cut open our children's naked bodies and leave them to the birds and wild beasts to eat. Do you do that with your children?"

All the chiefs shook their heads when Frank Partridge said this.

"No white man would do such a thing," snapped the governor. "We are civilised. You are savages. We do not cut people to pieces. Why – even my eagle chief here is also a priest!" Evans pointed at Chivington.

Frank was working out a suitable adjustment to the invective when Governor Evans poured on, softly now, "You are in alliance with the Sioux against the Wasichu."

"What did he say?" asked Black Kettle, even when the words came out in Cheyenne, so Partridge had to say them again. The governor was smiling.

"Who has told you this thing?" demanded Black Kettle.

"Damn you, with your 'Who said these things?'," shouted the governor and made to rise from his chair, but dropped back and wagged a finger at the leader of the Indian delegation. "The action of your people proves it – you are the leader, so your action proves it! You are responsible. Sioux and Cheyenne have killed the whites together. Together! Do you hear me? We know this to be so. We have proof in the feathers and the arrows, and the sights of bad things that our good scouts have seen with their eyes."

All the chiefs spoke at once. Black Kettle turned to them and heard from them that there was no alliance. He knew there was no alliance. The Sioux were like brothers, but there was no alliance. There was no agreement to make war. Sitting Bull was against war, he had said as much. He was a great warrior but he knew that war was the father of more war, and the Wasichu were dangerous, stupidly dangerous. What was this talk of an alliance?

"Tell this Wasichu Bear Coat Governor there is no war alliance against the Wasichu," Black Kettle's voice had risen in power. His back straightened, all the chiefs nodded and sat with their chins held high with the truth of it.

The governor saw there had been a startling anger in Black Kettle's eyes and voice, exacerbated by his previous gentle manner.

This was going very well indeed. The governor threw dry sticks onto the blaze.

"I also hear that you know that we Wasichu have a war of our own. You know that we have a big fight over in the East." Frank was careful to turn the ordinary language into appropriate Cheyenne turning 'East' into 'from where the sun comes up'.

Several chiefs nodded for this was true; they had heard of it.

"So you think you can attack us here and drive us out of our lands." Evans voice turned brusque, threatening.

Black Kettle chose to avoid an argument over whose land it was. No man can own the land; it is there, it cannot be picked up and taken away. So he said to the Wasichu leader who seemed to know nothing, "We wish to share peace with you in this country of our fathers."

"Well, Mister Chief I'll tell you this for sure measure – our Great Father in Washington has soldiers enough to drive out every Indian that ever lived here or anywhere and every Indian who lives here right now. He has soldiers enough to drive you all from every damned inch of the plains – and whip the damned Rebs at the same time!"

Black Kettle looked the governor full in the eyes, "We have many braves too. But we wish no such war."

The governor gave a sigh of exasperation. The damned Redskins had no idea what they were up against. He kept his eyes locked into those of the chief, with some difficulty and said, "Then there is a way for you. It is better you turn to us in peace, and come in to the forts. You must hand in your guns and your bows and your arrows, also your horses."

"We must hunt."

"All of your horses."

"All?"

"We shall feed you!"

"White Antelope speaks," announced White Antelope, oldest of the chiefs, friend of Black Kettle, famed warrior of an earlier time. What the Wasichu chief was speaking was a mad thing and it had to be stopped.

White Antelope said, "I went to see the Great Father and thought him a good man and I too want peace. I have heard all the words that have been said and I am for peace now and for as long as the sun

172

rises and sets and for as long as the buffalo moves with the seasons. That is what I think."

"You speak wisely," smiled Governor Evans sincerely, for the first time.

"I am pleased to be here and meet the chief of the whites in this place. I was proud to meet the chief of all the whites and he gave me this!" White Antelope banged the medal on his chest. "This medal is for peace."

Governor Evans saw that Black Kettle nodded in agreement, and caressed his own medal. All the chiefs nodded except for one, the lowest ranking. He sat impassive, watching, listening, also doubting – you could see it on his face. This was the one who embraced Partridge, the one called Yellow Hair – Partridge said something about him being a sodomite amongst his people. Savages. The wizened chief was still speaking. The governor looked to Partridge for the words.

"White Antelope said that from the time he got that medal he became the brother of the Wasichu, the white man," said Frank.

Old White Antelope would have begun to sing a peace song, but instead a truth came out of the wisdom in his heart and he added, for Grey Eagle to tell the Wasichu, "Now the soldiers do not shake hands, but hunt me instead, and want to kill me. They would kill even me – an old man – soon to pass through the screen to the other side. Soldiers are at this moment out there looking for my people, and will kill them if they find them!"

Black Kettle looked coldly at White Antelope, but Frank Partridge was faithful with the words.

"This is possible," said Evans, and hoped that it was true.

As the words were translated White Antelope nodded firmly, and then said, "But still we have come, as if through a great storm, to talk with you of *peace*. This is not the action of cowards! This is not the act of men at war."

Governor Evans thought back to the kids in the saloon, dead and naked, "But what about the killing of the settler families? Fires were lit on their bellies, their scalps were taken, and many of your braves tore at the bodies of the women whether they were young or old. Is that peace? Is that courage? Is that the kind of peace you bring to me?"

"The soldiers killed our boys first, caught them swimming in the river," explained Black Kettle.

"And were they not the braves who had earlier that day taken a whole herd of cattle from a ranch. It was they who started this thing, your people, not my soldiers."

"The Wasichu take down the cedars!" called out a chief.

"And the buffalo are taken for their skins alone!" called another.

"The beavers are all gone," said White Antelope.

"You sold them for whisky," snapped the governor. "It is you who take the pelts of your blessed beavers and sell them for hot spirit water!"

"Before you came to these lands we did not have these problems," said Black Kettle quietly. "But we must begin with now. We must begin with our today, not with what bad people have done in days which are now dead. There are bad Wasichu and bad Cheyenne, and bad Sioux, but we can still be together like brothers, like the bars on my honour flag that flies alongside your own flag outside."

"But the Indians also stole about forty horses," snapped Evans. He had to keep the fire from losing its heat.

For a moment, there was silence and the chiefs looked at one another in a kind of anguish.

"He is not listening to us," whispered White Antelope.

"He is himself a very bad Wasichu," hissed Yellow Hair and caught a growl of agreement from all of the chiefs.

"This is not going well," said Black Kettle.

"What are they saying?" asked Governor Evans.

"Can't catch it Governor, they'm a whispering."

"Tell 'em to speak up," ordered Colonel Chivington.

"They were Sioux!" said Black Kettle suddenly. "We have heard of that incident, and it was with the Sioux, this killing of the families."

"What are the Sioux going to do next?" snapped Evans. "If you know the past, do your know the future?"

Yellow Hair spoke, "The Sioux are also angry with the Wasichu. They want you out of the country. I am against that because I know you are strong. I also want peace. I would stand with the Wasichu if necessary, for peace." Yellow Hair was surprised at the ease with which he had lied to bring a calm to the discussion.

Black Kettle's face was impassive but thought that the winkte was a clever liar. There was still too much woman in this one.

174

"I have never harmed a white man," said Yellow Hair. He waved an arm at Frank Partridge. "I know this one and fought alongside him and hunted with him. He will tell you these things."

At the end of the translation Frank Partridge also lied and said, "It's true."

"I hope, Mister, that you also are on *our* side," said Colonel Chivington.

"Aye, Colonel, you can wager on it."

"More than a wager, I trust. We look for certainties today," said Evans. "Ask them what else they have to say."

"Tell him," said Black Kettle, "that we want peace and that is all."

"Now Colonel – do you have anything to add?" Governor Evans gestured towards the big colonel to give him the floor.

Chivington had been standing behind the governor's chair, huge and imposing, neatly barbered, uniform brilliant with its golden sash and hanging sabre. He came round from behind the chair and towered above the sitting chiefs. They looked at him impassively. Yellow Hair felt a curious need to put an arrow down his throat from a short distance though he did not know him. There was a wildness in this man's eyes. The Bear Coat Governor was a hawk to this man's eagle, bad dog and worse wolf.

The big man pointed to the eagle on his shoulder, "I am not a big war chief." He paused and looked down on the Indians; this was the enemy. He whispered to his soul that the day would come when he had them all in the front of a regiment, begging for quarter and not getting it. One day he would have them all.

"We have many soldiers beyond the rising sun. But here, beneath the mountains we all can see outside of this teepee, every soldier does what *I* say. I tell you this – my soldiers will fight you until you lay down your arms and honour the Wasichu Army. That is my rule – we fight to your death! But if you want peace then you can go to Fort Lyon with your people and lay down your arms to Gold Leaf Chief Anthony of the soldier horses, who is there in command. That is all I have to say."

Yellow Hair hoped that there would come a time when he would meet this man sitting on a war horse rather than standing in a peace teepee.

When the meeting was over, as the chiefs moved away, Yellow Hair took great pleasure in catching the eye of the Arikara boy. He felt a hint of lust, for the boy had a good face for an Arikara and was neatly shaped and would become a good warrior for sure. He gave the boy a look of death to hide the hunger and was pleased at the daring challenge which came back from his dark eyes. Yellow Hair thought that he would rather meet this boy between buffalo hides than on horseback – but whichever way Yellow Hair knew he could teach the boy more than the little Arikara could dream of.

"What is between you and Yellow Hair," asked Frank Partridge as the chiefs rolled away from the camp in the flatbed.

"Nothing," said Little Knife.

"You lie," said Frank.

"I know," smiled Little Knife.

)( )( )( )( )(

The Deer Rutting Moon the Wasichu called November in 1864, the place still called today, Sand Creek

Old White Antelope woke to the barking of a dog. His ears were sharper than his eyes. In the darkness of the teepee he listened to the dawn. Outside he heard the dog again and it was saying that something unusual was out there. He listened again and heard the call of a dog wolf too. He smiled as the animals threatened one another with their words. He stared hard at the gap at the top of the teepee and saw that the blackness of night had altered to a tint of grey. The dog barked again.

The old man eased himself from out of the cocoon of warm hides in which he had just dreamed. In the blur of dreams he had run without pain and ridden a war horse at a wild gallop; had been young once more. These days the warm hides were the best place to be. Now the liquids in his belly demanded release and he must hurry. Even so he dressed old-man slowly, once falling across the hides as he lost his balance and giggled to himself, warning again that he was not the man he was. His bladder was fit to burst, so he struggled back to his feet and made for the rounded entrance of the warm teepee.

He bent and lifted the heavy flap to one side and was out in the fresh cold with a thin covering of snow on Mother Earth. The chill was pleasant and without a moment's hesitation he opened his clothes and began to urinate into the darkness, having to wait a painful moment until the trickle came and then thankfully changed to a rush, but not like in youth.

"Oh Great One, maybe this is my last winter," came an idea with the sound of his water. "I am not sad to come to you through the screen that divides us. My time has come." The urine stopped, the relief was pure. "But, maybe, not yet awhile," he said aloud, but no-one heard.

He stretched and staggered slightly with the effort of it and then heard the barking of several dogs, a warning bark. He pondered whether he should go back and pick up his rifle but decided that he would not. They were safe enough in Sand Creek.

They had done what was required, the Cheyenne and the Arapaho. The main camp had switched to the Wasichu Fort Lyon, and the Wasichu had fed them. But as the moons slipped by the food was not enough. It was a surprise when Gold Leaf Anthony said that all the young men could go out and sweep for game. Wise old Black Kettle sent the famed winkte with them to keep them in order. Gold Leaf Anthony had said that he heard many buffalo were close. The hunting was good, not that a Wasichu knew anything about buffalo. But if there was a herd then the winkte would find it.

Five days after the young ones had gone whooping from the fort Gold Leaf Anthony had summoned the chiefs and announced that since meat would soon be coming in with the hunting parties the Wasichu food supplies would halt. Then he said that the old men and the sick warriors, the young and the women should all leave the fort and go to warmer camping down at Sand Creek, in the shelter of the hills, for there was no warm space in the fort. He smiled all the time.

He told them they would be closer to the setting sun, from where the young men would return from the hunt. He said he trusted the bands of the good Indians. He gave them some of their good weapons back and some ammunition. He seemed to be a good Wasichu.

The seven hundred who remained in the combined bands of Black Kettle and White Antelope moved out quickly, happy to be away from the fort and the sickly smell of the Wasichu. None of them took notice of three riders leaving the fort. One was headed for Denver, the other two for the field camps of the battalions of the 1st and 3rd Colorado under the command of Colonel James M. Chivington, thirty miles south-east. This was the setting of the trap.

꘡꘡꘡꘡꘡

Colonel Chivington shook the hand of Major Anthony on the steps of the officers' quarters at Fort Lyon. It sounded like a market place outside the fort as over six hundred men of the 1st and 3rd made temporary camp.

"Well Major, you asked for reinforcements to attack the Indians and here we are!"

The colonel's arm was round the major's shoulders as they stepped into the yellow light of the interior of the officers' quarters. At once all present came to attention and presented their compliments to the District Commander.

"Good evening gentlemen, are we ready?"

A growl of confirmation greeted the burly man.

"Are we ready to take some Indian scalps, eh lads?"

They were. Their faces spoke it.

"By the gift of the Lord, lads, we shall be wading in their gore before the week's out!" roared the colonel.

A few jaws dropped but he was cheered to the rafters.

"We shall ride out the day after tomorrow gentlemen. A company will join us from this fort."

"We'll bring along a battery of 12 pounders, with your leave, Colonel," smiled Anthony.

"That will do very well, sir!" said the colonel. "We shall turn them all inside out by God!"

"We know the exact location of the camp," said Major Anthony. "All the people of Black Kettle are there, but we managed to get the warriors out of the way, hunting. We shall punish them severely."

"Sir?" A young officer, Cramer, stood by the major to get his attention.

"Yes young man?"

"Those Indians were said by you to be in a place of safety."

"And so they are! Safe from raiding our ranches and roads," snapped the major.

"Looks like we are setting out on a road to murder, sir!"

"What was that sir?" shouted the colonel. "Did you say 'murder', Mister? Did you say that?"

"I did sir, I did. Any officer taking part will be dishonoured. We are not..."

The colonel, huge inside his uniform, stepped right up to the young man who was standing by a supporting beam reaching into the roof. The colonel's fist flashed by the young man's face and walloped into the beam, "Damn you, sir!"

"Sir?" The young officer's face showed fear and astonishment.

"Damn you and any man who shows sympathy for the Indians."

"But..."

"We have come here to kill Indians, you hear me?"

There was total silence from all in the room; the wood on the fire hissed, the only sound.

"I believe it is right, by any means, to kill Indians. All Indians. Wipe them out to the last living one of them. I say this is right under God's heaven! And damn you for thinking otherwise. Where is my sleeping space?" The last was almost bellowed at Major Anthony, and led by him the Reverend Colonel Chivington swept out of the room.

)( )( )( )( )(

"You was at Gettysburg?"

Merle Clinton, wearing the chevrons of a sergeant in the 3rd Colorado Volunteers, temporary attached – permission given by the Regular US Army adjutant back at Camp Weld – turned in the saddle of his USA mount, a big chestnut. "What's it to you?"

"Now don't get ornery," pleaded the soldier at his side, one of the townsfolk who signed up for a hundred days. "It's just that I don't fancy fighting in that regular war like, and feel respect for them as do."

"I did not see too much."

"But you was there!"

The soldier threw his head back and took a long swig from the whisky jar.

Volunteer Sergeant Clinton said nothing about the drink. He had tried before, to no avail; told off the men for their drinking, and been shouted at by the colonel himself who said the lads needed the heat of the stuff for what was coming. Half the regiment was already drunk, thought Clinton to himself. Pity Custer was not in command. That would shake them.

Then from somewhere came an order, and the regiments, riding in a ragged column of fours, came to a clumsy halt with some men

179

thumping their horses into the next one in column. A soldier was thrown when his horse was kicked by the one to his front and then reared in defence and anger. Chaos broke out in that portion of the line.

Lieutenant Cramer, grim faced, came riding down from the head of the column with orders to deploy. The eastern sky was turning into dawn and they were able to see their way better. One by one the companies turned or wheeled from the column, men grumbling, horses protesting; officers calling for quiet and being ignored The companies moved into battalions to work round the village and then, part way through the manoeuvring, a general stampede developed which turned the regiments towards the sleeping village.

Clinton saw a small pack of wolves scatter as the horses broke into a trot and he heard dogs begin to bark and the next moment he found himself going in at a panic gallop. First cavalry charge for months!

He had his Colt in his hand. One of the old hands riding with the escort which brought him to Denver had counselled him that a good six shooter was better than a sabre at close quarters, but that he was to mind not blowing his horse's brains out.

Ahead, quite suddenly, in the snow, he saw the teepees, lots of them, hundreds it seemed. Incongruous, in the half light, he saw an Indian waving a big American flag. He was the first man that he shot at. Then he swore at himself for firing from so far away. Then, as he closed with the flag waver he saw a figure at the waver's side. Clinton fired as he passed by. He saw a woman's shape thrown back by the impact and said to himself, "A woman!" And felt bad about it.

Then he was in the camp, surrounded by soldiers and Indians. The crackle of firing was everywhere. He heard the artillery open up and a shell burst inside a teepee he was passing. Parts of people flew through the air; and Clinton fired again, this time at a man. He knew it was a man, because he was naked and waving a club strung with feathers. Suddenly Clinton was through the village and out the other side, unscathed. He fought the chestnut to turn it, and charged back into the melee.

)( )( )( )( )(

White Antelope saw them coming, plenty soldiers. He began to walk towards them. He saw they were coming at speed. He paused for only a moment, then he walked again and waved his arms at

them. He knew the Wasichu word and called out "Stop! Stop!"
They came on.

All around the combined camps he heard gunfire. The Wasichu
had come with death in their minds. There was nothing that he
could do. Maybe they would stop. Maybe they had made a mistake.

He stood and waved his arms wildly, calling to the Wasichu.
They took no notice and he saw that several had levelled their rifles
at him and were firing. They are not very good, he thought, for not a
bullet came close to him.

He stopped, stood, looked at them, and then quite slowly the old
man folded his arms. He began to sing to himself: *"Nothing lives
long, only the earth and the mountains."* A bullet hissed close by his left
ear. So he did the only thing that a great chief could do: he began to
sing the song again, out loud, for all to hear.

)( )( )( )( )(

The boy White Hawk ran with the sick warriors who, with the
youngest youths, had not been allowed on the hunt. They ran
between Wasichu horses and heard the hiss of longknives. They saw
laughing Wasichu trying to kill them, but they missed. They shot
back at the Wasichu and they missed too in the excitement. It was
the boy Bear Dog who saw the depression in the ground first, where
the river used to run but was now empty. He ran to it carrying his
old one shot musket, ready loaded.

He threw himself into the depression and turned, lying down,
making the place a shooting pit. White Hawk dropped alongside
him. Bear Dog was the first to kill a Wasichu, a Wasichu with a
beard. They saw the man's head pop like a fruit, hit at close range
with the big musket ball. They cheered and then other Wasichu
came at them, lots of them, firing at them from their horses. But the
pit was good and the Wasichu were very bad with their guns and
had no bravery in them, refusing to close. They came back again and
again, and many bullets were fired.

A Wasichu was unhorsed and his rifle flew from his grip. Bear
Dog leapt out of the pit, half way through re-loading the musket, to
get hold of the man's rifle. He hit the soldier hard on the head with
the butt of the musket, but as he was bending to take ammunition
from the man, another Wasichu came up with a longknife and cut at

181

him. Bear Dog did not get to his feet. The longknife soldier swerved his horse away from the pit.

Little White Hawk saw this, struggled up from the pit and ran out to him. When he got there he saw that Bear Dog was smiling. But his head was a hand's reach from his body, clean severed by the longknife.

The boy picked up Bear Dog's musket and the Wasichu rifle but found that the rifle was broken. He turned to the Wasichu warrior who was beginning to wake from the blow he had received. He pulled the Wasichu's six shooter out of its pouch and found some ammunition and began to load the gun. As he did so he saw the Wasichu turn onto his back and groan. Then he saw fear in the man's face, and that made White Hawk feel good. He dropped a sixth round into the vacant chamber and snatched the gun closed. He levelled the gun and pointed it at the Wasichu soldier's moving face and fired. The face stopped moving, ejecting a spray of carmine.

White Hawk raced back, followed by another longknife soldier on his horse, but the Wasichu turned away as arrows from the pit came close to him. The warriors hugged the boy and he felt very good, but they took the six shooter off him, and the musket and the ammunition. So he waited to see if another Wasichu might fall. It was then that he realised he had forgotten to take the scalp and felt very stupid.

He decided to stay in the hollow shooting pit and either live or die. If he died he would be a warrior for ever, if he lived he would have an evil story to tell his winkte father who should have been there.

$\rtimes\rtimes\rtimes\rtimes\rtimes$

Many of the people rushed to the teepee of Black Kettle as he waved his flag. They gathered round him getting closer to him to be protected by the honour flag. They saw his wife lying at his feet, still moving. The soldiers rode round them, continually firing into them. Many were hit, and the wife of Black Kettle was struck four more times, and still she moved. Some of the men fired back. It was then that fires began in the teepees.

The morning light, fast gathering, joined with the light of teepee fires, and in that light Black Kettle saw the big man on a horse with other Wasichu around him. He saw it was the black beard eagle chief who said all the soldiers would do what he said. It was the one who spoke of giving up their arms. He could see him now shouting at his men, seeming to try to stop them. He was shouting and screaming at them, but they took no notice. Then the eagle chief saw the leader of the Cheyennes and pointed towards him in recognition, with a longknife.

Black Kettle began to give orders that the people were to withdraw to the river and stand and fight. It was going to be a long day. But perhaps they were safe now that the Eagle Chief had seen him.

ЖЖЖЖЖ

Chivington could see the main chief. He recognised him – he was the one who boasted of the flag being red for the Red Man...

"Got you now, Mister Chief!" he snarled into the uproar.

A dozen riders with crazed eyes, shooting left and right went by.

"Stop that wild firing!" bellowed Chivington. "Don't waste your bullets lads – get in close!"

They were taking no notice of him. Too many of the Indians were on the run.

"Shoot 'em down. Let none escape!" bellowed the parson turned colonel.

Looking back at the Indian chief he thought he saw a look of relief on his face.

Two more troopers came by, "You two!" Chivington pointed with sword. "Try to cut down that bastard with the flag!"

ЖЖЖЖЖ

The sun was just above the horizon when two soldiers fired again and again at the chief. All missed him but they brought down others close by who fell across his good old wife, who lay heavy with the five bullets in her. Black Kettle pulled two dead men away and helped a wounded man move so that he could kneel at her side. She was still alive.

"This is a bad day," she whispered.

"It is a good day to die," he said, and put his buffalo robe over her.

Black Kettle stood and saw that the soldiers had moved back a little, for the old men, even the old women, had begun to fire back and the action was getting hot. The Cheyennes fought the Wasichu

183

for the rest of the day. Some Cheyenne slipped away in the gloom, some stayed on the outskirts of the burning village, but at the end the Wasichu claimed to have killed five hundred, and took many more away captured.

"That," said Chivington, looking back at the smoking encampment, some fires still red in the poor light of the bloody afternoon, "should teach them all a lesson for the future. A damned good lesson."

)(̶)(̶)(̶)(̶)(̶

Towards the end of the afternoon the chestnut stumbled and threw Clinton. Before he could remount the horse, it was away. He followed it on foot.

The young girl Little Feather saw this and thought that if she caught the horse and gave it to the Wasichu she would be safe. As it trotted by she grabbed out at the reins from her hiding place in a thicket. She held the horse.

All Clinton saw was a young Indian grab his horse to steal it and was so close he was on him in an instant. Clinton brought up his heavy Colt. The Indian began to fiddle with his robe and draw something from it. Clinton fired. Even as he fired he saw beautiful breasts and said, "Shit! Another woman!"

She staggered back, her garment coming away to reveal her utter nakedness. There was a gash above her right breast just above the nipple; not much blood came out. She stared in astonishment for a moment at Clinton. Then she dropped to her knees and pitched forward, still holding the rein for him. Clinton darted across to her and retrieved the rein.

"Sorry," he said, and mounted the chestnut, not watched any longer by two huge young eyes.

)(̶)(̶)(̶)(̶)(̶

Frank Partridge and Little Knife heard the gunfire. They were out twelve miles or more from the action. The breeze had stiffened to carry the sound, as it usually did as the day wore on, and Frank Partridge guessed he was too far away to take part in whatever was happening. But the firing continued for several hours. He had strict instructions to scout east and look out for the hunting parties. There was nothing to be seen of them. Towards evening he saw small

184

groups of Cheyenne and Arapaho on foot, moving as fast they could, north-west. Several were nursing wounds, bad wounds. He stayed well clear for some were armed.

"There has been a bad battle," said Little Knife.

Frank nodded.

"I go speak?"

"Leave it! We'll skirt round and head back to Sand Creek. They're safe down there."

And they did. But they stopped three miles short. They camped away from it because a cold night came down with flurries of snow, so that it was the following morning when they rode through. There was a burial party there; some of the cavalry had fallen. Little Knife was very silent as they rode through the camp. There were dead everywhere. Little Knife pointed at one.

A half-naked woman lay, as if asleep, but she was part disembowelled and at her side was an infant, attached still by its cord.

Then they came across a small cave with half a dozen women dead around the entrance. Just in front of the entrance lay a little girl, shot to pieces. Then they saw an old man, almost completely naked, his privates gone.

"Damn," said Frank Partridge, "that's old White Antelope."

"This is very bad," said Little Knife.

Frank Partridge said nothing; the shame of it silenced him.

They caught up with the drunken singing regiments half a day later. Several hundred Indian prisoners were trudging in a sullen compact group, idly watched by some of the soldiers. The hatred in the Cheyenne eyes was life itself. Frank could not look at them, and Little Knife looked only ahead toward the soldiers, thinking that maybe he should kill one of them.

Frank saw that many of the soldiers had scalps. One of them waved a scalp at Little Knife and the Arikara had to remember that it was a Cheyenne scalp and that he had one himself, and that these were his sometime enemy. Then he tried to think of nothing at all.

When Frank saw that one of the soldiers had the private parts of a woman hung on his saddle pommel he did not point it out to the young warrior at his side; instead he said, "Friend, we are riding north."

"Where?" asked the Arikara boy.

"Away."

)()()()()(

Five days later the scalps were on display in the little theatre close by the saloon where the homesteaders had lain, and the people of the town were triumphant. A reporter for the *Denver Chronicle* visited the saloon, talked to the troopers and wrote notes as he looked and listened. He returned to his desk and wrote in a neat copper plate hand a long and vivid account.

Then he pondered on his final sentence. He scribbled on a note pad and crossed it out. He got up and paced a little then sat down again. He hit on the thing, exactly the right final touch. Neatly he wrote for the typesetter:

"Our boys have returned, and all acquitted themselves well!"

9

The Hated Fortress

(The Sioux Moon of When the Cherries are Ripe,
the month called July in the Wasichu Year of 1865 –
Fort Rice on the Missouri western shore, Lieutenant Colonel
Charles Augustus Ropes Dimon, 1st U.S. Volunteers,
Galvanized Yankees, commanding)

Hot hot hot! Charles Dimon stood on the narrow veranda of the regimental office and looked across the neat parade ground. Pride oozed from his manner, his stance, his appearance – complete with white-gloved hand on the pommel of his ceremonial sword, for which the men had put up funds. The blade, out of sight in the gilded scabbard, was engraved in gilt with his name, and that of the regiment. He wore it at all times.

The sound of the sentry at the regimental office door stomping the butt of his rifle to the wood floor as he finished his salute brought a glance from the youthful colonel. Then his gaze took in the distant walls of Fort Rice and the neat lines of sod-roofed barracks. It was good.

He sucked in a breath of arid air, and decided to stay in the shade. The large thermometer behind him showed a temperature of ninety degrees. As he moved his legs he could feel the dark blue material warm against his flesh. He wriggled his leg to feel the touch. The sound of the material moving and the creak of his riding boots were the only outside sounds on the veranda. Inside there was a dull chatter from the three clerks, but that was all. The entire post was quiet after the midday meal.

A large hound at the end of the walkway on Dimon's left made an idle slap at one of a score of irritating flies attempting to find drink in the flanges of its nostrils. They immediately returned and the dog flopped its shaggy head down again, hopelessly. It was a thoroughly filthy hound. When or how it had joined the regiment was a mystery: some said it was when they had first disembarked from the *Effie Deans* in September '64.

She had run aground some two hundred and seventy miles from Fort Rice and Colonel Dimon had led the regiment to base on foot – a cold, miserable, autumn march, marred by deaths from illness, a single execution, a score of desertions and a handful of vainglorious clashes with hostiles. Now, with two more seasons gone, the regiment was in good order, the fort neat and tidy and General Sully could come yesterday, today or tomorrow and inspect until he dropped. The boys of the 1st U.S.A. Volunteers were more than ready.

The sound of Sergeant Clinton's horse leading the colonel's favourite grey came from his right and added to his pride. Dimon felt himself lucky to get young Clinton, whose regiment had been mustered out whilst the sergeant was out in Colorado. 'Young' Clinton – Dimon was only two years older! The colonel's epaulettes gave him extra years, an inner maturity, a certainty that he was right. The silver oakleaves on his shoulder made him feel much older.

Clinton was a find because he had taken part in the Chivington fight, but was too modest to talk much about it. He had experience fighting Indians – that was the important thing. He had also been at Gettysburg and ridden with Custer – a *real* find. The Galvanized Yankees might have had battle experience back East, but their Indian contact had been slight. Their actions had been limited to sighting hostiles in the distance, close enough to waste ammunition, too far away for a hit. Clinton was also Union Army proper and a breath of fresh air for that.

Dimon liked him from the start and gave him his regular USA stripes on the spot at the mustering of the regiment. It was an easy decision. He had the establishment for a headquarters' sergeant and the personal letter from General Butler asking that Clinton get a stripe clinched it.

"Is the Colonel ready for his ride, sir?" came the soft voice of the young Irishman.

"He is," said Dimon, and stepped out into the heat of the direct sunlight.

He took up the reins and within moments found their warmth penetrate his riding gloves. He removed a glove and found the reins hot to the touch. The back of the animal, already glistening with sweat, seemed comparatively cool. He patted the animal's neck and replaced the glove. His spurs touched her flanks.

He let the horse lift its head up and down as it adjusted the bit. His boots, grafted into the stirrups, shifted and again he gently touched both flanks with his spurs: not a jab, just a touch, a caress. The horse snorted and moved forward without a word of command.

The cur on the walkway looked up, but without serious interest, to watch the colonel mount and move off. The dog shook itself, half got to its feet to follow, thought the better of it, flopped back onto the shadow-coated boarding. Immediately, the flurry of flies returned to pester. It watched the two riders trot, watched out of one eye, then closed it to join the other, and fell into a dreamless lazy dog's sleep.

The riders cantered across the parade ground. With a click and snap, arms were presented by the brace of sentries at the gate. Then they were onto the level ground outside, cleared of scrub for an open field of fire for both carbines and howitzers. Beyond the gate, the Missouri was blue, unusually so that day, capturing the azure of the cloudless day, its waters dappled with streaks of silver-white where the sunlight caught eddies in the currents. This movement of light was framed by the green of vegetation on the opposite bank, beyond which, far mountains, then the sky.

"Magnificent!" said the Colonel Dimon loud enough for Clinton to hear.

"It's as dry as the Libyan desert!" said Clinton.

"What?"

"Dry, Colonel, very dry."

"What do you know about the Libyan desert?"

"Read about it in a book – this looks like what the book said. Dry, sir."

"Yes it is Clinton, very dry."

"Like the Libyan desert," pressed Clinton.

"So it is," said the colonel thinking he had never seen a desert and neither had the sergeant, like as not, but if a desert were to exist anywhere it must look like this, except for the river of course.

"Except for the river," said the colonel.

"Yes sir," said the sergeant. The colonel was mighty sharp, he thought.

To the left of the fort, itself dominated by the incongruously gigantic flag pole made from a mature fir, painted white, and sporting the largest Union flag in the West, were more than a hundred teepees. Dimon was both pleased and anxious at the sight. He was pleased, for it took the fort's collective mind away from the death of young Mrs. Cardwell, poor soul. She was Private Cardwell's pretty wife – died of birth fever, the infant too. He was anxious, at the Indian numbers growing at such a pace as to outmatch the fort in a few days' time. But old Sully, One Star Sully, wanted a council with the tribes and they sure were taking notice, gathering in their hundreds – except for the Sioux.

There was just a handful of Sioux teepees. Sully wanted the Sioux there, especially the Hunkpapa. They were the most powerful of the warriors and led by an obscure villain who called himself Sitting Bull. Each morning the friendly Yantonai chief, Two Bears, and his plump little sidekick, Bare Rib of the Hunkpapa Sioux, would canter away from their little circle of teepees outside the main gate and 'count the people', reporting back to the colonel after breakfast. Dimon was specially attentive to what Bare Rib had to say – there were only a dozen Hunkpapa lodges close by the river. Sully wanted a hundred; he wanted the most dangerous group properly represented.

Dimon was proud of his association with these two, fostered during the winter as they camped near the fort, hoping for and getting provisions from the Wasichu foot soldiers. He enjoyed his conversations with them and felt a certain confidence, fed by their insistence on calling him their 'great capitan'. The relationship had been firmed and when hostiles had threatened the fort, the colonel had sent some mounted infantry and a howitzer in support of three score of the two chiefs' warriors who set off to chase the hostiles. He trusted the chiefs. Their advice was good. Dimon had won a clear victory. He wrote a lengthy report to Brigadier General Sully and told him so. He was confident that Sully would be pleased at what he read.

҉҉҉҉҉

"Hell's blazes!" Sully yelled when he read the neat report in the commander of Fort Rice's own sweet hand.

His bellow made every horse in his waiting escort either start or flick ears forward. They knew that voice and expected men to jump into saddles, and reins and spurs to give signals for a gallop. Sully's clerk looked up from the correspondence strewn on canvas beds and the field campaign desk.

"Bad news, General?"

"Bad news....... bad! Holy Jesus! I'm gathering in the tribes for a damned chinwag and damned Dimon chases the beggars back into the damned hills."

Sully formed the view that Dimon must go. Oh, he was a good boy. But too young. What was it? – twenty four – one of Ben Butler's favourites – political general, political choice. They said he was a stickler for salutin' – so am I – but not with arrows in me bonnet. Brave! Sure of that. Turned the regiment into a regiment, but should not have shot that damned lad for desertion. God damn, he only *said* he was *going* to desert. No damned authority to do it! But he did it. Sort of fool thing Butler would do. Dimon would have to go. Ease him out. Do that after the peace talks with the tribes.

The trouble with Dimon was his lack of subtlety. He had beaten off attacks which might not have been attacks. He could see no further than that. He had created a regiment out of dissident Yankees, who had been taken out of prison camps to form the 1st Volunteers; trained Reb soldiers they might have been, but they were not a unit, not until they marched behind Dimon. But making a regiment jump on parade was one thing, keeping it alive was quite another. Command and leadership had more to it than drill. A bit of cunning was called for. Dimon was not cunning. Dimon would have to go.

)*()*()*()*()*(

As Dimon rode with Clinton by his side, the colonel levelled his shoulders with pride, lifted up his young man's chin, and reminded himself he was colonel of a regiment and commander of a fort. Were he to hold such a command in the proper war he would have been a brigadier, nothing less. A star on his shoulder, the gold braid trailing his horse blanket. Someday! At this rate – soon. An establishment for the rank could be asked for. He would write to Butler about it. Sully would be bound to agree once he had read the report. Dimon was very happy.

A steamboat call distracted the riders. The sound came from either the *Deer Lodge* or *Yellowstone* – both about to push off downstream before the summer river dropped much lower.

Both vessels would have gone earlier but heavy thunderstorms the previous week kept the level up, giving them a chance to take on extra cargo. The hint of green growth which followed the downpours was burned out within a day or two. This was a warning that the worst of a long dry summer was about to begin. The river had turned yellow as a result of the added water coming off the solid broiled earth and raised the water level a foot or more. Now the rise of water was ended, the mud had settled; the summer was biting back once more, sizzling, lacking in mercy.

The boom of the signal gun back at the fort brought both horsemen to a halt. Clinton noticed a soldier on the lookout post above and by the gate waving his arm and pointing north. There was a dust cloud there, low. Hostiles?

"Hostiles?" queried the young Irishman eagerly.

"Another clan coming in is the more likely," muttered his clever young colonel.

"Guess so, sir."

"Let's go look."

They broke into a canter in the sun and within five hundred yards realised that the dust cloud was being raised on the east bank of the river. They saw that the run of dust was strict in its shape and suggested a column of soldiers rather than Redskins, who usually moved in open order with a lot of scouts strung out in front.

"It's infantry," called back Clinton, now half a dozen lengths ahead in his eagerness.

The sound of a bugle calling the fort to arms caught their ears. Then came the distant call for the honour guard. Lieutenant Colonel Dimon was pleased at the initiative; he was keen on salutes and honours.

As they got closer to the river they saw a column of foot – perhaps three or four hundred strong, a battalion of four companies according to the fluttering guidons. They came tramping close to the edge of the water where the 1st Volunteers had made a clearing earlier in the year – now a dust flat. A group of twenty horse led the way. Unmistakable, in the lead, rode a trooper with a one-star guidon fluttering, and just behind him was the tall gaunt figure of the commander of the Missouri Northwest Division, Brigadier General Alfred Sully: Indian fighter, sour faced, goatee-bearded, thin to the point of being gaunt, and respected by soldier and brave warrior alike.

Dimon glanced over his shoulder and hoped they would prepare a suitable general salute with the howitzers. Dimon waved to the advancing troops, was seen, and ignored.

)( )( )( )( )(

"Why is it you hate the fort called Rice?" asked Frank Partridge, trying to catch the eye of the *wicasa wakan*, the great spiritual leader of the Hunkpapa Sioux. He tried to make the question appear casual – an afterthought to nothing. You had to be careful talking with Sitting Bull; he missed nothing and always seemed to know your thoughts.

At first the sometime war chief, now looked on for wisdom and leadership in a wider realm, and the most powerful of medicine men, said nothing. He looked up from the pipe, glowing from a strong pull, looked at the Wasichu warrior who, sadly, thought himself a Crow.

How can he hope to be a Crow when his hair is shaved to nothing? He did not look like a Crow in any way. Perhaps this was a good thing. The Crows have fine hair, although they style it in their effeminate way, as is their nature. They were handsome it was true, but they used their beauty to slime their way into the greedy hearts of the Wasichu star chiefs. Sitting Bull found it difficult to accept that there was anything good in the Crow people at all.

Why was it that this Wasichu Crow had now declared himself to be a lover of the Cheyenne and thus a good friend of the Sioux? Why should this question come out of the air from nowhere? Perhaps the question itself was a chant of warning from the Great Spirit.

Sitting Bull nodded several times as he called the name of the *Wakantanka* in his mind, secretly. He drew deeply on the pipe and, to confuse the Wasichu, he passed it to him, in peace; which gave him even more time to formulate a proper answer to the Wasichu snake question.

"Take," he said to the Wasichu, "from a good friend."

Sitting Bull was not his good friend; he did not trust this pale one with the shaven head and the many weapons. Even the word of Yellow Hair, who claimed to be a friend of this Wasichu, did not remove his doubts. Sitting Bull wanted something more than words. A winkte can be tricky as a person; half woman but with the insight of a man into the heart of a man – very tricky. It was

193

important that the words of Yellow Hair be stored in the mind and unravelled at leisure.

The Wasichu took in a long draw on the pipe; he coughed out some of the raw smoke, but controlled his cough. His eyes began to water. He cleared his throat, "What worries you about that place?"

Sitting Bull took back the pipe and lifted it to his lips, "Many things."

"What?"

This Wasichu was direct. He asked the question very directly. It was necessary to think at length on any answer, and this Wasichu was full of questions. This might be magic, bad medicine. Sitting Bull was uneasy, but did not show it.

"The fort the Wasichu called Rice is close by the great river," began Sitting Bull.

"Yes – it is."

Again Sitting Bull paused. He knew something of the fort, but not enough. His loyal cousins Bare Rib and Two Bears were there, watching. They were to co-operate with the Wasichu, pretend to have influence with Sitting Bull, promise to bring him into the fort; they were to squeeze good things out of the Wasichu. But above all they were to watch. And if they could confuse the Wasichu, then they were to do that too.

"Yes – it is by the river. Does that matter?" Frank forced himself to be very patient.

The Hunkpapa's large eyes narrowed and he leaned forward as if to pass on a confidence of enormous importance, something very secret, "It was not there before!"

Frank also leaned forward, "Many places of the Wasichu were not there before."

"Yes!" said Sitting Bull.

"And when the Sioux march from camp place to camp place, their camp places were not there before..."

"Ah!" Sitting Bull cut in. Then he said nothing.

"You are the same," suggested Frank Partridge.

Sitting Bull shook his head and laughed, "No, friend, no. The Red Man comes and then the Red Man goes. We leave the place of staying to recover in a season. But the Wasichu fort is there like a bad wound. It grows and sends its poison through the body of our Mother Earth. The Wasichu lodges stay for ever like a festering arrow strike which is nothing in itself but as it remains its poisons multiply and kill the body itself, so that, in time, even the arrow rots. We must cut out the wounds that the Wasichu make. We must wipe out their forts – leave them burning so that nature can return."

How would the Wasichu-Crow-Cheyenne-Sioux react to that? Sitting Bull smiled and waited.

"It is not easy; this of the 'wiping out', it is not easy," said the Wasichu failing to hide a little discomfort, which brought a smile to the face of the Sioux leader.

"This I know," said Sitting Bull, looking pensive, letting a fresh cloud of smoke escape from his lips. "Of all the warriors, the Shoshone, the Cheyenne, even the Crow, of all of them, the Wasichu whites are the best behind a tree. That is why they make the forts. They try to move forests. But really they kill the forests. Their fort has eaten many trees for them to hide behind. They take the living forests to build forts for the making of death. It is because they are good behind a tree – that makes up for them being only Wasichu."

"We can hold a fixed position, it is true," said Frank and for a moment a vision of the Russian guns flaming in front of the 17th Lancers leapt into his mind. Had the Russians been behind ramparts, instead of in the open, it would have been different. But they were not behind ramparts, and history was made.

Sitting Bull nodded and said, "They stand and hold ground and are dangerous for it. I tell you this fort is made of many trees for that reason." Sitting Bull sensed that the Wasichu was not listening. "You are thinking of other things?"

Frank forced the carnage of the Light Brigade out of his mind and said, "No, my friend. You are right, we Wasichu are trained for standing and waiting to kill or be killed."

"It is in their blood then – this standing to the death?" Sitting Bull was wondering if the Wasichu ever ran away. Seeming to run away was a trick of war, but would the Wasichu ever run in panic, like the buffalo – to be ridden down like game? Or perhaps they could be encouraged to stand and waste their bullets on the circling braves, and then, unarmed, be slaughtered.

"Standing is not in their blood, Great Leader in Battle, but in their training. They prepare for such battles and if the battles do not go the way of the plan then they try to create circumstances that make the battle change direction. That is what the star chiefs try to do."

"Then we *shall* wipe them out," said the Chief, emphatically.

Frank sighed. "There are many soldiers at Fort Rice – a hundred, eight times, maybe more. They are good soldiers, experienced in war."

"I hear they are also prisoners," said Sitting Bull, feigning astonishment at the idea.

Frank nodded, "They were."

"Prisoners with guns – the Wasichu are a mystery."

"Wasichu are one big nation – but a nation divided in hatred. They have a big war."

"I have heard about this big war," nodded the Sioux, also smiling broadly. "Tell me of this war. For why do the Wasichu fight each other?"

"For..." Frank thought of ways to explain.

"For horses?"

"Not for horses."

"For what?"

"For men."

Sitting Bull looked blank.

"For slaves."

"Ah! We have taken slaves in our wars. Once we took a beautiful Crow lady..."

"It is different. All of our slaves belong to another tribe – the black tribe."

"Ah! I have seen a black Wasichu but once – they have the hair of a buffalo, and skin like old tanned leather. They do not make good scalps I am told; I have never seen one from a black Wasichu."

"Our war is fought because half of my people want to keep these black slaves and the other half say all men should be free."

"Free?"

"To come and go as they wish."

Sitting Bull thought that such a state of life was so obvious it was difficult to understand why the Wasichu thought about it at all. But he had to know more about the fort. The young men wanted to attack it. He thought an attack dangerous. But if he did not let them attack the fort they would attack it any way. They would be without direction and that would be even more dangerous. Sitting Bull had to know more of the power of the fort.

"But tell me – tell me of these soldiers in the fort – how did they get there?"

"It is because of the war in the East. One half began to win, the tribe of the South. Many prisoners were taken. Then the other side began to win, the Northern people, and took many prisoners. Some prisoners were exchanged."

"For horses?"

"No, Great Chief, for other prisoners."

The Sioux leader raised his brows in astonishment.

"Northern Tribes of the Wasichu had many extra captives, so they were offered their freedom in a different way, filling the forts in the West. The captives hated the prisons and agreed to come out of America towards the setting of the sun..."

"To serve those who captured them?"

"Yes."

"No horses exchanged?"

"No."

"The Wasichu are definitely a mystery."

Frank nodded.

"So these 'prisoner' warriors came to make war on the Red People, to take our land, to kill the buffalo and the antelope for no reason other than blood." There was a sudden edge to the Indian's voice.

"This is true."

"So – the Wasichu admits the wickedness."

"I admit the truth."

"Then we shall wipe them out. We want to live in peace with the Wasichu, but if they harm us then we shall fight."

"Such a war will be difficult for you. The Wasichu are many."

"All the Wasichu that I see are in the hated fortress."

"There are others."

"We hear of them. Our Dog Soldiers track them. There is a Wasichu one star chief named Sooli."

"Sully."

"Yes, Sooli. We know where he is. He goes to Fort Rice and then out again. But those at the fortress, we can wipe *them* out. When Sooli is gone, we shall do it."

"You do not have enough braves," Frank waved his hand over his shoulder to encompass the village behind and around them.

Sitting Bull nodded.

"And I hear not all of your people want a war; you are divided like the Wasichu are divided. I hear that the wise leaders search for peace, but the young hot-bloods yearn for war."

Sitting Bull nodded. This Wasichu had big ears.

"But," said Frank, leaning forward in emphasis, "the Wasichu will not always be divided as you are." Frank saw Sitting Bull bristle.

"Nor will the nations of my people always be divided," said Sitting Bull thinking at the same time – except for the Crow and the.... perhaps the Wasichu was right. These were dangerous times.

"You should not attack the fort," said Frank.

This was an easy thing to say, thought Sitting Bull. Outside there was a sudden whooping of young Indians racing by on their ponies.

"We cannot be stopped," said Sitting Bull with a secretive nod towards the noise outside. "They need to be blooded."

"The fort is dangerous."

"They see it as an easy way."

The smoke from the pipe dwindled and ended once more. The Sioux medicine man looked down the stem. He thought of loading a little more tobacco. He changed his mind and in a deft movement got to his feet, but swayed slightly with the suddenness of his rise and the effects of the deeply drawn tobacco and the usual stiffness from his old leg wound.

Frank rose with him, in respect. Sitting Bull reached out and placed his hand on the white man's shoulder. He gently steered him towards the open entrance of the great teepee, for he had something to show this Wasichu who thought he knew many things and believed himself to be a Crow – and thus lacked much in the way of wisdom. The Crow, in the mind of the Sioux, had little to say and, beyond that, were good for nothing at all. He should have chosen to be a Sioux.

⚓⚓⚓⚓⚓

Sitting Bull called for his favourite pony. It had an unusual colouring: almost red, save for a single white flash on its left rear fetlock. Its tail, left long and flowing, was also white – he called it White Tail. Frank still rode Ben who, at the very sound of Frank exiting the teepee, stamped with his front left hoof and then pranced briefly with a zealous welcome.

Mounted, they trotted out of camp with half a dozen naked youths, just out of adolescence following them on ponies, circling them, galloping ahead, trotting behind, but always keeping a respectful distance. The little party moved away from Sitting Bull's village and travelled about three Wasichu miles before coming on a low valley, filled with good timber. They dropped into it, scattering game and amused squirrels, until they joined a shallow river with a firm sandy bed which they used as a roadway. A further mile was covered before all of the youths broke into a gallop and went whooping and calling out of sight round a sharp bend in the waters. As the two mature men followed more leisurely there opened to Frank's eyes an amazing scene – a huge village.

"Many teepees!" said Frank with a hint of admiration in his voice.

"A hundred – five times!" The rounded face of Sitting Bull was smiling in pride. "Here are the rest of my Hunkpapa! Some Northern Cheyenne too. And over there are the people of Black Kettle – they are here still tending their wounds."

"That was a bad day," said Frank Partridge.

"I hear you were there," said Sitting Bull coldly.

"No – it was afterwards. I was with my friend the Arikara. We saw it all and went away. Then not far on our road we changed our minds and went to help. At first they drew arrows on me but a Cheyenne boy, White Hawk..."

"He is here now, somewhere."

"Oh – that is good. He told them I was a friend of the real people and so we helped. It was a bad day."

"It brought fresh war," said Sitting Bull.

"I know it," grunted Frank.

They rode in silence until, as they approached the village, a crowd surged out to greet them. Many more youths galloped round them; older warriors, some with coup feathers in their hair, held back and cried salutes as the pair approached. Frank felt as if he were in the presence of some Roman general at a triumph or riding with a king – and so he was.

It was then that he noticed the tall figure of a warrior about the same age as Sitting Bull. Old enough to lead, perhaps, but no longer in his prime. There was a rush of images in his mind, and suddenly Frank realised that it was Yellow Hair, beaming and holding up a hand in greeting. Frank looked at once for White Hawk but could not see him in the whirl of riders and shouting people, a richness of colour that was astounding, distracting.

Wherever he looked there was colour: from the blue reflected in the water to the multitude of patches on the teepees, almost all decorated with sharp primary pigments, from bright garments, from the sheen of human skin kissed by the sun, from the fluttering feathers of a hundred head-dresses. Even the colouring of their ponies caught the eye. Then there was a continual movement, almost a bustle, which served to accentuate the colours.

All was set against the lush green of the woodlands which gave way to the wide area of water meadows beside the river. Here were the Hunkpapas, set in circles of clan and rank and society, each teepee entrance opening toward the western sky.

"Hello Wasichu," a Cheyenne voice from behind his shoulder startled him. He glanced round.

The eyes, the glittering eyes, the open face, the lips broad and sensuous, the shoulders of a boy putting on youth's power greeted his eyes. Clad only in a thonged breechcloth sat White Hawk on a pinto so sheened with a curious brown pigment it looked like fresh chocolate.

The youth was shimmering with water, his hair unbraided and drenched. He had been swimming when the party had arrived. All of his decorative paint was gone. He sat on his excited chocolate pony, both of them blending into a single being. Frank put out his hand.

"Welcome!" called the boy and immediately hissed into the ear of the pinto and was away, passing within a finger of the standing Yellow Hair. Yellow Hair did not shift an inch. He grinned at the closeness of the encounter.

White Hawk wheeled away, and as he did so other youths followed. They were like a burst of starlings pursuing the unknown leader of a huge flock. They swirled this way and that but, instead of being in the air, these young men flew on excited ponies through the shallows, sending a shower of water over each other, turning the sky blue surface into disturbed yellow.

The visitors dismounted in front of Yellow Hair who was immediately lost amidst a growing group of war chiefs and elders, come to greet the great man and his strange companion who they already knew was staying in Sitting Bull's clan village. Yellow Hair had said this was so. They had not seen this Wasichu before, yet they had heard of him, having listened to the stories of Yellow Hair and heard the contrary interruptions of White Hawk in support. Both said that the Wasichu Warrior had an Indian heart, though none of the listeners believed it, for such a thing cannot be. A Wasichu is lost at birth.

The gathering dignitaries moved to a place close by the Teepee Of The Arrows and sat. Pipes were brought, special pipes for the occasion; they sat in a large circle in the warm afternoon and prepared to smoke.

That Sitting Bull had been there only two days before made no difference to the hospitality. Fresh buffalo meat was produced from a kill that morning and roasted or eaten raw and the introductions were long and honourable. A great deal of talk took place about things which had happened and might happen, and it was only when a rare lull took place that Sitting Bull turned to Frank Partridge and said: "I have brought you to show you this thing."

"This?" Frank waved his arms to encircle the enormous site – an Indian city rather than a village.

"This! Here we are many. Over that rise..." pointing to the north, "there is an encampment of the Teton, and beyond that a Kiowa group. We are many. I have brought them here. I have called the people."

"Why?"

The sudden coldness in Sitting Bull's face warned Frank that he had been too direct. But Sitting Bull decided to make an allowance for this poor Wasichu. He would test him. Just how strong was the Indian heart of this traitor to the Wasichu who would be a Crow, and perhaps a Cheyenne; maybe soon he would want to be Sioux. Thus he should not be trusted at all, but he could be used.

There was a pause as some of the gathered ones chattered confidently about the numbers of the people and the safety they had in that size. They made comments springing from Sitting Bull's words to the strange Wasichu.

"We shall wipe out the hated fortress," said one, firmly.

"We shall," said Sitting Bull softly, catching their mood, drawing smiles of appreciation from several other leaders.

Two things happened. There was an uneasy movement among some of the elders for they clearly did not agree with the idea; this was balanced by eager hisses and grunts from those close to Sitting Bull's apparent views. At the same moment a dust devil was given birth on the outside of the group so that all eyes turned its way as it went spinning off to the river, soughed onto the water and died. Curiously, this seemed to silence those who agreed with Sitting Bull.

"A displeased spirit," suggested a young war chief, Big Wolf. He had a rough face and already sported a hatchet gash across his brow so that his left eye appeared to be permanently open in an expression of astonishment.

"Did you see the direction of the Spirit? asked Sitting Bull of everyone, whilst glaring at the young war chief.

Much muttering confirmed they had.

"It was towards the south!" declared Sitting Bull.

More muttering greeted this announcement.

"Fort Rice lies to the south," observed Frank.

Sitting Bull smiled at Frank and said, "Even the spirits direct us..."

He was interrupted by a flurry of sound from the south; a movement of humanity from the low hill which rose above the tree line. On its crest were a group of warriors waving lances, and a puff of smoke preceded the distant crack of a Spencer. Frank Partridge knew the sound very well.

The riders plunged down the hill and disappeared from sight into the deep woods which lay between them and the village. The gathering of chiefs abruptly ended; all got to their feet. As a crowd they began to hurry towards the river. There was a general movement in the village behind them; an alertness swept through the lodges as each teepee emptied.

As they arrived at the water's edge six horses broke out of the woods, crashed into the river and came jerking towards them. One horse went down, pranced back to his legs; the rider struggled to remount, did so, and trotted his mount lamely after the rest. All the horses were clearly close to their last wind.

Frank heard the words in Sioux coming clearly across the freshly yellowed water, "Slaughter!"

They came closer and with the tired horses gasping, wheezing, throwing jets of foam from their mouths, the riders threw themselves to the ground. One, with a fine suit of doe-skin, wet with the river and flecked with horse foam, gasped out: "The wagon guns fired on us. Fired on us as we left the talk-of-peace-place. Many wagon guns. Just as the people were coming to the fort. They made to slaughter us."

The young warrior dropped from his horse, and paused to catch his breath, then he said, "One Star Sully called us in and as we approached they opened fire on us. They tried to kill us all."

"What did the spirit say?" called Sitting Bull. "Have you not seen enough, have you not heard enough? The spirit warned us ahead of these riders, and has pointed the way!"

He spoke directly to the chiefs – it was as if Frank Partridge was not there.

"We sent many lodges to talk with One Star Sully: we kept our word; we rode to join big-talk, we made no war – and now they use the wagon guns on the people!" Sitting Bull was shouting now; jagged veins stood out on his temples. He felt a surge of power over the rest of them.

"Rub them out!" shouted Big Wolf. "Let Sitting Bull lead us!"

There was a bellow of agreement.

"When I say we attack then we attack!" shouted Sitting Bull.

Another roar of agreement.

"But when I say withdraw, we withdraw."

The young braves were equally enthusiastic. They all shouted that they would come and go to the words of Sitting Bull. No matter what he called upon them to do, they would do it. They leapt and danced to the dreams of counting coup in his honour and to the bringing back of many soft Wasichu scalps to adorn the lodges.

Sitting Bull smiled.

So, he had them. They would get their moment. But he must lead them with care. They must not ride into a massacre. If he saw the power of the fort was too great, then they would withdraw at his command. If there was no power in the fort...? Then it was good. The warriors would indeed wipe them out. A little more revenge for the dead of Black Kettle's people.

That was the beginning of it. The news of the firing of the wagon guns flew through the encampment like a hail storm – and the news was embellished by its journey and became a tale of massacre. With speed, a will to war took hold.

"We shall dance then," said Sitting Bull. "The time has come to dance for war."

"I will ride with you," said Frank Partridge.

"Ah – He Who Shaves His Head will ride with us," said Sitting Bull.

Frank engaged the eyes of the chief, feeling a sudden discomfort. The chief's gaze seemed to pass through his own eyes and strike right into his brain, into his soul. He felt the look grip him, searching for truth.

"At least – I know the Wasichu way! I know how they will fight."

"We shall talk on this, " said Sitting Bull, seeing no lies in the Wasichu's eyes.

"The eagle chief at the fort is a boy," said Frank. "He has no experience. You must draw him out of the fort. He is hungry for a fight."

"We shall talk on this," said Sitting Bull.

"Let me ride with you."

"By my side," said Sitting Bull, and caught the eye of Yellow Hair and nodded to his red pony, but saw that it was already being brought towards him together with Ben by the bronzed hands of White Hawk.

"Then it is done," said Frank.

"You shall tell me the way Wasichu fight. What we do not know, you can discover at the fort, and then we shall rub them out."

)()()(

The negotiations had been going for some hours. General Sully was pleased with the progress and let a rare smile display his mood. Young Dimon had said next to nothing and that could not be a bad thing. He looked so damned smart in his perfect uniform and that damned fool presentation sword. Maybe the Redskins were impressed. Sully smiled to himself at the memory of the smoking of the long pipe: three good puffs to the Great Spirit and then he'd passed it to the boy colonel who took three gulps and went silent and green for half an hour. Sully enjoyed that. He coughed to himself to bring his mind back to the discussions.

"We must be brothers." The Yantonai translator was speaking the words of the leader of the Kiowa contingent.

"All my friends are my brothers," replied Sully.

General Sully saw that his words were immediately translated into three tongues and signs were made too – for the security of the idea. He knew the signs well enough and could tell that his words were being relayed with truth.

The sign language of the Plains Indians was narrow in its vocabulary. The general had learned it during a dozen years on the frontier – about a thousand gestures – but it was a wonderful internation means of trading and greeting and supplementing half-understood languages.

The Redskins have something to teach us, the general had thought on a hundred occasions under the stars or in a hard snow, talking and hand-signing himself out of one spot of trouble or another. But they were uncivilised and heathen in the eyes of his other world – the Washington War Department – and that was enough to employ him at what he did best, holding a thin line against his 'brothers'; 'hostiles' in the eyes of the Washington.

Now that fool Chivington had thrown everything into the air. He had done more to unite the nations, and turn the whole lot into hostiles, than any hot-head war chief.

Sully caught the eye of one of the small group of Hunkpapas. The Crow scouts had told him there were hundreds of Hunkpapa Sioux lodges to the west – perhaps thirty miles out – an estimate of three or four thousand souls. The Hunkpapa Sioux were very influential in sheer numbers. If he could gather them to his side then he might bring something more than a pretence of peace and counter the growing power of Red Cloud.

Word of Red Cloud's successes had worked through the tribes – many Wasichu had died at the hands of the Oglala Sioux and allied Southern Cheyenne, that was the word on the air. The situation was dangerous, for these wild people had learned that the white men were as vulnerable as any other tribe. Would these Hunkpapa Sioux leaders try to emulate the cunning of the Oglala leader?

They might – but their senior leader was not there; Sitting Bull they called him. Sully had heard that as a boy Sitting Bull had had a different name – Slow. Maybe he still was.

"So – Bare Rib, War Chief of the Hunkpapa – you have more lodges to bring in to this place of peace?"

Sully watched the fat chief's reaction. If the general could get the bulk of the people close by the fort and offer some supplies, ammunition and promises, he could perhaps get them to let the wagons through, and maybe stick to the reservation that was being planned. They were going to get licked in the end, now the big war was coming to a close. The Indians had no notion of the overwhelming power in his East, bulging towards their West.

It was not possible for the Red Man to resist the White Man – manifest destiny, that was the name of the business... damn it, it was already written on the wall. But at the moment he had a couple of thousand indifferent troops to hand and these damned savages could muster five thousand for sure if they had the will.

Thank God the *will* did escape them. They were unable to unite; they fought as individuals, no corps discipline, no regimentation. They were, at best, good irregular cavalry. Yet they fought with insane courage. You had to give the savages that – but courage was not enough against a modern howitzer.

By the end of the Eastern War there would be more artillery pieces available than the Indian nations could put riders on horses. They could not win. They were doomed and did not know it. Thank God indeed – praise the Lord for the manifest destiny.... but keep the powder dry for the old muzzle-loaders for the next few months. Sully smiled at the Hunkpapa who was leaning back and about to speak.

"One Star Wasichu – you say you are a friend. We have two hundred Hunkpapa lodges coming to visit this place – they wait over the sunset hills – they wait for my signal. We do not trust you. We think there is a trap. We think you will want to wipe us out when you see us. Am I right to say these things, Wasichu friend?"

So Sully smiled and proceeded to promise them the earth – or so it seemed to them. He gave them his word. This meant a lot to Sully and though the gathered chiefs respected him they knew it was only the word of a Wasichu and thus very limited.

They did not believe him at first, but they held him in respect as a warrior. He in turn dangled a dozen more pledges in front of them: repeating rifles, good food as a gift of honour, many lovely things. Had the War Department not said that it was cheaper to feed the

Redskins than fight them? Slowly they were convinced that there was no trap. At the end, as they rose to depart, Sully went to the leader of the Hunkpapa, singling him out, and he put his arm round his shoulder. He felt the warrior tense, and then Sully said: "I want only peace."

The Hunkpapa Sioux looked firmly at Sully and said, "I have already given the signal! The Hunkpapa will come."

Beaming, Sully smacked the chief on the shoulder and walked towards the line of waiting horses, in the company of his staff, and Dimon. He took hold of Dimon's grey and called to Two Bears. He gave the handsome grey to the Indian. With a great yelp the warrior leapt onto the unfamiliar saddle. He gave a sharp nudge with his spurless heels. The big grey reared and burst into an immediate gallop towards the river as if it had carried this man on its back all its life.

Dimon's face was seared with astonishment, combined with a frustrated fury, which brought bitten-off smiles to the faces of the general's staff officers.

"Same Army," said the general, "one hos is as good as another."

The colonel swallowed the protest that he had bought the grey out of his own money and with considerable grace said, "General, the officers of Fort Rice would be honoured if you would favour our table this evening together with the officers of your staff."

Sully knew this request was coming, and that his dress uniform would have to be dug out by his servant, but he oozed fatherly charm as he replied, "Why Colonel Dimon, sir, we'd all be most pleased to accept your kindness. You may expect us at six before sundown. I shall bring you a replacement mount."

)()()()()(

Sully and his staff let the reins of their horses go at almost six o'clock exactly, so their animals could pick their own way across the shallows to the north of the Fort. A handsome jet black stallion, the general's second mount, without a rider, fully equipped with saddle and a Spencer in its pouch together with an issue sabre on the other flank, was led by the guidon bearer. The general was mighty pleased with himself because to the west he could see, clearly silhouetted against the falling sun, a large body of Indians on horseback and foot. Many of the horses were walking and drawing travois. The Hunkpapa lodges were coming in at last. They were as good as their word.

At the half-point across the river, a signal gun roared out from the fort. All of the mounts crossing the river jerked in the water, the experienced ones out of memory, those not battle-trained out of sheer surprise. As the officers snatched for the slack reins and shouted at their animals the air was ripped with thunder as all the artillery in the fort opened fire as if in counter bombardment volley fire.

"Goddaaaamn!" bellowed the general, controlling his rearing horse.

Seconds later the heavy guns fired again. He saw that an entire battery had been lined up in front of the fort and was blazing away in thunderous rhythm. He could tell that they were double-charged with powder, for the best signal effect. The loud noise but lack of 'crack' in the explosions told that they were blank firing in honour of the approaching general. The general also saw that on the skyline there was utter confusion which rapidly swept into a definite shape as the entire incoming force of Indians turned tail and fled.

"That cursed idiot!" snarled Sully. "The slimy creeping young fool – he's scared 'em all off with a damned salute! Damn, damn, damn. Gawd DAMN!"

Brigadier General Sully rammed his spurs into his horse's flanks so that it took off like a rocket towards the open gates of Fort Rice, Lieutenant Colonel Charles Augustus Ropes Dimon at *present* in command.

10

Colonel Pattee

*(The Sioux Moon of When the Cherries are Ripe,
the month called July in the Wasichu Year of 1865 –
Fort Rice on the Missouri western shore,
Lieutenant Colonel Pattee, United States Cavalry, commanding)*

To the left of the entrance to Fort Rice, on the parapet, stood a timber block-house with a rifle-slit cut into each face. A rickety ladder gave access to the top and an even more uncertain balustrade served to remind a man on duty that the ground below was all too easy to fall towards. Colonel Dimon had insisted on a total rotation of command and even the Headquarters staff had to do picket and guard duty. It was one of few 'Dimon arrangements' still intact.

The 'arrangement' brought Sergeant Clinton to his favourite regimental duty at the 'high gate post', which was the name given to the man required to stand at this, the highest point in the fortress, save for upper reaches of the gigantic flag pole. Here, the duty sergeant had a view to the river.

With the telescope which the duty provided, Clinton could see the coming and going of the river paddle steamers, occasional small river luggers, and the even rarer canoes either carrying mountain men with beaver pelts or Indians with other trade goods. With the fort situated on the west of the river bank the whole panorama of the prairie could be seen in the distance beyond the body of the fort itself, with some low hills to the north. It was in that direction, the sun at his back, that Clinton was staring. He saw a movement and blinked.

He was not certain whether it was merely a small dust devil or some animal movement. He lifted the telescope and knelt down, putting his elbows on the balustrade to steady himself. At once he felt the tacky sap stick on his elbows. He swore, took his elbows away, looked at the sap stuck on the heavy cloth, swore again and put his elbows back in a different position. The perfume of pine entered his nostrils, and he swore again as he focused the telescope.

The shimmering blue of the light in the multiple lenses combined with the heat coming off the ground made sharp focusing difficult. He persevered and gradually caught a point which was balanced and so studied the subject, the image slightly vibrating as he stared. The image swam into the shape of a single rider, approaching at a canter.

From time to time Clinton pulled away from the telescope which was getting hot to the touch in the brilliant late morning sun. Each time he returned to his spying, the figure became clearer. At first he thought it was an Indian, then he saw that it was a mountain man, then he saw that the figure had no baggage, and his horse was of an Indian breed.

"Rider from the west!" he shouted down to the duty officer.

There was no answer.

As the rider came closer Clinton could see clearly that he was well armed, with two rifles, one on either side of his horse's neck. He also appeared to be carrying an Indian bow pouch. Clinton looked steadily again and confirmed the impression.

"Which way the rider?" came a call from below.

"Rider from the west – just one – comin' in easy-like."

He heard the news being passed across the parade ground to the headquarters' office and saw the colonel come out on the veranda. Funny thing – he did not look like a colonel. Well, he did not look like Dimon, and Dimon had 'gone on leave' – General Sully sent him back East with dispatches.

All to do with frightening the Indians off. That was the word in the post. The general was pissed off and mad about that. Dimon was fine and dandy – at least Clinton thought he was fine – except for the execution. The regiment never forgave him for that, but it pulled everybody together – more out of fear than respect. The new one was different.

Lieutenant Colonel John Pattee was a cavalryman; Limey Canadian he was born but he knew the Redskins well enough. He understood them. Dimon *thought* he understood them. That was the difference – that and uniform.

Clinton thought Pattee looked a sad sight, appearing half Indian with his buckskins and moccasins instead of regular high boots and a sword – like you would expect from a cavalryman, a gentleman and all. He had stopped the regular parades and the men liked him for that, though some began to wonder if the regularity and order they experienced under Dimon was not something dangerously lost. At least Pattee was not a boy – with his beard and whiskers touched with grey, plus a little tobacco juice edging the corner of his mouth. Clinton saw him spit from the veranda as he stepped out to the sound of news of a rider coming in.

The colonel dropped lightly to the ground almost skipping down the veranda steps and strode towards the gate. He saw Clinton looking through a telescope, watched him lower it and then follow a movement outside the fort with a turn of his head. Then he leaned forward to look down on the entrance, through which the rider burst into the colonel's sight, sending up a cloud of dust as he swept into the fort. The sergeant was hurriedly descending to join him at the gate.

As the rider trotted up to Pattee, the colonel recognised him at once and his eyes narrowed more than the sun demanded.

"Mornin' Colonel!" greeted Frank Partridge, reining in before Pattee, thinking at the same time – holy hell it's Pattee.

"Mornin' Mister – you still a captain, Mister Partridge?"

"Not exactly," said Frank Partridge and patted Ben to something close to calmness.

Frank's eyes ran across the fort and he saw a couple of privates from the 7th Iowa lounging by the nearest barrack block. So there *was* some cavalry present – must be, stands to reason, with Pattee in the fort – he was their colonel. The fort had more punch than Sitting Bull had imagined.

"Changin' sides, Frank?" asked Pattee, not smiling.

"You know me, Colonel. Come in to see the commanding officer – is Colonel Dimon present?"

"He is not."

"On patrol is he?"

"He is not."

"Sick?"

"Nope."

"He ain't dead is he?"

"He is not."

"Well where..."

"I am in command, Frank."

"Well – I'll be damned, for sure."

Frank had met Pattee before up close to the Canadian border. He knew Pattee had been passed over for brigadier and held Grant responsible. He was a good Indian fighter but the Army did not rate him for high command. Like old Sully he was kept in the backwater of the West. Pattee was smiling, an unlit cigar hanging from his mouth.

"Damned for sure," smiled Pattee. "And you are under arrest... for certain!"

)( )( )( )( )(

Frank Partridge had been dragged from his horse, yelling that he was on official duty, but there was no easing in the rough handling and failure to listen – on a nod from the colonel he was in the blockhouse, the nod had been enough.

As he was dragged away Frank had shouted, "The Redskins are on the warpath. I can tell you their whereabouts!"

He saw grins and heard jeers. They threw him into the cell – the kick cracked against the small of his back.

"I'm a tellin' you, damn it!" bellowed Frank Partridge from the stinking floor.

"You can tell us a better yarn than that, y'bag o' dung," called the ginger headed sergeant from outside the cell. Frank heard him move away, laughing.

The blockhouse was oven hot and alive with mosquitoes. His buckskins gave some protection and the insects seemed less interested in his baldpate than his forehead on which they produced a mountain-range of lumps. Frank ignored the bumps until a young sergeant looked through the bars of the blockhouse door – the same one that had given him a kick from behind when he was thrown into the cell. He was back, a smile on his face.

"For sure, you've bin wearing a crown o' thorns recently," sneered the sergeant.

Frank Partridge spat with unerring aim at the grill and the contents of his throat spattered the sergeant's nose.

"See you later," snarled the sergeant wiping away the spittle with disgust.

"In hell if you like, you red headed bastard!"

"The colonel'll want to see you, later, and I'll come and get you!" he threatened. "I promise – you Limey southern bastard!"

"Hey – heard this was a southern regiment anyway!"

"Shut your mouth – I'll be back I tell you!"

"Bring an army!" snapped Frank Partridge.

When he came back a second time it was not with an army, but it was enough

They came back to the darkened room an hour later, the sudden opening of the door bringing in a dusty coolness at once. Frank was not in irons so he stood up. A second lieutenant stood back at the door and let the tall ginger sergeant lead the way flanked by a private whom the sergeant called Hurtz. The private had arms the size of a buffalo's butt but whose face was that of a boy.

"We gotta search you," said the second lieutenant. He had more troopers behind him.

"You can try," snarled Frank.

"Strip him!" snapped the second lieutenant from the sun-lit doorway.

Frank hit Hurtz full in the mouth, but his fist had the same impact as a bullet on a rock. The others were on him in a moment. The young sergeant gave him a quick knee and Frank fell writhing to the floor. They ripped his clothes off. Each garment was searched.

"Here – lookee at this!" Private Jermaine from Saint Louis suddenly stood up and stared at the breechcloth which Frank had on under his buckskin trousers.

"He's got Injun knickers!" laughed Clinton.

"He's jus' another Nigger lovah," said Jermaine with his southern twang, and kicked at Frank's rib cage. Frank saw it coming and managed to move with the blow.

"Nigger lovah!"

"Injun suckah!"

Frank played half dead, his lip already split and his left ear singing from an encounter with a rifle barrel. The papers would clear him; they were better than a suit of armour.

They stood aside for him to get dressed.

"The colonel'll see you now," said the second lieutenant.

"I said I'd come back," said the sergeant with a toothy smile.

"What's your name mister?" snarled Frank Partridge.

"None of your damned business," smiled the sergeant.

Jermaine and Hurtz took an arm each and half dragged Frank out of the blockhouse. Frank was sharp and fit enough to rip himself clear and make a run for it, but he played the part of the beat-up man. The young soldiers were not aware of the danger they were in, but Frank reasoned that he would not make it to the garrison gate before some fool shot him, so it was better he played half dead rather than become real dead.

Pattee was waiting for him, sitting behind a desk, an unlit cheroot in his mouth, the end being chewed. "Thought I'd give you a taste of the blockhouse." Pattee was mirthless.

"Best tastin' blockhouse I've ever know'd."

"Good to hear it. What's this passport?"

The colonel tapped a yellowing sheet of paper in front of him. It had been taken from Frank at the outset. "What's this?" asked the colonel.

"That there's my authority!" Frank snapped.

"The only authority here is me," Pattee replied, matter of fact tone to his voice.

Frank did not rise to the calculated calm. He had decided to be cool and icy himself. He knew of Pattee's reputation and attitudes – a Colonial's hatred of the English. A brief acquaintance on the Canadian border a year back had done nothing for Pattee's views – other than give him the knowledge that Frank Partridge knew the Redskins better than he did. And he knew some.

Pattee was smiling, his cheroot drifting from one side of his mouth to the other. He sat back behind his desk, arms behind his head, his shaggy grey moustache, discoloured by tobacco. To his right stood Second Lieutenant Armitage, acting adjutant, who had just led the search of the prisoner; two other young officers were on the colonel's left. Their hands were resting on their Colts with holster flaps cleared. The colonel was taking no chances. Three officers, a sergeant and a brace of giant privates should be enough.

"Sit," he said, and Jermaine forcefully guided Frank into a wooden armchair on the opposite side of his colonel's desk.

"This here paper," said the colonel tapping the document on his desk.

"Like I said, Colonel, that there's my authority."

214

Frank pointed at the scrap of paper. He turned and spat a mouthful of blood onto the floor, without apology. The colonel glared but made no remark.

"Forgery more like!"

"Colonel I would advise you to study it, careful like."

Pattee had done so. It had a seal – an embossed mark – the seal was rounded, the edges sharp but the words could not be read. The neat spidery writing of the signature was clear. *Ulysses S. Grant.* The wording was stained, the ink was smudged through sweat, water, rain, snow, whatever, but was legible:

"The bearer of this document, Captain Frank Partridge, has my authority to be anywhere, in whatever clothing he is wearing, and bearing whatever arms he sees fit by my authority."

"I *have* studied it, Frank. There ain't no date."

"And?"

"I reckon it's a forgery."

"That's Grant's own hand!"

"You say!"

"I do!" This was snapped, hard and certain.

Pattee scowled, tapped the paper again.

"Say it is – what you doin' out there with the Redskins?"

"Spyin'!"

"That so?"

Pattee fell to examining the document again.

"Yes, that is so – I've been hangin' out with the Sioux – there's a big war party heading this way – they think you've been trying to slaughter half the nation with the wagon guns."

"Sully was right then," muttered Pattee.

"What?"

"Thought the Hunkpapa were scared off by the blamed fool salute given by my honoured predecessor for his genial general, scared the shit out of the Injuns!"

"That's as maybe – but I'm here to tell you that the fort's to be attacked."

"When?"

"Tomorrow."

"How do you know?"

"Been sent here."

"Who by?"

"Sitting Bull – he trusts me – spy out the land for him."

Pattee nodded. He was one of the few officers who understood the importance of the Indian leader.

"Sitting Bull know *I'm* here?" asked the colonel.

"No."

"You spyin' for everybody?"

"No – just for Grant. But the Sioux *think* I'm doin' it for them."

"But now you're caught – by your friendly enemy!"

"That document makes..."

"Ain't worth a buffalo dump."

"Lookee here, Colonel Pattee, I'm tellin' you – several hundred Hunkpapas are going to be here tomorrow, and..."

"Take him away!" the colonel cut in, and with a wave of the colonel's hand Frank was dragged out yelling his honesty and credentials.

When he was gone the colonel began a comforting chobble of his cheroot. The two young officers and the adjutant stood looking at him. There was a forbidding silence in the room.

Then the colonel said, "Don't believe a word!"

"No sir," agreed the adjutant, "he's just a damned renegade."

"Lieutenant Armitage." The colonel looked up at the young adjutant.

The adjutant drew himself to attention as he might have for Dimon. "Sir!"

The colonel frowned at the crack of boot-sole on floorboard. "Double the guard. Put an extra picket on the horse herd. Send out the Yantonai police scouts, and the Crows as well – all of them – have them scout out ten miles in all directions. Send them in twos – they are to run back at the first sight of Hunkpapa, or any other hostiles. I want to know how many and how close!"

"Then you believe him."

"Maybe, mister."

"At what time should they leave?"

"An hour ago!" snapped the colonel.

When the room was empty the colonel stood up and carefully tore the battered sheet of paper into shreds. "Don't believe a word of it," he lied to himself. "Sure he had a note from Grant. Now the note ain't nothing." He placed the torn paper in a broken earthenware pot he used for cigar ash and butts.

The colonel struck one of the few remaining English Vesta matches he had in a small drawer of his desk. He lit the passport from Grant and then used the dying Vesta to re-light his long cheroot.

"On the other hand maybe I do believe it. The scouts'll find the truth. Then I'll know – my way." This was said aloud, and then he nodded to himself in agreement.

He sucked on his cheroot and the blue smoke he blew away mingled with the last of the burning passport. Grant's handwriting disappeared, the same handwriting that had not been used to secure a brigadier general's star on Pattee's shoulders.

The colonel sat in his chair, put his moccasin-clad feet onto his desk and sucked deep and hard on his cheroot. He smiled with the pleasure of it all.

〉〈〉〈〉〈〉〈〉〈

Little Knife the Arikara scout was dressed as a Crow. Snow-on-Her rode with him with leggings, like a warrior. They went directly west. Little Knife was annoyed for he heard tell that Frank Partridge was in the fort. Little Knife had been ordered out to scout, with no chance to see the Wasichu warrior.

The sky was clear of cloud so the moon was strong enough to give them light to see their direction, but they left the detail of the navigation to their ponies. They walked them for three hours and guessed that they were about ten Wasichu miles from the fort.

They had arrived on a butte, higher than most of the surrounding land. This high ground would give them a panoramic view of the territory for almost five miles, at dawn. To their rear they could make out a few distant stretches of the Missouri where the moon caught the surface and there was no interfering timber in the way. Ahead of them was nothing but night.

They dismounted, but kept their horses on a long leash attached to their wrists. They settled to rest and wait for the dawn. Little Knife agreed to sleep awhile, then Snow-on-Her would have a doze whilst Little Knife stood watch. It was the noise of a gathering of prairie turkey, protesting the arrival of something dangerous, that woke Little Knife. The uproar woke Snow-on-Her as well.

Little Knife instinctively knew that Snow-on-Her had slept, and lashed at her back with the end of his horse leash. She dodged the light blow with a grin at his angry face. The sound of many horses on the move came to both of them at the same instant. Dawn was already in the east. With thumping hearts at their sudden waking they were on their horses in a single movement.

As soon as they were mounted they saw in the gathering light that there were hundreds of warriors on the move to their left. Without speaking to each other, both knowing what to do, they trotted their ponies off the summit of their butte and down the reverse slope keeping the hillside between them and the horsemen. As soon as they had dropped a hundred feet they broke into a canter. They found a coulee, which ran directly east and had the dry bed of a winter brook meandering through its bed. In the poor light they eased their horses, quite fresh and rested from the three hours pause in the darkness, into a loping gallop to get ahead of the band of warriors.

"Whey, hei!" The challenge was shrill, and ahead, and in the dialect of the Hunkpapa.

Little Knife had a repeater in the right hand pouch, but he left it, favouring the silent bow, already strung across his lap with a war arrow nicked into the string. There was only one horseman in front of them, challenging. He had been moving in the same direction, but at a walk. Now he had stopped thinking they were friendly scouts out of position. Clearly he was a flanking scout, the very edge of the advancing horde.

"Whey, hei!" called Snow-on-Her back at the lone Indian in perfect Hunkpapa dialect. They moved in on him. He appeared to rein in as they came close in the morning gloom, confused for a moment by her woman's voice.

They were on him before he could reply and Little Knife's arrow went cleanly into his heart severing the aorta. The unknown warrior was dead before he hit Mother Earth. Little Knife swore a very evil thing as he was aware of Snow-on-Her circling back to take the Sioux pony. She would get them both killed.

As they came out of the coulee they were seen at once. The coulee had taken them across the path of alert warriors who were acting as lead scouts to the main body. Several wore the wolf head-dress of an experienced scout. The larger following could be seen against the morning sky. Little Knife felt a rush of fear, which he subdued with a will, as he guessed there must be a thousand warriors pressing at his back.

The main body ignored what appeared to be two fleeing Crows, but three of the wolf scouts broke rank and began to follow them; a little further along the line two more cut away and joined the pursuit. Little Knife and Snow-on-Her broke to go in two directions. The last two wolf scouts followed Little Knife; the other three pursued Snow-on-Her. The Crows must die, for they were known to love the Wasichu – besides they were the hated Crow and should not have been born.

The party of three were led by a hefty warrior wearing a beaver cap beneath his wolf head-dress. This was the first time that he had chased a Crow in battle. He hoped the soon-to-die-Crow did not know him.

)(()()()(

Sergeant Clinton, with Privates Hurtz and Jermaine, 1st Volunteers, were spread out over a distance of close on half a mile. They were just in sight and hail of each other. They were on horseback and picketing the mounts of the horse infantry of the 4th Volunteers, the spare horses of the officers of the 1st, and another hundred mounts and spares belonging to the 7th Iowa. The word was out that a war party or horse stealers might come in with sunrise.

All three men – Clinton was the oldest at 22, the other two, 19 – were facing east watching the glory of the dawn. Jermaine thought he saw Redskins out of the corner of his eye, a shoot of fear rising as soon as he was sure. Hurtz knew at the same moment when an arrow whacked into his back, shooting him through. His yell of agony alerted Clinton.

Even as Hurtz was fingering the hot fluid from his chest where jagged flint protruded through his jacket, the Indian was on him, smacking at him with his bow, trying to unhorse him. Hurtz did not know the joy of the warrior as he counted coup.

Somehow Hurtz kept his seat trying to draw his Colt. He ducked fresh blows. From his left Clinton came galloping, screaming in fear as much as aggression. Hurtz heard the crack of Clinton's Colt and saw a second Indian closing in, but as Clinton fired again both of the savages turned and fled. Clinton turned after them and chased them up a rise, firing until the chambers were empty. He missed every shot. He drove his horse on. One-handed he tried to reload the Colt, giving up with but one round in a chamber and three more dropped on the trail.

He had gained a lot of ground on them and the first was two lengths ahead. Hollering like a Redskin himself, pure aggression now, Clinton spurred on. The Indian pony ahead of him was alive with tassels and feathers. The warrior himself was naked, clinging to his pony, head held low. Both he and the pony were lined with paint, mostly red. Clinton was to remember that red figure until the day he died.

Getting closer, Clinton leaned forward to draw his sabre as they both reached the brow of the hill. As he hit the brow he yanked his horse back with such a savage pull he almost went over its neck. Ahead was a group of twenty or more Indians. He spun his horse and raced back to the herd, aware that the man he had been chasing was already wheeling to come after *him*, screaming and hollering, fitting an arrow into his bow with dextrous ease.

)( )( )( )( )(

Private Henri Pierre, whose grandfather fell at Waterloo, whose father fell at Gettysburg and who, as a captain in the 3rd St. Louis Carabiniers, was taken prisoner at the opening of the Battle of the Wilderness, was now a Galvanized Yankee. He had drawn the lot to be final night lookout at the high gatepost. When he heard the shots from the area of the horse herd picket he shouted for a call to arms.

Even as he yelled, he saw from the same direction one of the Crow scouts galloping like a fiend with a couple of hostiles close behind. He saw the Crow turn and fire his Spencer, one-handed, at his pursuers. When he was within four hundred yards of the fort Private Pierre brought up his own Sharps carbine. Then he stopped and adjusted the sights to an extreme 600 yards. The .53 would carry that far, might even take a man out. He took a careful sight on the approaching hostiles and, hoping he would not hit the Crow, fired. He continued to fire as quickly as he could get rounds into the breech, but hit nothing. Only once did he ease his frustration by seeing a kick-up of dust to the right of the pursuers. He knew he was a damned rotten shot, but this was confounded bad.

Down below bedlam raged as the entire fort woke to the discomfort of boots being in the wrong place. But a half-dressed troop of the 1st was soon belching out of the open gate to form a skirmishing line; the colonel was with them in shirtsleeves, a drawn Colt in his hand. Men followed on and were shouted at to extend the line. Whether it was the shots from Pierre or from the men on the extending line, whom the Indians must have seen, the small war party wheeled away leaving the lone Crow to come on.

"Troop, ready to fire!" screamed Armitage as the single rider came on at a frenzied gallop.

"That's a Crow!" shouted an elderly 1st Volunteers acting sergeant (who had commanded a Confederate brigade eight months earlier).

"Do *not* fire!" came the colonel's clear voice.

"Told you!" snapped the sergeant and received a sheepish smile from the baby officer.

With a great whoop the Crow crashed through the scattering soldiers and was in the fort. He was laughing. His horse collapsed, rolled to its side, kicked, and was still. The Crow, Little Knife, in the guise of a Crow, was already on his feet looking down on his dead Elk Dog. He whispered a farewell to it, and another to Snow-on-Her, whose hair would already be on the lance of one of the Sioux Dog Soldiers; already her beautiful eyes glazed. She was gone to hunt with the rising sun on the other side of the sacred screen. Kneeling by the hot dead horse, Little Knife told him to go find Snow-on-Her and serve her well in the other real world.

They had split up as a natural in-bred tactical move. He had ridden hard towards the fort and expected her to reappear, to come in from his left; she was well mounted. She never appeared. As he rode closer to the fort his pursuers had wheeled away as the shots from the fort cracked overhead and got too close. Snow-on-Her was still out there. She could not survive. Little Knife felt bad in his heart, a coward; he should have stood and fought. As he thought this he saw a pair of moccasins in front of him and looked up.

The new silver leaf chief was standing in front of him. Little Knife scrambled to his feet and gave a courageous attempt at a salute and said, "Many many Sioux – a hundred hundred."

"Slowly," said the colonel in almost perfect Crow, "I am a Wasichu, not a Crow.

"I am Arikara, not Crow.

"Your hair..."

"I am made to look like a Crow," cut in Little Knife. He looked at the Wasichu chief, took the measure of his eyes and liked what he saw. He had heard from his woman Snow-on-Her that this new silver leaf chief spoke some Crow. That thought bought her back and he bit his lip. He concentrated on the man in front of him and forgot the woman, lost. This one was better than the child chief who had gone, and who did crazy things.

Little Knife gave another clumsy salute. "Plenty big Sioux. Ten hundred Sioux." Little Knife's hands waved in excitement, waved in awe of the great numbers out there. He was interrupted

From no-where, it seemed, soldiers came in at the gallop

"Jeeees," said the colonel jumping out of the way of three mounted infantry riding in, one with an arrow between his shoulders.

"Sir!" came a yell from his left. The chief clerk came running up with disarrayed bracers at his elbows, one boot on his left foot, the other in his fist. "The prisoner's gone!" he gasped. Eyes wide, looking into the colonel's, he was searching for mercy, though the loss was not his fault.

"Jeeeeeeeeeesus!" said the colonel, and glanced down to see if he had both moccasins on.

)(·)(·)(·)(·)(

Frank Partridge hanged himself.

He did it carefully with strips of his jerkin, undoing the securing leather. He stood in the middle of the cell in the combined light of the falling moon, the coming dawn and the lamp, which hung at the doorway. Together they cast an eerie glow about the room. He stood with the jerkin strip hanging taut from the rafters, with his head flopped to one side and his tongue sticking out. The strip actually ran down his back and through his legs and Frank was pulling hard on it so that it appeared to be under tension. Frank Partridge *looked* as if he had hung himself, awful in the mixture of gloom and light.

It was one of the many teenage Confederate soldiers, captured at Gettysburg who found the hanging man. Having marched five hundred miles with Lee's Army without a shot being fired anywhere near him, he had often been in boyish trouble. He was a kind of runt of a soldier, born to be terrified. The youth had seen but a single hour of battle before being overrun by Union cavalry on Lee's left wing. He was a young soldier spared much of war, but not spared the fear of rank.

When he looked through the doorway bars and saw the half-Indian renegade, who had been his responsibility, hanging from a beam, he dropped his Sharps in panic, threw the door bolt and was inside in a moment. The image of a soldier, a friend he had sunk rye with, being shot for *talking* about desertion nine months before, had hurtled through his mind. He was in trouble now, serious trouble. He was in serious *trouble*. Like as not he would be shot.

As he reached up, knife in hand, to cut the prisoner down, the man's knee shot upwards and caught him very hard between his legs; then a fist blow between his blue eyes sent him backwards at speed. His head hit the wooden wall, even as the wicked pain in his groin seared his soul. By then Frank was on him and struck him hard on his temple with the side of his hand, a swingeing blow that brought sparks into the boy's eyes and then darkness, temporary freedom from the yellow-sick groin pain. Those pains returned ten minutes later as he came-to, out of concussion, with testicles the size of 2 pounder shot.

By then Frank Partridge was outside the fort languishing for his guns, carrying the boy's Sharps with a single round. He cursed the loss of his guns, passport and Ben, but heading at a steady run towards the west and contact with the war party of Sitting Bull which must now be close to the detested fort.

He was a quarter mile from the fort when he saw a lone Indian heading in. He was being chased by some Sioux. Gunfire echoed from the fort. Frank dived into a hollow as the rider hurtled by, then as he rose he saw that the followers had turned away and were whooping insults from a distance. He rose to his feet and walked slowly towards them with the Sharps held high above his head.

)(	)(	)(	)(	)(

"It's Sitting Bull's Wasichu!" said the wolf soldier.

"Are you sure?"

"Yes – see – he has no scalp."

"You're right – hey Wasichu! What are you doing here?"

)()()()()(

Frank looked ahead as he trotted on the pony, behind the young wolf soldier, holding tight with his legs to the rear belly of the pony, one arm round the young man's waist. He was aware of the smell of buffalo oil on the young warrior's body. The musty scent of the wolf's head-dress made him keep his face clear of the young man's shoulders. They were headed towards the war party of Sitting Bull, the fort behind them.

With the light of dawn he saw the mounted Indians deploying towards the fort. They were forming an almost perfect arc of moving men, running from north to south at the rear of the fort. The fort was 'trapped' between the river and the approaching war party. Frank thought they had already come in too close. If the fool Dimon were in command he would have come rushing out to clear them from the hills and find himself in a mess, but Pattee was a cavalry man and knew he had nowhere near enough horses to take on the mass of Indians. Anyway the white soldiers would be out-ridden, out-gunned and out-numbered. Frank knew exactly what Pattee would do.

Frank pulled on his companion's belly.

"What, Wasichu?"

"Hold a moment."

"Why?"

"Just hold."

The warrior eased the pony to a halt and both men looked back at the distant fort. Frank Partridge's thoughts were correct – the whole garrison appeared to be outside the fort, but they were chasing no-one. The regiment – the Galvanized Yankees – and elements of other units were shifting and easing into a line with the handful of cavalry placed in the south, a deep skirmishing line maybe a mile in length already. Pattee was good! He had even moved some wagon guns into his centre.

This was a concentration of experienced infantry; battle-hardened most of them, not alarmed by the approach of irregular cavalry after facing regular brigades in the East. With a secure stockade behind them to withdraw into, and a cool head in command, the Indians would never break them.

Sitting Bull was just as damned clever. He did not really want to attack the fort, but he knew his hot-head young warriors wanted a battle. So he declared he would 'wipe them out'. All he wanted now was for the fort to know that he was coming so that they would be prepared. There would be a confrontation, but not a slaughter. He had sent his Wasichu Crow ahead for that very purpose for there was no end to Sitting Bull's cunning.

The hot-heads would have their moment, a few coups would be scored and the Wasichu would glimpse Sitting Bull's own power, but not all of it. That would come later, in a better place and at a better time without a fort for the Wasichu to hide behind.

"Go on," said Frank.

"You have seen enough, Wasichu?"

"Yes – and Sitting Bull must know what we have seen."

The wolf warrior was pleased at that. He would deliver the Wasichu of Sitting Bull to the great man. And that would please Sitting Bull.

Frank turned his back on the fort. He was smiling to himself, for he believed he'd saved a lot of lives – provided the Sioux did not decide on suicide. And they might do just that if he did not get to Sitting Bull and let him know that the fort was not only prepared, but was commanded by a good silver leaf chief, not a young idiot.

A woman's scream of anger, incongruous in that empty morning place stopped the riders in their tracks on the edge of a steep-sided coulee. It came from below. He heard cursing in the Hunkpapa dialect and saw the shadowy shapes of three naked men, fighting.

11

Rain Dance

(The Sioux Moon of When the Cherries are Ripe,
the month called July in the Wasichu Year of 1865 –
Fort Rice on the Missouri western shore,
Lieutenant Colonel Pattee, United States Cavalry, commanding)

The sun was rising in a cloudless sky and could not be stared into without pain and a myriad black specs floating in the eyes afterwards. Next Dream tried it and did not like the effect. For a moment he could not see the young Crow who was about to fall into his clutches. There had been two and they had split. The black flecks dissipated and he could see the quarry clearly.

"Chase! Chase!" he yelled. "Get him!"

Two young warriors looked to Next Dream for leadership that morning. He had a hold over Running White Horse and Eagle Flies since the day the winkte stopped their pleasure. Both were Southern Cheyenne who had been running with the teepees of Sitting Bull for more than a year. They both looked back on that day as a good day in their memory. The more they contemplated it, which was often, the better it became. They had taken the souls and bodies of some Wasichu in every way they could and escaped a large party of hunters immediately afterwards. They had even backtracked the hunters to watch where they went and seen the winkte do the same. The winkte had not noticed them; they were proud of that. Since then nothing so exciting had happened until today. Now they were scouting ahead of a huge body of warriors under Sitting Bull himself. They were going to wipe out the Wasichu in the hated fortress; and already they had a treacherous Crow scout to play with. But he was getting away.

Next Dream could see the fort in the morning dimness and sensed that the Crow would escape. It was then that the Crow's mount went head over hoof, throwing the Crow forward in a heap. They heard the crack of the horse's leg breaking. The horse was screaming as it tried to rise. The Sioux were on the Crow in a moment. Running White Horse was first, and counted coup, only to be thrown to one side by Eagle Flies. As he went sprawling he had instinctively clutched at the Crow's jerkin and grabbed a handful of flesh before he lost his grip. The Crow had felt curiously fat, but did not look that way as he had ridden.

The Crow had begun to fight, shrieking like a woman.

"It's a squaw!" gasped Eagle Flies to himself and jumped back off the prone Crow.

Next Dream was slipping from his pony's back. He watched as his two comrades went back at the struggling Crow and began to strip him. Next Dream was about to say, "Never mind the clothes, take the filthy scalp!" when, in the gathering light, he too saw two beautiful breasts. At the same time he recognised her.

"Leave her," he snarled as the other two were ripping away their breechcloths. "Leave her!"

"Go hunt owls!" snapped Eagle Flies over his shoulder and yelped as the edge of Next Dream's bow whacked low across his belly.

"Leave her!"

"Why?"

"She's mine!" His bow slashed at the top of Running White Horse's legs.

"You want everything first!" complained Running White Horse nursing his pride, glad that it was still there, big and jumping. He wanted this thing this time, very badly indeed. And he was going to have it.

Eagle Flies got to his feet and put one of his feet across the girl's throat.

"We're having her, now!"

It was Next Dream's step forward that did it. Both of his allies went for him and knocked him to the ground. The three of them rolled in an embrace, which including frantic searches for hunting knives. Next Dream found his.

Snow-on-Her struggled to her feet, out of the way of the three young men, and saw, just on the rise of the slope leading out of the coulee into which she had fallen, two men on a horse. She knew at once that one of the riders was Frank Partridge and waited for the crack of his rifle or Colt. She scrambled up the slope towards him. It was her frenetic movement, which caught the eyes of Eagle Flies, his hands already round Next Dream's throat, his mouth biting into his shoulder. Running White Horse was struggling to keep Next Dream's knife away from Eagle Flies' throat.

Eagle Flies gasped, "She's getting away."

The Sioux knife was edging closer to Eagle Flies' throat.

Running White Horse bit the Sioux's right wrist. Blood ran onto the blade before he dropped it. The Sioux's eyes were bulging.

Running White Horse got to his feet and said, "Let him go!" and kicked Eagle Flies to get him to move.

Eagle Flies let go and jumped clear leaving Next Dream coughing and retching on the dawn-wet prairie grass. "I'll kill you both," he snarled between his struggles for breath. He dropped onto his back and saw the girl had scrambled up the edge of the coulee. He saw two men on a pony. As she got to them one dropped down from the mount and Snow-on Her was in his arms, whilst another wolf soldier appeared and circled them on his pony.

All three in the coulee judged the intruders to be enemy scouts and turned towards their weapons. Frantic in the half-light, they looked for fallen knives, bows, quivers. Then they had to chase after their spooked horses. The laughter from above stopped them. Then an order came, sharp and clear, in good Siouan.

"Cut that sad horse's throat, boys!"

They looked up at the man on foot and saw that he was laughing again. They thought to kill him at once then, in the same thought-time, in the growing light, saw that it was the Wasichu who had been riding with Sitting Bull and there were two wolf scouts with him. The good day was turning bad very quickly.

With a shrug of his shoulders, Eagle Flies went to the weeping horse and cut its throat.

⋊⋉⋊⋉⋊⋉

"Go check the perimeter," said the colonel, just after the battle.

"Sir?" queried Sergeant Clinton.

"Just check it out. Git the Injuns away from the walls. I reckon we'll see no trouble but I don't like their damned wigwams close by my walls."

The colonel had noticed a dozen teepees near to the gate on the day of the skirmish with the Sioux. Clinton was not concerned because they were lodges of some of the Crow and Arikara scouts. But the colonel was right: they might get in the way of the field of fire if there was another attack.

The scouts grumbled, the squaws looked thunder, but they moved. What struck Clinton was the speed of the move once they had decided to co-operate. In less then an hour the dogs had been called in, the horses found, the teepees taken down, the cooking pots loaded on to travois poles and they were off.

As Clinton pretended to supervise from horseback, great bundles of artefacts and buffalo robes were piled high on travois and horses. A couple of kids even fitted two of the bigger dogs with poles and they carried some of the cooking pots. The dogs seemed to accept the confinement with pleasure, tails wagging, yapping with excitement. Clinton watched them move to the specified area, about a mile from the fort, closer to the river. The colonel's will was done.

It was when Clinton turned away that he saw the lone Indian, curled up by the entrance to the fort. He looked as if he were asleep. In Clinton's mind's eye he had been aware of the bundle earlier but had taken it for a pile of discarded old blankets. He had kept his eyes firmly on the group of lodges and their departure; his back had been towards the pile and the lone figure had missed his attention.

"Hey!" said Clinton, and eased his horse towards the figure.

There was no movement.

"Hey!"

Clinton felt a slight flush of irritation. He was already something of a veteran. Civil War battles, courier for generals, survivor of two battles with Indians and long marches across the plains. Who was this 'bunch of rags' taking no notice of a three-stripe war chief?

"You there! Waken up!" This time it was a shout and the Indian stirred.

From out of the blankets came a face with red eyes staring out of deep copper skin. The hair was jet black, well cared for. It was a handsome face, with good cheekbones, a thin face rather than a gaunt one and the nose was beginning to take on the power of a man. He had his hair in the style of the Arikara. Clinton recognised him as the man whose horse had dropped dead on arrival at the fort, fleeing from the Sioux.

"You gotta move," said Clinton and he noticed that the face was marked with dried tears which had run through gathered dust on the skin.

The Indian looked at him for several seconds, seeing confidence in the Wasichu. As Clinton was about to yell out for a couple of troopers, the Indian stood. As he did so the blanket dropped away from him revealing the body of a young man clad in breechcloth and leggings. Clinton was put in mind of the statues of Greek gods he'd seen on some great building in Dublin, flat bellied, etched with unattainable muscles. A patch of porcupine quills guarded the Indian's chest, he had a thong across his right upper arm; other than these slight garments his torso was unclothed. A low-slung belt carried a knife and the warrior's leggings revealed a gap at the top of the thighs, the outside cheeks of his rear open to the air. The flesh rippled as he stepped towards Clinton, making him feel as scrawny as a plucked chicken half starved to death.

"You sergeant – give me horse."

"What?"

"I want horse."

"Get your own horse."

"No horse here. Me horse dead from Sioux."

"Ain't got no horses."

"No horse from you. Take me to lodges."

Before Clinton could react the young Indian had stepped forward, raised his hand to Clinton's belt and, with a yank that all but unhorsed the sergeant, had pulled himself up behind him. Clinton's horse pranced in surprise.

"Steady!" snapped Clinton, and the horse calmed.

"Get off!" bellowed Clinton.

"Please."

Clinton was surprised at the way the word was formed, a kind of plea, half a command, an expectation. Clinton could smell the Indian, a sweet mustiness, not unpleasant. He could feel the hand of the Indian come round his side and rest on the buckle of his belt, and as it did so the Indian slapped the hip of the horse, and it began to move. Clinton let it be, allowing the horse to go forward, then touching its flanks with his spurs and turning the head towards the wide half circle of lodges. He began to follow the column of displaced Indians who but ten minutes before had been packing their belongings.

"You got a horse over there?"

"Many horses."

"You're the one that came in on the dying horse."

"Yes."

The smell of the Wasichu sergeant was singing in Little Knife's nostrils. It was a bad smell, like the smell of an old man dying; maybe a hint of the belly water of a man, the odour from his armpits, a whisper of soil from the back of his trousers, sweat; a nasty Wasichu smell. Frank Partridge did not smell that way.

"I hear Frank Partridge dead," said Little Knife. He already knew the story was that Frank had escaped from the fortress, but he wanted to learn what the Wasichu were saying.

"Who's that? Frank who?"

"A white man – from Sitting Bull."

"Oh – him! He ain't dead. He hung hi'self, pretended to be dead and then beat up on the soldier who found him. Got the lad a week of drill. He went off. Escaped."

"Him bad-man-white-man," sang Little Knife happily.

"He sure is."

Little Knife's heart felt big, as, at the mention of Frank Partridge, he also thought of her. She it was who brought the tears. He had to know what happened to her. He had to gaze on her vulture-corpse. He wanted to know. The time for tears was gone. He must look to the bones of his love woman and put them in a high place.

"You knew him – I saw you with him one time."

"Yes."

"What's your name?"

"My name is Little Knife."

"You Crow?"

"Arikara."

"Yea – thought so – I can tell you Indians from your hair."

"That is good, Sergeant, you good man."

Little Knife wanted to lose the sergeant, get him off the horse. This man needed to go swim for a moon or two. Little Knife squeezed the sides of the horse with his knees, instinctively trying to turn it to the right where a small herd of Indian horses was grazing. The sergeant's horse was momentarily confused. Clinton sensed the movement and said, "You want to go over there?"

231

"My horses there."

Clinton flicked at the reins and eased the horse into an altered course and less than five minutes later they were mingling with the herd. A Crow youth, half-asleep in the short grass, slowly got to his feet. He recognised Little Knife.

"I want a good horse," said Little Knife.

"There's one of the Sioux horses over there," he said with a grin. "It's a good horse."

The herd was mixed, some of them Crow and Arikara, and some Yantonai, but a bunch of Sioux horses from the crowd of lodges that had been in the area two days before had been run off from the withdrawing Sioux and half a dozen had been taken during the battle.

One was a fine pinto, a stiff stallion, asleep on his feet, his mottled brown and black snake jerking with the rhythm of his heart. He was maybe six or seven years old. The colouring was largely without pattern, a blending of yellow like buffalo grass before the onset of the Fall. The colouring tapered towards the tail turning to cream with the tail itself, so light a cream it was almost white. He was prime. His flesh flickered with the arrival and departure of busy flies. He was dreaming, as he stood, left rear leg relaxed, of racing with the buffalo, for he was a buffalo chaser. He had been used in battle, but he was matchless in the buffalo hunt. To his captors he was just a very good pony. They knew nothing of his training. As he looked at the beautiful animal Little Knife wondered what his Sioux name had been.

Amongst the tribes horses were owned, but it was a loose ownership. It was known that a horse or horses belonged to a given lodge or warrior, that the horses could be passed on as gifts; but in time of stress, in the moment of a hunt or battle any man could take any horse. This was a horse taken in conflict, or at least by default. It belonged to everyone until it was 'given' by a chief, or favoured by one of those who used it.

"Who favours this horse?" asked Little Knife.

"Many," said the boy. "But the chiefs have not yet decided how to divide them. They are talking about it."

Little Knife approached the animal and it woke. It blinked at the warrior standing in front of him, did not back off or prance, or move to one side. The horse looked into the eyes of this man thing and liked him. He moved his head forward, up and down as he did so, and he gave the man thing a push which made the human step back. He saw on the man thing a change in the face which meant good and felt the hand of the man thing touch his muzzle and caress his lips and open them.

These men things liked to look at the teeth of horse people, and though it was strange and beyond the comprehension of the brotherhood of horses, it was not unpleasant. The great animal allowed the man thing the pleasure of the look and heard the sound of delight come from the man. Then the man caressed the horse's great head and whispered in his ear and blew into his nostrils. The horse smelt the man too and liked him. He was pleased when the man sprang on his back.

He felt the legs encircle him and the heat of the man as both their bodies touched. He let the little man thing who had been with the herd put the halter on because it might be that they were about to chase the horses with horns. But this was not to be.

Instead, wonderful pleasure, he was told by the legs and the hands of the man to fly, to gallop, to rush across the ground, and he did so, loving the sound of the whooping that the man thing made. That was how the horse, ridden by a Sioux who had been cut down in the battle of the fort, came to fall in love with Little Knife the Arikara who gave him the good name Star.

)()()()()(

Little Knife had ridden back to the gates alongside Sergeant Clinton. They said almost nothing for Little Knife was busy feeling his new horse, sensing the animal's mood and movement. Every so often he would change pressure on the animal and it would swing into the gentle gallop they made, sensing what his rider wanted. Once the sergeant snatched at his own horse to avoid a gofer hole and the horses would have smacked into each other, but Little Knife's horse simply glided away. It was then that Little Knife guessed that the horse was a buffalo hunter. That was very good. They were the bravest, they were the most honest of horses. Little Knife was happy.

At the gates the pile of blankets were still there. Little Knife jumped from the stallion and went to the blankets. One he threw round his shoulders, the other he placed across the horse's back. He would ride on the blanket alone. He hated saddles; even the small Indian saddles made him feel insecure. He liked to be part of the animal. A saddle came between them. A quiver, his bow, the old Spencer and lance were there, close by where the blankets had been.

He drove the lance into the rain-soft soil and picked up the weapons, strapping them with care across his shoulders. Then he leap-frogged onto the stallion's back. He lifted the lance from the earth and without a glance at Clinton turned the head of his animal away from the fort.

"Where you going?"

"Away."

"But you ain't got permission."

The Arikara directed his eyes toward the rise of land which formed the edge of the prairie. The single being, that was himself and his horse, made off for the hills. Somewhere there he expected to find the corpse of Snow-on-Her, or whatever was left of it.

Clinton wondered whether to shoot him off the horse, but decided to report to the colonel instead.

)(()(()(()(

Sergeant Clinton reported to Colonel Pattee that the perimeter was clear of Indians and their lodges. He told his colonel that the heathen were all quartered safely in, more or less, one place, close by the banks of the river where at least there was fresh water and some grazing, especially if the rains came. At that point it seemed it would never rain again.

"Well done, lad," smiled Pattee and moved the cheroot to the other cheek. He really liked the young Irishman and Clinton felt it.

"They were no trouble, Colonel, but there was one who behaved a bit strange."

"Oh?"

"Remember the one who came in on a shot-through horse? He was riding with that Partridge man one time."

"His name was Little Knife I do think," said the colonel. He blew a long cloud of grey smoke from his mouth.

"Yes sir," smiled Clinton. He tasted the smoke on the air and wondered how people, even colonels, could find pleasure in the habit. But he was impressed with the colonel. Pattee was known to

234

remember the names of the entire regiment, but to include the scouts as well was a surprise.

"I knew him from another time. Its another story, Sergeant, it will have to wait."

"Yes sir."

"So what about him?"

"Seems he had a squaw who got herself killed yesterday and he left her out there, and now he wants to find her."

"Won't be much left," smiled the colonel.

"But he still went off to look," shrugged Clinton.

"They'm a bit like that."

"Sir?"

"Emotional."

"Yes sir."

"You wouldn't think Indians was emotional, would you, Sergeant?"

"No sir."

"Well they are, Sergeant, they are. And I'll tell you what – they'm also true to their word."

"Yes sir."

"It'll be their downfall."

"That it will, sir."

"Aye lad, that it will. He's gone off without leave you say?"

"Sir."

"I'll put him down as a deserter – doubt if he'll come back now Partridge has gone."

"Sir?"

"They're like brothers."

"That's disgusting, sir."

"Aye lad, that it is."

)( )( )( )( )(

There was a dead person close. Little Knife was certain of it. But when he breasted the edge of the next coulee he was almost disappointed to see that it was the corpse of a horse, half consumed by scavengers, wolves, maybe a bear, certainly fat vultures. The ugly birds were still feeding and squabbling, with screams of annoyance at one another, flesh hanging from their sinister beaks. They were almost careless of his approach.

He searched, he scoured all about. He studied the ground and counted the marks of feet and hooves. On a low section of the coulee he saw that two people were walking and three horses trailing them. He also found a streak of vomit and some fringes from a calfskin jerkin; it was soft enough to be a woman's.

For some time he sat close to a brook at the bottom of the coulee and played with the mud. She must have been taken into the Sioux village. How could he get in, there were thousands there? He stroked his face and to his surprise found that the mud had a taste to it, almost sweet, completely contrary to what he…

Even as he thought, he saw that a patch of sweet basil, close by, had lost many leaves into the mud. That was the reason for the perfumed taste He thought about that – seeing the mud and not knowing of its scent, not realising that it was something more than mud. That would be the way! All they would see would be a warrior entering their lines, a warrior who was a stranger, but untouchable in the magic of his nature… a man who was no man… a contrary.

He began to search in his *wakam* pouch for colouring clay. He took a long time daubing his face with the sweet mud, streaked with the pigment from his pouch. This would make a good beginning. He sighed as he thought how he would have to cover his entire body, and that of the horse as well. He would have to explain to it first. But this was a good horse, and would understand his quest. He had to look like a contrary, and the horse had to be disguised too.

)()()()()(

To say that Sitting Bull was like one struck by lightning on the open prairie, scorched by the finger tips of *Wakantanka*, would not be sufficient to describe his shock. He stared at Snow-on-Her as if she were a black bear sleeping in his teepee and come awake with Sitting Bull mistaking it for a cured skin to snuggle into.

"You were gone!" was all that he said.

"I found some braves fighting over her," said Frank Partridge, armed folded, smiling. "Those three!"

"She's mine," said Next Dream.

"Hold your tongue," said Sitting Bull, for she was his.

She was everyone's. It had been done to her. This was a big problem. It was as well that the coming together was in this safe gully where his war party was regrouping, tending the wounded, and beginning to sing a song of victory, making ready to parade into the great village of the teepees of many nations.

Frank Partridge had refused her demands to return to the Fort because he knew the three warriors would not have it. She was their prisoner to be taken back for the pleasure of her destruction or slavery. He planned to negotiate with the big belly chiefs on her behalf for she belonged to Little Knife, a good warrior even though he rode with the Wasichu as a scout.

The two Cheyenne had refused to take her with them to the small circle of Southern Cheyenne that was grouped in the centre of the great village. This was because Next Dream would not have it. Suddenly their spirit of oneness had disappeared and all three had blood in their eyes. It was all to be a matter for resolution by a big belly chief, and no wiser big belly chief than Sitting Bull existed, the Cheyennes said, even if his big belly was really very small. And now he who was so wise, and had the best words for all moments, was speechless.

Sitting Bull wished he only had to deal with war.

The fight was over. The losses had been slight, the warriors were satisfied, the Wasichu soldiers did not pursue, which was unfortunate because Sitting Bull had laid a trap. But already the rings of lodges were starting to break camp against such a pursuit, ready to go in every direction away from Fort Rice. Later each group would divide again, spraying out across the vast grasslands so as to give no pursuer a large body of people to destroy. Meanwhile the Dog Soldiers would fan across the rear of the bands ready to die in their defence, also ready to turn back on the Wasichu. If the white soldiers followed they would be certain to keep together and make a fine target to snap at – like a herd of dumb buffalo.

The victory parade would not take place unless the breaking of camp was stopped. Messages must be sent to stop the great village breaking up completely. There was so much to do. Now this.

The return of this woman.

She must be got rid off again, for she was poison.

"Let me take her," suggested the Wasichu.

Why does he want to take her?

This was Sitting Bull's immediate thought. He wants a squaw, this Wasichu, was the next future phantom that came into Sitting Bull's mind. This Wasichu had no squaw. This in itself was odd for one who moved amongst the Red People, for Wasichu were much favoured by some of the women, especially those who had lost their warrior in battle. Perhaps he preferred Yellow Hair. Sitting Bull smiled at that. Such things were known amongst the mountain men.

"Never!" snapped Next Dream.

This young man was getting difficult to handle. Sitting Bull looked towards him. "Never? What is this, 'Never!'?"

"She stays."

"She is already exiled, gone from us. She goes again." Sitting Bull was firm.

"She..."

"She what?" asked Sitting Bull, startlingly irritated. "You are our friend and my son, I have taken you into our place of living, wherever we are, and you are one of our bravest of the brave. But you too can go as well. You can return to your filthy Crow people if you want this..." He waved his favourite Spencer in the direction of Snow-on-Her.

She snorted, "I want none of you. I want to go back to the fort, to my man."

"Shut up, woman! Perhaps I should blow your head off," said Sitting Bull sweetly. "Well?" He turned to Next Dream. "Is she to go or are you to go, or both of you? What is it that I should say in this thing?"

"I shall go," snapped Next Dream, half turning away at the thought.

"Then perhaps we should search for your scalp in one of the Cheyenne teepees for you to take back with you. I think you might need it when you go back to your people," said Sitting Bull. He looked for a threat from the young man. At once he regretted his cruel words, but was ready to defend himself.

Next Dream felt his heart explode and saw a hundred laughing faces from his own people. He could not leave. Sitting Bull knew that he could not leave. Here with the Sioux there was honour; with the Crow there would be an unhappy return. The wretched visions of jeering faces came once more. Then neither could she go away, he thought. Next Dream fingered his hunting knife. A sudden leap

238

and she would be nothing. That would be a way out of this evil happening.

At first they did not notice the contrary warrior riding by.

He had just entered the circle of Sitting Bull's warriors. Many had been drawn to hear the argument, others were gathering to learn whether the parade was to be or not. Others were reacting to riders coming back from the lodges to say that the women and children and the old people were indeed striking camp and moving north. There was a complexity of movement going on, attention was on other things than a single naked warrior who was mad and sacred at the same time, just passing by. That was what they did, the contrary warriors, they passed by.

Scouts were returning at the same moment confirming that the soldiers were staying where they were; even their cavalry was not venturing out. The Hunkpapa lodges were safe that night, but they were already on the move. Sitting Bull sent riders to stop the movement. Turning, he noticed the contrary.

"Goodbye, good morning," greeted the contrary warrior.

Sitting Bull ignored him and called for more riders to hurry to the lodges and tell them to stay put. There was no threat. Perhaps the parade could take place and a victory dance mingle with the wailing of those who had lost good people in the fight. It was fitting that the day should end that way.

"No greetings to a little peace chief!" called out the contrary warrior.

Sitting Bull nodded. Contrary warriors could be a nuisance, but he understood their sadness, their turning everything round the wrong way, which was the right way. This man had said, "Greetings great war chief!"

Sitting Bull said, "Where are you from?"

"Nowhere between the sun and the stars and your small toe."

It was impossible to gain a firm impression of the face. He was young, yet maybe not. Sitting Bull looked at him with care and respect as did those around him.

They looked up and saw a figure, with a young man's grace, obscured by wipings of mud. He wore all of his regalia back to front. He sat facing the rear of his horse. His bow was unstrung but an arrow was placed against the string, by its barbed head, the feathers protruding in the direction of fire. He had a Spencer in the pouch but it was placed the wrong way, the butt in first. His entire body was a multiplicity of paints which meant nothing whatsoever, congealed with the coating of mud. His horse, a good stallion, was equally caked with mud, looking uncomfortable and matted. The contrary's features were hard to ascertain because of the gaudy colouring. He had the hairstyle of the Sioux, but his plaits were tied across his nose to form a hideous moustache, and at the front was a tuft which could have been Crow or even Arikara, dirty little people.

"Who are you?" growled Next Dream.

"A proper warrior who is here today."

Suddenly he looked at the squaw standing with a glint of anger in her eyes. "That is a man – I want him now – I am a winkte."

Frank Partridge was losing the conversation; nothing seemed to make sense. Sitting Bull muttered in his ear, "This is a contrary..."

"I can see that, my friend."

"He wants this woman, or maybe he does not."

Sitting Bull said, "Hey – warrior – will you give this man back to us?" For the contrary this would mean, "Will you take this woman away from us?" But it might mean nothing at all to him; a man can never be certain what a contrary would do, or say, or think.

"No, peace lover."

Sitting Bull smiled and hoped that the contrary would see it as a look of anger. Sitting Bull desired peace, but was no lover of it.

"Then give him to us," Sitting Bull nodded towards Snow-on-Her.

"I'm not going with that!" snapped Snow-on-Her.

Sitting Bull clicked back the hammer on his Spencer, fire in his eyes, and she saw it.

"I do not want this man!" shouted the contrary and held out his hand for her.

Hesitantly she stepped forward and was all but snatched onto the hindquarters of the horse, with her back to the contrary, facing also the rear of the horse. The contrary eased himself backwards towards the horse's neck and his arm snapped round her waist and pulled her towards him with a jerk

"Now I come back!" said the contrary.

He eased his mount, with a twist of his legs, towards the outer circle of warriors and moved east to take him away from the circle, away from the direction of the teepees and away from the warriors.

As he did so they heard the curses of Snow-on-Her declaring her disgust at this closeness to the lowest catfish. She spluttered hatred of the Sioux and all of manhood, for it was well known that a contrary would have nothing to do with a woman, and now he was taking one. What would happen would be beyond disgust. Yet she did not struggle. This was indeed a contrary moment. Sitting Bull shook his head with puzzlement, but was much relieved to see her go.

Frank Partridge hid the smile in his head, for the contrary warrior had failed to hide the quality of his voice.

Next Dream also watched the contrary go. He bit his lip and went for his horse. He mounted and moved off with his friends towards the gathering parade, for messages were coming back that the lodges had been halted. That night though, he planned to ride east, alone, away from the celebrations.

As Little Knife rode away his heart was thrusting at his chest, for he had seen two ghosts. His Wasichu – what was he doing with the Sioux? Secret things, always he was doing secret things. This Wasichu was everywhere, everyone's ears and eyes. Did he not know that ears can be cut off, and eyes put out? But the Wasichu knew what he was doing... one day they would laugh about this... he did not know that his Little Knife had done this brave thing, right in front of him. Ah! Little Knife was good. Little Knife would have much to boast of when next they met. But the other! The other ghost. He knew the face. It was Runs Fast. He remembered the weight of his body, as he had tried to move him, on that day long gone. He had been dead, but still warm. Little Knife remembered the wonder of that and had thought it was because of the beating sun. Somehow he must have lived... but those wounds... how could he? Little Knife closed his eyes as Star walked further away, feeling that if his eyes were closed he would be invisible and Runs Fast would not recognise him. He concentrated with his fingers on the belly of his woman; she pressed her back hard against his groin as the horse walked on. It was too much, so he opened his eyes and saw, far off, that the Sioux were no longer looking his way.

)()()()(

The strange pair and the muddy horse were gone from sight. All the warriors mounted again and the whole war party was heading towards the place of the lodges, hoping they were halted and the celebration could take place. Sitting Bull sat proudly in the lead with his Wasichu on his left-hand side, White Hawk and Yellow Hair were close by.

The Wasichu had grumbled as they rode that they had won a battle but that he had lost his best horse and his favourite weapons.

Sympathy was offered then White Hawk, his horse just trailing that of Yellow Hair said, "I want to be a contrary warrior."

"You already are!" said Frank Partridge, but could not help a smile. "For we are talking of other things and you are interrupting."

Sitting Bull nodded, having had enough of contrary warriors for one entire moon and was not smiling at all.

Yellow Hair growled, "You have not had the right suffering. A contrary has suffered something, something rich and strange which causes him to be touched by a special spirit."

"As does a winkte," said Sitting Bull.

"A winkte is *born* a winkte. That is our special power. We are born with two spirits."

"And such men-women are dangerous," grunted Sitting Bull.

Yellow Hair smiled sweetly.

For a time they rode in silence. The dry air across the prairie was moving in a steady breeze which brought little coolness.

"I think that soon we shall have rain," said Yellow Hair.

"Another of your powers?" smiled the Wasichu.

Sitting Bull sniffed the breeze.

"I sense it too," said Sitting Bull. "What do you think, Wasichu? What do you think, my Wasichu with no hair and no guns and no horse and not even the bow that you were so proud of."

"I think it will rain too."

"When?" asked Sitting Bull.

"The rain will come this day – when the sun goes down."

Yellow Hair nodded at that.

"I see Yellow Hair agrees," said Sitting Bull.

"Grey Eagle, the Wasichu, is right. The rain will come with the night, good rain."

"And the guns, and the bow and the horse?" smiled the great war chief. "Those which were taken from you by your own people."

"They are gone," said Frank Partridge. "But there are guns enough in other places. I will rearm."

Sitting Bull reached behind him and brought forward a bow, his own; one of his favourites, beautifully formed, very accurate, hard to pull, causing am arrow to carry many strides of a horse.

"Until that day, take this," smiled Sitting Bull.

Frank took the bow, lowering his head in gratitude. He examined it as they rode and saw that it was very fine. He turned to show it to White Hawk. He had gone.

"Where did he go?" asked Frank Partridge.

Yellow Hair smiled, "Away."

"Where?"

"He said he wanted to take some water to the Wasichu – maybe he *will* become a contrary boy."

"He's too clever for that," said Sitting Bull.

Both Yellow Hair and Frank Partridge smiled, for different reasons, and said nothing.

Sitting Bull said, "Now tell me Wasichu, how is it that the Wasichu longknives do things together to the sound of their iron flutes – how did they learn to do these things? We saw them do it again at the fort."

"That," began Frank, "is a complicated thing, and will take long in the telling – and the lodges are close."

"Then you can talk to us until we reach them. And then some more when we do reach them."

Frank sighed and began to tell of men who were kings of war. For the first time Sitting Bull and those gathered heard of Alexander the Great. They tutted with approval at the taming of Bucephalus and were pleased to hear that Napoleon had a white horse and that Wellington a big chestnut. But they had much difficulty when they heard of the dead at Waterloo. So many – the Wasichu were wondrous strange to kill each other in such numbers.

"But why did the Frenchies not break camp and flee in all directions into the night across the prairie?" asked Sitting Bull.

"Because there was no prairie," said Frank Partridge.

They had much difficulty with that and even stopped once and spent time on geography and maps of Europe drawn in the dust, but it meant nothing to the Sioux or the Cheyenne – this was a Wasichu thing.

)( )( )( )( )(

Early in that long lecture, further away than a long ride by a well-mounted warrior, Snow-on-Her twisted round to look at her mud caked man. She stayed twisted round, and said awkwardly in his ear, "I love you."

He said with a pretended contrary growl mingling with a giggle, "I hate you very much."

So she put her hands behind her, reached up, and finding his good flat nipples, she pinched them both, very hard.

)( )( )( )( )(

For Next Dream the trail was not difficult to follow, almost carelessly laid. He sensed a trap. He sensed cunning, sensed that suddenly the trail might vanish, and indeed it did disappear.

He followed the spore of a single horse until it arrived at a broad tributary of the Missouri, known as Bear Creek. It has since dried up, but then it was shallow and prone to turning into quicksand and mud pools in the summer.

Next Dream saw two sets of footprints alongside the horse, marking where it stopped to drink. He saw the prints toe to toe. He saw smudges on the edge of the mud which were the length of a single body, and within the smudges were the remnants of body paint rubbed from flesh in the half dry soil. The area was disturbed as if a fight had taken place, but it was not much of a struggle. He felt anger surge at what the gouges in the mud told him.

The footprints rejoined the horse which had moved to some lush grass on a small water meadow. The spore then went back to the water and as the level grew deeper the marking disappeared. He followed the embankment on both sides for a considerable distance, half a day's riding, but he never regained contact. After a week of searching he made his way back to the Sioux lodges which had already moved north leaving good wide tracks.

Little Knife and his woman were already well to the south-west moving towards another of the Wasichu forts they called Riley. He planned to put his mark to paper again, for they were sure to want the eyes of a real person to help them do what the Wasichu had to do, and that in itself was a mystery – but it carried Wasichu money and that brought many good Wasichu things.

)()()()(

On the afternoon of the day after the battle, Clinton blinked as the Indian boy approached the gate. The young sergeant was not on duty. He was outside the fort leaning against the main wall to the north of the gate. He kept in the shade thrown by the afternoon sun. The colonel, for no apparent reason, had given him one of those long cheroots he seemed to chew on at all times. Clinton had been smoking in the shade for five minutes and his head was spinning. At first he thought the boy was an hallucination coughed up with the smoke being cleared from his inexperienced lungs.

The boy was dressed in feathers, or at least it looked that way, from head to foot; his pony also had feathers in its tail and mane. It was as if a dwarf chief in full regalia was about to visit the fort. His handsome pony was painted from one end to the other in patterns as gaudy as they were numerous but did not detract from the superb condition of the animal. A travois was trailing behind the pony; furs were heaped on it, full buffalo robes, fine beaver and a wolf-skin complete with head. The boy's ambling beast halted in front of Clinton and the boy looked down, smack into Clinton's eyes. Clinton gulped.

The lips, full and sensuous, pouted with a smile. The face, half painted red on the left, the other side browned by the sun, was at once open and daring, yet there was a hint of menace. Naked arms emerged from the decking feathers of a sleeveless shirt, arms which were a boy's arms, but were muscled like a child acrobat in a circus. The boy was talking some kind of Indian yatter. Clinton shook his head and made a sign to show that he did not understand. The boy laughed and talked on with words which sounded like water running over pebbles. Clinton was stunned by this gaudy youth. Other soldiers strolled over to stare.

Two Yantonai came trotting up. They had seen the lone rider coming in. Noting that he was but a boy in dance regalia they had not rushed at him. They saw that he was talking to one of the

Wasichu. They wanted to hear this. They were some distance off but saw that he was Cheyenne. How come a lone Cheyenne boy was out here by himself in this festival way? They quickened their pace.

"Hey!" they shouted in clumsy Cheyenne. "What you want scorpion-child?"

"Nothing, masters," replied the boy.

The boy dropped from his horse.

Finally satisfied that he was but a kid, the two Yantonai began to relax, but stayed mounted.

He was polite, respectful. They looked at him with their hands on their hips. There was an almost feminine air about the child, but he seemed very sure of himself. Green Leaf was the first to notice that there were two eagle feathers in his blue-jet hair denoting that he had killed two men; there were three first coup feathers too. Absurd. This was wearing decoration for effect. It was typical that the Cheyenne allowed such a thing.

"Why you here?" asked Dangerous Wolf, the younger of the pair.

"What's he sayin'?" asked the Wasichu, in Wasichu, which Dangerous Wolf could speak very well.

"Don't know soldier."

"I have brought gifts for silver leaf," said the boy.

"He say he bring things for colonel," translated Dangerous Wolf.

Clinton was alert now, and dropped the sleeping cigar into his tunic pocket.

"Why you present bring silver leaf?" snarled Green Leaf.

"Sitting Bull speaks that I do this," said the boy sweetly.

Both the Yantonai swung from their horses, keeping the reins in their hands.

"You name?" Green Leaf leaned forward and touched the face of the boy in an insulting way.

"My name is for my companions," hissed White Hawk. "As is my face."

"Ohhhhhh," laughed Green Leaf and thought to take his knife to this pretty face; instead he removed his hand, sensing menace from the boy, strange in one so young.

Clinton was watching the exchange and did not like it, "Bring him along with me!"

Clinton turned on his heel and walked into the sudden hit of the direct sunlight. He glanced back to see that the boy was following with a Yantonai on either side of him, his be-feathered horse trailing behind, between the Yantonai mounts.

The colonel came out of his private quarters as soon as he was called. He had been dozing and his shirt was out of his trousers. He had picked up his half-chewed cigar, snapped off the beat-up end and shoved the fresh half into his mouth. He looked at the boy they just brought in and wondered why he was dressed for a dance, Sun Dance, Moon Dance, some damned dance. The colonel had once had it explained to him by Frank Partridge in that border time, way back, before the bastard had taken to the savages lock stock and barrel.

"Has he come to dance?" he asked the Yantonai in English.

"No, he come to trade," replied Dangerous Wolf.

"Trade? What trade?" snapped the colonel.

There was a flurry of three Plains' dialects and waving of arms and still greater chattering until the youngest of the Yantonai spoke. The colonel knew him and fought for his name, and lost it.

"He want horse and guns," said the Yantonai.

"The hell he does."

"He will bring some rain, and plenty skins."

"Rain?"

"Him come to dance for rain."

"We don't need no rain," lied the colonel.

The one thing Fort Rice needed was rain. The river was shallow, the fort's wells were dry, and the whole plain was fit to burst into flames. They needed rain.

"Him bring plenty good skins, and him dance for you."

The colonel looked at the skins. They were the finest. They were worth perhaps three horses – certainly three half-worn cavalry mounts – a thousand dollars. There were some spares – they could let him have the nags. He looked up at the boy. What a face! He felt the eyes on him. The eyes were trying to get into the colonel's head. The colonel countered and stared the boy down, stared, saw the beauty of the eyes, saw a bird high in the blue, flickering white and found that the boy had averted his eyes – the little bastard. He had not been stared out; he had averted his eyes so that the colonel could not follow the vision any further

"We'll trade," laughed the colonel

"Silver leaf will trade," said Dangerous Wolf.

"How old are you? Ask him his age! What name?" the colonel nodded.

"Me Dangerous Wolf."

"No! What's *his* damned name?

"Me is Dangerous Wolf," the Yantonai grinned at the colonel

"Yes – I know that – but what's *his* name?"

"He says his name is for his companions," smiled Dangerous Wolf.

"Tell him I would be his friend."

"Boy, Silver Leaf Pattee wants your winters and your name."

The boy frowned, thinking for a moment that the Wasichu chief was going to kill him, take away his time from him, then understood the badly translated question.

"And the silver leaf says he want you his friend… so you can give him your name, you cheeky Cheyenne boy."

The boy smiled, "Better a cheeky Cheyenne boy than a fat Yantonai fool."

"Were we in the open I would cut off your future pleasure thing, Cheyenne doglet," smiled Dangerous Wolf – this boy was so cheeky he was born to die before he made milk.

"To put in place of your own, little Yantonai ant?"

The Yantonai laughed – the boy should have died at birth.

"What the damned hell is going on!" snapped the colonel. "What's his name?"

"I am White Hawk, son of White Hawk and son of Yellow Hair of the Southern Cheyenne, people of Black Kettle our War Leader and wisest of men, who is friend of the Wasichu and Peace Chief."

The Yantonai did not know it but Pattee understood it all.

"Your winters!" snapped Dangerous Wolf. Who was this boy to call out a warrior's boasting?

"I am holder of two Wasichu scalps, and three First Coups, shooter of a straight arrow, and good friend of the Wasichu Warrior we call Grey Eagle and the Sioux call The Man That Has His Head Shaved, the friend of Sitting Bull. I am sent by them to dance for the silver leaf and bring him gifts, and so to trade. My name is White Hawk and I am a Contrary Warrior and have lived for ten winters and one more." White Hawk held up both hands and then a single finger.

Dangerous Wolf and Green Leaf looked at the sturdy boy in front of them, then at each other, and Green Leaf said, with studied insolence, "You lie, prairie pig, eater of old men's weapons."

White Hawk's eyes closed partly, but the smile remained, and then he said, with an almost most perfect Yantonai dialect, "Honoured warriors, lickers of Wasichu balls, why do you fear me?"

They both started towards the boy to slice his sweet throat, stopped only by the colonel's bellow, "Stand still, you bastards!"

Clinton was in front of the boy at once, not knowing what was going on, but getting between him and the colonel's Yantonai. The boy lifted Clinton's arm and his grinning face appeared from beneath the armpit.

"He say bad things!" screeched Dangerous Wolf.

"I'm doin' the tradin,'" snapped Colonel Pattee having caught the drift of the insults. "Clinton! Call up three of the third rate mounts. He shall have them."

Clinton was gone, replaced by the sentries from the HQ veranda who had moved in as they saw the heated argument in front of their colonel.

The boy was smiling and speaking, "Tell the silver leaf I shall dance now."

The boy turned and from his waist he drifted left and as he did so his right foot rose and beat the earth, and he turned and swayed and beat the dust with a different foot to each countered sway. Within seconds a sheen of sweat began to appear on every part of him that was exposed to sight: his legs, arms, the displayed parts of his shoulders, back and waist. As he danced he sang a secret song, chanting to the beat of his own feet, in a voice not yet broken.

After ten minutes the colonel retreated to the veranda, and flopped onto a rickety chair and watched the boy dance on. He danced for an hour in the sun, a spectacle of movement and a drumming chant from his own throat, calling on the Great Spirit to bring water to this place, for no reason other than to show these poor Wasichu that he, White Hawk, had His ear. A crowd gathered and chattered, pointed and laughed, but gradually the grace of White

Hawk's movements entranced them. An unexpected thing happened too.

Dangerous Wolf leapt on his horse and galloped out of the fort. He returned quickly and with him he had a drum in his arms, guiding his horse by knees alone. The drum was about three times the size of a military kettle and in constant danger of being dropped.

The Yantonai swung his leg over his horse's head, leaning back as he did so. He dropped lightly to the ground, the drum in his arms.

As soon as he was off his horse he was kneeling before the dancing boy, and began to beat the drum. He was joined by Green Leaf to whom he handed an extra pair of sticks held in his belt. Together they followed the dancer until at a sublime moment the drum took over and White Hawk began to prance and turn to its call. The prancing and the bowing and turning, and the beating of the enemy drum formed a cascade of sound and movement. It was an enemy drum, but not a Wasichu drum; it was a drum of the people. It made them one; for a time, they were one.

The moment came for the dance to pause, or to end, or to continue, an opportunity for change. *Thump, thump; thump thump – thump, thump; thump thump...THUMP!*

The beating stopped

The boy stopped.

He froze, only for a moment, and then he stood, smiling again, perspiration cooling his skin.

The boy pointed at Pattee.

"Tell the silver leaf he shall have his rain, and the furs. But I do not want those sad creatures." He indicated the three nags which had been produced. "I want the horse and guns of the Wasichu Warrior, Grey Eagle, in return."

"So that's it!" growled Pattee. "Frank Partridge is too chicken to come get his own gear – sends a kid."

"Does the silver leaf agree?" asked the boy through his sweating enemy friends, the Yantonai, who loved him enough to knock him on the head before they cut his throat, or even to make him their slave.

"It's a deal," said the colonel. "After the rain comes."

He whispered to Clinton, "Give him grub and stick him on the porch 'till dawn. We'll let the little sod go at dawn anyway. I like his God damned feathers."

)( )( )( )( )(

Clinton was on his *least* favourite duty. He was Night Orderly. He had the task of waking the colonel in times of emergency. Now was an emergency.

He bent over the colonel and shook him. The man stank of tobacco. His hand stayed on the colonel's shoulder and was shrugged away. Clinton was surprised at the power of the sleeping man, a gristle-like hardness. "Sirrrrrr!"

"What the…?"

"Sir – the Indian boy's gone!

"The boy?"

"Yes, sir."

"So what? He was going at dawn. What in hell's tarnation time is it?"

It was a moonless night, the brilliant crescent of the new moon long gone out of sight in cold pursuit of the setting sun in the west.

"Two in the morning, sir."

"Two is it?"

"Yes, for sure it is, sir."

"So – the boy has gone."

"He's a hostile, sir."

"Clinton, he is at least a hostile, maybe something more; he's also a darned treasure to some damned mother and father."

The colonel paused, turned to his left and spat the grunted contents of his upper chest, with great accuracy, considering the darkness, into the spittoon set close to his bed. "Is that all you woke me for? Ain't the hostiles returned in force?"

"No, sir – but he's taken the horses, sir."

"They were his'n."

"He's taken the renegade's horse an'all."

"The little devil."

"And the guns!"

"God damn!"

"And the three mounts for the orderlies; he left the three nags."

"He what?"

"And the furs he left for us – he left them behind."

251

"The little bastard."

"The Yantonai want his skin. They're mounted outside. Ready to go."

The colonel raised his hand for silence. He listened and smiled.

"Tell 'em to go to their lodges – let the boy go."

"But sir!"

"Jeeees! Do you not hear me?"

The colonel was on his elbow, about to flop back into his bed

"But sir."

"Listen!" snapped the colonel. "Will you damned *listen!*"

Clinton could hear nothing but the rain.

What the hell was the colonel talking about... my God! It's raining.

"Sir!"

"Yesssss?"

"It's raining."

"Jeeeeeesus Christ!"

)()()()()(

Brigadier General Sully placed the scrawled report on his campaign desk and leaned back so hard on his sailcloth chair it threatened to break, even under his trim weight. Outside the tent rain was pelting down, the canvass of the tent was roaring in sympathy.

"Well, God damn me to hell and back," he growled, "for being a lucky varmint."

"Sir?" said the staff major.

"Me, lucky me."

"Sir?"

"Putting Pattee into Rice!"

The staff major, grey-haired and hunched with more years than he cared to admit, nodded in agreement and waited for the report to be handed to him. Instead the general slapped the document firmly onto the campaign desk with his broad but skeletal hand. "Nice little action!"

"May I read it, sir?"

"Sure," said the general, picking up the two sheets of poor handwriting and passing them to the major. "Read it aloud so that I can go over it again without a struggle – you'd better ignore his damned syntax and foul hand... he's a fightin' officer! Canadian an' all, so he's hardly educated don't you know? Can't write a sentence without a smudge and a word writ wrong... here – read it!"

The officer huffed agreement and adjusted his pince-nez and read:

"To: Brigadier General Sully USA

From: Command at Fort Rice

Sir, I have pleasure to inform you that this day the officers and men under my command was attacked by a large force of hostiles led, we do declare, by one Sitting Bull and various War Chiefs including The Man That Has His Head Shaved. This man is a renegade bastard..."

The major raised his eyebrow, coughed and continued to read.

"...we succeeded in arresting. He was once an aquaintance of mine. Now he is a traitor. And claims to be a capt. of foot (and was English!). He had forged documents in his hands which was destroyed. I regret that this man, who goes by the name Frank Partridge, excaped custody, though he may have fallen in the later action. The enemy attempted to lure us from the fort. Instead we formed a powerful defense line and fort off attack after attack. We lost one man killed and ten wounded. I fear one boy struck through by an arrow in the darkness at the start may die yet. One Crow squaw who was scouting for us failed to return Another scout has deserted. The heat of our fire kept the hostiles away from our line. Many hostiles fell in this action, but their dead was picked up and taken to their rear in acts of admiral bravery. Some of these galant savages road their horses standing on their backs. Despite heavy fire they succeeded at the opening engagements to come close enough to our line for blows to be exchanged. But they was quickly withdraw as each section of the line was reinforced. My officers had to warn our own men against cheering the daring that took place before them. The action took place along a line at times almost two miles in length and lasted quite three hours. The hostiles withdrew and I ordered that we continued to fire our howitzers at extreame range over the hills beyond which the enemy had withdrawn. The hostiles did not return in force. This concluded the day very much in our favor. Our only concern now is the heat and the lack of fresh water in the butts

Pattee, Lieutenant Colonel, USA"

"At least he's got his rain," said the major.

"He has, we all have – what do you think of the action? Nice little fight, eh? Well?" growled the general

"As you say, sir, '…a nice little fight'."

"Yes," said Sully, and thought to himself how very annoyed young Dimon would be when he heard talk of the action. Better that than dead!

12

Silver Leaf

(In the Wasichu Year of 1866 – November – Fort Riley)

To the west, the Republican River was edged with beaches of frost for the first time that fall; to the south, the Kansas ran like oily steel reflecting the doom sky; in the fort, streams of grey-blue smoke rose vertical in the chill of the morning from each of the barrack huts, and every soldier bemoaned the icy air. The outlying stands of timber were rich in hoarfrost so that chattering ravens were like flecks of coal as they made their senseless trips from one equally desirable branch to another.

"Bad winter come," said the Arikara scout, dragging his riding blanket closer about his broad shoulders. His warm breath was turned instantly grey about his face and then drifted to nothingness.

Sergeant Clinton had difficulty in catching what the Indian said, so he replied with a nod of his head and a curt, "Yes, guess so."

The scout was leading the two horses which had broken out of the stockade the night before, in a panic over something in the darkness. The commanding officer had called Clinton to go get them back; he asked to take the Arikara with him.

"What for?" asked Captain Benteen, his flowing grey hair billowing beneath his hat.

"Against me being me'self lost, sir!"

Clinton liked the company of the Arikara and had sponsored him as a scout, though he was supposed to have deserted back at Fort Rice. But no Indian could be told from the next. Anyway, it was a connection with Rice, which for Clinton had been a good posting. He had been disappointed when the Galvanized Yankee regiment was disbanded and regular troops started to head out. Even Pattee was to go elsewhere. Pattee had suddenly put his arm round the Irishman's shoulders, reaching up to do so.

"Damnit Clinton, you're as tall as the damned flagpole."

"That I am, almost."

"Clinton, how'd you like to get back in the cavalry, proper like?"

"Hell sir, I would like that."

They're forming some new regiments – 7th through to 10th I hear. How'd you like a posting?"

"Yes, sir."

"Right – I'm sending you over to Fort Riley. The 7th is going there. They say Custer'll be lieutenant colonel."

"That is real fine," said Clinton.

Pattee was pleased too for Custer was now junior to him in the lieutenant colonel's list – Pattee fancied he might get his star in the end.

Clinton felt six Christmases had come with the posting. Five weeks later he was at Fort Riley, ahead of Custer, but arriving at the same time as the senior captain who was in temporary command. Being a veteran, Clinton was well received by the temporary commander, Captain Benteen. Benteen went through the young sergeant's records and was impressed.

The lad had been with General Custer in the war, and then fighting Indians; he even knew the department commander, Sheridan. He had served with one of them damned Galvanized Yankee outfits and then volunteered for the regulars when his regiment was mustered out up north. Been at Sand Creek. Very interesting. Keen as mustard, that was obvious. He'd clearly fit into the 7th Cavalry. Benteen wrote him into the roll as a substantive sergeant in Company H.

The arrival of Benteen's Company H had brought the newly formed 7th Cavalry, United States Army, up to strength. Now they awaited the arrival of their first commanding officer; when Benteen's temporary command would cease.

The organisation of the post-war Army called for a Colonel of the Regiment, more as a figurehead, and a lieutenant colonel in field command. The 7th was proud to have Andrew Jackson Smith, brevet major general, as their colonel – one of the few Union cavalry leaders to beat that old Reb Nathan B.Forrest – stopped him dead at Tupelo back in '64. Even more exciting to the men was the knowledge that the famed Boy General Custer, was to be the lieutenant colonel in the field. He held the brevet rank of major general too – but of volunteers, which placed him junior to Smith's regular brevet.

"Eagle chief come," said the Arikara.

"What?"

"EAGLE CHIEF COME!" the Arikara shouted at the stupid Wasichu who could not understand his own tongue.

"Silver leaf chief!" corrected Clinton as he realised that the Indian was talking about the rank insignia of the commanding officer.

"New colonel is a silver leaf chief, no eagle chief!" he added for emphasis.

The Arikara looked blank.

"Me sergeant, you scout, him silver leaf!" Clinton pointed to the strips on his arm. "Me three stripe chief, little war chief."

"Me Little Knife!"

"Ah, me still Clinton – Jo!"

"Hello Still Clinton Jo!"

"No – Jo Clinton!"

"You say, 'Still Clinton – Jo!'"

"No – me Jo Clinton. Me American, me teach you English."

The Wasichu were clearly insane, American but their language was English. It was like saying the Arikara speak Comanche. Little Knife was careful to appear stupid for he had learned much more English from Frank Partridge than he cared to reveal.

They eased their horses closer to the fort, keeping a tight grip on the ropes of the recovered mounts. The gloomy entrance to sprawling Fort Riley emerged from the cold autumn mist. They saw that the regiment was paraded outside the walls. Hell, there was some kind of inspection going on. They saw the guidon of a major general fluttering behind a group of officers. As they got closer they could make out Benteen with his greying hair, as ever, bulging from under his hat escorting a stiff backed man with the silver and gold of a general catching the occasional appearance of the sun out of breaking clouds. He had long hair too, golden blond. Clinton recognised him at once.

"New silver leaf come!" he declared to the Arikara, and kicked his horse into a trot so that they would track wide of the parade, close by the stands of timber to the west, and pass round the back of the fort to where the horses were stockaded. No sense in getting caught up in inspections.

Little Knife glanced at the tall figure of the silver leaf and wondered why it was that if he were a silver leaf he was showing as a two star chief. He shook his head in irritation.

)(X)(X)(

George Armstrong Custer was alone in his quarters. He sat back in a large wooden armchair – regulation issue to a commanding officer. Regulation issue – the war was really over! He stretched out his legs so that the blazing log fire heated the leather of his riding boots. He felt the heat ooze through his gold-seamed riding pants, into his pink long johns and finally caress his flesh. As the boots warmed he decided to leave them on. Damn! It was damned cold already, and only early November. Custer hated the cold. And he did *not* like Benteen.

They had never met before. There was something about Benteen that made Custer's flesh creep. He had the aura of the aristocrat about him, a cultured cynic with his hair turned grey too soon for his forty years, all coiling and curling from beneath his hat. With his curling hair he looked a mite too much like an old woman. There was a pipe in his mouth at all times and a smile on his face, a smile you could not get beyond. He also had cool blue eyes, and Custer did not like that at all. Custer had cool blue eyes.

Captain Benteen had commanded cavalry in the war too. At the close of the war he was given a coloured regiment for a spell, but with that also mustered out he was relieved to accept a posting as senior captain to the 7th. Private Green, his black servant, was all that was left of his previous command. The days of glory were over.

Custer had casually laid out the divisional log books of the 3rd Cavalry Division and many of his papers and listings. He reckoned to put Benteen in his place. He had shown Benteen the documents from when six thousand men stood at his back and the captain had smiled politely and said, "Most impressive... General." That damned blue-eyed sneering smile.

There had been a sickly pause before, "General."

Benteen should have been more impressed since he had never made a grade higher than brevet colonel. True he had on several occasions commanded a cavalry brigade and was known for his courage and extraordinary coolness under fire. He was offered the grade of major in the 10th Cavalry, one of the two new Negro cavalry regiments, but chose to go to his substantive rank of captain in the 7th. Maybe it was something to do with his father being a slave owner one time. In fact his whole family were Rebs. Custer had taken care to read up the records available on the man he was replacing, but who would remain within the command. And now he had shown what he was about – he had *grinned* at the sight of Custer's divisional papers, as if they were not worth a cent.

Well!

Well, Benteen was a captain and Custer was his colonel, and captains should not laugh at colonels, not if they wanted to stay captains. Custer reassured himself with that thought.

Benteen had not made much of a start either. The regiment was slack. They lacked sharpness. As Custer sat back he dreamed a series of parades, drills, patrols, standing orders, discipline. By the heavens – the 7th was going to be the finest cavalry regiment in the whole damned Army. He would have them drill at his command. Command.

He let his mind run, briefly, over the surge of power that had been his when thousands of young horsemen were dashing to his call. The 7th was just 700 – but what a sight they would be – the savages would know soon enough that Custer was out West – Custer and his 7th – the guidons fluttering in the western breeze and a regimental band in the lead, scouts ahead, a force to be reckoned with. He would make them go down in history. He intended to make his name anew with them.

He heard calls outside which announced that his first command had been obeyed. The regimental band was on parade outside his quarters beginning to strike up something jumpy. Custer had his own ideas on what tunes they would be playing. They would practice and practice so that they could play on the move. There would be no regiment like it in all America.

Custer got to his feet and picked up his gold-braided major general's hat, faltered for a moment, then placed it with the rest of his general's tunic. Instead he picked up his colonel's braided hat and moved towards the door. Let's see if Freddy Benteen laughs this time.

)( )( )( )( )(

In columns of four the 7th Cavalry came to a halt for night camp. Spring of '67 was slow in coming. Custer had been away in Washington on staff training and had come back to make himself a throne of tyranny. The regiment was sharp with his training routine, but the men were wearying of the constant training which seemed to be at nothing less than a war footing. And all that happened was that Indians slipped through their fingers. Custer seemed unaware of the rumblings, and was entirely wrapped up in himself. The trouble was he had never commanded a regiment before and was treating them like a division, like toy soldiers, like formations which had no feeling, which were numbers. He liked the Indian scouts though. As they halted one of them pointed at the colonel and said something, laughing.

"What did he call me?" asked Custer. Custer had an amused and quizzical expression on his face for, if he heard correctly, then the epithet was entirely inaccurate, for his behind felt like a sponge of burning chilli powder.

"Iron Ass!" Frank Partridge, chief of scouts, translated the words of the Arikara scout at his side.

"Well, I'll be damned if that ain't only a margin wide of the mark," grunted the colonel and with much effort to make his movements look smooth he swung his leg over the rear of his saddle and dropped to the grass.

"What's his name?" asked Custer, nodding at the Indian.

"Little Knife," smiled Partridge.

"Ain't he the scout whose got that pretty squaw with him? Came along with you that night back East."

"Snow-on-Her, General. You've got a good memory."

"That her name?"

"It is."

"They have a quaint way with names."

"Their names mean something. Ours have to be remembered for what we've done. Their names describe them or tell us what they've done – their names mean something."

"Got it. So what's Snow-on-Her mean?"

"No idea colonel."

"And Little Knife?"

"No idea."

"Well that's helpful."

"You'll have to ask them."

"Benteen!" called Custer, now appearing to lose interest in the Arikara. But both Frank Partridge and Little Knife followed the young commander, an almost respectful three paces behind, on horseback.

"Where did your name come from?" asked Frank in sweet Crow. Little Knife did not smile.

"Well?"

"It's an old name."

"So..."

The Arikara laughed.

"What you laughing at?"

"What the name described is not true any more."

Frank looked puzzled.

"I have a very big knife now!"

The senior captain approached and dropped from his horse. He did not move towards Custer, but awaited the colonel's approach.

Minutes earlier, they had ridden in between the rough encampment streets where small fires were already being lit against the chill of the spring night to come. The damned cold winter was over. Custer had hated it. Now the spring threatened never to really emerge from the melting snow and ice. But for the last three days there had been warm sun and the old white snow had all but disappeared. In the sheltered areas such as the flood plain where they were presently camped, the new grass was a couple of inches up; even the earth seemed to be drying out.

"Have the horses kept in close – but take the saddles off so that they can roll a piece." Custer spoke to Benteen over his shoulder, as if he were speaking to the air. "The men can make camp. We'll stay here over night."

"Will do," muttered Benteen, biting his tongue because he had already given orders to the effect of Custer's wishes. Custer thought he knew the lot. He knew a touch, and that was all. Benteen watched his commanding officer amble towards his tent, already being erected by a couple of troopers, and whispered to himself, "I've got to learn to love that bastard." He turned to watch the troopers carrying out the command.

Within seconds of the saddles being taken away the mounts were collapsing with grunts of joy and rolling in the fresh grass. There they were kicking legs, and scratching the unspeakable horse itchiness and dried sweat which had accumulated under the leather seating of the troopers, scratching by rolling and wriggling their backs on the earth. Benteen turned from them and watched Custer standing by his low hunting tent, Partridge and a scout still with him. Benteen shook his head and strolled towards his own quarters where the card table was sure to be readied by good old Green.

Custer's tent, already pitched by his servants, was large, easy for a man to stand in, even a tall man. Custer stood at the entrance and with his hands on his hips, stretched his back straight for all he was worth. He became aware of the scouts still standing there, on horse.

"So!" he said. *"Iron Ass* is it now? Was *Long Hair* – kinda liked that. Redskins fonda changin' names?"

The question was not directed at anyone.

"Names get given early," said Frank. "Then a brave does something real bold and he gets his name changed."

"Like bruisin' his asshole!" grunted Custer steadying himself to duck into the safety of his tent. He glanced at the Indian scout, "Well – thanks for the name, Bloody Knife."

"Me Little Knife."

"Damn me, so you are – getting mixed up with the new one just joined."

Frank was surprised. Here he was, chief of scouts, and knew nothing of it.

"Sorry, colonel, what was that?"

"Oh – yes, Mr. Partridge a batch of recruits came in with an experienced scout, name of Bloody Knife. Like the looks of him. He's to be the corporal."

"Well, thank you sir," smiled Frank Partridge, hiding his annoyance for the allocation of ranks should have been his.

"It's nothing, Captain Partridge."

"It would have been useful if I'd..."

"It's nothing, Captain, nothing." Custer turned on his heel and ducked into his tent.

"My Frank, I know of this Bloody Knife – him a heap of warrior who likes whiskey," said Little Knife, pulling at Frank's elbow.

"Bad man?"

"He's Arikara."

"Is he bad?"

Little Knife frowned and said, "He's Arikara."

Frank glanced over his shoulder, thought about it, and just shrugged.

)( )( )( )( )(

A sudden swoop of warm air wafted across the plains and through the woods, sending ripples on the broader expanses of the rivers. It killed the last of the snow, except in the high places. The sky was sweet blue and the troopers were happy with the return of warmth, even if it did waken empires of insects.

Half of the scouts had stripped down to breechcloths and oiled themselves against the flesh nippers. Custer astonished the troopers by ignoring this lack of uniform. The scouts blended with the landscape and out on patrol looked a lot less Army. The colonel liked his scouts more each passing day, enjoyed the quality of their horsemanship, the flow of their bodies which seemed to unite with their horses more closely than any trooper. But then most of them had been horseriding since the age of four or five, in some cases starting strapped to a horse. They could almost speak horse.

Two had especially caught his eye – the one with the chief of scouts and the new one, Corporal of Scouts Bloody Knife, older by several years than Partridge's young warrior.

Bloody Knife was very much the man, good looking for an older Redskin who tended to grow big noses and wrinkles and fat bellies, as far as Custer could see. Yes – Bloody Knife already had a strong nose. His body was running to fat but it was a sleek fatness with an even covering, like a coat. He rippled as he moved. The muscles shook as they might on a horse's flank when pestered by flies. Custer liked to watch him move. He was also a crack shot.

They said he had counted coup many times and the blood of scores of men were on his hands. Custer wondered how he himself scored against the man, and for a moment his mind slipped back to the numerous charges he had led in the war, the decisions he had made, the men lost on his order, the men killed by his command – all might be alive but for him. The colonel had certainly counted coup galore and had blood on his hands the equal of any of the infesting Redskins. Iron Ass could look any Redskin in the eye. The stumbling of his horse as it placed its leg into a prairie critter's hole, grunting and recovering without injury, pulled Custer's thoughts to the moment.

He was walking his horse on the right flank of his column, a full mile ahead of H Company – Benteen's – which had point that day. The terrain ahead was undulating, rising gradually about seven hundred feet above the greater expanse of the plains. Custer sensed that it was the dip slope of a long butte that would fall away to low land about a mile ahead. The essence of good cavalry command was to sense what the geography would do *ahead*. A cavalry man had to read the terrain. So far Custer had been right, always having a view of what the land would do before he got to it.

Custer reckoned that beyond the dip slope would be another slope, going down, then another either longer or shorter, scrub and tall grass covered, then there would be a creek. The rolling land, like some vast solid ocean appeared to go on for a marching eternity. This was an overpowering, dull, and magnificent country with a vast bowl of sky which seemed to rear upwards so powerfully it both sucked up the observer and pressed down at the same moment. And all the time there was a wind, at best a breeze, but usually strong enough to lift a scarf away from the face when a man's mount was at rest.

But it was the awesome space, a huge surround of space, with, at times, nothing else whatsoever that impressed the colonel. Custer wondered if it would drive him mad, that and the wind. He wanted to get used to it, and hoped to do so. There was a sudden break in the continuity of view.

A group of riders appeared ahead, waving, frantically waving.

Custer considered his eyes were as good as they were blue and saw that they were Arikara scouts, and were his own, Bloody Knife in the lead.

He also noticed Little Knife with a lavish trailing sash which dropped from his shoulders where a slit in it allowed his neck to contain it to his body. The sash, made of regular strips of hide, linked at intervals, marked by fringes of hide strips, threatened to get entangled in the legs of his horse, but never did. The colonel felt a curious surge of pleasure at the sight of his savages; for all the world, knights without armour.

Custer flicked the flanks of this horse with spur tips and it surged forward at the loosening of the rein and his matching command. Within moments he was with his scouts and saw smiles on their faces. From the left three more scouts were coming in with Frank

Partridge in the lead. In an almost choreographed moment the standing Indians, the colonel and Frank Partridge's little outfit came together at the brow of the slow slope, before it dipped.

"Cheyenne hunting party ahead!" said Partridge.

"Numbers?"

"Ten!"

With a burst of energy the colonel's horse was spurred forward and he was gone.

"Holy Moses!" shouted Frank Partridge. "Git with him!"

The chief of scouts swept his hand across the group of eight Arikara, and they were off, with Little Knife and Bloody Knife in the lead – chasing their silver leaf chief. Frank spurred down the hill towards the approaching column to get them moving up in support.

Within a mile and a half the trap was sprung. Out of a thicket of shrub and half dead timber a party of twenty Cheyennes appeared, hitting the group racing after Custer in the flank, downing two of the Scouts and cutting off the colonel. Little Knife saw Silver Leaf Chief Long Hair pull his horse down and fall from the saddle in a single movement.

"Come on!" he heard Bloody Knife call and the older man kicked his pony towards the colonel. Little Knife followed.

He saw that the colonel had a carbine in his hands and was already behind his kicking horse as sixteen or so of the Cheyennes were racing towards him, likely to run him down. Three shots rang out in quick succession. One of the Cheyennes went down, his horse giving a mortal scream.

The Cheyenne rider rolled clear and was immediately picked up between two other riders. The colonel's carbine cracked again and one of the Cheyenne rolled backwards in his Indian-style saddle as if to perform a riding trick, only to turn away clutching his shoulder. Bloody Knife had reached the colonel and leapt from his pony. The pony raced away towards the Cheyennes and one of them pulled away after it.

Little Knife kicked his pony forward. Even as he did so he was aware that his brother scouts had turned away and fled.

Little Knife knew that the rest of the Wasichu warriors would be close behind. He would distract the attackers, already wheeling to return to the kill. Little Knife pulled his pony to a halt as soon as he was between the Cheyennes and Custer and Bloody Knife. He held his lance in the language of a challenge and with his battle cry he threw himself off his horse about fifty yards in front of the colonel. He could hear the Cheyennes yelling; "Now you're going to die, Arikara coward!"

"I'll kill you all!" screamed back Little Knife, thinking that this was not a good day to die. An intense feeling ran through his veins that he would live, count coup, kill Cheyenne. This was a good day to live.

"Come back here!" He heard a yell from Bloody Knife. Little Knife became deaf.

The Cheyennes were halted at the challenge and then began to trot round in a distant but decreasing circle. Their movement and their jeers and the waving of their horses' heads gave the impression that their horses were laughing. There was a double *crack-crack* as he heard the colonel and Bloody Knife fire and their bullets passed by his head on their way towards his taunters.

One of their horses pitched forward, threw its rider, and then tried to rise up only to go into a collapse as its legs crumpled. Its rider struggled to his feet and began to hurl Cheyenne abuse at Little Knife.

"I'm here, Cheyenne woman!" screamed Little Knife.

Another round from the colonel cracked overhead.

Seemingly unconcerned the Cheyennes moved in closer. Little Knife saw that they were all young warriors – dangerous, but stupid. He would take scalps today, for sure. Two were riding, standing on their horses, yelling at the colonel that it was a Wasichu death day. Another horse went down, the standing youth being tossed into the undergrowth as the horse pranced in death. The taunts turned to anger. The colonel was targeting the horses.

The Cheyennes scattered and withdrew out of effective range. Little Knife could see them arguing, then they began to form into a rough line. Three of them began as if to charge towards him, excited. The rest followed. This was disgraceful, thought Little Knife. – for Little Knife had challenged them one by one. The Cheyennes had no courage. They had to do it together.

Little Knife drove his spear into the end of the long extension of his battle sash. He was trapped. Only a friend could rescue him or he would stand and die, or he would kill them all. He had announced his intention to die fighting, but knew that many

Wasichu were not far away and he was protecting their silver leaf chief. They would come. Little Knife felt sure this was not the day, but when he saw the double line of Cheyenne thundering towards him his mouth went dry.

"I stand and die," he declared to *Wakantanka* who, Little Knife hoped, was listening with appreciation.

The Cheyennes surged round him, leaning towards him to touch him, to count coup on one who was soon to die. As they did so one of them spun from the back of his pony as a bullet from the colonel or Bloody Knife passed through his rib cage and chewed up his beating heart. His squeal of pain was very short for the young man was dead before he hit the ground.

Little Knife stood firm with his small shield in his left hand and a long hunting knife with a bear's thigh bone turned into a firmly fixed handle in his right hand. His knuckles were white with the grip. The Cheyennes, wavering, rode round him. They seemed to be startled each time the colonel fired. Much of his shooting was to no avail since the riders made poor targets, but even so too many hot bullets were finding their targets. They should have ridden over this filthy Arikara and gone straight for the Wasichu.

Then two of the Cheyennes came hurtling forward. Both had lances and were going to pass him on either side. Little Knife saw that a third rider was behind them, also racing in. As the pair were about to strike the Arikara he threw himself forward and down. Both lances passed over him. The twin horses, seeing the fallen Indian, flew over him. He was not touched by lance or hoof and was on his feet in a moment.

The third rider was upon him, a very young one, and so close he was unable to draw back his lance for a strike. Little Knife's blade slashed through his thigh and he felt the *crack* of its edge cutting into bone. The rider, in attempting to avoid the cut, toppled sideways, fought for his balance, but was down. His horse sped past the colonel and was away with wild excitement.

The first pair of riders were coming back at speed, yelling to their colleagues to go for the Wasichu. Instead they all turned towards the Arikara. He was too brave. He had to die.

Little Knife turned to face them. As they thundered in they suddenly veered away from Little Knife and on to the fallen Cheyenne who was already on his feet but unable to run. They passed either side of him and leaning down scooped him up, one to each arm. But he slipped from their gasp. The two went away towards the rest of the band, whooping derision at the lone Arikara to whom they would soon return. They had skilfully kept the murderous Arikara away from their injured friend. But now they had dropped him.

The sound of bugles caused Little Knife to look behind him and he saw a mass of horse soldiers galloping towards them. There was a flurry of blue-white smoke as a dozen of them fired in the direction of the Cheyennes who were now fleeing. None fell. The range was too great. It was over.

As Benteen's men came up they were already reining in. The horses were winded, tired from the long march, blown by the sudden sprint up the long hill and the furious ride down the reverse slope only to face two more such ventures before they came in sight of their colonel at bay.

"No need to chase them," said Custer, finding it difficult to hold the barrel of his carbine, almost red-hot.

Benteen looked at him coldly, thought to ignore him, then with forced politeness, "You're right colonel, the mounts are blown."

Frank Partridge ambled over on a completely exhausted horse. He dropped from the saddle, and immediately loosened the girth to help un-wind the animal.

Suddenly Bloody Knife sprinted by Little Knife, "Come, come!"

Little Knife jerked his lance out of the ground and followed the older man. He ran straight to the young Cheyenne who had been left behind.

As Little Knife came up to the older Arikara he was holding the young Cheyenne by the throat.

"Do not kill me," said the youth, who was Running White Horse.

The blow from Little Knife's blade had wrecked the muscles in the young man's thigh, and cracked the great bone. There was much blood. Bloody Knife placed one foot on the youth's throat and the other on his damaged leg – the pain kept him in position like a trapped snake. His strength was ebbing fast. The scream as Bloody Knife's blade took the scalp stopped Little Knife in his tracks.

The youth was sobbing as Bloody Knife then took hold of the youth's hand and cut round the wrist to the bone.

"I will die," gasped the Cheyenne. "Why kill me like this...?"

"It's a good day," growled Bloody Knife.

He took the other wrist and severed the hand completely as the youth screamed and writhed. He threw it to Little Knife.

"Trophy!"

The young Cheyenne shuddered, a look of bewildered terror on his face, and passed through the screen without his hand.

Bloody Knife took up the scalp, attached it blood-dripping to the hip of his belt and said, "Come!"

Little Knife looked at the man who shared his tribal blood. He looked at the broad back as he sauntered away towards the Wasichu soldiers. He must let Frank Partridge know that even though he was Arikara... he was bad. He stared at the young Cheyenne. Carefully he knelt and pushed the hand back where it belonged and whispered to *Wakantanka*, "Let him use it on the other side."

Little Knife began to walk back to the Wasichu.

)( )( )( )( )(

Custer swallowed hard when Bloody Knife swaggered up and said, "Good scalp for colonel." Then he just stood there, holding it out, so Custer said, "Well done! You can keep it."

Bloody Knife smiled and hung the scalp back on his hip.

"Mr. Partridge," said Custer, easing the hammer back on his Spencer and holstering it as his horse got back to its feet, on command, grumbling like some eastern camel, "Mr. Partridge did you see what that young scout did?"

Frank Partridge looked across at the approaching Little Knife. Frank had seen him pull his lance from out of his sash and knew the significance. He felt glad he'd brought the troopers up in time.

Beyond the young Arikara the fleeing Cheyennes were moving along a distant bluff, except for a pair stopped on the skyline, seeming to call the Wasichu on to a fresh chase.

"Looks like he was ready to die! That's what they do, Colonel," said Partridge.

"Damn near saved my life!" said Custer.

Partridge nodded.

Benteen looked on, a faint smile playing on his lips.

269

"What do they call him? I do not recall... tell me once more," muttered Custer, dusting himself down.

"That there's Little Knife."

Little Knife was by now walking towards the colonel. He paused, bent, and wiped his hands in the grass. His torso was running with sweat, his heart was still racing, his mouth was dry.

"You should be called Bloody Knife the Second," declared the colonel.

"Hey – Little Knife!" called Partridge in Caddoan-Arikara, "Silver-Leaf-Named-Long Hair says you are no longer Little Knife – you are Bloody Knife."

Little Knife thought about it.

"No – only *he* is Bloody Knife," said Little Knife, pointing at the older man.

Bloody Knife smiled, coldly, wondering where the hand was; this was a squeamish one this young Arikara – he did not deserve such a name as his.

13

The Good Medicine Flag

(1868 in the Sioux Moon of the Falling Leaves)

Yellow Hair woke to the scent of another's breath.

Into the blackness of the teepee the embers of the central fire cast a glow from beneath the red-grey covering of hot wood dust. The forty-five winters winkte-warrior, he who was the holder of stories in his head and Keeper Of The Arrows, twisted his ageing bones and reached into the cold air for fresh fuel.

He poked the fire with a half-burned aspen twig to catch the air. Reaching out from the warmth of his blankets he laid sticks so that they crackled in their dryness. Small flames appeared, licking away the crinkled bark. Lice and beetles, coma cold, suddenly jerked to life by heat, threw themselves into the bright embers, hissing to death. Sparks of light broke the shadows of darkness on the walls of hide. As Yellow Hair did these things and saw these things, thinking nothing of them, he felt a human nakedness at his side.

Turning back to re-enter the warmth of the buffalo blankets he looked at the shape which was close to where his own head would lie. He saw a vague image, a head with flowing hair, and heard the gentle snore of a youth. White Hawk, vulnerable in his sleep but at peace, lay there. The widow Sweet Water lay sleeping beyond the fire.

The older man smiled, and shrank down into the skins. He turned the warmth of his back towards the sleeping youth who had evidently crept from his own pitch on the other side of the teepee to enter the warmth of his fathers' blankets, without the old warrior knowing.

"Perhaps I shall beat him after the sun is up," considered Yellow Hair, "for his impudence."

Then as the youthful body turned and arms enfolded his old broad shoulders and he felt the shape snuggle up to him in utter trust, he smiled in the gloom. The old hungers were there but his love for White Hawk transcended them. He simply lay and enjoyed the closeness and certainty of the boy's simple affection. Briefly he stared at the apex of the gut-sewn buffalo skins which protected them from frozen fingers. As he watched the coils of smoke escaping into the outside cold his eyes closed. They were all safe inside this warm place.

Outside the ice devil ruled. Inside were the embers, the air-heat of the people, warmth. They were safe from the freezing touch of the winter dealer in death. The ice hand still had time enough, and more, to search out their bones, but they had good stocks of fuel, were surrounded by more, good water was to hand and a plentiful supply of meat was stored from the hunting season. For the moment they were secure from winter's greed. Time meant nothing for them other than it being a night in the long season of winter. Had they been white-eye men they would have known that it was just before dawn on the 27th November 1868.

Yellow Hair's eyes opened.

He found that he could no longer sleep despite the pleasure of the warmth. With his eyes still open he had heard a dog bark. It was not a careless bark or a snap of anger, a warning to some other restless hound. Or was it? Then he heard a baby cry. The dog did not bark again. Yellow Hair's senses relaxed once more.

His thoughts began to dwell on the wise words of his good friend, his warrior brother, Chief Black Kettle, whose camp this was, close by the river called Washita. This was a safe place. This was a good place to be, nestled down, protected by the hills, running water close by, despite the frost which edged the stream with pack ice. The winter was going to be a hard one yet – his wounds told him so. The broad scar on his face, which still marked the blow from a Crow club, ached: throbbed slightly, enough to worry the edge of dreams. Even so, it was only the cold that threatened, for the hunting had been good that summer. There would be no hunger this year. There was no fever. The longknives were far away.

Soldier men did not fight in the winter. They were known for that. But Yellow Hair was disturbed at the thought of them. There had been dreams forming on the edges of his thoughts each dark night, for the scar did not always throb. Yet the mind-pictures had been imperfect. They were wonder-dreams which lacked focus. Half dreams, not visions. He saw them when he slept and could not understand them. This troubled him. Each time it was the same.

The half men were there and he -Yellow Hair of a hundred battles – was running through water, or was it snow? Running and running but making no progress. Behind him, always came a slashing longknife warrior with blazing eyes on a horse with wings of fire. The wings of fire: that was the mystery of it.

In the dream Yellow Hair could run as well as when he was a youth, chasing after the buffalo, the air streaming in his face, leaping through the long grass. That was how it felt. That part of the dream was good. But it always changed.

Suddenly he was not running. At each step, fast or slow, the blade warrior on the steaming horse was coming closer. This part was very bad, in the dream. Yellow Hair fought to wake. He felt the pounding of the horse behind him. He ran like an old man; ran, but made no progress. Yellow Hair felt the slash of steel across his back, in the dream, for the first time. He woke again, covered in a film of sweat.

He woke. It *was* a dream. He had slept. He had dreamed. He had dreamed *the* dream. It had come again. He had not been awake. Yet it was real. The spirits of the world that lay just beyond the real world, behind it, through the protective skin of death, had searched him out once more – to terrorise, to warn. But it was not clear. He shuddered. The meaning was not clear. Yellow Hair was no longer the receiver of visions. Now, he thought to himself, I am an old man. Waves of sadness swept over him.

The startled movement of his body in the skins, as he had leapt out of the dream, out of the world behind this world, in his terror, had disturbed the boy. Boy! He was all of fourteen winters. How fast the winters came, but they also went.

Yellow Hair felt the youthful hands caress him and the body move closer still. In the blanket-blanket, in the darkness-darkness, in the warm-warmth, his gnarled hand sought out the shoulder of the boy and he touched it. He gently squeezed it in reassurance at the moment an explosion of gunfire erupted into his head.

Screams came and dogs yelped and gunfire followed gunfire, and more gunfire ripped the air.

There also came the sound of many horses, shod horses.

Naked, old Yellow Hair was on his feet, startled White Hawk also. At his side in the darkness there was a crack and splat and he felt hot things come splashing over him with force, unexpected, unreal, hitting him in the darkness. Sweet Water was thrown against him so that he fell with her in his arms and in reaching to touch her face found a kind of heat, like cooked food. He felt no face beneath his fingertips. Instead there was a ragged flesh-hot terrain. Meat.

He knew she had a terrible wound and that perhaps she was already on her way to the good hunting places of the spirit lands, already joining her husband and her sons. He struggled beneath her. With his strength, all of it, he cast her to one side, unmoving. She was gone. Safe now. Outside he could hear the voice of Black Kettle shouting.

In a moment he and White Hawk were both outside and were aware of but ignored the new sun, which was butchering the eastern tree-lined sky. Horses ran, and dogs fought dogs knowing there was threat, each protecting its teepee, assuming there were intruding hounds all about, panicking.

Warriors, almost all half dressed, or with nothing upon them at all, few with weapons, raced this way and that. Horses were everywhere. Men on them. Firing guns. Soldiers. A soldier was off his horse, on his knee aiming at Swift Deer, the four winter's child of the next lodge, which was burning. He fired, and missed, and the little one was running away towards the river. More horsemen came passing by, firing like demons into every teepee. Men were cut down as they dived from the entrances, or crawled from under their hides. The kneeling soldier was reloading.

A black horse, its eyes white with fear, came towards them, its rider firing at them with a hand gun. The thump of air that touched the face of Yellow Hair was good news. The man had missed. Yellow Hair snatched at the gun-holding hand as it came towards him and held the man.

The moving power of the horse and the strength of the man was too much and Yellow Hair was flying through the air and smashed into the side of his own teepee, to roll and fall into the soft snow. Behind him in the light of burning hides the kneeling man fired and missed again and Swift Deer just kept running.

A second soldier threw himself from his horse a little way beyond his kneeling comrade. He threw his shooting stick to his shoulder and fired at the child.

Yet another soldier was hurtling towards White Hawk, who snatched a bow from nowhere as he rolled in the snow towards

274

Yellow Hair. White Hawk thrust the useless bow into the old man's hand and was running back to be in front of the next of the soldier horses – to face them.

A horse came from out of the half-light, rushing. The great Elk Dog, its soldier man shouting and firing into the nearest lodge, appeared to smash White Hawk to the ground, plunged over him and was gone. Almost. But the boy was up at once. He had thrown himself beneath the horse; the legs and hooves had missed, save one. Its left front hoof touched the boy, the most minute of touches; yet that touch, together with the gathered frozen snow on the horse's fetlocks had been enough for it to cross its legs at the gallop and go hurtling over its own head throwing the rider out of the saddle. The horse was up and was gone, away into the darkness and confusion, screaming.

At that moment, both kneeling soldiers, close by, fired. Swift Deer of five summers, come the summer season, was thrown about by the impact – like a doll – and down he flopped, infant spine shot through, heart ripped out. No pain, no dreams, no hunting in the buffalo summers, no unborn woman to moan beneath his manhood of the future years. All stolen. White Hawk searched for a weapon and as he did so he saw the high chief.

Black Kettle stood there with his wife, transfixed. He had seen it happen to the infant and his hopes were slaughtered by what he saw. He also saw his own son shooting already and bringing down a soldier, fifteen years, but a warrior now.

Old man old man. Near seventy years. She, old woman old, with gashes from another morning of dread death dawn, not four years before. Seven holes in her then, when the priest-butcher Chivington led his drunken scum to murder sleeping children in the night, but the Great Spirit smiled and kissed her that time; now her holes and broken bones were stiffened and repaired and filled with life. She watched him, her man, and saw what he saw and knew that death had come.

He was doing a curious thing, with death all around; he was signalling as might a chief with a buffalo robe signal a change of charge to his braves at war, or cause his hunting party to encircle a herd of buffalo. He was not holding a buffalo robe.

He was waving the flag of America. He had been given the flag again. The sacred flag again. The protection flag again. The Good Medicine Flag again.

"Whilst this flag flies you and your people are safe!" They were the honour words of but a few days before. The men with flowing white hair and silver beards, with smiles of assurance and some very good gifts had also given the honour words with the flag.

They said, "This is the flag of all the nations, all the states, all Americans. It is a stopper of bullets, a peace flag for a peace chief." So they said. It was a mighty present to be given, also to receive. Black Kettle had swelled with pride at the taking of it once more.

Now the Wasichu were riding him down. This was no talk. Their presents this dawn were the wasps of death, balls from soldier guns. He threw the flag to the red snow earth.

He began to flee. He stopped.

He was a warrior. Frantic, with old woman old, hanging on to his arm like his mother, he looked round. His horse was there, prancing to the gunfire, tethered by his peace chief's teepee.

He called his horse. Ears back it obeyed. Good horse, good horse of plenty fights.

Old man old man. Old woman old woman.

He helped her up behind him in the growing flames of his safe place.

White Hawk saw this as he searched for weapons, saw it out of the corner of his eye, and wondered that the great chief would not fight, but seemed to turn to run away. White Hawk found a broken lance and picked it up. He spun, to search for a wicked Wasichu.

White Hawk found the soldier whose horse had gone over. He was moaning on the snow soft earth. One leg was strangely bent, a ridiculous angle, broken on the snow.

This man from Maine, broken legged and mean, saw a naked boy with cold-shrivelled jewels and a black tuft of hair above them to show he was not a child. He still held his Colt in his hand. He pointed it at the boy. The boy, his back to the east, had sunrise round his head. Face beautiful. A kid. Filthy savage. Blow it to bits. *Click.*

"Shit!" The man from Maine looked at his Colt in fury, and then looked up for his last time.

Boy running, running forward. Lance in hand.

The soldier, as he lay back on the sodden snow, felt the blade rush into his lower jaw, under his chin. He was surprised at the lack of pain. For but a second he sensed it travel behind his tongue. As it swept its flint head up into his soft brain he felt nothing, for he was already dead, killed by a youth. More horses coming. Soldiers, soldiers coming.

White Hawk was running now and saw that old Yellow Hair was up. The old man was still holding the bow without an arrow. He also ran. He saw the high chief and followed. Black Kettle was ahead, in the growing light, riding for the river, his old old wife behind him and the cracking of bullets like summer bees coming close and fast, filled the air with their anger and death-sting threat.

Black Kettle's horse entered the freezing mud of the river's edge. Old woman, old, she fell screaming, as bullets went through her, chipping, slashing, cutting, bursting, spurting – so she fell.

He who was a warrior and a peace chief, he who had enough honour to believe in the sacred flag – for the white chief had said it was a thing of truth and a powerful medicine – pulled up his horse. He hesitated in his flight.

He began to turn his horse, in his love of she who shared his blankets, thinking to retrieve her. Many bullets hit him and brought down his horse dead in its tracks. His master was dead before they both hit the mud. They all three lay dead.

Soldier men were immediately trampling over them in their pursuit of others. As they did so their horses were streaming sweat-hot air and nostril smoke which, on capturing the red sun of the dawn, seemed to form into wings of fire.

Yellow Hair was in the same soft marsh of willows, struck to stillness as he looked at the heap of death and the oncoming horses. White Hawk's hand suddenly snatched his fist and pulled him away, pulled him into a frantic run. White Hawk realised that they were both naked but he felt no cold.

"Run!" cried Yellow Hair, as they ran. "There are wings of fire on the horses – they are here!"

It was never clear who held the hand of whom from then on. They simply ran together, that bloody dawn. They ran from death and the slaughter of the horses behind them. They did not see the chief of those who came with the dawn laughing, as he shot the cringing dogs who stayed faithful to the encampment, stood by their lodges, their tails between their legs – not knowing what to do. Some thought to follow the fleeing people, but they stayed with their lodges and died.

The two saw nothing more of the old and young, men and women, nor thought of the dogs. It was too late. They ran on through the snow. They ran and they ran. They heard the screams. They heard the shots. They saw massacre only in the fears within their heads. They collapsed into a drift and saved their lives, as moments later a bunch of soldiers led by a young yellow leaf chief, shouting his men on, crumpled through nearby frozen snow at a clumsy gallop, with the sun at their backs.

Panting, Yellow Hair snatched the boy to him in the snow and hugged him so that the boy thought his ribs would break. "Remember this dawn until you die, and avenge it!" snarled the old warrior. "Come!"

They set off in the tracks of the soldiers, trotting as if they were on a long journey in search of visions. But their panting lungs and beating hearts settled into a rhythm and despite the ice which ruled the air they moved steadily forward, the old man leading the way. Though old, he was a teacher of the fighting arts and a carrier of stories. The boy was but fourteen, so they were matched for speed.

"Why chase them?" gasped the boy. "Do we look to die?"

"To kill!" snapped back the old man. "Stop!"

They stopped. The old man knelt to steady himself. The boy was by his side.

"Listen!" said the old man, holding his breath for a moment, despite the pain, the urge to gasp. Breathing killed the power of the ear, so for a moment he controlled his panting and hearing returned.

Far behind was the sound of heavy gunfire hanging on the cold clear air as the destruction continued, drifting from where Black Kettle's safe place had been.

"If we hear that – so do they of a thousand teepees!"

Yellow Hair pointed towards where the group of galloping soldiers had gone. Not a mile away, directly in their path, lay the rest of the gathered tribes. They were there part by custom, part by the call of hunters and the wolf scouts, lone men who consult the spirits in the forest and carry news of where is the best place for winter camp. The nations were together for the protection of numbers. There was a fine gathering there, a thousand lodges. Black Kettle's people had pitched on the outer horn of a four-mile curve of lodges. The Wasichu had attacked a city not a village.

Much of the rest of the Southern Cheyenne had raised their lodges along the valley. There were Arapahos too, many Kiowas; even Comanches and Prairie Apaches out of the reservations. At least a thousand warriors had been woken, by the sound of gunfire.

They thought only of the protection of the women and children, perhaps of a little glory too. But even now they would be cutting through the snow and willow trees surging in the opposite direction, certain to meet the soldiers. Instead of fearful quarries the longknives would be hit by hornets. There was a sudden rattle of gunfire ahead.

The man and boy did not have far to go. They saw, now in full light, the soldiers were already off their horses. Their animals were scattered or down, kicking or still. Round the closed circle of men, lying heels together in defiance, there crawled and galloped an ocean of braves. The soldiers died one by one, some with courage some with unimaginable fear. The braves rushed in to take their souls.

It was then that Yellow Hair and the boy appeared, like ghosts out of the sunrise, walking as if dead, walking hard, but stumbling in the snow-covered undergrowth. It was the absurdity of their total nakedness in that bitter morning air that made brave men stand aside.

One warrior of the Southern Cheyenne recognised Yellow Hair and, jumping from his pony, snatched the steaming blanket from its back and gave it to him. The old man let it drop into the snow. Instead he held out his hand. From his mind there passed a message and the knife of the Southern Cheyenne was placed in the hand of Yellow Hair. They stood at the circle of the dead, and near dead, troopers. The action had been swift. They paused, and as they did so it was a young Kiowa who placed his blade in the hands of the boy.

Although the scalping and the stripping was already begun, they all stood aside and screamed encouragement, as Yellow Hand with White Hawk, ice in their hearts, noticing the tongues of cold on their flesh for the first time, went to work. They ensured that not one of these men of morning murder would take their manhood into their own paradise, except in their mouths.

They took out the bone-like apple in the Wasichu's throats and threw them bloody in the snow; dead eyes were gouged and placed outside the head, grotesquely staring. All the time Yellow Hair wished they were alive to feel it all, but at least they would not be able to enjoy their own Promised Land beyond touches to the skin – they would be blind for eternity, without voice and without their organs of joy.

Meanwhile scores of warriors raced by, heading for the sound of gunfire and the columns of smoke, which rose steeply on the morning air above the Black Kettle village. There were many more longknives to kill.

Afterwards, shivering, both accepted horse-warmed blankets and went forward to the camps of their good friends. Not for some time, not until the chattering of their teeth stopped, and their frozen tears had melted, were they able to tell their story. But when they did, the spirits of Black Kettle and his old old wife lived again for a moment, only to fall again with the telling. At least *they* would never have to return to this land of the real people awash with Wasichu lies. They would not return to this place, where dawn conspired with evil to paint the white snow red.

14

The Death of Dogs

(The same bloody day, but earlier)

Benteen was alone. He had checked the pickets and now stood with his back to his resting battalion. Looking out it was as if he were lost in the wilderness, not a soul in sight. He closed his mind to the muttering of men behind and wondered what it would be like to be in this place, really alone. He would have to be a Redskin to survive.

Snow was gathering on his chest. The brim of his hat was down so that his head had to rise to peer beneath it, only to see a thinly wooded vista through large wind-carried flakes. Earlier in the day he had never seen such huge flakes, now they were less impressive. Behind him his battalion of three companies of the 7th Cavalry was resting, universally grumbling at the weather, cutting and scraping the accumulated snow from their horses' hooves. The packed snow had turned to ice and was making the horses stumble. It was their turn to bring up the rear, protecting the wagons and packhorses. Consequently they were blind to the expected action at the head of the column. That always made them nervous. It made Benteen very nervous. He shivered.

His hands were in his greatcoat pockets, seeking the warmth from himself, buried deeper beneath the thick wool cloth. The collar was edged with bearskin and its fur ruffled in the wind; fresh flecks of snow were alighting, then blown away, continuously.

Within his head he cursed his commanding officer, likening him to the rear orifice of a buffalo with dietary problems. It was the fool's clear intention to divide the command, yet again. Ahead was a village of unknown size in unknown terrain, with unknown numbers of the enemy. Ahead there were savages to be admired for their courage and hated for their butchery of the dead; worse, their evilness with the dying. No reconnaissance had been made, other than Custer's own. Custer's notion of reconnaissance was to glance and charge at once at whatever might or might not be there. Benteen wished he knew the hell what was going on.

To Benteen's right a dog yelped. A sudden, furious fight broke out between one of Custer's hounds and another that had attached itself to the soldiers ever since leaving Camp Supply. They had trotted out to the ripple of 'Garry Owen' – damn the sound of it, every God damned night. "What?" asked Benteen of the icy wind pulling at his face from the distant sunset. "What *am* I doing here?"

"Watchin' the night, Colonel?"

Benteen knew someone had come up behind, despite the wind blowing the sound back into the trees. He did not know it was Trooper Green until he heard the deep sweet sound of the Negro's voice.

Green had addressed his captain by his Civil War brevet rank of colonel. It amused Benteen, but did not serve to flatter him. Green had been his servant in that conflict and never failed to address him so. Benteen had commanded a full brigade in battle, brilliantly, and was loved by his men beyond measure. Trusted. Respected. They were proud of their leader and knew him to be a great card player with a smile as impenetrable as the meanest poker face. And he could drink. He was not a drunk, but he could drink a dried out mountain man under the table. But it was not so much that, as the way he was steady under fire. He did not seem to care that there were bullets in the air. Maybe that was why shot never hit him; they took out his horses, but his own life was charmed.

Not a trooper forgot how Benteen, when his 10th Missouri failed to advance on some ill used guns, had galloped with sword drawn backwards and forwards across the front between the opposing sides until their courage returned and the whole brigade swept forward and took the positions and the guns.

His men were not in awe of him – they simply belonged to him, for he led from the front. So did Custer. But Benteen led them for their safety; Custer led them for his own glory. With Custer they were drawn towards the gates of jeopardy as well as glory. With Benteen they were secure, and might find glory. The styles of both commanders had had their place in the Eastern War. This chasing and worrying of the Indians was a different war; a war that called for more caution than pursuit of glory. There was more to this business than capturing artillery; even though not a cannon was fired at Benteen's command that he did not capture.

Benteen smiled as he thought of that, for it was a truth. It was exactly the same thing that Custer had boasted, about his own outfit, when they first met at Fort Rice. Benteen knew his own claim was true. All Custer had left of his command was his blasted papers. At least Benteen had Green.

"You, is it?"

"Yes Sir."

"Damn cold, Mistah!"

"Sure is, Colonel sir."

Silence. Green was hanging around for some reason, shuffling his feet.

"Something on your mind, Green?"

"Sir, the General says we must kill the dogs."

Benteen said nothing.

"All of them. They all gotta go."

"His an' all?" Benteen faced the black man with the question

All he could see were eyes peering out of a scarf wrapped round and round his grizzled features, leaving those eyes, looking young and bright. Brilliant flakes touched his black brows, paused, then began to melt. Benteen knew the black man had a cur of his own. He was attached to it.

"All?"

"That's right, Colonel!"

"Gawd damn!" said Benteen. "Why, I do declare our sweet natured old Goldilocks is using his brain instead of his little old toe nails."

But Green bit his lip beneath his scarf.

A screech rather than a howl carried against the wind.

"They've started then! I heard no shot. He *is* being very clever. I declare I am surprised he is not shooting them, seeing as how he intends, it is my certain guess, to slaughter the curs to make them less noisome. Shoot 'em to make 'em quiet, in the face of the enemy, is what I would expect of him, but the dear general is getting it right for once."

"He intends they should not alert the village, Colonel. We have to use blades, sir!"

"Crossed my old mind, son, kinda struck me that way."

"I's already gone done mine." Green said it almost as an afterthought to a priest – saving the worst sin until last.

"Have you now?"

"He went very quiet," said Green.

Benteen did not speak, but let the man tell him: "I got him close and said things to him. Held him tight. Cut his throat quick. Not a sound – kinda trusted me. Animals is like that. You know what, Colonel?"

"What?"

"Dogs trust ya 'cause they don't tell lies theirselves."

Benteen nodded.

"You know what, Colonel?"

Benteen's eyes called for the next words.

"He was real warm of a night."

"Who was?"

"Ma hound dawg – he was real warm of a night, Colonel."

Benteen nodded.

They heard the call to mount.

"The General gives another order!" said Benteen. "Unusual – I'd got kinda used to following the horse-arse in front of me, just speculating on what might be coming next."

"Was it necessary?" Green was still troubled.

"Was what necessary?"

"The dogs."

Benteen put his arm round the broad shoulders, "I'd have advised the general to give the same order if he had not already done it."

"Then that's fine, sir," whispered Green. "If you think it's right, then that's fine."

Benteen removed his arm, shrugged against the cold and walked back to the lines of his battalion. Without another word the black trooper followed, head down against the wind. The tears which had rolled from his eyes froze an inch below his eyelids.

The hollows in the snow where they had paused filled with new snow, sped by a sudden swirl of surface flakes picked up by the biting wind. The sun was almost nothing, a slit above the peak of hills. The dark night had come, heralded, it seemed, by the smears of a dead and bleeding day.

)()()()()(

They had marched, ridden, and staggered for three days over the snow-covered territory. Twelve hours earlier Major Elliott, second in command, had taken two companies forward and found tracks. Large group, he had reported. He estimated the tracks belonged to a large war or hunting party – maybe fifty riders.

"War party!" Lieutenant Colonel Custer had decided, and smiled, for the first time in two days.

Custer had been riding well ahead, with only Frank Partridge, his chief of scouts at his side, but in sight of the main body. Everyone in the regiment felt excitement grow. They knew that there were Indians near. They knew it, and were pleased, for they had come to kill Indians, a lot of Indians if they could. They had seen a few, a handful of buffalo too, foxes, some wolves, an occasional antelope and once they thought they heard the eerie call of an eagle just below the cloud cover, but it might have been an Indian scout. Perhaps in hours there would be a solid contact. More Osage scouts were pushed forward to join, somewhere ahead, Major Elliott's advance guard of a score of picked men.

Frederick Benteen quite liked young Elliott. An administrative matter of his having an early commission in the regular army had placed him senior to Captain Benteen though Elliott had once commanded a company in the 10th Michigan *under* Benteen. Elliott was young and dynamic and would be a general one day for sure. He had been a school superintendent before the war and had a certain young schoolmaster air about him – as if he expected to be obeyed and followed.

Elliott had had a shock a year before when Custer sent him out to round up some deserters and had had a pot shot taken at him. It had ended with the deserters being shot. Custer was out of line on that one. Benteen had seen one of them brought in with a belly wound screaming with the bumping of the wagon across the roadless terrain. Custer had drawn a Colt on him and threatened to shoot him. When the outrage of the shooting of deserters got out to the press and politicians, it had cost Custer a court-martial, a year of seniority and a suspension without pay. Elliott had command for that time and was fine at it for a lad, but tended to ride off with the boys in the wrong direction.

Word came to Benteen offering him the command. But he thought, the hell with it, and recommended that Custer came back early. He did, at the behest of Sheridan himself, and ought to have changed, but had not. Custer did not know that Benteen had asked for him back. Benteen never mentioned it, kind of felt ashamed that he had done it and was damned if he would let Custer have the pleasure of the knowledge. But all that was wind blown on the prairie now. The truth was, Custer was not worth a nickel in a poker game, and there was an end to it.

Suddenly Elliott's outfit came cantering up spraying the covering of newly fallen snow like a squadron of ships, racing in choppy waters. Custer spurred forward to join them.

"More tracks, General," he called to Custer.

"Show me!" said Custer and made them turn and dash forward beyond the regiment's head.

They found the tracks with ease, and then slowed. They walked their horses on top of the tracks themselves. They almost stumbled on the campsite.

Dropping from their mounts and crawling forward in the snow they peered at a mass of distant teepees with smoke universally drifted from their peaks, dozens. Each column of blue wood-smoke was caught by the fickle wind and thrown about like jagged sprites. An Osage scout whispered, with a hint of respect, that it was the village of Black Kettle for he could see his sign on one of the teepees.

"What was that, Captain Partridge?" asked Custer. "What did he say?"

"He says, General, that this here is Black Kettle's camp. Black Kettle is a peace chief, I think...."

"No such thing, Mister. We licked *him* at Sand Creek," said Custer. "Well, sir, we'll lick him again, right here and now. He's been on the war path since Sand Creek."

"Not so."

"Not so, sir, not so? I tell you so. His young braves have been seen – right down towards Texas."

Frank knew it was true, but it would not be of the old man's making. Each young warrior could do as he pleased. They only worked together when they all saw the same thing as their personal pleasure. It was the downfall of them. They could not run as a battalion.

"Did you hear me, Mr. Partridge?"

"It's true enough, General, but Black Kettle..."

"Is the chief, and that's it!"

Frank Partridge shook his head but was ignored as Custer returned to staring through his field glasses.

Frank Partridge got back on his horse with the rest of them and stared into the distance, counted the triangular shapes. A couple of dozen, a couple of score, maybe more. There were trees behind the encampment and the river turned twice and was caressed by more trees. There could be more lodges behind the thick stands of timber edging the river. Frank Partridge wished he were inside one of the lodges out of this damned cold.

The chill knifed its way through his thin frame. Better to be warm with people, a central fire carefully tended, kids chattering, old granny telling a tale of love whilst making a blanket maybe, peace in the warmth.

Frank Partridge shrugged, not so much against the cold, but against the thoughts of what was about to take place, this coming destruction of treasures passed down. Those possessions in the teepees had taken days, even weeks of careful construction. They would go up in smoke in moments. This was not to be looked forward to.

Frank felt nausea in him, guilt. When would it stop? He had thought that were he to ride again with his own people he could modify the brutality, bring an understanding. Lecturing the officers on the way of the Indian was not enough for them; he had been sucked once more into taking command of the scouts. Maybe this would be the last time.

"I think a few hundred souls, General," he said quietly. "Scarce worth an attack."

"I hope more, sir!" snapped Custer. "We need a famous victory – put some fear in their murderous hearts – Sheridan expects it. We shall certainly attack."

Little Phil Sheridan. Custer remembered leaping from his horse and taking his little master into his arms and twirling around as if in a dance after Cedar Creek in '63. Now the two star was in command of the District of Mississippi and had the brilliant notion of a winter campaign. The savages were an infestation: damned old fleas breed in the winter and the spring's nits would make new summer fleas. Bloody Chivington had put it well. The Redskins, quite simply, would never expect a full winter campaign. They would be hit at their most vulnerable time. They would be unable to spray away onto the prairie and escape as they could in the summer.

They would be cold and hungry in their lodges, and for sure some would be digging each other in their blankets, naked, as they always were, the dirty heathens. Hit them at dawn. Kill the whole damned lot. Better than cutting down a deer – deer don't beg for mercy, ain't so much entertainment. "Go get 'em! Any way you want!" was Sheridan's command. That suited Custer to the core.

Custer liked the savages in one moment – naked on a horse – streaming feathers in the wind, howling bloody challenges to the world; hated them the next, as he envisaged them carving up his wounded lads, tearing at their white men's bodies. Custer shuddered when he thought of it. He had seen the remains. A man turned to ribbons by a shell on the battlefield was one thing, but when another man takes a hatchet to another man's knees, and a knife to...

"It's a good day to die!" That is what they chanted, so Frank Partridge had described.

That also suited Custer very well. "Damned if it wasn't also a good day to kill – any damned day!"

They would hit them hard at dawn. Let the half light come, enough to see the ground. The snow would help, catching the light of the coming day. They must be careful – not a sound. Benteen would approve of that.

Benteen. Damn those big eyes looking through a man. Damn his hand of cards, the lucky devil. Just damn him. Damned Brevet Colonel damned Benteen. Why, God damn it, he was Custer, brevet major general of volunteers – seen more action than Benteen. What did he know of anything? A lot! Damned good soldier. Damn him to hell.

Custer turned his horse away from the direction of the village. As he did so his mind again filled with the sound of hooves and the majesty of two brigades of cavalry wheeling across half a mile of land because he, their general, had said go this way or go that. Damn the cold. Damn the savages. Damn the dogs. Damn Benteen. Especially damn Benteen with those woman eyes and money in his pocket whenever he put his hand there.

He was such a woman. Got him to telegraph a hundred dollars to sweet Mrs. Custer when he went back into barracks whilst the regiment was in the field. Weeks later Benteen had asked for ninety-one back, because Custer had let him have some notes in a game of cards. One of the rare occasions that Freddie Benteen lost. Custer sent him ninety-two dollars, saying his accounting was different. Damned if Benteen did not pass him back a dollar bill. Custer used it to light his pipe.

)()()()()(

Custer's first vision of the attack was to be followed. He would cut the village off. Arms would enfold it, squeeze it. Destroy it. His officers stood in front of him in the darkness. They hustled together; unconsciously trying to catch some warmth from one another

"By my calculations, gentlemen, the village is north and a touch east from here – two miles. I want you, Mr. Elliott to take companies G, H and M, skirt the village to the east and work your way back to strike in on a line coming south east. Captain Thompson you will take B company and F company to the east and then strike up by a left turn to drive in on a line north west. Try to come in more from the east. You, Lieutenant Myers, will follow Thompson and then turn off so that you drive directly north. You shall keep company E and company I, with you. I shall push in from here with HQ and with Colonel Benteen here on my left, having brought his battalion up from the wagons. We shall surround and destroy. Is that clear?"

They nodded, they shrugged their shoulders, staring at the map the general had drawn in the freezing morning snow, dimly lit by a flickering hurricane lamp.

"Wait for my bugle call, gentlemen, and then... destroy the enemy... we cannot hope to do less, for we have them by surprise!"

)()()()()(

The confusion. The call of horses entwined with the rattle of gun fire. The screaming of the frightened and the dying. Benteen had difficulty in handling his horse and found savages surrounded him. Then they were gone. They made no attempt to harm him.

They were running in a blind panic, half of them naked. He shot at some, but missed. Then his six shooter ceased to fire, empty. Reloading was difficult. He slid it into his holster, reached forward for his sabre. A tremendous blow enveloped his back and he knew an Indian had leapt onto his horse's rear.

)H)H)H)H)H

The fifteen winter's son of Black Kettle saw his father fall, and he saw his mother fall and he saw the shod horses of the soldiers ride over them. He decided to kill another soldier at once. A man rode by on a big horse. The boy sprinted through the snow after him and leapt into the air with the power of anger that made it possible for him to vault onto this big soldier horse. In a single movement he wrenched at the man who was already reaching for his longknife.

The man thumped down from the horse onto the snow with the boy on top of him. The man was still for a moment, enough for the youth to have his hands on the man's throat to take away his life. There was joy in this thing.

The power of the blow to his face came from nowhere. The knee between his legs sent him soaring over the Wasichu's head, but gave no pain. The speed with which the man was on his feet surprised him. As he was getting up a new blow to his head angered him. Then he was looking at a six-shooter but felt a great sense of relief when he heard a click, followed by a click. He would kill this man now... which was when the boy saw horses riding across the sky, and a great wind rising in a black column from the earth, twisting into a thousand stars of blackness and...

)H)H)H)H)H

Captain Benteen felt himself falling out of his saddle. He instantly feared and felt the huge *thump* of himself hitting the snow. Hands were on his throat. He looked into a face which was that of a youth. Benteen smashed his fist into the face. The glancing blow served to drive the hands from his throat. Bringing his knee up, he caught the youth in the small of his naked back and he pitched over Benteen's head.

Rolling to one side Benteen lurched to his feet to receive a new assault. He snatched out his six-shooter and brought it smashing down on the boy's head as he was getting up and knocked the lad down again. Benteen pulled off a glove and broke the six-shooter open. His cold fingers searched for rounds in his pocket, pulled out a handful, started to reload, dropping rounds into the snow at his feet.

He got two into the chambers. The boy was rising. He snatched the gun shut.

Click, click.... *blam!* the boy's head cracked open and he was pitched backwards by the power of the round tearing through his forehead. Benteen fired again, *click*, then *blam!* The bullet tore the boy's heart, though he was already still.

Benteen looked round for his horse. Horses were suddenly by his side. He recognised the grinning teeth of Green, in the half-light, looking down from his own mount. He had his colonel's horse by the bridle.

"You lost somethin', Colonel, sir?" He offered Benteen the bridle, speaking through a couple of Sharps carbine rounds held in his teeth.

"Damn the horse, I damn near lost my life!"

"So I seed, Colonel, then get back up on your damned hoss... sir!"

Benteen put his foot in the stirrup and, horsed once more, felt safer. He looked down on the dead youth, peaceful, for the world like a reclining nude in some classical painting. A prince. Wasted.

"Wasted," hissed Benteen to himself.

He was conscious that his mouth was bone dry and his heart was thumping. He inhaled an immense breath of cold air to steady himself. He looked down on the dead Indian again. He thought how young he looked, so incongruously naked in the snow, his blood so very red – a youth, a boy – oh shit to this business!

"God damn!" he said, and that was all he said aloud.

Benteen turned his horse, looking for a fresh kill, thus still prepared to exercise his vocation. But he realised that almost every Indian now in sight was a child or a woman, and they were being gunned down. He grunted and spurred his horse between the shooting soldiers and the dying innocents.

)( )( )( )( )(

From his horse Green saw an old man and a youth running into the outer darkness which was not yet morning. He snapped off a shot at them and saw that nothing happened, not even the kick of a bullet in the snow or a branch falling from the trees they were headed for.

He ejected the empty case, and snatched his last shell from his teeth. He pushed it into the open breech. Up came the stock. He fired, but nothing happened. The strip of caps which fed the firing nipple had come dislodged. He adjusted them quickly and re-cocked – they were getting too far away for a sure shot.

Target the man. Squeeze. *Crack*. Nothing again. That one must have the protection of their Great Spirit or whatever they call their source.

He slid his carbine out of his way by the belt across his shoulder and drew his sabre. He spurred after the two, but they had disappeared. Wheeling round he saw a small group running between the teepees. Turning his horse, more by knees than bit, he drove at them. Riding by he cut down at the first and she fell away with a fleck of flesh spinning off the side of her head.

Damn, a woman! He saw it was a woman, cursed again, but galloped on.

His horse rode another down and twisting in his saddle he slashed his blade down onto the head of a man who looked to be old. He felt the blade crack his skull. The man staggered away holding his head. An arrow thudded into his saddle horn.

He looked for the author of the shot. All that he could see was a teepee burning, huddling groups of half-naked squaws with their arms raised for mercy – and kids.

Something went by his cheek like a horse fly in August. He saw flashes from a line of timber; there was a crackle of musket fire, old muzzleloaders. He saw figures there. Then they were gone. He saw Major Elliott calling to men about him close by the trees.

"Come on – who'll come with me?" His horse was turning and turning. He was waving a sabre like the pictures Green had seen of Union and Confederate generals rallying their troops. Some of the men, a dozen or so of them, were joining him. The sergeant major was there, bellowing. Green thought about it and decided not to go – there was enough going on in the village.

Then Green distinctly heard the major laugh and yell: "Death or a brevet!" and go ripping into the timber that led down to the river, followed by close on twenty or more yelping young troopers and the sergeant major behind them, excited, blood up.

"Chasing Injuns in timber ain't lucky!" thought Green, pleased that he had decided not to follow.

He looked round to see if he could locate Colonel Benteen again. He saw at once that his colonel was to his right, facing half a dozen soldiers, with a group of squaws behind him. He was yelling at the soldiers to stop further slaughter. Green spurred in his direction. Looked like the old man needed help again.

)( )( )( )( )(

It was all over. They had stopped the killing. Benteen saw to that. Custer rode up and glowered at him, but did not countermand.

The regiment had at least a hundred of the enemy standing in mingling groups, heads up in defiance. The troops had let them snatch blankets from the teepees before they put them to the torch. They were howling in grief or were sullen quiet, staring at a herd of ponies passing by.

They were about three hundred ponies Frank Partridge had found trapped in a gully. Other stray Indian horses were making their way into the encampment. Benteen had heard tell that they were trained to do this when a village was attacked but had never seen it before.

A series of bullets hissed over head and yells came from the northern end of the village. There were numbers of warriors on horses moving in and out of the trees, firing, and retiring. Others were moving in on foot.

"Sir," called out Frank Partridge, "we can't hold these horses under fire – we'll have to move 'em out."

Custer looked round. He saw Benteen with the squaws. He saw several Indians wounded or unmoving, and some troopers dead, not many, others wounded. Teepees were beginning to go up in flames. The sun was clear of the trees. It looked like the beginning of a cloudless day. Another array of bullets flew around, peppering the snow, cracking through the air when close.

"Kill them! Shoot the whole damned herd down!" yelled Custer.

Frank Partridge made no move.

Custer snatched his silver butted Spencer out of the holster behind his saddle and snap shot at one of the ponies. He saw blood spurt and the horse reared. His second shot broke its neck and it went down.

"Shoot them. Shoot the lot! You men, move up there and shoot them."

A platoon of soldiers formed at once, under the shouting of a corporal, and knelt and opened volley fire.

"There are men of ours over there!" shouted Benteen. He was pointing beyond the animals. "Cease fire! You fools."

Custer glared at him. "There are enough horses in the way. Keep firing, corporal!"

Custer turned his horse away to watch the firing from the north.

"Damn you, corporal, hear me! Get the men into the horses, and shoot them close up," snapped Benteen and they knew damned well they had to do it Benteen's way.

The firing into the horses slackened. The corporal told the men to slit the throats of the remaining horses and those wounded.

The ponies sensed danger, smelt the curious odour of the white men, and shied out of their way as they got in close. Three troopers seized one of the horses and the knives went in, but it took at least two minutes for the animal to stop kicking and bleed to death. The sight of it served to worry the rest of the animals. The smell of blood spooked them and the men were in danger of being trampled. Custer rode up again.

"Shoot them, lads, I told you to shoot them," he hollered and brought up his own rifle again. An animal fell as if pole-axed. Then another. He began to take them out standing still or moving, galloping or rearing, never missing. A dog went yelping by and Custer half blew him apart so that the front half, still seeming to live, dragged the end parts through the snow, trailing blood, yelping, yelp, yelp, yelping.

Meanwhile Benteen had spun his horse away, and joined by Green and a grim faced Partridge, began to hustle the women and children towards the south end of the village. He passed the dog dragging itself along on front legs only.

"Shit! said Green.

Benteen heard Green's voice and glancing back saw the Negro pull out his Colt and drop the wounded dog.

"This here's a bad day for dogs, Colonel."

"It's not a good day for anyone," grunted Benteen, but no-one heard him except Green.

Then the destruction began in earnest, as the men of the 7th Cavalry took out the remaining animals of the lodges of Black Kettle. Before that last animal collapsed into the snow the soldiers began the systematic destruction of the lodges and any dead and dying within.

When it was over, all that remained were the frozen tears of the children who looked up at the laughing soldiers as they rode by. One by one, the smiles disappeared from the Wasichu faces. It was as if shame hung on the frosty air, waiting to be breathed in from the steaming breath of the staring children.

)( )( )( )( )(

"Where the hell is Elliott?" Custer asked.

There was firing to the north and it was clear that large numbers of hostiles were moving in ever closer. Custer feared that he had touched an encampment larger than first estimated.

He pulled his regiment together with messengers and bugle calls. He was satisfied that they had completed the thorough destruction of the village, despite the threat of other warriors being seen in the woods, closing in.

Every teepee was destroyed. A huge fire was made and clothing, frozen buffalo meat, arrows – thousands of hand-made arrows – so much for a 'Peace Chief'; all were thrown into the growing flames.

One set of arrows, finer than the rest, bound up in beautiful skins was shown to Custer. He thought to keep them, changed his mind, and from his horse he threw them into the flames. He saw Frank Partridge nearby shake his head.

"Well?" he asked the scout.

"Sacred Arrows, Colonel."

"They were," said Custer. "And they ain't no more."

Frank Partridge shook his head again, but said nothing.

Bows went too, shields, saddles, painted skins, drums and beautiful secret things. All went into the flames. They found quantities of powder. It was laid down, black on the snow, and flashed to oblivion so that even the experienced horses prancing nearby, used to death and noise, reared at the sudden hiss and flare of light.

The air became sickly with the embroidery of smoke. The smell of burning flesh both from the skin walls of the teepees and those dead inside, soaked every nostril. Gunsmoke, the smell of it acrid and unique, like rotten eggs, mingled with the perfume of blood, so that both could be tasted on the air. The swirling smoke obscured the carmine sun, then it flickered into sight and, for a moment, its shape seemed broken into that of a beating heart. Frank Partridge noticed it and shuddered, remembered the sacred arrows being thrown into the flames.

Custer surveyed the destruction, and considered it to be a neat little victory which would teach the wretched savages a lesson for months to come. Frank Partridge rode up.

"What is that dark look on your face again?" asked the colonel.

"Well now – it ain't so much a dark look, General, it is more a pitiful look."

"How so?"

"Well now – it is a pity because this here village *was* Black Kettle's"

"And?"

"He was a peace chief, I told you."

"Was he now?" smiled Custer and nodded towards a huge surge of light as the final kegs of powder were put to the torch. "Then I guess the four thousand arrows, four hundred guns...."

"Four hundred and fifty two!" corrected First Lieutenant Cook, adjutant, at his side.

"Indeed sir. I guess all this equipment and armoury was just for fishing and shooting geese?"

The chief of scouts shook his head with the dark look still there, turned his horse away. He could still hear Cook calling out the inventory as he walked his horse toward the timberline.

"We've killed a hundred warriors, or more, General."

Frank looked around and saw clusters of bodies. Maybe the number was right, but sure as hell they weren't all warriors. Too many kids, he thought to himself, too many bloody squaws. This ain't no victory; this here's a slaughter. And he was part of it. The unfamiliar nausea of guilt welled up into his throat and blended with a dangerous idea.

"I've had enough, enough," he muttered to himself. Old Ben's ears went back, listening to his words.

Custer watched Frank Partridge talking to himself as his horse meandered through the ashes and the trampled snow, and thought that maybe Mr. Frank Partridge would have to go. Distant firing to the north stopped his thoughts. That's where some of the boys said Elliott had gone.

)( )( )( )( )(

The 7th rode out of the Washita Valley with guidons rippling in the cold air. Custer kept the troops together detailing a brisk charge in one direction or the other when the war parties came too close and the arrows hissed by. He had the band play. Despite the hatred that seared the air, manifested in the war calls and threats, despite the hunger for revenge, the 7th only had to contend with threat, and an occasional lucky sharpshooter or an arrow at the weak limit of its flight. Custer had secured his reputation anew – not just as a leader of cavalry, but as an Indian fighter – and one to be wary of.

Benteen, wrote a letter to a good friend, many weeks later, wherein he praised his leader for his courage and the quality of his sharp shooting. Such a great warrior, taking out pet curs and riderless horses, entrapped as they were in a place they had thought to be safe. It takes much courage to shoot a defenceless dog does it not?

As Benteen penned the letter with a hot fire close by, he said to himself: "I loath that man – though I must follow him to the gates of somebody else's hell, I pray to God it is not mine in disguise." The letter took a long time to pen. Eventually it was passed, anonymously, to the *St.Louis Democrat* and then was blazoned in the *New York Times*. The letter did much to take away the glory that had never been there in the first place.

Captain Benteen was well pleased by that. Custer was enraged. Custer threatened to horsewhip the man who wrote the letter. He dared the man to step forward. Benteen did so in front of half the officers, his holster flicked open against the whipping. Custer turned away, no whipping took place. The rift between them was confirmed.

There had been a postcript to the letter which, not published with the rest, had read:

I have omitted to relate that when we held roll call to count the heroes who remained we found that the chief of scouts was missing. No one saw him fall. But then no one saw Elliott fall either. But whereas we later found Elliott's outfit, in bits, eventually, some two weeks later, our brave scout was never seen again.

*"After he has lost his country, and finds himself
compelled to remain on reservations, his limits
circumscribed, his opportunities of hunting abridged, his
game disappearing, sickness in his lodge from change of
life and goods, and insufficiency of the latter, and this
irregularly supplied, and the reflection coming to him of
what he was, and what he now is, and pinched by
hunger, creates a feeling of dissatisfaction which...
starts him on the war-path again."*

**Lieutenant General Phil Sheridan, Commander of the
Division of Missouri**

Part Three

Dreams, Paintings and Warpaths

15

Snow Dreams

(In the Wasichu Year of 1876, in January; the Centennial Year of the founding of the Republic)

It was the smile on Crazy Horse's face which pleased White Hawk more than anything. It was a form of salute. Crazy Horse was one of five Shirt-Wearers, selected by the Oglala Sioux to lead in war; highest of honours. Tired, angered, sickened by the onslaughts of the Wasichu, the Sioux as a whole were determined to protect their hunting grounds. The re-institution of the Shirt-Wearers was part of that determination. The people must be brought together, with good leadership.

The word was already running through the scattered peoples that during the coming summer there was to be the biggest gathering ever known in the valley of the Little Big Horn, along the run of the Greasy Grass. Even though it was winter there was excitement in the thoughts of everyone, an expectation of something wonderfully spectacular coming with the new seasons. The Wasichu would be shown that the real people were many. And all the leaders would be there, including the Shirt-Wearers.

The piercing eyes behind the smile were looking into White Hawk's twenty-two winters' head. The young man felt, almost physically, the penetration of that stare.

The battle leader's gaze came from hawk-eyes. There was no laughter in them, just the impression that behind them were secrets. White Hawk had the eerie sensation that their gaze could explore White Hawk's own secrets, sucking them out by a crossover of their spirits. Crazy Horse's eyes were sunk beneath handsome brows and looked out from above powerful cheekbones which served to the accentuate the broad face, an apt setting, for those eyes. It was an engaging face, but formed a wall rather than an entrance to the man. Crazy Horse's gaze never left the young warrior. He raised his sinuous arm in further salute; saying nothing. The enigmatic smile would have to be enough.

White Hawk slid from old Breeze's back. The horse's head was already drooping from the efforts of the final hunt. Breeze was the survivor of the pair of mares that Yellow Hair handed to the boy a decade before. Winding Storm had fallen in a buffalo hunt five years later.

"Here – they were your father's. Let them return to he who has his name," the winkte had smiled.

Breeze was no longer young enough to take part in the buffalo hunt, but was good for travels, and White Hawk could hunt antelope from her back for she could still carry a good buck across the base of her neck. That was how White Hawk had arrived in the large village of Crazy Horse, the hundred and fifty lodges curving in a circle, facing the frozen flood plane of the Little Snake River.

White Hawk looked at Crazy Horse with an almost boyish grin of pride as he struggled with the dead antelope, pulling it from across his horse's back. The horned creature's tongue lolled, now at an unreal angle for it was frozen stiff.

White Hawk presented the thin buck to Crazy Horse, almost dropping it at his feet. He had carried it five miles or more, flopping across tired Breeze's shoulders until the carcass froze. The young warrior's arms were outstretched at the presentation and he fought the dead weight of the animal. The buck's eyes were open, a glaze having long set in, and its death blood was frozen stiff on its shoulder where the wide head of the hunting arrow had passed through.

Crazy Horse immediately called in the crier to take it away for the people, but he stipulated which lodges; for he knew which of his people had little left of the dried buffalo from the summer hunt; he knew whose need was greatest. Like all true leaders – he had a picture of all his people in his mind, their needs, personalities, even personal possessions of special significance. His head carried many secret things. Mostly it carried a terrible fear, an insight.

Crazy Horse beckoned White Hawk into his teepee. The young warrior stooped and followed, ducking through the entrance. He turned briefly to secure the flap against the cold knowing exactly what to do though this was not his home. He was shivering – from reverence rather than the bite of the icy air. This was the Moon of the Snow-blind and it was well named. The world was an unremitting white, punctuated only by the tall trees dressed with frost. The interior of the teepee was another world.

Outside the air was ice, inside the air was warm. The walls of buffalo hide provided a welcome relief from the harsh white light of packed snow. He was greeted by gathered relatives who smiled, but said little beyond the greeting and a gentle touching of his cold buckskin.

"Ah," said a fine old woman, "you are covered in cold."

A sough of laughter met her words and then quiet, for Crazy Horse might be about to speak to this new friend they had not seen before. Crazy Horse had bidden him enter – that was more than enough for them all.

Crazy Horse stood close to the fire in the centre of the teepee and called White Hawk to him with a gentle gesture, sitting down as he did so. As was the custom, White Hawk was careful not to walk between the fire and those sitting round it. He passed behind them until the site allocated to him was reached. It was by the side of Crazy Horse, his right hand side.

As he came close, Crazy Horse reached up and touched his leg to have him sit. Once White Hawk was down Crazy Horse placed the back of his hand, his knuckles, on the young man's face. Then his fingers felt towards the young one's left ear and he pinched it gently, cold to the touch.

"She's right. I am grateful, young friend, you have brought a little life to us. There was no need; yet there was great need. I have many hunters out this day. Let them return, even with thin meat such as you have brought, and we may yet live to see another spring and summer."

"What did he bring?" the old woman asked.

"A buck," answered Crazy Horse.

"Too thin," said White Hawk.

"Anything will help," sighed the old woman, who had known worse winters… but not many.

Warm food was passed to him by the women of Crazy Horse. There were smiles, but no eyes met. They saw that he was Cheyenne, and marked as a contrary warrior though he seemed ordinary enough.

White Hawk wolfed the tough strips of last summer's buffalo. As he did so he glanced at Crazy Horse and saw the smile again, so that his chest swelled with the honour of it.

White Hawk had not seen Crazy Horse for almost a year, not since the day of the skirmish with the white-eyes that the Wasichu called 'The Pryor Creek Fight'. At that time, White Hawk had heard of the Oglala leader, but had not seen him.

Yellow Hair's band had joined with the teepees of Crazy Horse whilst the warrior was out with the war party seeing off the Wasichu who had come too close. A sudden rush of excitement ran through the village as they heard that the warriors were returning.

They had three scalps, still wet, for it had been a dull day without heat. There were two dead Sioux warriors across their sad horses, going back to the people to be laid to rest. Several others in the raiding party had minor wounds; one nursed a broken arm already in a splint. He looked grey, but was upright on his horse, a grim smile playing on his face.

He rode *next* to Crazy Horse because he had made an astonishing ten coups in the fight and killed two Crows who had been with the Wasichu. Crazy Horse was announcing the man's successes as they rode through: "This is Young Wolf who killed two Crows and took ten coups, this is Young Wolf, my good friend, my brother..."

"That!" said Yellow Hair, "is Crazy Horse."

"Oh!" gasped White Hawk and stared.

Crazy Horse looked more worn than his twenty-seven winters; there was a curious maturity about him, as if he had been that age for ever. He was dressed in breechcloth and moccasins only. From his hip hung a war-club with a stone head set in a long bent stem of ash. On the bare flesh of his hip was a faint redness from the friction of the stem. His bow and arrows were slung to the left, neatly stored; a repeating rifle was balanced across his loins; in his right hand a lance was held almost perfectly vertical, its head of rusted metal, dulled by morning dew. Objects of honour graced this weapon.

White Hawk was surprised to see that the hero seemed so slim, but not thin. The tight muscles of his body were sinuous; each block of muscles on his stomach appeared carved with a hatchet. His back was very straight, his head was held upright, his jaw thrust forward. Proud proud.

He was painted with patches of white, some of which had run with moist sweat and buffalo grease. There was a lightning zigzag, red on white, painted on the left of his face. A single eagle feather stood out from the back of his head, seeming to give more height to his straight stance. His hair was flowing free, not in braids, and on his head was fixed the body of a red hawk with its wings outspread. As he rode in he looked neither to the left nor to the right and did not sing as the rest of his warriors did, other than to call out their honours. Never did he mention himself. The blood songs of those in his train did that.

Gathered people, toddlers to crones, watched in delight for here was one who had been touched by *Wakantanka*, and they were glad he belonged to them. Yet on his lance were no scalps; rarely did he take a scalp.

That lack of scalps was even more impressive than were ten to have hung dripping from his lance. The children jumped up and down in admiration, dancing and spinning almost through his horse's legs. White Hawk only looked on, but felt like jumping up and down too. He remained absolutely still; only his eyes followed the warriors as they passed him by, for he was already a contrary warrior, determined not to smile when everyone else was overjoyed.

Yellow Hair stood with arms folded at the warriors' approach. Crazy Horse, seeing the Cheyenne lodges were Yellow Hair's, halted his raiding party so that the famed *wicasa wakan* could tend the wounds. The villagers surged around but Crazy Horse backed them off so that the Cheyenne could do his special work.

Yellow Hair said, dealing with the broken arm first, "You all hold him tight."

Four of them pinioned the warrior with the broken arm. It was a good break from a longknife cut. The blade had been blunt and the long bone above the elbow had cracked rather than severed. As the warrior groaned the *wicasa wakan* firmly explored the fracture, tested it for it being slightly out of line, checked for shatter and found none. "Here!" he said, and put an arrow between the young man's teeth. "Bite!"

They all heard a kind of 'grind' as the bones aligned. The young casualty groaned and his eyes turned up into a half faint and then opened and he said, "That hurt."

"Young men today are so brave," whispered Yellow Hair, thinking that he would have neither groaned nor passed out had it been him as a young man. "But then," he whispered, "I never broke an arm."

They put the splints back under Yellow Hair's approving gaze then Yellow Hair said, "No love making for a year!"

They all laughed at the look of horror on the young man's face as the pains suddenly appeared to retreat.

Yellow Hair helped the young man to his feet. Crazy Horse was there too, looking diminutive alongside the big old Cheyenne. Then Crazy Horse was pulled away by the press of his people, going to his own lodges.

Yellow Hair said, "Come with me," as the crowd passed by.

"Where?" asked White Hawk.

"To meet my young friend properly," said the old man and nodded towards the one touched by *Wakantanka*.

White Hawk's jaw dropped – his soul-master had spoken of Crazy Horse, but never had he hinted that Crazy Horse was his *friend*. True, Crazy Horse had taken a Cheyenne for his wife, a cousin of Yellow Hair, but to be a friend as well! Yellow Hair's friend was Crazy Horse! And Yellow Hair was the father-teacher of White Hawk. The young man began to float.

When they met, the amazement grew! Crazy Horse *embraced* the old man and called him father.

"And who is this?" asked Crazy Horse, as if he had never heard of the son of the winkte. Crazy Horse's face broke into a smile of such unexpected warmth that the boy was his slave immediately.

"My contrary warrior."

"A contrary warrior!" declared the great one, noticing the markings on White Hawk's face and chest. "A hero man, a hero, a hero-hero." Crazy Horse smiled and for the first time he placed his hand on the youth's face, and let his fingers caress the left ear, in that unique way.

"I have heard speak of you, White Hawk. You cut away the manhood of the Wasichu who slew Black Kettle and his wife – revenged them, alongside this ancient one." He glanced at Yellow Hair with mock contempt. "And then there was the Elk River fight, and then the young Crow, then the wagons, then the fight with the longknives at Silver Creek. You are a great warrior already." He glanced up and down the young man's elegant frame and saw the not too far off vision of a chief of warriors, an inheritor, a Dog Soldier

White Hawk disappeared into his own soul, feeling that he would explode with the gift words that were pouring from the lips in front of him.

The moons, since then, had gone by all too quickly, the seasons running just as fast. The hours of light seemed to grow shorter, the winters colder, the summers briefer. And as another year went by Crazy Horse looked even thinner in his face. The bone structure protruded. His eyes seemed to be deeper sunk. It was more than just the winter look.

When the spring came, the man, with the rest of the real people, would become sleek once more. But at this time there was clear relief that even the small amount of meat brought in by White Hawk was available for some of his poorer people.

"Will you stay this night?" asked Crazy Horse.

"I have nowhere to go."

Crazy Horse gave that rare smile once more, then raised his head to point with his jaw to the south, "There are Cheyennes of Chief Old Bear – sixty lodges – that way – closer to the banks of Powder River, where the beaver used to beat the waters. They are but a day's march away. We have all been hunting. The villages have spread to follow the game. But we are anxious, for we know that many soldiers of old Three Stars Sheridan, the Wasichu war chief, are lurking in that direction too."

Crazy Horse paused for a moment as if a weight was upon him.

"We think the Wasichu ride in the winter once more. That Sheridan is a bad Wasichu and drives us hard."

White Hawk nodded.

"Tomorrow we shall begin to bring the villages together. The Hunkpapa of Sitting Bull are to the north. We will all move in that direction. He will wait for us. We have agreed. The Wasichu may strike us at any time; they like to come at us in the cold times now – they know that is the way to hurt us."

"We are too careless," said White Hawk.

Crazy Horse hardly nodded but his eyes agreed. "The Wasichu are no longer fools and remember, they have no honour. They want *all* we have. Nothing less will satisfy them."

"They cannot kill us all."

Crazy Horse turned and looking into White Hawk's eyes and said, "They would like to. I think they would like to do that very much. Then all that we have would really be theirs. We have to fight them off. We shall have need of plenty warriors soon. It is better that we are come close together. We must not make it easy for them. When we are small villages they like to kill us when we sleep and make love, if they can. You have tasted that."

White Hawk nodded and saw in his head the fire wings of horses in the dawn. He blinked the memory away.

Outside the wind was getting up and the whole of the tent talked to the passing air. A flurry of snowflakes entered from the smoke opening at the apex of the teepee and for some spirit reason White Hawk saw himself again: running through the snow with Yellow Hair; whilst death, in the sun's rise, mingled spiralling snow flakes with hot lead. A curious feeling ran through the young man, and he looked into Crazy Horse's eyes and saw nothing, for the smile had gone. Perhaps it would happen again – the Wasichu at dawn. No – it must never happen again.

White Hawk shook his head as a swimmer might, on surfacing from a dive into a deep pool. It must never happen again.

)()()()()(

Three nights of warmth, talk, laughter, daytime riding in the late winter-cold sun, passed by. Three days with Crazy Horse and his cousins, resting and hunting.

They found a small family of half-starved buffalo and chased them through the snow. Screaming and crying with delight, they chased them. They loved the animals for bringing them life. The bull stood and let them shoot it to death, stood as if he wanted to die, thinking in his buffalo mind that the others would flee. But they were too weak. All five in the family were killed.

They butchered them in the pristine snow and made drags from willow branches to take the carcasses home. The chunks of carcass froze solid as the hunters rode, stiff backed with pride, into the village as if they had wiped out the entire Crow nation.

That night there was feasting, singing, and much dancing round a celebration fire which sent sparks into the frozen black sky. The ice of winter was in its own death throes, but spiteful in death, it descended on them when the dancing stopped. Would he never go, the winter one? They finished the dancing early as the winter spirit sent more flurries of snow and the temperature dropped quickly.

As White Hawk lay in the warmth of the teepee, his young belly distended from the feast, he wondered if this was to be a Wasichu night? White Hawk felt it, clawing at him; the sudden sound of gunfire, the pounding of charging horses. He sensed that Crazy Horse was watching him.

The great warrior said, quietly, "We have scouts out tonight, far out in the darkness, watching, wrapped in many blankets."

"Watching?"

"Watching for wolves with two legs."

White Hawk nodded – accepting the reading of his thoughts.

He thought of the scouts out in the bitter air, so cold a tear of laughter could freeze in eye-corners. In the lodge of Crazy Horse the oldest of the women placed three thick logs on the central fire. She watched Crazy Horse and the contrary Cheyenne whispering to each other and she heard that the chief wanted the contrary to stay until the spring. She saw the young Cheyenne shake his head.

White Hawk looked around at the cocoons of skins, so inviting, but was firm, even as they were all about to snuggle down in teepee-warmth, that he would move to the camp of Chief Old Bear, close by the Powder River. He had heard talk amongst the people of Crazy Horse that Yellow Hair was visiting there. He would go at dawn.

Crazy Horse said, "I heard *that* old man was with the *other* old one – Sitting Bull – in his big teepee to the north."

"How do you know this thing?" asked White Hawk, frowning in the darkness.

Crazy Horse looked surprised at the question and said, "I know."

White Hawk, with a daring smile, caught by the flickering fire, said: "*I know* he is to the south."

"You go south?"

"Yes."

"Yellow Hair is to the north."

"I go south."

"Thou art a contrary boy," smiled Crazy Horse and pushed him so that he fell laughing and stumbling onto the buffalo bedding, scattering the old women.

"Would you attack old women?" screamed the mother of Crazy Horse and, totally naked, leapt at the young man. She was followed by others.

Everyone in the teepee assaulted the warrior and with many hands holding him, they tickled him with gnarled fingers until he screamed for mercy. They felt his flesh and loved his youth and power. But they were too much for him. He laughed until he could not move. The noise was like a hundred ducks landing. Others, in hasty blankets, came from close by and looked in, despite the cold, and laughed as no mercy was given to the contrary one – until everyone in the warm place was alive with mirth and joy. Then they slipped, giggling, into the skins and blankets, all in places according to their station and their loves.

"Come to me for warmth," whispered the mother of Crazy Horse.

To her astonishment he did, for the night was truly cold, but nothing happened other than dreams.

The calling of several steaming dogs involved in the raping of a bitch, just in heat, all yapping at the rising sun, and the promise of spring, woke White Hawk from the deepest of safe dreams. He listened for a moment only. It was no Wasichu attack. He began to ease himself away from the sleeping form of Crazy Horse's mother.

Crazy Horse, awake at his movements, watched him from the warmth of his mountain of hides.

Clear of the robes White Hawk pulled leggings onto his feet and up to his thighs; each had a winter moccasin attached. Then came his breechcloth across loins and upper legs. He attached the thongs of the separate leggings to the waist band. White Hawk then threw on a fine doeskin shirt, warmed by the fire, and over that a heavier shirt; both hung well below the bare flesh between leggings and breechcloth Then his sheath knife, bear-bone handled, slid into a belt around his top shirt, the strapping remade the previous night by Crazy Horse himself when he saw that those already there were worn.

He had admonished the boy.

"You will feel for this knife when you are about to die, and it will not be there, and you *will* die, and your young scalp will dangle from a smelly Crow's waist. Worse – a dirty little Arikara."

"No Arikara will ever…"

"Then have your knife safe and ready for they come behind you, unseen like a Wasichu illness."

Crazy Horse now struggled out of his blankets. His wife, half in a dream reached for him in her sleep, but he disengaged her arm. He was naked for a moment and then pulled a great blanket from the bedding, wrapped it around himself, containing his warmth.

He watched as White Hawk picked up his own buffalo-robe, throwing it round his shoulders. He shrugged himself to greater warmth and made for the flap of buffalo hide which led out to crisp coldness and new morning.

Outside, with head drooping, standing close to the warm side of the teepee, protected from the wind, was Breeze, her chestnut face white with snow, old and wise. Quickly, in the cold, with Crazy Horse assisting, the horse was prepared and the young man skipped onto its back, facing its rear, for he was a contrary warrior and was making his statement of belonging to that society, that honour.

The animal made a soft protest, uneager to move that morning. White Hawk spoke quietly to his friend Breeze over his shoulder, and the horse moved slowly into the sharp morning. The snow cracked at each step, its surface freshly frozen in the night. Below the surface lay packed powdery snow, and beneath that, out of sight, the first minute fingers of spring as the tough needle grass began to show new life.

Crazy Horse watched the contrary appear to glide through the snow towards the outer line of teepees and move down to the river, where there was good marching ground, flat and hard.

Crazy Horse raised his arm in a distant salute, but the salute was not returned, for this was a contrary warrior. Crazy Horse wondered at the affection that he had for this young man he had known for such a short time. But he knew it was because of the vision. He had told no-one, and certainly not the boy.

Out of sight of the village White Hawk swung his leg and body in a single graceful movement and was facing forward. He leaned so that his lips were close to the animal's ears and said: "We have lived through the dark night. Today will be a good day, a good day to live and even a good day to die."

He said that to his pony every morning, no matter what the moon.

Breeze snorted and raised her head up and down with sheer delight at her master's words. She did not understand them, other than they were the words to begin a day, but they were words from her master, and had affection in them and were good for that, despite the tiredness she felt.

}({)({)({)({

Crazy Horse was quick to slip alongside his woman, and he pressed his hardness against her and she murmured, snored. He smiled in the gloom and began a slow rhythm against the small of her back. The snores grew less and she began a purr. Crazy Horse pressed slowly and then stopped as the vision slipped across his mind again. He was able to recall it as might the teller of a tale remember the words to the beat of a drum.

He had seen it first, sitting, half-starved before a cave in the Black Hills; rocking in the sunlight he had seen it.

Now he wanted the young man to hear what he had seen, but that was not possible because he had gone into the frost-mist morning. He wished he could tell him but instead he lapsed into a morning doze, warm inside his home.

}({)({)({)({

"His eyes are moving," came a gentle whisper.

The eyes of the young Cheyenne in the blankets were moving. Those eyes looked, and saw other eyes, huge eyes seeming to smile by themselves, then the smile was a face. White Hawk felt cool water on his lips and saw it was the face of a beautiful girl which was smiling.

"Hello, little warrior."

He understood the words and knew that he was alive. It was all a dream. In the dream he had heard the words of Yellow Hair whispering, "It is all a dream, it is all a dream; do not worry, it is all a dream."

Now he was awake, confused.

Her hair was in the Cheyenne style, he realised, and her words were Cheyenne too. A beautiful face was there in the confusion of waking from a dream so deep...

The flaming snow was gone! Looking up at the smoke-opening he saw, through the spiralling grey-blue smoke, a sky... his eyes took in the face again. She was stroking him, gently with her fingers, caressing his lips, so that his tongue, with a love-snake movement, touched one of her fingers, and returned inside his mouth at once, shocked at itself.

"Ah – you are alive, with your rattler's tongue."

He felt himself smile. She was so beautiful, this stranger with her clean dark hair, small eyebrows, broad face and eyes of jet. Her lips were parted, still in the smile he had woken to. She was looking at him, exploring his reactions, reading his soul-thoughts. He wondered if she could see the flaming snow which hurried across his thoughts once more. A surging fear and hopelessness came over him for he knew he had lost the meaning of the dream for ever – it was more than a dream, it was a vision.

"Did you see..." he began, but knew the question to be hopeless.

"We saw you in the snow."

He gave a start.

"Lying there."

"Where are the soldier men?"

"What?"

"They killed... they killed him..."

"Who?"

"The boy – I could not put him back together again."

"Which boy?" She laughed at the panic in his voice so that she felt she must stroke his face. With a mischievous grin she ran her hand onto his neck and the bare flesh of his shoulder she had grown to know so well.

"It was a vision," he whispered. "But it was so real."

Suddenly White Hawk realised that he was wrapped in a bed of furs in a teepee, naked, throbbing, being caressed by... by a beautiful girl with parted lips, and white teeth... and...

"Where am I?" he muttered.

She threw her head back with a burst of mirth and said, "In Running Snake's lodge, brother of Old Bear." Surely the whole world knew, she seemed to say. "This is the camp of Old Bear," she explained as if he were an infant.

"Old Bear?" He seemed surprised.

"Yes, this is the camp of Old Bear," she continued, and her hand was on his forehead, caressing again.

He pulled his right hand from the skins. He reached and touched her hand and looked into her face. His left hand cupped, then held, then stroked, the secret thing beneath the skins, as any young warrior might, rapidly gathering wits, to take advantage of the blood-rush opportunity, forgetting he was a contrary.

"How did I..." he began

"We found you, two mornings ago, in the snow. You were inside your pony."

He blinked.

"He saved you."

"Inside! Inside?"

She nodded.

He remembered, and a river of anguish touched him, and he felt the hardness drift away from his left hand as the vision of his good friend Breeze going down in the driving snow returned to haunt him.

It had been night already, Crazy Horse's camp was a slow snow-march away, and White Hawk knew that he was only a mile, maybe two, from the village of Old Bear. He had caught the scent of distant fires. But it was the warmth of death that he felt on him. He knew that if he could simply lie down, just for a very short time, he would regain his strength and all would be well. He did not want much from his life, or anyone. Crazy Horse would understand. He had just wanted to sleep for a little while.

So he had let go, and fallen asleep. For about a hundred paces of his pony he lolled forward, still on the animal's back. The pony stopped, and awaited a signal. For Breeze the stopping was the final touch. A feeling of intense tiredness driving away all sensation of cold swept through the old beast, and in that moment her great horse-heart stopped.

Her spirit leapt from out of the frame of flesh and without a single farewell to her master she was through the screen and away from the ice. She left the world behind, galloping away down a lush green meadow which led to a summer river; she was gone into a shadow land of shadows, and was young again, for ever. This saved White Hawk some further time in this world.

The girl was speaking through smiling lips, "We found you inside your horse. You had opened it and crawled inside for its death-warmth; you were almost stiff with cold, and we could not wake you. I have slept with you for a day and a night. My brother slept on one side, and I on the other. It was the only way. You were dead. You took life from our bodies' warmth." She gave a slight cough. "You are a beautiful man!"

314

"I..."

She leaned forward and kissed him.

"Leave him alone," came a voice from the other side of the blazing fire. A grinning young warrior aged perhaps eighteen winters was toasting a piece of buffalo meat, frozen; it had little fat in it, but what there was flared in the fire.

"I am Big Horse," said the young man by the fire.

"And I am First Snows," smiled the girl.

"I am White Hawk of Yellow Hair's clan of the Northern Cheyenne, the real people." He did not tell them he was a contrary warrior. But they knew that already from the markings which were now almost worn away, but had been there when they found him.

Again the girl caressed his face and as she did so his mind tripped back to Breeze's legs collapsing and himself falling, suddenly awake in the snow. His teeth became a chattering agony of cold so that his jaw was aching stiff. He remembered seeming to hear Yellow Hair shouting in his ear. Screaming in his ear. He had seemed to feel the slash of the old man's bow on his naked back, but he was fully clothed. Out of the dreams of time the phantom of the old man had been on the air, calling into his soul boy's brain to stay awake, and live.

"What are you thinking?" asked the girl.

White Hawk smiled and said quietly, "Nothing."

)( )( )( )( )(

Far away to the North, in the teepee of Sitting Bull, Yellow Hair had been sleeping when suddenly he was flailing in his dreams and calling out, and woke everyone.

"What is wrong?" Sitting Bull had snapped.

"A dream," mumbled Yellow Hair.

"Go to sleep!" came a woman's voice.

"Go to sleep!" called a cheeky boy, out of the darkness, thinking that no elder would be able to tell who it was, but they all could and smiled at his insolence, though he did not know it.

The teepee went silent, and all of them, in their places, in the warmth of themselves and others, rolled over, or curled up and in the safe darkness drifted back to peace.

All, except Yellow Hair who was wide awake, for he had seen such a thing... a white place, with blood everywhere. He had seen

315

himself there too, standing in a blizzard, late for the time of the year, standing there with a waving bow; and he had seen a horse steaming in the snow. He saw his love, his boy, fighting for life in the deadly cold. So he thrashed his shoulders with his bow and the young warrior staggered to his feet and searched for his knife, and found it. In a moment horse entrails were strewn across the white, hissing with warmth. A cavernous warmth was formed and into it White Hawk crawled. Yellow Hair wondered whether it had been a vision or a dream. He decided it was a dream.

That boy was truly wicked coming to him in such a dream. He should have a bow broken across his naked back. With a broadening smile on his face he slipped into an empty sleep until he woke long after sun-up when old Sitting Bull kicked him and said that he was a lazy old winkte fool.

)()()()(

The stinking entrails kept their warmth for some time and held off the cold. As the snow drifted across the entrance to the stomach wall White Hawk was protected from the wind. He bit his lips and talked aloud to stay awake. He knew he must stay awake. Curious thoughts came to him as he drifted towards sleep, and gradually as he lost the battle he began to dream of...

...a white hawk with human eyes, a human face, standing on a snow covered hill. A huge army of warriors dressed in cloaks of albino buffalo fur sat on white ponies, many rearing in honour before the white hawk. A warrior without clothing, youthful, was kneeling in the snow before the hawk. From his perfect chest poured blood from the wounds made by eagle's talons – for he had clearly gone through the ritual of the Sun Dance. Slowly he got to his feet and danced before the warriors in the snow.

Suddenly flames came from the snow for no reason, turning into explosions as, from the ranks of warriors on white horses, came a mass of Wasichu horseriders, their teeth bared with the joy of slaughter.

Regiments of soldier men cut through the white-fur warriors and the snow turned into a sea of blood. The first of the Wasichu soldiers came racing down on the unarmed dancing warrior. He stood and faced them, his arms spread as if to stop the horses, like a brave man might halt a horse spooked by a bear. As he did so, the Wasichu horses turned into bull elks with mighty spreads of antler, from which there fell more soldiers. They tore into the young warrior so that in a moment he was being broken and trampled into the ground; all the beauty of his few winters being turned into... raw meat.

This made the white hawk angry, so angry he became a man, turning into a giant warrior as big as the elks. With a single yank he pulled a leg from the first rearing elk and all the Wasichu fell into the bloody snow. The warrior turned to wipe them out, snatching at the blade on his hip – but it was not there. So he ripped at them with his bare hands which became miracle knives. The beating hearts of the Wasichu were exposed, hideous in their paleness.

It was at that moment all the snow began to turn into flames. The Wasichu themselves had become burning snow, consuming everything. The snow became fire-dust, and in the dust, the darkness of the dust, the hawk man searched for the young warrior who had been torn apart.

He scratched into the dust which covered the earth, burrowing into it and found him, entangled and dirty with the fire-dust. In frantic panic the hawk man tried to put him back together, the blood hopelessly mixed with grit and earth.

As the hawk man was about to cease his struggle, the young warrior in the dust began to metamorphose into a human. First the shreds of face, which smiled a sensual smile and then an arm which lifted up his hand and touched the face of the hawk man, and gently pinched his left ear and then caressed his lips... and was the face of a Cheyenne girl saying, "His eyes are moving..."

16

The song they called:
"We have recovered all our horses!"

(In the Wasichu Year of 1876 when Spring was a few days closer; the year Brevet Major General Reynolds was dismissed for his failure at the Powder River fight)

The reporter from the *Bismarck Post* was very cold indeed. Bob Stanwyk hated the cold, but composed descriptions of it in his head to stay awake. Double coverings of pink long johns, an outsize old uniform over his worn suit, and a soldier's spare horse-coat, all failed to protect against the cutting breeze that always prevailed in those parts in spring, so the older soldiers said. There was no moonlight.

There was a terrible *deja-vu* in this business. The sounds were the same; the horses seemed the same. Even the men huddled against the cold seemed the same. Were the *Bismarck Post* man to have heard General Custer's voice in the gloom, or seen Frank Partridge pass by on a drooped-head horse, he would not have been surprised. But his time it was Colonel Reynolds in command and Frank Grouard the tracker and scout taking point.

Stanwyk could not see them, but Colonel Stanton, chief of scouts, and Lieutenant Bourke were up ahead, talking things through with Frank Grouard. Grouard was a wizard. He knew the country so well it was as if he could see in the dark.

To an extent there was borrowed light from the snow, and against the snow the dark shapes of stands of timber gave some points of reference. But that was all that could be seen by a normal eye. Yet the scouts were following tracks even in this gloom. Damned clever. These mountain men, scouts, renegade whites, call them what you will, were to be admired, thought Stanwyk. They might go over to the Indians and then come back, though some went for good like Frank Partridge and the sons of William Bent (half Indian, of course), but mostly they came back to their own folk. Even so the trackers did not see the Indians first – when they caught sight of them, the Indians were already pointing in *their* direction. That sent shivers down a few spines.

What made matters worse was, it took a trooper on the left flank picket to see the Indians, almost by accident, when he sneezed. His snow-caked hat fell from his head, and as he was brushing it clean of snow he saw them. The small group of blanket-wrapped Indians had been watching *him* long before the sneeze. He did not know this and thought himself an excellent soldier to have caught sight of them. He did not know that they were laughing at his carelessness.

That had been in the late afternoon, already dark, a whole night and day ago. The Indians were on a couple of ponies which seemed fresh, even frisky. The entire command was exhausted, and chase was not given. But as they made off whooping defiance without opening fire, they left a good back trail in the snow. Provided no heavy falls came they could be followed.

General Reynolds – he had been a brevet major general back in the 60s, now lieutenant colonel in command of the 3rd Cavalry in the field – had gone round talking to everyone, saying if they could push on through the night they were more likely to live than die. Everyone grumbled but saw the sense of it. Movement would drive off the cold. It had gotten so God damned bad they had to watch one another in case they fell asleep. That could be their end. Stanwyk saw one young trooper drop to his knees before the first-sergeant and beg the man for permission to sleep. He got the good sergeant's knee in his mouth. The blood froze before it ran an inch. But the lad stayed awake, bless his soul. God! It *is* cold!

Flurries of snow drove into Stanwyk's face. He hunched his shoulders and dropped his head into a sudden blow of wind, air that was black and icy in the utter darkness. Black and icy, and cutting; that was a fair description, was what he thought. Voices ahead.

He felt so wretched he ignored them, thinking only of why he had got into this loathsome situation.

Orders had come from an almighty level – from President Grant himself – directing that the savages were to go to the reservations, the whole sorry lot of them. The order went to Sherman, general of the army, and then to the second man, the lieutenant general in the field – Sheridan.

319

Stanwyk had met the little round general in Chicago. He was charming, even if his language was ripe. He had a clear view of matters military – and all things political – shitty! The damned savages had to be put out of the way of progress. The question was – how?

The general had put up his hand in an insolent Indian sign when he said, "...how?" His staff officers laughed, but the general was very serious. Fooling around with noble firefights was no good. The Army had got to go for the throats of the savages: their property, their food, their living, their way of life.

So, the answer was simple: slaughter the buffaloes, wipe out the horses, disarm the bastards; an unremitting campaign against them – but if they went into the reservation, then that was a different matter. Then they got fed, clothed and looked after – and kept quiet – civilised, if you like. And that was about it. The strategy, at least, was a simple one – surrender or annihilation. But for the present – they must not escape.

Sheridan said he never lost sight of where the tribes were. He had maps. He knew the rough location. All he had to do was send in columns; not one after the other, but co-ordinated across time and terrain. Sooner or later he would bag the lot. And what's more the drive was to go on throughout the year, no lone summer campaign; every season was to be a war season. Sheridan was going to win come hell or high water.

Hell or high water would be a better place, thought Stanwyk, because right at that moment there was frost enough to crack the nuts off a polar bear. It was cold and snowing as well – damn it, this hell was frozen and the high water was sheet ice. A couple of weeks before there had been a thaw; spring was about to arrive; then a sudden drop in temperature, followed by wicked blizzards, late for the season. But 'orders is orders', as they say.

Bob Stanwyk became aware that there was the faintest glimmer, a lesser blackness to the east. Thank God. Dawn. The sun. It would be late-winter weak, but it would be the sun, bringing light. For the moment this was the coldest spot in a twenty-four-hour period.

Despite the harbinger of dawn the air became colder still. As the dawn broke more positively, the air seemed to be solid and struck at the inside of a man's chest. Lips cracked and froze.

"Keep blinking your eyes, damn you all! They'll freeze sure as day follows night, if you don't blink," First-Sergeant Fuller had growled, riding down the line.

Fuller was a small man with a big voice and had been commissioned in the field in the last days of the war. He had reverted to a con-commissioned rank on signing up for the new regular cavalry. He had a mean streak which served to good purpose in these conditions. He kept the men alive. The men had begun to fall asleep on their horses. His crackling voice supported by a riding crop he was prone to carry kept them awake. *Whack!* "Wake up you bastard!"

"Jees, Sergeant, that hurt!"

"Hey, Steiner, you want a beating an all?"

"Nein, Sergeant!"

Whack!

"Speak English you German bastard!"

"Yahvole!"

Whack!

But the boy came sharp awake, untranslatable Germanic filth hissing from beneath his breath.

Command came from the colonel to dismount.

They led their tired mounts through the snow – good way to stay awake. The journey had taken them gradually higher. With the dawn came a spectacle of desolation – a great wilderness of woods, and hills, all capped with ice and snow. A blanket of mean country lay before them. Somewhere out there were the Indians who should be somewhere else – in the reservations.

"There is a enough land here for everyone," grumbled Stanwyk to himself.

Not a living thing seemed to be anywhere. But the scouts knew where they were, sensed the location and all but stumbled on it. They came back, staggering through the drifts, tripping on buried rocks. They reported to the colonel.

Stanwyk saw in the cold gloom that Reynolds, stiff and upright, back in the saddle, immediately set about talking to his staff together with the scouts. Then came the call for officers. Stanwyk moved over towards them, feeling invisible – for he received no attention, not even a courteous nod. Reynolds did not court the press. But that suited Stanwyk.

"Are you certain?" he heard the brevet major general say. They really clung to their old glory, thought Stanwyk.

"Sure am!" the half-breed scout coughed out in the cold. Stanwyk thought it was the scout Batiste – half Blackfoot, half Froggie – but was not sure with all the furs wrapped round his head. He sounded very certain of himself.

"How many again?" asked Reynolds.

"A hundred teepees or thereabouts, maybe less. It is the encampment of Crazy Horse."

The startling news brought a subdued cheer from the gathered officers. Good news.

Stanwyk ran a thought through his mind of looking down on the famous savage's corpse and describing it in detail, the cruel lines now at peace, the hands that pulled the scalps off women after unmentionable deeds. To take the scalp of one of their greatest of leaders in revenge! Maybe he could get it into a bottle of whiskey for preservation and exhibit it in Bismarck. Make a damned fortune.

He saw himself kneeling to sketch the detail of the face without hair, a horse soldier holding the grim trophy in his hand, maybe with a foot on the heathen's chest, hand on hip, scalp held against the sky. He hoped his fingers would not tremble in the cold. Such a sketch would drive Bismarck wild. Crazy Horse destroyed! And in the centennial year – what a story.

Only Sitting Bull and Red Cloud were greater. Red Cloud was already safe in a reservation – his own – or so he was allowed to think. Sitting Bull was somewhere. Somewhere to the north. He would be next. This morning's work was to be Crazy Horse; the most dangerous of the warrior savages – to see him skinned – what a story, oh boy!

Reynolds was giving orders already – he described his understanding of the village, from what the scouts had reported, and layout of the terrain. He spoke with brisk words and added a line drawing in the snow.

"See this, gentlemen – a creek lies across our line of march. It lies at right angles into the Powder River. The hostiles are on the west bank of the river to the north, on the other side of the creek. Steep hills lie here, to the west of the camp, hemming it in." He shuffled a draw of snow with his foot to mark the place. "On the opposite side of the river is a range of high ground. Between that ground on the river, cut off from the village, the scouts have reported a big herd of ponies – at least five hundred in number. Now listen, this is what we do."

The colonel told Captain Egan to take Company K straight into the village – they were on the lovely greys, looking more like albinos with their dressing of fresh snow. Egan was to charge across the creek and into the village through to the upper end – frighten the wits out of them, shoot into the teepees, frighten them out, cut them down, give targets to Captain Moore's lads who would be on Egan's left. There should be time to catch them sleeping, if they were lucky.

A battalion of two companies under Captain Moore was to move close to the village and take a position on the west side at the near end of the ridge, which overlooked the village. None of the Indians would be allowed to escape that way. "Shoot them down, Moore, shoot them down."

It was to be the task of young Captain Noyes to cut out the ponies and drive them back south towards the pack animals and the reserves. This would serve to take them away from the Indians who would either have to drown in the river, or struggle up the escarpment on the west, or run north – pursued by the greys.

Low laughs of approval greeted the colonel's orders. It looked good. Reynolds divided the scouts – about fifteen each to the three commands to make sure they did not lose their way.

"I'll go along with Moore," said Colonel Stanton, chief of scouts. The grizzled old warrior looked cold, up all night, half the time on his feet, tracking. His toes were numb, he tended to hobble. He was hoping that frostbite was not setting in.

Stanwyk resolved to mention him in his dispatches as a brave officer who would not give up. He watched him join Moore, carrying his long hunting rifle for the coming sport.

"May I also proceed with the greys?" Bob Stanwyk asked.

Reynolds eyed the reporter with little interest, and did not answer.

"Sir?"

"Of course, of course, go as you please Mr. Stanwyk," snapped the colonel and then turned back to his officers to check that all knew exactly what was required of them. Stanwyk resolved to be less kind to the colonel in his dispatches – unless it was a brilliant victory, of course.

The troops moved off, only mouth-bits and bridle making any noise, and even that was subdued in another flurry of the dying blizzard. The terrain was not easy: scrub and rocks, low trees, broken stumps, fox holes and entangled vegetation lay like grabbing serpents beneath the uneven covering of snow. Despite the excitement of the change from cold marches to hot action, the icy air bit into the struggling men's concentration. But they finally broke through the worst of the undergrowth as they came into clear sight of the village.

They stared through the weakening falls of snow. The collection of teepees appeared deserted except for a few horses tethered close to individual teepees, and a small pack of dogs moving through the west of the village. Steady smoke from each lodge, drifting vertically, showed life was present inside. They could smell burning wood, for the prevailing currents of air, having come from the north, were carrying the village vapours down to them. The wind had dropped a little, so the perfume of habitation lingered over their start-line area. This was good – the dogs would not pick up the scent of cavalry.

Moore moved out of sight on the left where he was to dismount and form a strong skirmishing line. The greys led point in the centre whilst the troops of Noyes, on the right, wheeled away and forded the river to move in on the ponies.

At a mile distance Egan saw that they had not been discovered. Redskins were never awake – not until after sunup in winter, and in half the summer too, docile idle people. Too much wild dancing before they slept – but surely not in the winter. The devils were just bone lazy. Even so the camp looked majestic in the growing light. The teepees, scores of them, lay between some fine cottonwoods just short of the steep slope, which was becoming the advancing regiment's left. A mass of willows close by the river formed the right. The movement of Noyes troops would be partly obscured by the willows.

"Check your weapons," came a whisper from Egan.

The men made sure there was a cartridge breached in their carbines, and the few who had repeaters of their own checked that the magazines were full. Revolvers were fully loaded; they would be heavily used for certain. Overcoats were removed and packed behind the saddles. The men were still shivering, partly from fear, and resented losing their protective coats. But without them they had greater control of their movements, and thus their weapons.

Through field glasses the forward terrain was inspected, and then the order came to move forward, quietly, on foot. Little more than half a mile short of the village the men mounted again, drew their revolvers, or cocked their other weapons, after leaning over to ensure that cavalry blades were lose in the scabbards.

"Move forward at the trot – in your own time gallop, if we're discovered, and go right into them. Pass it on!" Egan said quietly to his officers on left and right.

The order ran through the ranks of the greys. The horses snorted; seeming to know the importance of the moment, for their snorts were low, like whispers.

"Fooooorwarrrrd har," came the command, spoken, not bellowed.

The scouts had indicated a run of low land along the edge of the river, and the company moved along it. The company had been reduced by illness and minor desertions, and was little more than half its full strength. One hundred and five men moved forward.

From the right of the camp, as they approached, a lone Indian was seen to emerge from the willows. He saw the soldiers at once and gave a great yell.

"Charge!" screamed Egan. "Charge, my boys!"

)(()(()(()(()(

Whilst the Wasichu froze and advanced on the village, White Hawk was sleeping in the arms of a beautiful girl, at his back a warm young man. The girl had suggested it when the temperature dropped. Everyone in the teepee had giggled. But it was very cold. All of them were sleeping with others than night, but in twos.

All, except aged old Moon-On-The-Water, who lay alone in a darkness within the darkness of the teepee, within the darkness of the night, for she was blind.

After the jokes and the gossip, after the complaints about the cold, after the plans for tomorrow, when the sound of sleep overtook the air they shared, she listened to their breathing, their soft whispers and the hint of rhythmic movements. She focused her hearing on the three youth people; herself aroused by their pleasure.

Occasionally there was a sound of mirth, whispered. The old lady knew that they were exploring each other. Within her own warm hides and blankets she held herself. She stroked her flesh and thought of those good times when she could distinguish the blue sky from the clouds in summer, and see birds on the air.

She thought of her men, fallen to arrows or the hooves of bison in the hunt, she thought of her sons, and she thought of her granddaughter over there with her own young young brother and the stranger who had touched the old lady's face in greeting. The caress had been so smooth and gentle, like a woman's; but when she had touched his chest it had been that of a young warrior, firm and smooth, oiled with buffalo fat. He had felt beautiful. To see, oh, to see!

The blindness had come slowly, edging her sight, with a blackness round a hole in her vision, as if she were looking through a wrapping of fur. The edges of her sight shimmered, and then, gradually, with the passage through the autumn of her years, spots without vision formed, and then there came a blur overall, then blackness with occasional lurid sparks. It had been especially bad for her for she was the painter of the calendars – famous for her designs on the teepees when she was young. She would paint no more. But at least the paintings were still there, recording the passing of the years, for ever.

She heard a gasp.

It was the stranger; she knew his sound. They said he was a contrary warrior and Moon-On-The-Water felt a slight disgust with the way in which the young behaved in these upset times. In her youth no contrary warrior would have lain beside a naked girl. This wicked boy was between a girl *and* a boy. She smiled again in tolerant disapproval; this was a bad thing, a wrong thing, a very contrary thing... she thought about that – perhaps he *was* a contrary after all.

The old lady's hearing was acute, more so since her blindness. She felt as if she could hear the sound of skin touching skin. She could sense the sweat between them, the contact. Her imagination driven by the darkness which surrounded her very soul was a second sight. She drifted inside the darkness and was beneath the hides with them, touching all three, feeling their sexuality and their closeness. She fell into a dreamless sleep.

She woke with a start.

She thought it was the young men returning. The small scouting party of Wolf Soldiers had been sent out following news of Wasichu soldiers coming up from the south. The Wasichu were lost in the cold and the snow, but they might stumble on the lines of villages along the Powder River. She pictured village scenes in her mind's eye, pulling back the visions of the river in the summer: the antelope moving in and out of the woods, the ducks descending to the water, geese, she saw geese in her head.

She saw the huge herds of buffalo that the people said were disappearing to the slaughter of the Wasichu. All that she had seen, and had been, was in her head but was disappearing from the sight of the whole world.

She heard the drum of distant horses.

She listened for the young ones making love, but there was silence, she could hear the three of them breathing. She could hear her younger sister breathing to her left, coughing the persistent winter cough from time to time in her sleep. She could hear the children too, early morning bickering between begging to be left alone to sleep a little longer. All was happiness.

Yet, surrounding the happiness like the commencing of her blindness, there was a something which should not have been there.

She picked up on the smell of smoke, she sensed all eight souls within their warm home as individuals, everyone sleeping in the circle of buffalo hides set upon their willow frameworks to lift them from the still frozen earth. She could hear footsteps outside too.

She tried to picture who it was and knew it was old Beaver Man going out to pray. He was a foolish old man. He was too old to risk praying at dawn in this bad bad bad weather. He had wanted to marry her not so long ago and she had refused, for she was good for nothing and he prayed too much. But once, once, there had been a time...

Old Moon-On-The-Water turned on to her side, smiling in the warmth of her hides and heard the sound of horses, even felt it coming from the earth.

The sound of horses. Many horses. Far away. She heard horses.

"I hear horses!" she said.

Silence from everyone.

She heard horses.

"I can hear horses." Her voice rose slightly so that the others woke or moved towards the flaps of consciousness.

"THE SOLDIERS ARE RIGHT HERE!" An old man's shout came from outside.

She heard everyone come awake.

Crack!

She heard a gun fired too close. Screams cut the air, and the thunder of horses, coming in fast, meant slaughter. Plenty horses. She held tight to herself in her nakedness. She felt with certainty that this was to be the morning of her death, so she began to struggle out of blankets to face it as best she could.

Wasichu voices. Horses. Screams. *Bang! Bang!*

Bang! Crack! Bang! The sound of firing was a crackling of mighty hailstones on teepees. She heard them hitting the teepee, whizzing through the teepee.

They were all up. They called to each other.

Terrible noises.

Frantic, she reached for a robe, which would be exactly as she placed it. A child ran by and she felt the sudden icy air of outside coming in as someone rushed from the teepee and left the flap open. She found her robe. It was on her in her darkness within the darkness of the dawn within the darkness of the lodge, a darkness in which she could see only with her fingers.

On hands and knees she set off for the opening. She suddenly realised that she was alone. They had left her. All of them. Now her world was darkness and death, and the laughter of the Wasichu.

She had never seen a Wasichu. The darkness came too early. But she had a vision of them in her eyes. They were white like ghosts in snow, and had eyes which were blue like the sky, and their smell was evil. She had never smelt a Wasichu. People said it was a bad smell. She stood at the opening, sensing that the sun was up with a cold dawn, and she sniffed at the air which carried the sounds of war. A smell came to her that she had never smelt before. So, she thought, that is the perfume of the Wasichu... it was not so bad.

)( )( )( )( )(

The three of them ran west. The whole village was a confusion of galloping horses and screaming people. White Hawk felt an anger with himself that he was helping no-one. He was just running with the rest. It was panic. It was all happening again. They were like a herd of buffaloes stampeding; everyone was running because everyone was running. Running. Where to? Away!

A huge white horse swept by. A Wasichu rider with a handgun was firing into each teepee. He fired at a child and missed. He fired at a woman and missed. He fired at White Hawk and missed. Then the gun was not firing. He was pointing it and firing, but it was empty. He was laughing.

A second huge white horse went by and White Hawk felt the hiss of a longknife pass his head. He threw himself into the snow, rolling away from beating hooves and found himself next to a repeating rifle and was on his feet in a moment. He jerked a round into the breach, snapped it to his shoulder and fired. Nothing. It was empty. The round had been a phantom. Then he noticed that the barrel was bent, so he threw it to one side in disgust.

Another Wasichu horse went by and White Hawk felt a splash of warm blood on his face and he saw that the animal was spurting death from the great vein in its neck from which protruded the flight of an arrow that had passed through the animal. The horse went a few lengths further then collapsed, no rider on its back.

It was light now.

He looked back and saw the fight. There was utter confusion with hundreds of the real people fleeing like ants from an armadillo. The soldiers were riding this way and that firing their weapons. White Hawk was surprised to see no-one was dead. There were no bodies. Then he saw one of the horses go down. All of the horses were white or grey, their blue-clad riders contrasted sharply against horse and snow; only the teepees with their brilliant designs, one of which was already on fire, brought brightness to the scene.

White Hawk saw a bow in the snow. It was not strung. He picked it up and with a push of his knee set the gut-string taught. He looked for arrows. In that moment there were no soldier-men near.

He dashed into the last of the teepees before the ground rose towards a steep incline. Masses of Cheyenne were struggling up the incline, some on ponies, most on foot. Some had already turned and were singing songs of death and calling out that it was a good day to die. They had begun to fire down on the soldiers riding through the village. Inside the teepee he found a quiver full of good hunting arrows. They would do.

Outside, and he ran towards the rise in the ground where he saw a soldier on foot firing up the hill. To his left he saw three Cheyennes; he did not know their names. He threw himself beside them. They had taken cover behind some fallen trees. Bullets were in the air.

"Kill him, kill him!" he snarled at the three of them – two of them had guns and were doing nothing.

He fitted an arrow to the string. He looked at the soldier. The range was too far.

"Shoot!" White Hawk shouted at the fools with guns.

A bullet from the soldier sang overhead.

One of the braves had a repeating rifle. He had set the rifle on its butt in front of him and was passing his hands along the barrel, muttering, preying to give good spirit to the rifle. Then he said, "My medicine is good; watch me kill that soldier."

He brought the rifle up, cold barrel to his fingers. He squeezed the trigger, the butt slammed into his shoulder. The soldier was just standing there, firing steadily up the hill. Fearless. A warrior too.

"You missed!" shouted White Hawk.

"Watch me!" said the other one with a gun. He had a muzzle-loader, an old musket with a long barrel, which used only good old black powder. He aimed with care. The pan flashed and the old gun kicked.

The soldier had turned away to check his weapon, and to pick something up from the snow. They saw the ball smack into the back of his head. He pitched forward to his knees and all four of them ran out to attack him. They kicked him and as he turned on his back to face them one of them stabbed him and another clubbed his face. He was soon dead. With bullets wasping between them they stripped him.

One took his jerkin; the others snatched what took their fancy. White Hawk picked up the soldier's gun. It was a single shot rifle. White Hawk felt in the pouches lying in the snow and found nine rounds of ammunition. He felt in a smaller pouch and found caps. He opened the breach and put in a new round, and capped the nipple. He waved the rifle in the air and called out to *Wakantanka* with a scream, which startled the others.

"*Wakantanka* – where are you?"

They recognised him as the contrary stranger who had been found inside a horse. Did he not know that *Wakantanka* was everywhere?

But when he ran towards the hillside they followed him because he was a contrary warrior and could not be killed by bullets. It would be lucky to be by his side even if he did not know of the presence of God.

)( )( )( )( )(

Noyes' company forded the Powder River south of the junction with the east flowing creek. The Indian herd was not tended – it must have been the cold. The troopers circled left and right and then edged the chilled and sleepy animals south. There was some hesitation when they came to the river but the noise of gunfire from the village put some life into the animals. Then First-Sergeant Fuller raised his voice and lashed a stallion on its flank. The brute kicked back in protest but jumped into the icy water. The rest followed, pursued by yelling soldiers.

A few spent bullets sang on the frosty air making the troopers feel that they were part of something, but the freezing water in their boots kept more of their attention. They passed the colonel, horsed and proud, watching the action in the village through his field glasses and gave him a cheer. He took off his hat and waved them by. Reynolds estimated there must have been six or seven hundred ponies in the herd, and the savages had given up the village without a fight. There might be a star back on his shoulders by the end of the year.

He brought his glasses back up to his eyes and watched the rout. Something to his left caught his attention and he panned round, whispering to his horse to stand steady, damn it.

)( )( )( )( )(

The panic was over. White Hawk led his three braves part way up the hill then they turned to fire on the soldiers. There was already a grizzled warrior in position, firing steadily from a venerable sporting rifle, captured by an uncle, years before, from a wagon train.

"Aim!" White Hawk shouted.

The much older warrior gave White Hawk a dark look, "I've put two down already! I *am* aiming."

"You just missed!"

"I've got two!" the older man snapped back.

White Hawk suddenly realised that it was Chief Old Bear himself and said nothing more to him.

331

The barrel of his long muzzle-loader was hot to the touch, nice to feel in the cold of morning. The rifle had gold etching along the barrel and lock. The stock was smooth and tanned to a bronze sheen. There were deep grooves in it – ten. Seven had been carved by himself.

He hammered home the ball. After putting a fresh percussion cap on the nipple he steadied himself and looked for a target. A group of horsemen were close to the north entrance of the village. It was a long shot. But they were milling around and he felt lucky for the group made a large target. They were setting fire to the teepee of Two Bears – the one painted by Moon-on-the-Water before her sight went away. He recognised it from that famous painting which had taken the woman two weeks to complete on the outside of the skins. The whole village was proud of that design. They said it was her best. He pulled back the hammer.

Resting with his back against a fir he steadied the barrel with right elbow pressed into the inside of his right knee. The target was at extreme range – perhaps half a mile – but he had put in an extra couple of pinches of black powder from the horn, in anticipation of a long shot. The barrel was steady, unwavering, his arms were strong, he was relaxed and happy. He squeezed.

Crrwam!

The smoke cleared. A pause. One of the distant horses reared and suddenly dashed from the group, spilling its rider. The man was on his feet in a moment and chasing after the horse, which suddenly fell forward and was on its back, legs kicking in the air. They watched as the Wasichu rider pulled out a revolver and shot into the animal until it stopped moving.

"See," said the Old Bear smiling up at White Hawk.

The contrary was also smiling and said, "But you only hit a horse. Anyone can hit a horse."

Old Bear grunted at the impertinence and began to reload, smiling.

}(}(}(}(}(

The colonel trotted between the burning lodges. Shots were buzzing through the village like hornets in anger and a line of Egan's skirmishers was firing back up the hill. Moore was not moving to his left as he should have been, to clear the hill. The whole encampment was in flames. Everything was burning. Damn! Damn! Damn!

A scout came in from the north end of the village and reported a war party of fifty or more was gathering at that end of the village. A shot sang over the colonel's head.

"We appear to have punished them enough," he said to no-one in particular.

He noticed Stanwyk sketching a burning teepee and reined his horse towards him.

"We've given them a thrashing, Mr. Stanwyk. I trust you will record it so, sir!"

"I shall, Colonel." He did not even look up from his pad. "Any sign of Crazy Horse?"

"I have not heard."

The colonel glanced over the reporter's shoulder. The sketch was remarkably accurate. He had recorded a pile of native artefacts: furs, robes, amazing head-dresses with eagle feathers – all going up in smoke.

"Each damned tent is an exhibition house, by God," the reporter remarked, for his trained eye had valued what he sketched.

"And they also hold a damned arsenal of supplies," snapped the colonel.

The reporter nodded.

"And they are damned teepees, Mr. Stanwyk, not damned tents."

"I stand corrected, Colonel."

A bullet kicked up snow between them. The colonel looked towards the western ridge. There were scores, hundreds of them up there, with sporadic firing puffing from between the trees.

He looked round and saw that several greys were down. He watched a trooper deliver the *coup de grace* to a fine animal – took three shots, waste of ammunition. Damnation to the man.

A sudden irritation ran through him as yet another bullet, from its whirring, almost spent, went so close to his head he felt its wind on his face. A whoosh of flame leapt from a teepee as an emptied keg of powder was fired.

"What the hell was that?" asked Stanwyk, still sketching.

"I said the victuals were to be spared!" shouted Reynolds as he suddenly realised that masses of dried meat had been put to the torch. All of it! Damn!

"Mr. Egan! The men have burned all the damned meat! Enough for a brigade for the rest of damned winter."

Captain Egan had ridden in to be greeted by the colonel's wrath.

"My apologies, sir. They are too eager and annoyed – we've lost some men!"

"We needed those supplies, damn it! How many lost?"

"Three dead, three or four wounded sir."

The colonel thought on his epaulette of stars.

The herd was taken; the savages beaten. Many must be dead, though he saw no proof of that beyond one naked figure in the middle of the village with two exit holes cratering his back. The village was in flames. Their supplies were destroyed. Pity about the damned meat. Time to pull out.

"How many did we get, Egan?"

"Hard to tell."

"Well – tell! Hazard a God-damned guess, man!"

"Forty, sir – maybe more."

"Where are they?"

"Must have carried them off, sir!"

The colonel grunted.

"Bugler! Where's the damned blamed bugler?"

"Bugler!" shouted Egan for his colonel.

A trooper spurred forward from Egan's company.

"Sound withdrawal!" snapped the colonel.

It was then that the colonel saw two troopers trying to shoot an old woman, so he turned his horse that way.

"Egan – get those men away from her and back to the skirmishing line."

)()()()(

Moon-On-The-Water heard the Wasichu voices. She did not understand them. She stood there at the entrance to her teepee with her arms outspread for this was a very good day to die, and about time. She stood smiling, pale eyes staring at her memories.

"Hey Steiner – look at that old bitch!"

Trooper Gerber, eighteen years old, without a hint of hair on his face, his grey horse prancing, pointed to the squaw in front of the teepee. He aimed his Colt at her, sighting with care; he chose a chest shot. She made no movement. He could hear her chanting with a squeaky voice. He pulled the trigger. Misfire. He cocked again and fired. Misfire. He looked. God daaamn! No ammo!

"Shoot her, Harry!" said Steiner with his German snarl. "I'm out of ammo."

"I'm out too."

But Harry Gerber felt in his pouch and as he did so his horse turned on the spot and reared. He had heard the bullet hit the animal. He looked back and saw that the hip had been creased. Nothing. Steadying his horse he found two rounds caught up in the leather of his pouch. He broke his revolver and spilled the spent cartridge casings and slipped in the two fresh rounds. He locked the gun back into position and turned to face the old woman again.

He heard Steiner shout, "Shee'z blind!"

Gerber, recruited for the famous 7th Cavalry, was displeased to be in the 3rd. But at least he was in action, killing Redskins. His mind was full of the certain fact that thus far he had killed nobody. The whole village had fled. The old woman would have to do. He pulled back the hammer.

"Shee'z blind!" shouted the German again.

It was the vision of an old relative, blind Aunt Maria, which caused Harry Gerber to lower his weapon.

They both moved in close to the woman and heard her chant, saw her body moving up and down very gently with the beat of her call. Sudden heavy firing from the west caused them both to look up. The old woman continued her chanting.

"Shiiiiit!" said the beardless boy and turned his horse at the approach of Captain Egan.

"You men get to work over there!" bellowed the captain and pointed to a line of skirmishers returning fire at the hillside which was now alive with smoke and flashes of light. "What's holding you?"

"Shee'z blind!" shouted the German boy.

"Go!" screamed the captain.

The two troopers pumped their horses towards the skirmishing line.

The colonel came up skidding to a halt, almost colliding with the departing troopers.

"How goes it now, young Egan?"

"Strengthened the skirmishing line, like you said!" Egan snapped.

"Well done!"

The colonel eyed the old woman. She appeared untouched.

"She's blind," said Egan, matter of fact, and in looking her way the colonel saw that it was so.

The colonel stared at the frail figure.

"Thought we'd leave her – and her teepee – did you ever see such colours?" said Egan, gesturing towards the teepee.

The lodge was covered with images of braves chasing buffaloes, dancing round huge fires, diamonds and streaks of colour winding though and around the characters – damned primitive as far as Reynolds could see, but magnificent.

"Beautiful," muttered Egan.

The colonel grunted assent and turned his horse to lead his battalion out of the burning village under cover of the skirmishers. One teepee left would accentuate the destruction. One blind woman spared – what possible harm could she do?

It had been a good fight. But those lost rations could have kept his and General Crook's men supplied for a week or more. Reynolds felt the prospects for a returning star begin to fade. But he still had the horses.

)( )( )( )( )(

As the troopers left, to the south, so the warriors and the people trickled back from north and west. When White Hawk met with Big Horse they hugged each other like brothers. They searched for First Snows, with growing fears they might not find her alive. They came across Wooden Leg, good friend of Big Horse, who had saved the chief's own pony (they learned later) and White Hawk recognised him as being one of the three who had killed the soldier with him. He said that he had seen First Snows alive and back in the village. They headed for where their teepee had stood.

Out of the smoke and stench of burning furs and meat they were astonished to see their teepee still standing. First Snows was there and in her arms was old woman Moon-On-The-Water. They were crying.

"What has happened?" howled Moon-On-The-Water.

They told her.

"I heard it, I heard it!" the old woman moaned. "I smelt the Wasichu – they are only men! You should have killed them all."

News came from all sides that the herd was gone. This was a cruel day. There was nothing to do. Each warrior had a view, everyone spoke at the same time, chattering, boasting, blaming each other. But nothing could be done. There were too many soldiers and the fighting men had no horses. Suddenly Moon-On-The-Water spoke, interrupting as she always did.

"Listen to me!" she screeched.

Those around took no notice, as always.

"Listen to me!" Her voice was a call like a swooping hawk. Voices stopped. How could the old woman make such noise?

"We are Cheyennes!" Her voice was a scream, ripping into the moment of silence, and the veins on her old neck stood out.

In her mind were visions of her people marching through their own history with spears held high and huge herds of buffalo fleeing. She saw the Crow and the Arapaho and all the others who loved or fought and feared her people. Saw it all in a moment, a life-time of life-times, and she saw the horses returned through the snow, saw it clearly, saw it in designs and patterns on a teepee of the mind.

"They can not take our horses!" she called.

Blank faces, for they already had taken the horses, but she had not seen.

"They've gone, old woman," said Old Bear leaning on his ancient Baker rifle, still warm, very warm.

"I have seen them returning!" came her broken iced voice, gasps of vapour leaving her gnarled lips, hissing past three broken brown teeth.

Muttering broke out.

"Go! Go young warriors! Get them back – I have seen you return with them – I am blind – but I have seen it – before the sun rises! Thirteen young braves must go – led by the contrary." She saw him in her mind's eye, saw his movement in her dead eyes.

Before the sun rises! Was it possible? Protests began.

Old Bear spoke, old chief, too slow to lead in a fight, but he spoke. All went quiet. He had heard the woman and sensed some magic.

"We have horses for forty braves – you, Wooden Leg and you," pointing to White Hawk, "and you." His finger was towards Big

Horse. "Take ten more good warriors and bring back the herd if you can."

"They can," she wheezed through tears anew, "I have seen it!"

Old Bear continued, with an unseen frown at the old woman, "The rest help the people and cover us as we withdraw to the lodges of Crazy Horse. He will give us shelter. He is not far to the north."

"I have seen it," she said again. "I have seen it."

As she spoke, she fell to her knees. Two young men bent to lift her. It was as if she meant to die.

But she did not die then.

Others took skins from her teepee and made a travois. It was the rescued horse of Old Bear himself which dragged her through the melting snow for two days to the camp of Crazy Horse. They re-set her teepee there in all its glory. It was there that she died, calling out that she could hear horses coming. But by then no one listened, for the ten young men had not come back. It seemed that everything was to be lost after all.

Moments later the dogs began to bark and they heard the approach of many horses, not ten, but hundreds.

As a pack, dogs and people ran to greet them, leaving the old woman in the teepee with the many drawings on the outside, once taken from her mind.

)()()()()(

They had taken only the silent bows and arrows. They followed the noisy Wasichu. Then on the last of the cold nights when the sentries were sleeping they whispered amongst the horse until they found the lead mares. Then the horses, sensing that they should be silent, began to follow the mares, ridden by thirteen young men, away from the Wasichu. That was how they recaptured the horses and returned home to their valley.

They passed through the burned out camp but did not stop. They looked ahead, weeping as they rode, thinking of the beautiful things that could never be again.

Two mornings later they came down on the village of Crazy Horse. As they approached, the people thought it was the Wasichu cavalry, but when they came out in fear their panic turned to cheers when they saw the horses. A song was written on the air which they called, *"We have recovered all our horses!"*

338

Singing, they went to see Moon-On-The-Water lying in death. They saw there was a smile on her face, for she had been the first to hear them coming.

That smile was a wonderful sight, and spontaneously, with much feeling of honour, they began a beautiful funeral chant. They developed it, adding it to their first song, as an honour to she who saw what would take place with her blind eyes.

17

The Awakening

(In the Wasichu year of 1876)

Colonel 'Sandy' Forsyth slapped the letter on the lieutenant general's desk. "We have it!"

Phil Sheridan studied the document and glanced at the date on the inkstand of his desk. February 7th. Memorable. He had authorisation from the secretary of the interior to go on the warpath against *any* non-reservation Indian.

Sheridan spent less than two days with his staff setting out the strategic detail. Three columns were to be released – one led by Brigadier General Terry, another by Brigadier General Crook. Colonel John Gibbon was to set out from Montana with the 7th Infantry and half of the 2nd Cavalry. They would be there in that area in any case since they had been ordered to get in position to block the buffalo hunt that spring. If the hostiles moved north he was to intercept.

Crook was to leave from Fort Fetterman in Wyoming Territory.

"When do you reckon he can move, Sandy?" Sheridan asked his chief of staff.

Colonel Forsyth thought for a moment. "March, I guess – he'll complain, but maybe he could move at March."

"What's he got?"

"About ten companies of cavalry – 3rd licking their wounds – and a couple of companies of infantry. There's some scouts with him. He'll have a thousand fighting men and a long baggage train."

"He's already messed up with that blamed fool Reynolds. That man wasn't worth shit on a damned dining table. Never shall I understand how he lost those damned horses to a handful of heathen. He deserved what the papers wrote – but I'm damned if the Army did. Crook filing for a court martial for Reynolds don't change a blessed thing – only doin' it to save Crook's own skin..."

"And reputation, sir."

"And reputation, Sandy."

Sheridan pondered for a moment on the time he had suspended Crook himself as one of his corps commanders in the big war. Not a pleasant job, relieving a friend. On that basis Crook would have had no worry about getting rid of Reynolds. There was no love lost there.

Sheridan strolled across to the big scale map covering the whole of one wall of his office. He picked up a long pointer. "They're there, you know Sandy, they're there; right there – I bet you a dime to a gold mine."

He pointed at the line of the Valley of the Little Big Horn. In fact, the Indians were not there; the valley was empty. But that was where the nations *planned* to be in the Month of the Ripe Berries – June. Sheridan's instinct would be proven sound.

"We've failed this winter to lock into the heathen. Reynold's fault, damn him. We have to have a steady and careful summer campaign. The Redskins will like that, sure to give us a run for our money. But we'll wear the bastards down. We have to have the best columns we've got – out in the field this summer, always working towards each other."

The chief of staff nodded thoughtfully, "We are bound to make contact somewhere. But it is important, sir, that each column is small enough to move quickly and big enough to look after itself."

"Agreed." Sheridan drifted across to the big window looking out onto the garden behind the headquarters building. Then he turned back to his chief of staff.

"Now then, how does this sound? Gibbon's to move down the Yellowstone, starting, let's say in April. Now then, Terry has a pretty well full 7th Cavalry, yes? They can move out of Fort Abraham Lincoln beginning of May at the latest. Reno is temporary in command, no damned good to man or beast. We've got to get Custer back. Damn it, I'll write to Grant, Sherman as well. We need the lad back. Custer is no Reynolds. He'll find them if anyone can, *and* grip them. Yes, we'll get Custer back in command, right?"

"Right, sir."

"Terry's column should march down the Heart River valley joining the Yellow Stone at Cedar Creek, or thereabouts." He pointed out the confluence of the rivers. "Now, once Crook is back at Fort Fetterman he can re-equip, and move out in early May too. Should get to the Rosebud River about June so long as he don't take time off to go fishing. They all ought to meet around mid June in the Big Horn Valley. If we have not hit the Lakota Sioux and their allies by then, or got them into the reservations, well, damn it to hell... you can eat my hat."

"Yes, General."

"Then you agree, in principle, that's the plan."

"In principle – and I'll get down to the details with the staff. When do I get onto the commanders?"

"Now."

"Of course – should have known. That means two days from now"

"Less, damn it!"

Sheridan filled two glasses with a fine sherry just come in from Spain. "To the damnation of the damned," said Sheridan, handing over a glass.

"You mean the Redskins?"

"I mean all those who are going to fall because we are making big decisions on little maps."

"That's a pretty big map, General."

"The country's a damned sight bigger!"

)()()()()(

(May 29th 1876 Sage Creek)

Lieutenant Bourke, on Crook's staff, double-checked the inventory of troops, equipment and supplies and made a record in his diary. General Crook strolled up. The approximation to a uniform he had worn at Fort Fetterman had already been replaced by buckskin, old and worn. He had also started to braid his beard again, certain sign of a long campaign.

"Well Bourke, what have we done, ten, twelve, what?"

"Well, sir, by my calculations the column has moved around eleven miles."

"Now that's not bad for a start, first day of a march."

342

"The column got a bit spread out. We were well over a mile long at one point. When we have open country we'll march in four columns, by your leave."

"Of course, but I fancy the terrain will not be that kind. Keep 'em up together as best you can. Pass the word as an Order of the Day."

The general walked away, there was a clear creek on the edge of the camp. He wanted to take a look at the trout.

)( )( )( )( )(

(June 15th 1876 Near the headwaters of the Rosebud)

Pursuing the woody perfume of the camp fire Frank Partridge was surprised to see a single mule tethered to a bush. There was no saddle or pack tackle on its back as it munched on some leaves. It was not feeding so much as tasting, searching out the most succulent. The mule did not find them to his liking and was in the process of spitting them out, lines of saliva hanging from mouth.

Frank Partridge did not see the mule in time to halt his movement through the undergrowth so the mule's ears turned in the tracker's direction. The animal stopped chewing and stared with baleful eyes into the timber. It could smell nothing. Frank Partridge was downwind. It could see nothing either for Frank had eased himself out of view. But it had *heard* something. Frank froze. With no further sound disturbing the air the animal forgot about it, began to move its jaws, its ears flicked back, it relaxed. It began to nibble again at another distasteful leaf.

Frank Partridge was Grey Eagle that morning.

He had not seen a white man for a year, living with the followers of Sitting Bull. He was wearing Indian clothing topped with a jerkin without paint-work, rather old and smelling of his own sweat; leggings were over a breechcloth and good moccasins protected his feet. He had left the huge concentration of villages and nations three days earlier, just wanting to get out and hunt, get away from the noise of all that merriment, for they had taken some good buffalo and were celebrating. Half a dozen of the young braves followed him. The Wasichu had good luck on the hunt.

He was armed lightly with a knife and his old Whitworth .45. He had planned to bag a deer, early in the morning, whilst everyone else in the hunting expedition was sleeping. He did it within an hour with a good clean head-shot. He took the carcass back to his friends and the day was spent in cooking and eating. Hell, how they loved to eat. He left them recovering from the following night of dancing and laughter after the buck had been finished and shared with three dogs which had followed them out of the gathering of the peoples.

Grey Eagle now wanted the patch of woodlands to himself. That part of the prairie was untouched by settlers and the woods which had colonised the small valleys had not been stripped naked for fuel and buildings. In some of these secret places humans were almost unknown even at that date. But it looked like he was not alone on this occasion. The fact that the animal was a tethered mule and not a stray elk suggested a white man's presence in the timber.

A parting in the run of trees exposed a small outcrop of rock, green with moss and rounded lichens. The outcrop had been worn smooth on one side by a stream. The sides were damp from the splashing of a brook's falling water which eventually broke out from the small patch of woodland and made its way into a deep coulee and then on to the Little Big Horn River about twenty miles away. Grey Eagle strained his ears and heard the noise of a fire crackling in the clearing. The acrid perfume of coffee brewing hung on the air as an invisible cloud. A thin column of blue wood smoke rose almost vertically until it dissipated into the air at the tops of the firs. This marked the place the camper would be sleeping or eating. Grey Eagle eased himself to his left, keeping an eye on the mule; he caught a glimpse of his quarry at the third step.

A somewhat gaunt man with a scraggly beard tied into braids, with what looked like some string, was lying idly by the side of the fire, his head supported on a crooked arm. He slowly turned a rabbit on a spit put across the fire, held there at each end of the spit by a tripod of branches. He was scruffy in his dress, old trousers and a jerkin with a tear in the arm.

Frank moved a little closer and the man turned his head as the mule gave a grunt and shifted position. It was not chewing at all. I'm a fool, thought Grey Eagle, for he had clearly spooked the animal.

The man, quite slowly, got to his feet, feigning unconcern. He was tall, slim, somewhere in his fortieth decade; there was a care-worn air about him. There was a double-action Colt in his hand but held to his side. Grey Eagle heard the working pulled back with an audible *click*. But the arm did not come up.

"Easy," called Frank Partridge, leaving the Grey Eagle in his head to one side for a moment.

"You come on out, Mister!" came a gruffish voice, but educated, cultured, out of the East.

"Take it easy – just huntin'."

Frank edged himself into sight, holding the Whitworth well to one side, with the hammer safely down, and moved towards the man.

"That's far enough."

Frank stopped. This man was defensive. He was not going to shoot unless Frank did something stupid and then, Frank sensed, he'd get a bullet in the heart before the stupidity was half completed.

The man looked him over and saw that he was armed only with a long sniper's rifle, looked like an old English Whitworth. He had not seen one of those since the war. He saw a white man without a hat, bald, long grey moustache hiding his mouth and drooping down either side. He was dressed Indian style and sported a big hunting knife in an Indian belt.

"You come forward now, easy like, and you can share my rabbit."

"That's kindly," said Frank Partridge. "Frank Partridge – the Sioux call me Grey Eagle. Kinda live with them these days"

"George Crook."

"Nice to... who?"

"You heard."

"You ain't *General* Crook?"

"Rabbit's ready."

"Gawd damn me if it ain't Three Star Crook himself."

"You familiar with the Army then, Mr Grey Eagle."

"Captain Partridge, Washington Volunteers."

"Hey! I heard about you. You're that Limey went over to the Indians," said Brigadier General George Crook, Brevet Major General of Volunteers and sometime commander of the Army of East Virginia. He was the victor at the Battle of Winchester on September 19, 1864, but had his command routed at Cedar Creek, and was captured by the Rebs in Maryland, exchanged within weeks, ending the war commanding a full division of cavalry. An Indian fighter before the war and an Indian fighter since, he was the most experienced general officer in the field in the West.

"Well, General, it's true I ain't been around much these days – given it up – soldierin'."

"Were you not with Custer one time? Have a coffee."

"One time. Thanks"

"Sand Creek?"

"Right."

"Since then?"

"Had my belly full of murder, General."

"It ain't all murder, Mister. So you weren't with Reynolds?"

"Nope. Served wide and far, General, but did not have the fortune to ride with Colonel Reynolds."

"That's as well, Mister – court martialled him. Left the service now."

"That so?"

"I'd ordered him to hold the village, and he pulled out."

"I heard he lost the horses he took too. Cheyennes took 'em all back."

"Sore point, Mister. Wasted the damned meat supplies he could have taken as well. Burnt the lot."

"Nobody got to eat it then."

"Right, went up in flames."

"Now there's a sad shame, General. Do you know how much work them Indians put into... damn, it don't matter. Fortunes of war."

The general nodded and touched the flank of the smoke blackened rabbit, "Looks ready to eat. Ouch! Damned hot. Fancy a morsel?"

"Sure do."

"Your accent, Mr. Partridge – you from Boston time back."

"No General, I was English."

Frank Partridge thought about that: "was".

"Well – captain of volunteers and all – you're American now."

"Feel more Indian at times."

The general nodded again, "Know what you mean – at times I envy their freedom... not that they've got much left."

The general took the spit away and, holding the rabbit on it, knifed off a large slice of the flank and an entire rear leg, passing it to Frank Partridge.

"Watch it Mr. Partridge, damned hot."

Frank took it with care switching it from hand to hand to cool it. Frank Partridge had heard tell that General Crook had a real liking for the wild. Like other general officers he was rarely in anything

346

approaching a full uniform and took advantage of the luxury of going off hunting some way from his command. Just like that damned bastard Lord Cardigan on his damned yacht whilst his brigade was in the line.

Had a soldier done what a general did he would have caught a whole load of trouble. Difference was, soldiers might desert; generals don't do that. And there are no other generals around to complain anyway. Sometimes it went wrong though, like the time Custer went thundering off on his own and tried to shoot down a buffalo. In his excitement he put the bullet through his own horse's head and it was several hours before Frank Partridge found him sitting forlorn on his saddle alongside his dead mount. Neither his scout nor himself was aware that a raiding party of Sioux passed him five miles to the north. That was not his good day to die.

"Who you with, Mr. Partridge?"

"Pardon me?"

"Which chief?"

"Sioux. Hunkpapa. Sitting Bull."

"Ah." Crook thought to ask him where the camp was, but the lads could do that soon enough, bit of smart interrogation.

Frank Partridge fell to wondering what a serving general was doing in the woods, where was his command, what was his command doing here anyway?

"What you doin' out here, General?"

"Well, right here and now, I'm taking my ease a little."

Frank looked around, a quizzical smile playing on his face.

"You're wondering about where my boys are?" smiled Crook.

"Well – generals are usually surrounded by an army."

" Mile and a half down the hill's my command."

"You on an expedition?"

"Why now, Mr. Partridge, you'll find my command down the hill. Maybe you already know it is there. You'd know its business if you saw it. You could see for yourself we are not on an exploration trip. You *know* what the Army's about. We have got to get the Indians onto the reservations, legally provided and agreed to by them."

"By force?"

"Don't reckon there is a better way since they have refused to come with good grace."

"General I gave up fighting the Indians after Sand Creek and I ride with them now. That's my pleasure. I care a lot about them."

"So do I. They're a fine lot of murderin' rascals. But I am also a servant of our Union and have got my orders. Wouldn't nothing please me better than to see myself at the tail end of a great column of Sioux and all the rest heading, all peaceful like, towards the appointed reservations."

Frank toyed with killing the general right there. But the general had his six-shooter close at hand. He was wary. Frank Partridge decided to become American, again.

"Do you know what's out there?" Frank asked.

"Millions of square miles of land and a few thousand hostiles."

"There's more, General, a lot more."

"Meaning?"

"There's a whole heap of warriors out there who want nothing to do with reservations."

"That's why I'm here."

"General I sure hope you've got a big army."

The general looked at Frank Partridge coldly.

"General, there'll be a lot to take on."

The general nodded gravely.

"A lot I tell you."

"I think, Mister, we'll cope with whatever they throw at us."

Frank Partridge found himself a man of two souls. Here was the best Indian fighter the Union had and not fifty miles away was the greatest concentration of prairie tribes that any tribesman had ever known. For sure Crook had to have an army down there in the valley, or else he was in trouble. But what if he did, a big one? Grey Eagle had to find out.

The sound of horses some way off stumbling up the hill caught both men's attention and the old mule began to call.

"Sounds like my escort," said Crook. "Bit late this morning – must have misjudged the slope, a lot of outcrops down below. Old Betsy managed it, ornery old she-ass, but those cavalry mounts are too windy for it."

They both bit fast at the rabbit, dripping with the warmth of wood. The coffee washed down the meat and they watched each other as they fed.

Finally the general said, "You coming down with us?" If he didn't then the general was going to put a bullet in his leg. This man was a renegade.

He was with the Indians. He already knew too much. Then he thought to himself that it would be a good thing for the Indians to know what they were up against since his command was one of three powerful contingents each with horse, foot and artillery. They were aiming to catch a whole lot of Indians in a military corral and coerce them into the reservations, if they did not go there of their own free will. If they knew what they were up against, maybe there would not be a fight. Crook could drink to that.

"You goin' to arrest me?" asked Frank Partridge.

"Never crossed my mind," grunted the general, appearing irritated.

"Well – I have to say it would be nice to hear a whole mess of English being spoken again."

The general grunted, "You'll also hear plenty of German and French and a whole lot more of Europe's babblings."

"I reckon the Union Army was always so," said Frank Partridge.

"Right enough!"

"I'll come along."

"Then you'll be my guest, Captain Partridge."

"Honoured, General."

Frank Partridge gave a weak rabbit-smelling salute, and a smile, as a dozen horsemen came labouring into sight out of the tree-line. In the lead, to his astonishment he saw the unmistakable square shoulders of Little Knife, a second class corporal's single chevron on each of his sleeves. What in tarnation was he doing here? The last he heard he was scouting for Custer. Frank Partridge felt his face break into a smile of welcome.

The smile was ignored as Little Knife yelled, "Hey! Three Star Chief – we've found very much plenty buffalo – many Sioux. Big fight come. Hey! Frank, what you do here?"

)+()+()+()+(

White Hawk opened his eyes. The reflex of his arm driving off a honey bee, come droning across his face, woke him. For a moment he gazed on the unbroken azure sky. The ceaseless chatter of myriad insects formed a second canopy on the air. He also caught the distant sound of a hawk smashing into a dove and felt the pain. Turning his head to the left and right his vision was quartered by the knee high prairie grass, fresh green in the late spring. Then he heard them.

He felt them rather than heard them. There was a resemblance to a family of buffaloes on the move, frisky, cut out from some vast roaming herd, for no reason. The feeling was transmitted through the thin soil and gradually turned into a far off beat on the air – horses.

White Hawk had fallen asleep – for how long? That horsemen had got this close? He had been running until his thighs burned. He had dropped, sweating, into the cool of the grass. He had carried a pebble in his mouth to encourage moisture, and it was still in his mouth when he woke, carried in the pouch of his cheek. It clicked on his teeth as he coiled his tongue round it to gain fresh dampness, and in doing so he moistened his pink lips with a pinker tongue. The sun had gone beyond its zenith – he had slept for some time, longer than he had intended.

White Hawk felt alarm run through him together with a sense of carelessness – what if they had been enemy on foot, moving like wolves, silent but for the whisper of fur caressing blades of still grass? But for the rhythm of the horses he might not have heard their approach. They might have stumbled on him. This was what happened when the Wasichu whisky water was in the blood. He felt a rush of shame, stupidity, both – for he had not sipped a drop of the Wasichu poison – so only he was to blame.

With care he eased his naked body up on his elbows, turning gently on to his side, his dream erection was already turning from bone to sleeping snake.

He brought himself to his knees and reached for his bow with the knife attached to one end, a contrary's bow. Even as he made that movement his right leg lifted so that his foot was on the broken grass ready to launch himself upright.

Slowly he eased upwards so that his eyes could see between the peaks of the swaying grass. He dropped at once. His heart increased its beat at the sight of the threat. He had expected to see a hunting party passing by, tired perhaps, returning to the encampment of the several families who followed Yellow Hair, Keeper of the Arrows Which Were Burned.

The teepees of Yellow Hair were a couple of Wasichu miles to White Hawk's rear. They were on the edge of a creek called, Fallen Horse. A place so-named because a horse fell there, and was found half in the water, half on the embankment. It was not known who the horse was or why it was there, but those who passed by gave this name to the creek. White Hawk hoped the soldiers would not go that way.

White Hawk, very gingerly, looked once more and saw that the soldiers equalled the fingers on three double hands, all in dark blue jackets and mounted on plain brown horses. They were cantering across White Hawk's front. Most wore hats and their blue coats had dark patches of sweat beneath their arms and across their backs. They were only half looking ahead, their heads mostly dropped; they were clearly tired and unaware. There was a carelessness about them.

Suddenly there was a sound to his right. His head turned. He froze. A solitary Indian of unknown description was coming towards him to pass ten or twenty paces to his rear. He too wore a Wasichu uniform, which was worn and ill-fitting but had a pretty gold stripe on each arm. White Hawk shrank, settling into a ball of silence, willing himself to be invisible as the four hooves trampled by.

As he crouched, he eased a broad headed flint hunting arrow into the gut of his bow. Had he already been discovered the rider would be screaming by this time, pulling at the shaft embedded in his living flesh. It would have hit somewhere – his face, his chest, his arm, his stomach, his leg. It would have driven in wherever White Hawk had sent the razor edged missile. There would have been no question of White Hawk missing. He would then have fought the rest to his death, to be remembered as a great contrary by his whole nation until the sun ceased to climb in the morning and the night stars stopped their singing in the heavens.

But the flanking scout passed by, close, but not close enough to die.

White Hawk uncoiled and stared with eagle eyes after the troop of cavalry. Certain they would not see him, for they had already shown themselves to be without sight or alertness, he was tempted to shout and wave. But he thought better of it. He watched them carefully as they created distance between him and them. The call of leather and harness, the beat of metal on metal, with an occasional call of a voice, grew less with the distance. These Wasichu were very strange.

None of them was naked, even in the heat. Not one of them wore feathers of honour, or crooks of rank – except at the front of the column was one man with a spear and from its top was a large Wasichu 'feather' made of their soft cloth. It was triangular, red and white with a black picture on it. Such a feather he had not seen before. Then he smelt them.

Had his brother the West Wind been blowing perhaps he would have heard them before he smelt them, but now they were upwind. Their scent had drifted across from their approach, carried over White Hawk and then beyond, as it was replaced by the following prairie air, rich with sage.

He caught the odour of alien horses, also leather, then there was an acrid smell. He knew it to be the smell of men, but it did not have the sweetness of buffalo oil; it was unfamiliar. This smell was that of rot, the sensation of evil, of cruelty, of threat. White Hawk felt the blood shudder in his veins. He also saw that the distant group were insane.

Why ride that way? Each man rode close to the next, both to his side and in front and behind. White Hawk had never seen this before. Every other time the Wasichu had been close to him it had been out of the dawn when they were in a wild frenzy of attack without this curious and regular order.

Crazy Horse, Lord of the Horse, Shirt-Wearer, Hero of the Spear, Defeater of the Crow, Dog Soldier, had said, and White Hawk had heard it himself: "When the great war party advances let it be many moving as one. Let each warrior be a war party, let each warrior lead, fight and be aware. Advance like a cloud. Surround like water. Death deal as one. Let every brave man see with his own eyes, and look to the opportunity for if each kills his man then we have the victory. But we must move at first *together*, like the mad Wasichu."

The gathered ones did not like that. It was not the way of real people. Real people move as individuals to gather-in an individual's honour. They did not move as one.

"But," said Crazy Horse, and there was that gentle patience in his voice. "The Wasichu can do this thing and drive us off, so why cannot we?"

When they killed Two Silver Bar Chief Fetterman, it was because they took advantage of the Wasichu moving the Wasichu way, as one man. The Fetterman Wasichu came as one and were hit as one by the compact warriors of Red Cloud. It was after this fight that the warriors began to think that Crazy Horse was right, though the tactic was as much designed by Red Cloud at the time. Fetterman came on as one sure that he could chase off the undisciplined mobs of Indians. But, and this was the difference, the mob also moved as one as they surrounded him and wiped him out. Not one Wasichu continued to breathe, in the shortest time. That was a famous day.

"Drive across the low ground, bring them on," Red Cloud had said to Crazy Horse.

Crazy Horse said. "I will bring them to you – but you must all strike together. No one must break out to count coup. We must take their lives today, not their honour."

"We will look for you," smiled Red Cloud.

"And we shall come!"

Later, after the attack, Red Cloud had said to Crazy Horse, in that strange lilting accent of the Oglala that they both shared, "I see you, my Rider of the Sky. You fooled them!"

Crazy Horse was proud of his twelve comrades who had tricked the arrogant fool Fetterman.

"We did; fooling fools is easy," said Crazy Horse.

"This will warn them!" said Red Cloud. And who would think that this great leader would soon become a Reservation Man, like a loafer.

"The game will come to an end after many victories like this," Crazy Horse said but there was a note of sadness in his voice.

"There may be other ways," Red Cloud had said, and perhaps that was the moment that he had begun to move away from the path of war.

Crazy Horse could think of no other way, except war, for any other way called for the keeping of promises, and the Wasichu were not good at that – even Red Cloud knew the Wasichu could not keep their word.

Later when Crazy Horse was conferring with Sitting Bull, wise old man, they had decided, with the other chiefs to make greater camps than ever before. In the winter the lodges would come together, and in the summer too. For sure the Wasichu would return, for they hungered for all the land. Also there was, deep inside their minds, the unspeakable fear that the Wasichu would prevail and soon there would be no opportunity for the great summer gatherings to come together, to talk, arrange marriages, to hunt and to dance. Maybe the Wasichu would take everything in the end. Perhaps that was the only promise they would keep.

Old Yellow Hair caught the danger, he saw it coming, he saw it at the ceremony of the signing away of the Black Hills, which Sitting Bull and Crazy Horse would have nothing to do with, but sent Yellow Hair there as their eyes. Yellow Hair had suddenly become angry in his heart, though he was no-one at that meeting. The papers were signed and the Wasichu could ride into the Black Hills and look for the yellow stuff they loved so much.

Yellow Hair suddenly gave a part chant, in irritation, "Hey, hey! Hey, hey!..."

He called it loudly and when all were looking at him he bent and snatched up some dust in his hand. He glared at the Wasichu with their high hats, and their pale faces, turned red by the sun. He threw the dust at them, and said, "Here – take this dust – you have taken everything else."

"What did he say?" asked the leader of the Wasichu.

But no-one would tell the leader anything, other than this was an old winkte who was crazy. They said this because they wanted the Wasichu gifts and the Wasichu promises. And this meant that they sold the Black Hills for nothing.

The Wasichu were clever at these things, so it seemed all the more strange to White Hawk that they were so foolish in war.

White Hawk, as he now stood, watching the troop of cavalry move into the distance felt a flash of anger. He studied the column of men, with a rider on each flank, one of them the Indian in white clothes. They disappeared down the slope into a hollow of dead ground and he thought, "Only those at the front can see to the front and those at the front cannot see to the rear – surely these men with hair on their faces ride in search of death." He hoped so.

⊁⊁⊁⊁⊁

The soldiers – a troop of B company 2nd Cavalry scouting out to the north-west of Crook's column – had also been seen by Big Horse. He watched from his buffalo pony's back, hidden on the reverse slope, as Crazy Horse had advised so often. He was out of sight, but for his head above the earth's edge – ten yards further away from the peak

354

of the slope – but close enough to see over and down onto movement in the valley. The troop moved slowly now and Big Horse continued to watch as they dismounted, together, but raggedly.

As they dropped to the ground and pulled at their horses he heard a command come on the air, distant, carried on the warm breeze – "Disssss – mount!" The order came after the movement – such was the distance.

It meant nothing to Big Horse – a call in the wilderness from crazy people.

He counted the men, both hands three times, and one more. He caught a flash of sun on metal and saw that one soldier had drawn his longknife, and then put it away again. This also meant nothing. The horses were a long time drinking and the men had turned from blue to red and then to white as they tore off their clothes and plunged into the water. A lone figure did not join them and even at that distance, Big Horse could see, despite the fact that he was fully clothed that this man was an Indian.

He saw that his hair was very long and in a style that he did not recognise. He watched as the man put a soldier hat back on his head. This man was aware, was alert even at the end of the day. He was watching. The soldiers were safe, though they did not know it. Surely these men were in search of death. Big Horse hoped so.

Big Horse yearned for a dozen Dog Soldiers under his leadership – a charge, sudden, swift, no war cries, and then there would be death-dealing, scalp-gathering, a winning of coup feathers. From the throat of the young Indian came a deep growl, not unlike that of a yapping dog, with a bone in its mouth. The growl was like that issued as a threat to the young in the pack who might dare come close enough to sniff and yearn, salivating at the hope of tasting the bone, put off by the low snarl and bared teeth surrounding the bone.

Turning his horse away he slipped down the slope, veered to his right and began to canter, first south and then west towards the encampment of Yellow Hair. He was half a mile from the teepees of his family when he saw the almost naked figure of White Hawk running swiftly ahead of him. He tapped Brown Back into a gallop and held his bow at length – he would slash at the runner as he went by, striking a friendly coup, raising a weal, winning an honour, taking an advantage.

White Hawk knew he was there. He had been aware of him before the horse had broken into the canter. White Hawk was breathing heavily but with power and rhythm for he could keep up the pace for at least a mile or more, even accelerating to rush into the encampment. He felt the almost limitless power of his youth, the blood coursing, the strength in himself as he cut through the warm air, scattering insects, making the prairie rats stay low at his approach. He now judged the beat of hooves and even as he heard the hiss of the bow, aimed for a coup, he had thrown himself forwards feeling the wind of the passing wood and was onto his hands, somersaulted back onto his feet, the horseman gone by.

"Woman!" he called after Big Horse, thinking of slipping an arrow into his bow which he had yanked from his shoulders a moment before his defensive leap so that his right hand had supported himself in a fist. He was so fit and supple that his somersault had scarcely needed support. At the time of the dance when the snow bled into water he had startled the elders when, at the moment the others were carrying out the sloping turn in the Spring Sun Dance he had thrown himself into the air, and turned over completely, without support. Some of the elders said that it was profane, others asked what else could be expected of a contrary – especially one whose father was a winkte warrior. A winkte warrior as a father; that in itself was a very contrary thing.

Panting, White Hawk came to an immediate halt as he realised that he had scattered three arrows from his quiver by his sudden movement. They were precious hunting arrows, straight and true. He gathered them in the afternoon sun, gulping air, cooling sweat running down his elegant frame.

He cursed Big Horse as he picked up the last of the arrows, keeping an eye on him in case he came racing back for some dark purpose. He called on *Wakantanka* to strike his manhood to become like the little finger of a new born child. Still panting he broke back into his run, easily, so that within a few steps he was running, panting, running, panting – the grass whipping his glistening thighs, snatching away the sweat. He could see that Big Horse was already dismounting at the gallop, throwing himself in front of the lodge of Yellow Hair, who was grey with age. Big Horse was too forward, impolite, hurried, insulting, and there first. He too must have seen the horse soldiers.

)( )( )( )( )(

Yellow Hair was asleep and dreaming, and the dream was of ancestors come sweeping on ghost horses. Their bodies glowed with youth and they whispered in the darkness as to how, when brother East Wind soughs across the plains turning the grass into watery waves, their minds turn to war, also to love. In his dreams Yellow Hair could see and hear it all clearly and he was one of them once more, but he also heard the sound of horses in his old wise head and woke at once. His eyes opened and the dreams were gone.

He counted but one horse. He closed his eyes again. He coughed. He got to his feet slowly. Only then did he open his eyes – dark eyes which had a grey edge to their colour now. Far things were not so clear to him with the passing of the years and the sun seemed to burn his eyes on a bright day. He stepped towards the streak of sunlight which led to the world outside and a youth almost collided with him but was on his knees in a moment, gasping apologies and reverence with a great insincerity.

"Is Big Horse mad with love?" Yellow Hair thought of Hands Quite Small whom Big Horse had offered many presents to and been rejected – for the moment, as was proper. Her good friend First Snows had whispered in the winkte's ear that more presents might make a difference. She had also pleaded with the winkte to tell his son that she herself would welcome presents from *him*. First Snows was very pretty and Yellow Hair liked her more than Hands Quite Small.

Yellow Hair had smiled and whispered winkte things in her ear so that she blushed, but she also knew that Yellow Hair would make presents appear. Soon they would come, for he had whispered to her that White Hawk was but a 'pretend' contrary, and that his strange ambition could be thrown to the winds for a sweet young thing like First Snows. First Snows heart had beaten very fast.

With all these things in his old head Yellow Hair did not first catch the urgency in Big Horse's voice.

"What is it – rushing boy?"

"Soldiers!" the youth gasped.

"Perhaps you are just mad – like a dog in the bright sun."

"Soldiers! Three double hands of soldiers."

"Soldiers?" Yellow Hair saw soldiers in his mind's eye, he saw gunfire and heard death, and felt a surge of fear. Soldiers always made him feel fear. Not fear of death for that was just a passage through the screen towards a forest of thighs and much eternal joy, but fear that the way of the people was under threat once more. He feared that the Wasichu had come for the last grains of dust which had slipped through his fingers that time as he threw them towards the white-eye leaders.

Perhaps it was his secret thoughts of the future which haunted him, like horrors of the past. The Wasichu soldiers brought fear, and Yellow Hair did not like the feeling, so he hated the Wasichu.

"Soldiers, you say?"

"Those with hair on their faces."

"Hair on their faces?"

"Those!"

"Where?"

"North – two gallops of a fresh horse."

"From where?"

"South."

Yellow Hair's mind drew fresh clean pictures from ancient memory. He sniffed the air and knew that no fires were burning. It was hot, so food would be cooked later, ready for the cool hours of darkness and stories round a central fire. This was a good place to be. It had felt to be a safe place. But so had the other places felt safe.

Yellow Hair shivered, despite the warmth. Yes, they had all been safe places to be. Perhaps this was also a place of future ghosts – perhaps that was what was haunting him. There was something to stop them though. It was the great gathering. Would it be enough to halt the soldiers if they came? That was the worry that began to eat him.

A huge pow-wow was to take place here in the near time. Soon the first of the nations would arrive at the Little Big Horn. Yellow Hair's five family band were perhaps four days ride from the meeting place. He had chosen the Fallen Horse, on the west bank, in the cool of the trees, for a day of rest. This site and the lack of smoke had ensured that the passing troop had not seen them. They had gone by heading north, oblivious to the small Indian encampment which would itself head west at dawn towards the meeting place of the nations.

A movement out of the dimness of the corner of his eye attracted his attention, a blurred image, like looking through curved hands at the moon, but with the edges of vision misting into a jagged blackness. Out of this mist White Hawk came panting. He could hear the youth pulling in the air, and could smell the sweet sweat of his exertions. He was on his knees before the old man and Yellow Hair's fingers felt down to touch his face and felt the warmth of the skin and the wet sweat and the old man said: "Do you flee from ghosts?"

"Future ghosts," gasped White Hawk, and he did not know where the words came from, nor did he know that Yellow Hair's heart missed a beat.

)( )( )( )( )(

When Big Horse felt the coup stick touch his shoulder, out of the darkness, he knew that it was White Hawk. He had glimpsed him coming, breaking away from his position on the flank. This touching with the stick was an unnecessary piece of humour. Big Horse had counted coup on White Hawk earlier – he knew he had – White Hawk denied it, said he had dodged the stroke. But Big Horse had felt the touch, he had scored the point. This touch from White Hawk was nothing. He had seen him coming, he had not tried to avoid the touch. This coup did not count.

Big Horse was walking in the black night with the moon already sunk. He was walking his horse a good gallop from the rear of the companions of Yellow Hair as protection from followers. Yellow Hair had decided to strike camp at dusk and travel through the night, pushing hard to place distance between them and the horse soldiers. With such a small number of Wasichu they may have been scouts for a greater force. And even this scouting force was too much for Yellow Hair's small travelling band.

Yellow Hair knew that ahead there were many family groups converging on the Greasy Grass plain close by the Little Big Horn and he was almost certain to meet up with them within a day or two. With only half a dozen warriors in his band they were very vulnerable. Big Horse he placed well to the rear and White Hawk to the rear and left flank. They were alert young men and no-one could come from that direction without the band being alerted.

Everyone, even the women, had weapons loaded, and good bows ready to string. If attacked his people would give good account. Meanwhile the moonless remains of night would provide a coat of invisibility. The Wasichu did not like to ride at night. He had heard this many times. Yellow Hair would have been less than pleased to learn that the young men were talking together and the flank was exposed. He would have been even less pleased were he to have known what had passed in the mind of White Hawk.

The young men walked their horses close to each other and though the night was moonless their strong eyes could meet in the light of the stars. All around wolves were calling, calling to wolves about wolf matters. There were no humans out there. The young men knew the calls.

"Come with me," came a whisper of conspiracy, as soon as the coup stick tapped.

Big Horse whispered back, "To where, my brother, to where would *you* bid *me* follow."

"You whisper! Do you fear the Wasichu are close about?" And White Hawk whispered too, for it was the dark night and anything could have been about.

"To where, half-contrary one?"

"Blind man-woman, great warrior, killer of ferocious rabbits and skunks – I would have you come touch the longknives with me, touch, make the coup and then flee with laughter and great honour!"

White Hawk squinted into Big Horse's eyes and felt a sense of brotherhood and the knowledge that his sister was the most beautiful woman in the world.

"You mean – go back – with you?"

"Yes."

"To make coup?"

"Yes."

"And something else?"

"Yes,"

"What?"

"A scalp."

"They're soldiers," hissed Big Horse.

"Two scalps then."

Big Horse looked ahead into the night as if to see if those friends they were following, out of sight, had seen and heard. He calculated the distances they had travelled in his head, the possibility of doing what was suggested and getting back before the sun came up. He saw that it could be done. He saw it in his mind's eye.

Big Horse smiled in the darkness. "I'll follow."

Silently they slipped onto their horses and turned back east, beyond which the sun was deep asleep, as were the men of Company B.

18

A Hundred Is Better Than Two

(June 13th 1876)

In Pierre's dreams the face was always real, as it once had been. It had been a pumpkin face with life in its eyes. They used to call him 'Pumpkin' Billie. He was bald. Even his eyebrows were gone. All of Pumpkin Billie's hair fell out after his first battle. In his dream that night Corporal Pierre dreamt only of a pumpkin with candle-light for eyes, until the pumpkin turned, in the dream, into the face of Billie again; his good friend, grinning and happy, young, freckled. He saw the ball approaching, just at it had at Gettysburg, and he froze within his dream, as it gently curved towards them.

"Get out of the way, Billie – watch that bastard ball..."

But they were mesmerised, until the missile smacked into Billie's head. The pumpkin face of his friend burst its brains and blood into Pierre's eyes. A sudden, clear, impossible, horror.

Corporal Pierre woke with a merciful start, destroying the nightmare war memory, and found himself staring into another young face. The face seemed surprised to find Pierre suddenly awake. It was a face with hair this time; hair topped with a feather.

A feather!

"InJUN!" Pierre bellowed and grappled at the face, battle instinct, fear, repulsion.

The Indian slipped out of his fingers like a fish and was rolling away in the long grass, into the darkness. Pierre made a violent snatch at a disappearing ankle and his ham of a hand closed round it. Yankee Hurtz, the trooper sleeping by his side, was on his feet and diving onto the struggling savage, pinning him down.

Pierre's left hand instinctively searched in the gloom for his sabre and at the same instant saw that it was in the Indian's hand, drawn. Not questioning why this was, he launched himself across the wrestling two and went with both hands for the free wrist which held the sabre. He got there in time to intercept the stroke which was already aimed at his own face. The keen edge was sharp enough for shaving. Pierre was known for the quality of his grinding; his father's father had taught him. That death-deadly edge came within a finger of his nose as he wrenched the slim arm of the Indian back against the joint. He heard a muffled yelp as the savage's arm almost broke.

Three other troopers had scrambled to their feet and thrown themselves into the struggle, punching and kneeing the Indian. Hands round his throat cut off the air to his lungs and he suddenly went still. Sensing that perhaps he was dead the soldiers eased their attack and began to get to their feet.

Others turned up with brands from the fire in their hands and in the uncertain light they looked down with contempt on the naked form. The breechcloth had been pulled to one side revealing his manhood. Pierre pushed the buckskin back into place, almost ashamed that the savage was also a man. Pierre became aware that one of the Indian flanking scouts had appeared out of the darkness, and stood behind Hurtz.

It was Yankee Hurtz who picked up the sabre and lifted it two-handed to drive it into the youth's chest.

"Hold it, Hurtz!" panted Pierre. "Let's watch the Indian scalp him first."

Little Knife, the Arikara Scout, tall, was smiling.

"What do we have here, soldiers?" his sweet accent sounded incongruous out of the beak nosed face. He bent over and looked at the youth, taking in the lines of his chest, slim, muscular, powerful, young. He studied the markings on his face, three yellow streaks. "Cheyenne. Contrary." There was an echo of recognition from somewhere. Then he knew.

"Kill the critter!" said a voice in the darkness, and there was a growl of consensus.

Lieutenant Engles, brevet lieutenant colonel from the war, limped into the scene, and said: "Corporal?"

"Injun, sir, tried to take my blade," said Pierre

"Dead?" asked the officer, unable to be sure as to whether he could see the creature breathing in the poor light.

"Alive!" said Little Knife and gave the youth a light kick in the groin. There was a groan and the figure curled and turned onto its side so that all the men jumped back, except Little Knife. Two of them dropped back across the boy and held him.

"Stinks!" said one.

"Greasy!" said the other.

"Buffalo fat," said Engles. "What's his tribe?"

"Cheyenne," said Pierre.

"Contrary," said Little Knife.

A couple of troopers, young, inexperienced, looked blank.

"Do everything backwards," said Engles.

Still blank.

"Don't sleep on beds, ride their horses facing backwards. Don't have women."

The troopers frowned in disbelief. Riding facing front was hard enough – but no women?

"Fornicate with men," said Pierre.

Little Knife shook his head.

"No?" said Pierre catching the Indian's expression, doubting it – for he had heard other things about contraries.

"Some," he replied. "They don't go with their women. They don't do things that other men do. We like life, they look for death. We eat, they will starve. We sleep. They run. They are great warriors. If they love, it is because ordinary men hate; if they hate then it is because ordinary men love. They dance when they are tired and laugh when they mourn. What we delight in, they ignore. Contrary. Doing the opposite."

"Fornicate with men f'sure!" snarled Pierre. "Turn him over!"

The troopers obeyed.

"Give it here!" Pierre snatched his sabre from Hurtz and placing the keen tip at the base of the youth's spine, then lowering to the entrance, he braced his arm to drive it home.

There was an explosion of movement. They should have heard the horses coming. Later, Little Knife, would go out, far on the flank of the column, take his knife and cut both his own ear lobes in punishment, but for the moment he was intent on saving his life.

He sensed the arrow coming and in the instant saw and heard it *zang* into the Lieutenant's mouth. It came out at the back of his neck, quivering for a split second before the man dropped to his knees. For a moment his arms fell to his sides, then he dropped forward with a single jerk, his spinal column severed by the slashing flint tip. His fall pushed the arrow further through his neck so that it seemed to be alive, growing from the base of the skull.

The second arrow came with the horses and embedded itself to the feathers in the chest of one of the men who had been holding the contrary. The soldiers dived in every direction. The contrary snapped to his feet and was spinning in the air as the horses smashed through the group. He made a grab for the flailing tail of a riderless horse and was jerked away. The other animal, a screaming warrior on its back, half jumped the fire. The last they saw of their captive was his figure, still holding the tail, being wrenched across the flames by the riderless horse.

Corporal Pierre stood with feet astride, sabre in hand, feeling a sense of frustration. He shook his head and cursed.

The sergeant was dead of a snakebite a week ago, the lieutenant was now gasping his last. Corporal Pierre, grandson of one of Napoleon's generals, was now in command of thirty men. This was no problem; he had commanded a regiment of infantry ten years before under Lee as a Confederate captain. Army was in his blood, so he signed up into the new United States Army, with the others of the Galvanized Yankees, who knew they had nothing to go back to.

He thought again. He looked at the now still lieutenant and the trooper choking up blood from the arrow in him; the kid's eyes were glazing already. He would not last the hour. His command had slipped to twenty-eight. Even as he thought that, he also thought: at least they will not be back tonight.

)( )( )( )( )(

Little Knife had to think hard once more. He knew that he could have got to the Cheyenne before he cleared the camp. He knew it. But he had not. Past times had stopped him in the instant. He had held that one in his arms when he was an infant. He was the winkte's boy. How strange it was that the paths should cross because of his woman and her Wasichu silver leaf chief. But for that he would not be with this regiment but with the 7th.

Snow-on-Her had caught Long Hair's eye. From the first the colonel had wanted her. Little Knife saw it in his eyes. Then he saw Bloody Knife, Custer's favourite scout, talking to her. Then Bloody Knife talked with Long Hair Custer. Then the scout talked with her once more. Then she came to Little Knife and said she was going to cook for the officers. Little Knife said nothing, and so she went, leaving him with wet eyes.

Bloody Knife, that favourite scout, was always looking at Little Knife, when they rode on the flank, with that smile on his face. He knew. He wanted Little Knife to know what he knew. Bloody Knife took him, one evening, down to a creek. He had a jar of whiskey with him and they got drunk. It was quick for Little Knife, for it was the first time Frank Partridge was not there to see no harm would come. He nearly drowned in the creek. Bloody Knife saved him, at least he said he had. Little Knife could remember fighting for his life in the water. Little Knife also remembered the drunken advice from Bloody Knife, given as from a brother – that it was better that Little Knife go away for a time.

Little Knife did not want to go – until he watched her enter the silver leaf chief's square teepee and heard her laugh. He knew that laugh, what it meant. That morning at role call Little Knife was marked as missing.

"Desertion? Has he deserted?" snapped Lieutenant Cook.

"Him go home," said Bloody Knife.

"Home."

"Him father dead."

The adjutant grunted, "He's a good scout."

"Heap good," said Bloody Knife.

"I'll have him marked as on leave."

"That good."

"Without pay."

Drifting, Little Knife had crossed the path of Crook's column heading for war, and been signed up for scouting duties. He had done well and was given a stripe. But her face was in his head even as the stripe was sewn on his sleeve. One stripe is a thousand battles from a silver leaf, and that is what she had turned to. Maybe she always wanted to be with a chief – after all she began with Sitting Bull. Finally, he shrugged his broad shoulders and thought: so, if that was what she wanted, so be it. Maybe the Sioux had been right: her name should have been Milk-on-Her.

)( )( )( )( )(

White Hawk and Big Horse left their ponies in a patch of scrub and moved back, keeping low, to the crest of the hill. Looking down on the scene from the long grass they had a good view of the camp, the fire, higher than before. The Wasichu were asleep again. Even the two Wasichu who were sitting further along the hill were asleep, oblivious of the two Cheyennes in the darkness.

Big Horse put out his hand to touch White Hawk, but he was gone. Big Horse felt a mixture of respect and irritation. He had no right, half-contrary or no, he had no right to go off without a word. Again!

Closing his eyes to a squint, looking upwards into the darkness to bring his best night vision into play, he caught sight of his comrade and watched him slip back into the encampment.

He had passed within ten paces of a sentry standing silhouetted against the firelight. Maybe he was asleep standing up. White Hawk could have killed the man, but instead he penetrated deeper into the camp. Big Horse watched him moving on his belly, flickering firelight catching his shoulders, as he snaked through the sleeping soldiers. Then he stopped close by a man sleeping next to one of their chiefs, a two-stripe chief. He saw White Hawk gently reach over the sleeping man to pull the longknife from the two-stripe's sheath and then retreat, out of the firelight and back into the darkness at the foot of the hill.

As he watched Big Horse broke into a sweat as he saw one of the Indian scouts raise himself on an arm and watch. The scout did nothing. When White Hawk got to the darkness the scout dropped back to the earth to sleep.

)( )( )( )( )(

Corporal Pierre woke for the second time. He pulled at his moustache, still cut in the style of a French dragoon, copied from the painting back in Orleans. He could see the steel grey of dawn in the east. He raised himself on his elbow. He looked quickly round the perimeter to check the sentries. All were there, including the two sitting on top of the rise. Scratching at his saddle-stiffened buttocks he got to his feet and went to the embers of the fire. There was a coffee pot there. It was hot to the touch; half an inch of coffee mud was in the bottom. He looked round to find a trooper to fetch water. He kicked the nearest. It was Hurtz.

"Wake up!"

No movement.

"Wake up you idle bastard!"

The trooper stirred in dead sleep such as some still have at dawn. Another kick. An eye opened to view the corporal and begin a struggle to get out of his riding cape, protection against bugs more than cold.

"Water!"

Growling at the injustice of it all, the trooper lurched down the slope of the narrow flood plain to gather fresh water. The sky was turning red.

Pierre checked the sentries again and drifted back to his own bivouac position. It was then he saw that his sabre was gone from the scabbard.

"The hellll!" he snarled. But it was gone. It was gone. He turned on his heel and went across to Little Knife. He awoke at the heavy approach. Pierre was a big man and walked with the weight on his heels. His footsteps thudded, even in the grass.

So as not to let the others hear he knelt by the Indian and whispered: "My blade's gone."

"They came back then." Little Knife was raised on his elbows, blinking his eyes into full power.

"My blade's gone."

A movement against the red morning caught Pierre's eye. At the same time there was a yell that Indians were on the hill.

A shot rang out from Pierre's left. One of the sentries was already taking aim again, his single shot Sharps reloaded.

"Cease fire!" roared Pierre and felt good when the rifle came down at once. Pierre could see the annoyance in the sentry's face even in the half-light, but he had done as told – that was the important thing.

He watched the figures on the hill and was amazed to see two Indians, first kneeling on their horses then standing, to rise higher above them. In front of them sat the two sentries on the hill, ignoring them. The two Indians were waving. One had an army issue sabre in his hand, the other a bow. At the tip of each weapon was...

"They came back!" hissed Pierre, nausea ran to his throat so that he had to swallow... the pickets killed and scalped.

He watched them turn their horses and disappear out of sight, into the rising sun, at speed. He could hear their distant whoops. The sentries up there still appeared to be sitting, their backs to the sun, so that its glow was red upon the white which was the tops of their skulls, the pristine bone clear of flesh, a further red slash, unseen, running across their throats. They sat looking west through sightless eyes, victims of their own youth and the skills of hunters who were warriors, savage in war.

"I did not expect..." began Pierre. Then he thought – twenty-six left.

"Contraries," said Little Knife, already saddling his horse, "Expect the unexpected, and even then..."

"Where are you going?"

"I must go out and kill them before they kill me."

"You stay!"

"No."

"You stay, that's an order!"

Little Knife suddenly stopped his attempt to get on his horse.

"That's better," said the corporal.

"Look," said Little Knife.

The corporal looked to where the Indian was pointing. His men were also looking that way. There was a smudge across the horizon.

"What the hell?"

"Boss – that's buffalo – plenty," said Little Knife.

"What a sight."

"We have to go back to the general," said Little Knife.

Pierre had that in mind, but asked, "Now why is that?"

"Plenty buffalo, plenty Indians. They will come to kill the buffalo – then we get them. That's what the general wants. We must tell him, big lots of Indians soon. Maybe big battle."

"What about your contraries."

Little Knife shrugged and grinned, "Hundred dead enemy is better than two."

19

Soldiers with no ears...

(7th-10th June 1876)

There is a sacred place on the Rosebud, close by the rocks where the ancient people made paintings before the horses came. That is where Sitting Bull made his Sun Dance.

The dance happened a few days after Sitting Bull went up to a high butte to pray. Sitting Bull, looking just a little old, said he wanted to speak with God. He did; the old man tried to make a deal with the Great One, with *Wakantanka* Himself.

Wakantanka gave the famous vision to Sitting Bull and Sitting Bull had flesh cut from his body in return, yet really it was the other way round. Sitting Bull promised a Sun Dance, and made it special. He kept the promise; he did it, and the keeping of the promise caused *Wakantanka* to be very pleased and look favourably on the people.

When Sitting Bull went to the high butte he took close friends with him. He chose Young Eagle, Jumping Bull and Yellow Hair. There was no surprise that the ageing warrior winkte was invited, for he was himself a holy man. But when young White Hawk followed, even from a respectful distance, Young Eagle turned on him – not only because he was merely a young man but he was also a Cheyenne, but not a *wicasa wakan* like his father.

Sitting Bull rested a hand on Young Eagle's big shoulders and said, "Let him come. He once saw a Thunderbird in a dream – maybe *Wakantanka* will be pleased to see him up there with us, and will listen better to what I have to say. And our friend the winkte is Cheyenne too, remember – so it does not matter. *Wakantanka* is for all the people."

"But Yellow Hair is a holy man, this one is nothing."

"He comes," said Sitting Bull. And that was an end to it.

So White Hawk followed, at a very respectful distance, for he did not want to offend anyone, not even Young Eagle.

Sitting Bull's hair was loosened from its braids. The raven jet was still there but there were grey whispers of age in the strands as the prairie wind, strong that day, lifted it across his face and shoulders. He had no paint on his face for *Wakantanka* can always see beyond decorations and Sitting Bull did not want to make Him think that he was trying to trick Him. Sitting Bull wanted clear thoughts to come to him from the Great One, because there were many Wasichu in their saddles and the people were under threat.

Word had come in that the Wasichu wanted all the tribes, *all* of them this time, to be on the reservations at once. At once! Who were these Wasichu with their 'at once!'? This 'at once' was very funny because many of the warriors who were already on the reservations had left to join their cousins for the summer hunting on the plains. The free people had been swollen by their numbers. Never had there been so many gathered for the season. The Wasichu would be disappointed. Even the Red Men in their grip were slipping away.

But the word was out that the Wasichu war chief they called Three Star Sheridan, whose teepee was far to the west, was determined to take everything, and give biscuits in exchange. He wanted to buy off the Red Men's souls as well as their land. He wanted every Indian in a place of his choosing. Some Indians went in and tried to look good in the eyes of the Wasichu. But most of them were old.

"Me good Indian," said one from the south. He was standing in front of Three Star Sheridan at the time. The big Wasichu chief had gone to watch them coming in to the reservation place, to hand over their guns and their horses for bags of flour.

Sheridan was a little warrior with a red face and hard bad eyes and was very brave because he was so small. He looked with those hard bad eyes at the Indian who had just given everything up to do what the Wasichu wanted.

"Me good Indian!" He had put his hand on his chest where his brave heart should have been.

The three star looked at him again and said, "The only good Indian I ever saw was dead."

No-one knows what the 'good Indian' said in reply. Maybe he did not hear the three star. Maybe he did not believe what he heard. But the three star said it, and he meant it. That was the man he was. Very dangerous.

It was said he never lost a battle. But as yet he had not fought with *Wakantanka* Himself. Sitting Bull wanted to make sure the Great One understood that the real people needed His help this time. The matter was serious.

That was why Sitting Bull undid his hair and smoked his pipe, wound round with silver sprays of sage, the perfumed herb which had been sacred since time began. That is why he went to the butte with his best friends, to pray.

But Sitting Bull was clever. He called out to *Wakantanka*, with great politeness, and the words have been recorded, even by the Wasichu, from that time. He said: "Great One, my *Wakantanka*, save me and give me all my wild game animals. Bring them near me, so that my people have much to eat this winter. Let the men on our earth have great warrior power, make all our nations strong and successful in the fight. Let them be of good heart, strong heart, make the lodges of the Sioux and all the tribes live as one and be happy."

Then he paused. He looked round at the others wondering whether he should call out what he wanted to call out. It is not possible to make a deal with *Wakantanka*, but He had to be made to understand the matter was very important and dangerous for the people. Sitting Bull said the words, "If you do this for me, I will perform the Sun Dance, two days, two nights... and give you a whole buffalo."

Sitting Bull wondered if that would be enough. But *Wakantanka* is not greedy so Sitting Bull decided it would be enough.

Afterwards, when they all went down from the butte, Sitting Bull lead them in a hunt at once and some good buffalo were brought down. Sitting Bull chose the very best, a most beautiful cow with a hide which was perfect in all respects. He told his friends what to do and they helped him. He had her turned onto her belly. Her legs, in death, were spread out to each of the winds; the head was stretched out too, towards the butte.

Suddenly Sitting Bull stood to one side and let out a terrible wail and raised his hands to the blue sky. "There!" he called. "I have not waited on you. Here is the beautiful buffalo I promised you. *Wakantanka* – here it is – even before the dance."

All of those watching later said they had felt *Wakantanka* was there, with them, at that moment. Far to the west, at the very edge of the world a single strike of lightning was seen, but there was *no* call of Thunderbird wings, moments after. That was very unusual.

Yellow Hair had smiled and suggested that it was a wink from *Wakantanka* and the others thought he was being profane as only a Cheyenne could be. Only Sitting Bull had smiled.

Sitting Bull did the Sun Dance differently. All the Sioux were there, for it was their Sun Dance; it seemed as if the entire nation was gathered. The numbers were swollen by the lesser tribes, the Cheyenne and the Arapaho and the Sans Arcs; even a few Kiowa were there, only a few Kiowa, for there were not many left by that time. There were many from the reservations too, pleased to show that they were no longer 'loafers round the Wasichu forts'. But only the Sioux took part, except for a single young Cheyenne and the Cheyenne winkte; the others watched as part of a gigantic circle of humanity.

When the word got round as to Sitting Bull's intentions there were intakes of breath, or clucks of approval and many anxious faces. He had decided to give flesh. He would not hang from the sacred pole. He would have skin and flesh plucked from his old man's body. He would give fifty pieces of flesh... from each arm.

No warrior *had* to do the Sun Dance and hang from his own body. There was no compulsion, but for many there was a need to show their courage as they searched for visions and the respect of all by taking part in the ceremony of pain. Sitting Bull did it the old way once when he was a young man. He was hung from the flesh of his own breast for almost a day. The way of doing it was sacred and did not change.

As the initiates lay naked on the earth, the flesh on either side of their hearts was pinched, then stabbed through with a good knife and a cherry-wood peg inserted through the wounds on either side. The holy men, the *wicasa wakans,* men who had themselves seen wonderful visions in the embrace of pain, were fast and careful, their fingers being warmed and made slippy by the quick-run blood. Once the peg was in place then buffalo-hair ropes were attached. The ropes led to a high pole in the sacred teepee and the young braves, whose blood ran good, danced round until they dropped or the pegs tore free through the flesh. It could take a day. It could take a day and a night. Even more.

As White Hawk lay there and let Yellow Hair cut his flesh he dared not call out for he was the lone Cheyenne. He saw that the old winkte was biting his own lip and knew that he did not love the mutilation of his beautiful son.

"Are you sure?" he had whispered to White Hawk.

"Yes – I must do it. I must do it so that First Snows will see that I am complete."

"For a pretty girl?" whispered Yellow Hair, thinking like a winkte.

"Yes," smiled White Hawk, thinking like one who is not a contrary.

"Then so be it – grit your teeth!"

As Yellow Hair cut and probed he wondered if he was taking away or adding to this single treasure in his life. But he did it; he cut deep and neat because it was what his White Hawk wanted. Sitting Bull watched and nodded in appreciation of White Hawk's silence and wished the youth were a Hunkpapa Sioux.

This time Sitting Bull knew that he needed to do something different. He wanted to show his people that he had everything to give, and would give it. He needed to see what was to come, and *Wakantanka* alone knew what that would be. Sitting Bull had to ensure he experienced a new vision. Sitting Bull wanted to give such marvellous gifts to *Wakantanka* that He would let Sitting Bull share His thoughts.

Those who knew about these things thought on what Sitting Bull was going to do, thought hard about it, thought of the veins and the muscles and the flesh. They thought of the pain of the tearing of the skin. A hundred pieces. Would he live? Did *Wakantanka* want so much?

Yellow Hair overheard that.

He turned on the old Sioux woman who had said it.

"*Wakantanka* did not ask, Sitting Bull is giving without demand."

"Why?"

"Because he trusts the Great One."

"To do what?"

"Woman – Sitting Bull wants to see into the future."

"Future?" snorted the old woman, who in her way could see already. "What future?"

So Sitting Bull had the flesh cut from each arm, Jumping Bull did it. He did not want to do it. When he heard Sitting Bull ask him, he said, "What? You want me to do what?"

"You heard, my friend, your ears are not full of grasshoppers yet."

"But a hundred!"

"You do it or I shall ask the Cheyenne winkte."

374

Jumping Bull had glanced at Yellow Hair.

"Well?" asked Sitting Bull.

"Will *you* do it?" asked Jumping Bull, looking at Yellow Hair.

"For my friend, I will do it."

"Then I shall do it because I too am his friend."

"But Yellow Hair must sit with you and do the counting, for all the nations must feel part of this thing," said Sitting Bull and had a good feeling about that.

The young men were pierced first. When they were hanging, leaning backwards, aching with the wonderful agony, weaving and straining on the ropes, all in position, then Sitting Bull went to his place.

The blood ran out of him so easily when he was being cut, it seemed eager to prove his word. As the blood ran it formed small rivers which took Sitting Bull to another place. At first he was aware of the pain. A steel awl was used and a knife with a very narrow blade, honed to silver-edge, very sharp. Sitting Bull sat right against the sacred pole from which hung the buffalo ropes, attaching to young men's backs and chests. The dancers touched the pole vicariously, through the ropes, the blood running down their rippling frames. Sitting Bull's nakedness was rested against the holy pole itself as his good friends knelt at his side and cut away.

Jumping Bull had not done this thing before and did not know where to start. Yellow Hair nodded at the wrists. With care, so as not to rip a large vein, the awl was used to lift the skin from the flesh and then a small slice was cut away. Jumping Bull took very small pieces because it seemed the right thing to do. He glanced at Sitting Bull who eyes were looking towards the roof of the big teepee of the Sun Dance.

Jumping Bull wanted to know if he was doing the thing right – he turned to Yellow Hair and received a nod of approval; so he carried on, lifting and cutting, lifting and cutting. Soon the blood flowed as it might were a man dragged across rocks by a mad horse.

Sitting Bull scarcely flinched, and as the cutting continued did not move at all. His legs were spread in front of him and his arms, one bleeding, one not, lay casually, his hands resting on his thighs. Then Sitting Bull began to wail. It was not a wail of pain, but a rhythmic run of sacred words, words which seemed to be a dance in themselves, throbbing from his lips. Then the next arm was cut in its fifty places. Yellow Hair made an exact count.

It was over.

The dance began.

Sitting Bull's friends stepped away. They made as if to help him to his feet but his bloody arms waved them to one side.

The two who had cut and counted had hardly been aware of the youths and young warriors who had already hung from the pole and had the flesh ripped from their chests with the strain of it. Now they were dancing slowly round the pole, all the time looking up into the sky where the sun was half hid behind thin clouds. They were dancing the Sun Dance, looking for visions.

Sitting Bull, the warrior chief, the *wicasa wakan*, joined them to dance for two days and two nights as he had promised. And he did not even remind *Wakantanka* of the help that he had called for. He would pay the price whether *Wakantanka* spoke or not, for who knows the ways of God?

He passed partly through the screen and saw wonders. He seemed to sleep even as he danced. Some thought that he had given too much flesh; too much blood. A few had worried looks for they thought he might pass right through the screen and not return. But he danced as if he were a boy.

He danced until the sun went and then to dawn. Very slowly the next day reached the point half way through. All were tired. Many of the young men had collapsed. Sitting Bull was still dancing but he was stumbling like a brave buffalo with arrows in his chest. Then he began to fall and those who were close ran to him and laid him down on Mother Earth, which was encrusted with the blood of the young men.

Water was thrown on him, and they made him drink a little too. He was saying something.

Yellow Hair put his ear close to the old man's face. Black Moon the war chief was there too.

"He's saying something." Black Moon said and pushed Yellow Hair away. He pushed gently, not to give offence, but making sure the Cheyenne gave way. Black Moon bent and listened. A smile came to his face. He listened again, carefully.

"What is it?" asked Yellow Hair.

Black Moon ignored the Cheyenne and walked into the centre of enclosure and called for silence. It took some time, because the people were excited and wanted to know if Sitting Bull was dead or not.

At first they thought they were being called to look upon the body of a brave old man. They expected to have to take him out to a place higher than other places, so that the body left behind could be laid to rest.

But Sitting Bull did not die. He had work to do for his people and for his *Wakantanka*.

So they listened.

"Sitting Bull has seen a wondrous thing."

"What?" the same old woman called.

Black Moon, whose good memory was well known, had heard what Sitting Bull had said, his exact words. So he called out and told the people.

)K)K)K)K)K

As Sitting Bull danced the day went and the night came and still he danced until he dreamed as he danced and saw things he had never seen before.

He greeted two Thunderbirds who called in his head and then swooped low about his ears and then were gone. But it was not the Thunderbirds he was after. For an ordinary vision-seeker to have seen them would have been a thrill and a moment of great importance, enough to change a life. But it seemed to Sitting Bull that it was only on the other side of the screen that he would find what he looked for. He thought he would have to die, and come back. But he was wrong. He did not have to go so far.

To him the moment of the vision seemed to cover an age but the whole vision happened just before the middle of the second day when his mind was gone and his body about to fall. What came was a brilliant sight as he stumbled upon the sacred screen itself. And there stood his father, looking very young and handsome with his arms folded as if in anger. Behind him stood a fine horse, a mare of great beauty and beyond her a line of green hills. Between the rolling hills was a river, so blue... but his father was speaking.

"It is not your time."

"I am looking for something very rich."

"No, no – you must go back. The people need you. You will come to this happy place presently. But not yet."

Sitting Bull wanted to touch his father, who seemed younger than himself, but was stopped by a sudden washing away of the vision of the screen and what was beyond. In its place he saw soldiers. Plenty soldiers.

Sitting Bull stood still inside his head and watched the soldiers. There were some Indians too, from every tribe, riding beautifully on horseback. It seemed that all the soldiers were placed against the sky and were falling, upside down. Their hats were dropping off. There were a few Indians too, falling. Soldier after soldier came down, as thick as grasshoppers on the move. All of them came falling into the lodges of the people in a huge camp. It was then he heard the voice of *Wakantanka*, who said, *"I give you these because they have no ears."*

The water on him woke him, and he saw the face of Yellow Hair and briefly wondered who he was. Then he knew. He began to tell the Cheyenne what he had seen but the words were muddled. Yellow Hair put a water skin to his lips. Sitting Bull took a sip as his eyes caught the face of Black Moon who was the teller of tales.

He saw Black Moon push Yellow Hair to one side, so he began to tell Black Moon what he had seen. Then Black Moon could tell the people. Black Moon's eyes grew wide as he heard.

Black Moon moved away to tell the people. It still seemed to be a dream as Sitting Bull heard Black Moon's voice describing the vision whilst the people listened in silence. Then he heard the sound of many voices as the people talked and shouted and Black Moon went racing off amongst the lodges to tell those who had been too far away and had not yet heard.

Yellow Hair was kneeling, back at Sitting Bull's side. A young man, one of the Sun Dancers, his chest caked with blood, had raised himself on one arm, recovering from his own ordeal and smiled at Sitting Bull. Sitting Bull saw that it was White Hawk, very pale, like a Wasichu and he hoped he did not look the same himself.

"Did you see anything?" asked Sitting Bull.

"I saw a bad winter, all I saw was a bad winter," White Hawk said anxiously.

"Don't worry," said Sitting Bull. "Maybe the bad winter is for the Wasichu."

"*I* heard the voice of *Wakantanka*," said Sitting Bull. He tried to sit up and Yellow Hair had to help him.

"The words mean something. I think He was telling us that the Wasichu do not listen to what we have to say, and we will wipe them out when they next come to our village. The only way they will enter is with their hats off ready for us to count coup and take their scalps. I think that is what it means."

Sitting Bull looked at the winkte and in his eyes was a question, "Do you agree?"

The Cheyenne winkte nodded thoughtfully, "*Wakantanka* spoke with you. The vision is good. I think we shall have a victory, a big victory."

"Good."

"Now you must rest and let us tend your arms."

"*Wakantanka* will help – they are His wounds."

Women and men came and carried Sitting Bull away to his big teepee. The old Cheyenne watched, then he turned to help the young man to his feet.

As the winkte put his arms round the young man's waist, and a hundred sensual thoughts shot through him, he asked again about the winter vision. The young man told him once more, with some hesitation.

"And in this bad winter what did you see? Did you too see the Wasichu without their hats?"

"No."

"Did you see Wasichu in the winter?"

"No."

"What *did* you see?

"A bad winter, a very bad winter."

"Just hills and trees with snow and river iced?"

"That I saw."

"And...?"

"I saw people in the snow."

"People?"

"Our people"

"What were they doing?"

"Nothing."

"Nothing?"

"They were stiff in the snow. I saw a very bad winter."

The Cheyenne winkte asked, "And did you hear the voice of *Wakantanka*?" He knew that the voice was the essence of the vision, the voice would bring the clue, the passageway to the meaning.

"No..."

The young man seemed to shake a little as he walked and Yellow Hair could feel the defined muscles on his flat belly tauten.

"I am not sure but..."

The young man stopped. He knew Yellow Hair as if he were himself, knew him to be a wise man and to be trusted; but what he had to say would not be believed.

As their eyes met Yellow Hair was surprised to see fear in those of the young man.

"What is it?"

"I think I *saw Wakantanka*," whispered White Hawk.

"Saw!" The Cheyenne *wicasa wakan* was aghast.

"I think so, I think so..."

"And what did He look like?"

"I do not know for He also was stiff in the snow..."

An End Note

On 17th June 1876 a large war party, mostly of Sioux warriors, under the leadership of Crazy Horse, met and clashed with Crook's column at the site now known as the battlefield of the Rosebud. Crook, though he claimed a victory, and may have caused higher casualties to the Indians than he suffered, withdrew from the field. Indeed Crazy Horse, some hours later, returned to the battlefield with some followers and picked up hundreds of abandoned cartridges which were later used at the Little Big Horn. It can be claimed that the Indians for the first time were handled in a regimental way, though such a statement has to be seen in the light of the way in which the Indians fought – as individuals. This time they worked *together* in large numbers across a much larger area than, say, the Fetterman fight. The Indians felt, properly, that they had won the battle, and celebrated accordingly.

Eight days later, in the early afternoon of the 25th June 1876, there was no doubt about who won at the Little Big Horn. Following a night march, and after moving forward in temperatures around 90F the 7th Cavalry came upon the great gathering of the nations in the valley of the Little Big Horn. Arrogantly dividing his command into three battalions Custer attacked what he thought was just another village and blundered into nothing less than a metropolis. The battalion under Reno lost large numbers during its panic retreat from its initial charge and came under siege. Meanwhile Custer's battalion was being wiped out. Only the troops under Benteen were relatively unscathed, and had he not come to Reno's aid, and organised the defence of the remains of the 7th Cavalry, the disaster would undoubtedly have been worse.

Sitting Bull remained within the 'metropolis' during the battle, actively calming the women, old people and children; the warriors being led largely by War Chief Gall, and Crazy Horse. Within days the huge encampment broke up and escaped into the plains. But it was the beginning of the end. That winter saw a further series of campaigns masterminded by Sheridan from Chicago. By the following year the power of the Plains Indians was broken.

Crazy Horse surrendered in 1877 and was shortly afterwards bayoneted to death. As he lay dying it was said that a hawk passed by, screaming. Sitting Bull took his people into Canada and later returned to join a reservation with the remnants of his band in 1881.

On surrendering to the commanding officer at Fort Buford he said, "I wish it to be remembered that I was the last man of my tribe to surrender my rifle, this day have I given it to you." In fact he did not personally hand over the weapon but first passed it to Crow Foot, one of his sons. He then said, "This boy has given it to you, and he now wants to know how he is going to make a living." The great leader was defiant to the end. For a time he took part in the Wild West Show of Buffalo Bill Cody. Eventually Sitting Bull was also murdered.

Frank Partridge remained with Sitting Bull to the end and then returned to Canada riding deep into the forests and was not seen again. Little Knife continued as a scout, was present at the killing of Crazy Horse and then served with various cavalry regiments. It is not known how he met his end. Snow on Her remained with him. What happened to White Hawk and Next Dream will be revealed in the sequel to this book which will deal with much of what is described above.

Lieutenant General Phil Sheridan was the nation's chief Indian fighter from 1867 until 1883 when he received his fourth star and became the commanding general of the United States Army. He died on August 5th 1888 and is buried at Arlington Cemetery.

And Yellow Hair... well, of course, he is, even now, on the other side of the screen, young and beautiful, with all the others, and rides a fine pony across plains of green grass where blue rivers flow. In the sun-caressed daylight he rides in the hunt with the warriors of his dreams pursuing swift buffalo – and at night... he gives and takes such pleasure as only a good winkte can, for ever.